TROUBLE BECOMES HER

Also by
LAURA VAN WORMER

THE LAST LOVER
EXPOSÉ
TALK
JUST FOR THE SUMMER
JURY DUTY
ANY GIVEN MOMENT
BENEDICT CANYON
WEST END
RIVERSIDE DRIVE

Watch for the return of Sally Harrington in
LAURA VAN WORMER's

THE BAD WITNESS

Available in hardcover November 2002
only from MIRA Books

LAURA VAN WORMER

TROUBLE BECOMES HER

MIRA®

ISBN 1-55166-847-5

TROUBLE BECOMES HER

Visit us at www.mirabooks.com

Printed in U.S.A.

First Printing: November 2001
10 9 8 7 6 5 4 3 2 1

For
Katherine Orr

With deepest gratitude to

Loretta Barrett, Megan Underwood,
Nick Mullendore and Alison Brooks
in New York

and

Dianne Moggy, Stacy Widdrington, Maureen Stead,
Craig Swinwood, Alex Osuszek, Tania Charzewski,
Shelley Cinnamon, Vivian Ducas and Katherine Chamberlain
in Toronto

You are wonderful.

PART ONE

New Yorker

CHAPTER ONE

Things have been going fairly well lately. This means I have managed to keep out of trouble, show up for my new job on time and not fall in love with anybody new—or fall in love with anybody of old, either, which is a whole other story I've gladly put on the shelf for the moment.

My name is Sally Harrington, most recently of Castleford, Connecticut, the small city where I was born. I went to college on the West Coast, did a stint at *Boulevard* magazine in L.A. (yes, *dahhhling*) and then returned home to Castleford when my mother fell ill, and I ended up staying a while, writing for my hometown paper. A once-in-a-lifetime freelance assignment for *Expectations* magazine led me to a part-time job with the DBS television affiliate in New Haven, which, ultimately, has led me here—to a job at DBS News in New York.

So here I am, the new cosmopolitan sophisticate, with an apartment in Manhattan and a cottage, as New Yorkers say, "in the country." And today is a very big day because my not-so-sophisticated canine pal, Scotty, is making his uncertain urban debut.

As our Yellow Cab rolls up to the gates of the West End Broadcasting Center, home to the Darenbrook Broadcasting System among other Darenbrook enterprises, the security guard hails, "Hey, Ms. Harrington!" and walks toward my window.

Scotty immediately goes nuts, barking his head off and jumping on top of me to protect me from this approaching threat.

"Oh sheet, ladeh!" the driver yells through the bulletproof glass from the front seat. "You tay da dawg not DOO anyting!"

"Scotty, enough!" I command, and Scotty instantly shuts up, but he also plunks his rear end down on my lap, paws resting on the armrest to keep guard at the window. Since I am wearing a navy-blue DKNY skirt and blazer, and since Scotty is eighty pounds' worth of collie (read, long-haired)-German shepherd-golden retriever mix, you can imagine the state of my coiffure. I have light brown hair—instead of Mother's honey blond—and have blue eyes that people seem to go for, but even these gifts of nature can't overcome a flurry of dog hair, lint and dirt.

I get a firm hold on Scotty's leash and manage to worm my left hand through his legs and chest to roll down the window.

"Hey, pooch," the guard says, unafraid, holding out his hand for Scotty to sniff. He ducks a little to smile at him. "First day, huh?"

Scotty tentatively looks at me and then back at the guard and suddenly gives him a big lick on the hand. I scratch the dog behind the ears. "That's right, my good boy," I say. "It's the first day of school, isn't it?" (When you don't have children, I'm afraid this is the kind of conversation you tend to have with your dog.)

"Mrs. Cochran and Mr. Rafferty brought their dogs in today, too," the guard reports. "The doghouse seems to be a big hit."

I should explain about this so-called doghouse. When DBS News first offered me a job as an undefined (albeit very well paid) assistant producer to the network's star anchorwoman, Alexandra Waring, my agent asked them to consider the possibility of building a dog run in the park located in the middle of the West End complex. I knew the kind of hours I was likely to keep and there was no way I could bring Scotty to live with me in New York, not if I kept him locked up all day and night after his entire three-year life had been spent in the country. I thought my future bosses would freak at the audacity of the request, but my agent insisted I ask, because she said you never knew, someone way up there might be a little gaga over animals too. Well, sure enough, my request turned out to spark a minor revolution, with two aforementioned executives (Cassy Cochran, president of the DBS network, and Will Rafferty, executive producer of DBS News) at the head of the line to get the dog run approved so they could bring their dogs to work, too.

The security guard is peering at Scotty's face. It is gold and brown, and his almond-shaped eyes are lined perfectly in dark brown. "What is he?" he asks me. "Australian sheepdog?"

When I adopted Scotty from the Castleford Humane Society, he frankly did not look like much of anything. He was one of those miserable, big-nosed scrawnies of about seven months that always seem to get abused in the inner city before getting dumped somewhere, but who, after good food, lots of water, love and exercise, often grow into rather magnificent-looking mutts. Today Scotty does look like some foreign, outdoorsy breed. "He's a New Zealand highlander," I say, joking.

"Oh, yeah, New Zealand highlander!" the guard cries. "Yeah, my sister's got one of those."

"I'm sorry," I say. "I was just kidding. I don't know what he is."

"I think he *is* a New Zealand highlander," the guard insists.

I reach over to grab an extra box of Milk-Bone from the supplies I've brought for Scotty and hand it to the guard. "So you can make friends." Scotty turns back to look at me as if to say, *Hey*, but another cab has pulled up behind us and we need to move on.

I'm hoping that Scotty and I can walk to work most days, because getting a cab with him is more than a little tricky.

Most cabdrivers in Manhattan seem to be from countries where animals the size of Scotty are more likely shot, eaten or worshiped, and they seem to be genuinely fearful of him. The only way I got this cabdriver to take us was to wave a fistful of dollars and swear that Scotty would never, as the driver says, DOO anything.

It is a few minutes before noon. I am not expected to be at West End until one, Monday through Friday, the time Alexandra Waring usually swings in. Alexandra anchors the news from nine to ten each night, and we get out of here usually around eleven. My job, essentially, is to be here when she is, and do everything my title of assistant producer allows me to do—rewriting stories, editing studio copy, supervising staff—without triggering union violations. (Anything with producer in the title, you see, means a job exempt from union rules, although I should explain I am also a card-carrying member of several of those same unions from my previous experiences as an on-air reporter.)

I overtip the cabdriver and it seems to square things, although the minute we get out, the driver jumps out too, checking the back seat as if he's sure Scotty's made some kind of mistake. Scotty, of course, now insulted, wants to go back and scare the driver and starts straining on his leash, barking and gnashing his teeth, desperate to get free. The friendly security guy on duty gracefully steers us away from the entrance of West End to the walk that goes around the side of the complex.

So much for Scotty's casual and sophisticated debut.

From the outside, the West End Broadcasting Center appears to be little more than a huge, gray, windowless warehouse of some kind, but when you walk around the side, you quickly realize you're walking around the middle section of a gigantic U-shaped complex of three buildings. And as you round that corner, going inside the U, your breath cannot help but be momentarily taken away. There is nothing but three floors of glass on the inside of these buildings, all looking out over a gorgeously landscaped park. And, beyond a grove of pines that screen out the West Side Highway, lies the vast beauty of the Hudson River. It is gorgeous here. A sheltered paradise amid the urban sprawl of Manhattan.

The complex also extends two and half floors beneath the surface. The park, in fact, outlines the perimeters of the actual television studios and production facilities below. Studio A is primarily used by DBS News and the newsroom, where I am usually found, branches off it. Studio A is where *DBS News America Tonight with Alexandra Waring* is broadcast, Monday through Friday, with weekend anchors on Saturday and Sunday. It is also where *DBS News Magazine* is produced, as well as a variety of news-related video and cable productions. Snaking out from the newsroom is a labyrinth of writing and editing bays, conference rooms and equipment rooms.

Studio B, not far away, is primarily used by *The Jessica Wright Show,* the nightly talk show for which busloads of people are brought in daily from midtown. The studios share the same Green Room (which is blue), wardrobe, makeup and hair and storage facilities, and Alexandra Waring's dressing room is next door to Jessica Wright's. The women are extremely close friends, a relationship no doubt forged when they were the sole programming sources for the network in its debut over seven years ago. To this day, as a matter of fact, the highest profit margins for the network still emanate from their broadcasts. Alexandra offers what has been nicknamed in the industry as "the exhausted yuppie news" at nine, and Jessica, "the exhausted yuppie late-night talk show" at ten.

Don't laugh, it works. The advertisers love their demographics.

I present Scotty and his shot papers to the dog run supervisor, who is actually one of the day care aides whose duties have been expanded. After a few minutes of barking, sniffing, growling and circling with a female blond Labrador retriever, a little wire-haired Jack Russell and an even smaller little black mutlett of unknown parentage, Scotty leaves me, happily occupied with his new friends, who have decided to begin the day's festivities by running as a pack from one end of the run to the other.

I swipe my ID through the security door of the central building of the complex and then clip it to my dog hair-covered blazer lapel. This center building, Darenbrook I, contains the corporate offices of Darenbrook Communications. It is the biggest, if not one of the last, media empires privately held by an American family. The building to the south houses the executive staff of the print and electronic divisions: the Darenbrook chain of newspapers and magazines, the textbook company, the chain of printing plants, the satellite company and, finally, the electronic retrieval and reference companies. DBS, the company's broadcast television network, sprang directly from the technology made available from the electronic and satellite divisions, and all of our offices are located in the facing building, to the north, called Darenbrook III.

The bigger the moneymaker, the higher the office. Standing in front of Darenbrook III, from right to left, all one sees is the reflection of mirrored glass, but behind it, on the third floor, the order goes like this: on the far right, the office of Denny Ladler, executive producer of *The Jessica Wright Show.* To the left of Denny is Jessica Wright's office. To the left of Jessica is Will Rafferty's office, which is kind of funny because he and Jessica are now married. (But then, the president of DBS, Cassy Cochran, is married to Jackson Darenbrook, the corporate CEO. Don't ask—it's a long story.) To the left of Will is Alexandra Waring's office, and then, guess who is now on that third floor, too, way on the end, in such high-and-mighty company? That's right, me. Sally Harrington from Castleford, Connecticut. And a day has not gone by that I have not been amazed that I'm here.

Actually, given the recent events of my life, I think we're all a little amazed I'm even still alive.

CHAPTER TWO

"Hi," I say to Benjamin Kim, Alexandra's secretary. Broadcasting, like so many other communications industries, is an apprenticeship business, and the caliber of secretaries constantly amazes anyone who's not in it. Benjamin holds a master's degree in English from Berkeley. He is a second-generation Korean-American and took a huge pay cut to work here, which is a triple whammy since Manhattan is outrageously expensive. But that's how it begins for us all. I, too, began as a secretary in Los Angeles at *Boulevard,* and had to bartend Saturday nights to make the rent. So Benjamin answers the phone, takes messages, organizes schedules, types correspondence, has no money and can probably recite *Beowulf* backward and forward.

"Oh, good, you're here," he greets me without looking up. "Alexandra wants to see you a–s–a–p in editing three." He glances up from his computer and does a double take, checking out my suit. "Are you, by chance, one of those Christians who was thrown to the lions?"

"Yes," I tell him, moving on to my office. I walk to my desk, drop my briefcase and open a drawer to take out a roll of masking tape.

There is a knock on my office door. Standing there is "The Kid," a college intern assigned to the news division. He is a senior at Columbia University. He is white and is nice-looking, with brown hair in an athlete's cut, large hazel eyes and a fresh, clean-shaven face. He's wearing the basic uniform of the rich kid: a button-down oxford shirt, gray chinos and loafers. He always has this slightly apologetic look on his face when he's around me and I'm not sure what that's about. Rather, I *do* know what it's about and wish I didn't. For some reason he has chosen me to have a crush on. You've got Jessica Wright around and Alexandra Waring, and so he picks me. Go figure.

"I'm so sorry for disturbing you, Ms. Harrington—" he begins.

"Sally," I say, simultaneously picking up my phone and turning on the computer. Holding the phone on my shoulder, I wrap my hand in masking tape. He always does this, calls me Ms. Harrington first thing in the afternoon, and by the time he blushes his way through the night, may or may not succeed in calling me Sally.

(I don't mean to sound so awful, but growing up I was not well-to-do. I landed a scholarship to UCLA but still had to work two jobs just to survive. I could never afford the luxury of even dreaming about an internship. My future was already heavily mortgaged with student loans.)

"Alexandra wanted me to bring you downstairs as soon as you got in," the intern says.

"I got the message already, thank you. I'll be right down," I tell him, skipping to get the highlights of the messages left on my voice mail with my left hand, while patting my blazer down with masking tape with the other. A lot of people are leaving me messages these days, from both inside West End and out in the field at the affiliate stations. Nobody knows what it is, exactly, I do, but they do know I work directly for Alexandra, so they're always giving me a lot of information whether I want it or not. I rip the masking tape off, toss it in the wastebasket and wrap another handful to attack my skirt.

"Um," the intern says uncomfortably, "Alexandra also wanted me to brief you."

"Hello, Sally Harrington, stranger at large," says the voice of my ex-lover, Spencer Hawes, on my voice mail. I hit the keypad to skip it.

The intern misinterprets my expression, thinking my displeasure is with him.

"I—Alexandra told me to. I mean, I know I have no standing..." A slow burn of red has started at his ears and is working its way down his cheeks.

"It's not you," I explain, hanging up the telephone and ripping the tape off my hand. I lean over to quickly scroll down through my e-mail. "Just one second...and I'll give you my full attention." Good. Nothing terribly earth-shaking. I glance over at him. "You never told me, Jim, how you got here."

He doesn't seem to understand the question.

"Who are you related to?" I translate, grabbing a notebook and pen in preparation of going downstairs. I don't, contrary to what I might appear to be doing, keep Alexandra waiting a minute more than I have to.

"Gosh," he stammers. "I'm not related to anybody. I'm nobody. I'm from over the transom. I started applying for an internship when I was a freshman. And this year they finally called me."

I walk around my desk, feeling more kindly toward him. I might have been wrong. "So how are you surviving?"

"Six guys, one-bedroom apartment," he says. He hesitates a minute and then adds, "Alexandra gave me a meal card for the cafeteria. I can have whatever I want to eat when I'm here."

Now I am genuinely moved, and I feel awful about my behavior. I put a hand on his elbow, steering him to accompany me out the door. "What's your last name, Jim?"

"Reinemann."

I nod, determined to remember it. "So brief me," I tell him. As we walk down the long hallway to the elevator, he explains that DBS News dispatched a producer down to Georgia to work on a story about a satanic cult in Atlanta. Alexandra, I know, is very big on compiling reports from the affiliates about the activities of any—how does she phrase it?—"organized groups of people whose beliefs appear to be contrary to the best interests of the United States." As you can imagine, we hear from the affiliates about every weirdo, wacko and misfit group around, and weekly sift through reports of terrorists, neo-Nazis, religious lunatics and other freak shows, looking for something that feels like a legitimate story.

With the advent of the Internet, you see, it has become increasingly difficult to determine the actual size of these renegade groups, or if they're even a group at all. We are always getting reports about what, on the Internet, for example, appears to be a massive movement of white Americans who have made a religion out of their race, but who in reality is always just this one same loser who still lives with his parents. ("There was no bigger loser than Adolf Hitler," Alexandra sternly reminded us at a recent editorial meeting. "I want you to keep tabs on this guy.")

From a ratings point of view, I can understand why Alexandra seems interested in these stories, but as a journalist I dread them. Take this possible story on a satanic cult. It's a terrible topic for TV because film footage is extremely scarce, or worse, the footage that is available looks staged—usually because it is. The only way something like a satanic cult can be adequately covered by electronic media, I think, is under the anonymity of radio. Nobody cares about a microphone, but everybody runs when there's a camera.

Why am I so opinionated about this? Because I come from the world of print media, and this is one of those areas where newspapers and magazines can beat the electronic world hands down every time.

At any rate, young Jim is explaining to me, something's gone wrong in Georgia and Alexandra is sure there's a story, but has lost faith in the field producer. Jim says he thinks she's going to send me down there, maybe today. She was pretty upset with some video she saw.

"Is that what she's working on in editing?" I ask, the elevator sinking to sub-level 2.

"No, she's working on something else, but she's still mad about the video that came up from Atlanta."

In the eight weeks I've been here, Alexandra has already sent me out of town on such errands five times. I keep a bag packed in my office closet for just such an assignment, but this time there is a complication. Scotty. I only just got him here to the city. We walk out of the elevator, through reception, and down the corridor toward the studio areas. "Do you like dogs?" I ask Jim.

"I love dogs," he says.

"If I have to go to Atlanta, would you be interested in house-sitting? You know, stay in my apartment and look after my dog?" I fight down the image of him looking in my underwear drawer. "And then bring him to work?"

His eyes light up. "Are you kidding? To have a place to myself for a night? In, like, a real apartment?"

"It's just a studio that I'm subletting, but there's a little backyard for Scotty."

"Oh, yes, please! Sally, I'd pay you to let me do it, if I had any money!"

I have to smile. He's a nice kid. And I am a bitch. "Well, good, maybe we can try it, then. Let's see what she has to say and then we'll figure it out." We've wound down the corridor to editing, where there are a series of soundproof glass booths with consoles inside. In #3 I can see Alexandra sitting with Carl Klieghoffer, a veteran editor.

I guess I should try and explain Alexandra's position here. She is not a goddess, exactly, but pretty close to it. She is and has always been the symbol of DBS News and its success. While Cassy Cochran and our CEO of the electronics division, Langley Peterson, and Will Rafferty probably deserve as much credit as Alexandra does for building the news division from the ground up, she is the undeniable star. When she was my age, thirty years old, she was the first woman to anchor a national nightly newscast in America, Monday through Friday. (Am I jealous? Hell, yes!)

At thirty-seven years old, poll after poll shows that while Alexandra Waring is not the most watched news anchor, the American public believes she is the most balanced and trustworthy one on the air. Democrats scream she is a closet Republican, and Republicans scream she is a closet Democrat, when, frankly, the only thing Alexandra's in the closet about is her love life.

She is very, very good at what she does. It is so easy, in broadcast journalism, to slip an opinion or bias or particular viewpoint into a story. Every word you use, the way you edit, the film or picture you choose to show—all of these factors present loaded situations. Alexandra goes strictly by the book when it comes to reporting the news, and viewers appreciate it. Her personal interests or biases can be sensed, at times, in her personal choice of stories she covers for the magazine show. But that's appropriate, because the magazine is a different vehicle.

But let's get down to brass tacks. This is America and we all know that a lot of DBS News's success stems from the fact that Alexandra Waring has one of the most telegenic faces in broadcast history. People love to look at her. TV-Q is a formula researchers came up with to measure the appeal individuals hold for TV audiences. It really has nothing to do with anything except, literally, face value. And Alexandra rates high.

This woman is no slouch, either, believe me. She's been a burning overachiever since day one, the youngest child of a nine-term Kansas congressman. Alexandra stayed on the family farm with her grandparents while her parents lived in Washington. She was a rich kid, no doubt about it, but even I can't resent her success (and I'm usually pretty good at it). She has simply worked harder and better than everybody else around her. For every success she's won in the past, nervous newsroom laggards punished her and sought to derail her career. Yet, she made it. Big Time. And I've learned more from Alexandra in the last couple of months than I have in the past eight years.

There is no way I can rationally complain about working for her. My salary is now almost exactly six times what I was making at my hometown paper (not including bonuses, if I survive the calendar year). I've paid off my car, I have a savings account with more than forty-two cents in it, I have a retirement account, and I'm doing my best to whittle those student loans down to extinction. I am, however, coming to realize why Alexandra has never had a right-hand person who lasted very long in my position. It's not that she moves so quickly—which she does—but it's that she moves so *mysteriously*. Half the time I don't have a clue as to what she is really up to, what she is thinking, what direction she is heading in, or what it is, exactly, she wants me to do. And to try to second-guess her, I have learned, is a complete waste of time. She is not a creature of any habit where schedules are concerned, and her energy level seems only to run on one of two speeds: HIGH and CRASH. If the latter is the case, she usually retreats behind locked doors until she's back on HIGH.

I knock once and slip into editing bay #3. On the editing screen, Alexandra and Carl are viewing a black-and-white still of two men standing in front of a factory. The younger man of the two is holding the hand of a small boy. Judging by the clothes and a Cadillac in the background, I guess the photograph dates from the 1950s.

Alexandra glances up at me. "Anyone look familiar?"

"Rocky Presario," I say, smiling, reaching past the anchorwoman to point at the younger man. "So that's got to be a young Frank, his son. You know, Lilliana Martin's father."

"The one-woman crime wave has arrived," Alexandra remarks to Carl, her eyes moving back to the screen. The anchorwoman has dark, almost black hair to her shoulders, but her claim to fame is the most extraordinary set of blue-gray eyes, the color of which, someone once wrote, is that of a stormy Atlantic. They were right. She has a full, generous mouth and a very fit, if not too thin, body. On TV her build looks perfect, but that is TV. It adds ten to fifteen pounds. Don't get me wrong, in real life Alexandra is extremely attractive, but it's only on TV that her looks take on the quality of a goddess.

"Keep Rocky and Frank," the anchorwoman says to Carl, "but since we don't know who that is—" she points to the middle-aged man "—take him out."

"I wouldn't," I say.

"Why?" She turns around. "Do you know who he is?"

"I think it's Longy Zwillman," I say. "He was a fairly big mafia figure, and when he went, Rocky Presario inherited a big piece of his New Jersey empire."

"When he went where?" she wants to know.

"To the great beyond," I answer. "He backed a character named Anastasia to take over the Genovese crime family, but that bet went south and Longy, here, supposedly committed suicide shortly thereafter. But," I add, shifting my weight from one foot to the other, "considering how difficult it would be to strangle oneself with a child's plastic jump rope, there was a wee bit of doubt surrounding his death."

I know all this stuff because I was recently nearly killed by an organized crime figure, one who was directly connected to the men pictured here. As it happens, that organized crime figure ended up being murdered himself, and I am rather intimately involved with the explosive trial that is about to unfold in Los Angeles. The press has dubbed it "The Mafia Boss Murder" trial, and I don't kid myself, part of the reason I was offered a job here at DBS was to do exactly what I've been doing—set up exclusive interviews with the principals of the case on behalf of the network.

How did I get involved in such a sensational case? Well, let's just say it began with a proposition for a vaguely scandalous sexual liaison in Los Angeles one night and ended up with a very definitive bullet through the head of Nicky Arlenetta, aforementioned organized crime figure. Arlenetta was the great-nephew of Rocky Presario, the younger of the two men pictured here, and the accused shooter, the production head of Monarch Studios, Jonathan Small, is Rocky Presario's grandson.

Alexandra runs an impatient hand through her hair, looking down at her notes. "I don't understand why research didn't identify him." She turns around. "Jim?"

The intern steps forward. Alexandra hands a manila folder to him. "Find out who worked on this in research and bring him or her to me in the newsroom, will you?" She turns to Carl. "You might as well put this away. I've got to get cracking on the newscast."

She gets up and looks at me, as if waiting for me to tell her what I want.

"You rang?" I say in my best butler voice.

"Yes, I did." Her face contracts a bit. "But forget it, I can't send you. I need you here. As a matter of fact..." She's walking out of editing and I am expected to catch up with her in the corridor if I am to hear the rest of what she has to say. "I think I may want to pull you off everything." She looks at me. "What are you working on?"

"Everything," I confirm.

"Well, I want you on this," she says, walking on.

"Um," I say, hurrying to catch up, "you want me on what?"

"On the Presario-Arlenetta story."

A reporter walks by and Alexandra smiles and nods to him as we turn into the newsroom.

"Alexandra!" Will calls. The place is already starting to hop with prenewscast jitters, the activity increasing at the desks and carrels. The closer to airtime, the greater the flux and flurry and fury of the newsroom. Right now the general story lineup is being assembled, but the order and segment lengths will change several times over the next seven hours. Many stories listed now will not make it to the air at all. Major stories will become minor ones, and events that have not yet even happened today could steal the lead.

DBS has 192 affiliates in the United States and just as many newsrooms. They are not, however, by any stretch of the imagination, first-rate. As the "other" broadcast network, our affiliates are, by and large, the stations ABC, CBS and NBC did not want. The quality control is all here at West End, where we're always trying to drag affiliate news stories up to national caliber, which, more often than not, means rewriting the story, reediting the visuals and rerecording the reporter's summary on a new sound track. We spend an inordinate amount of time in the satellite room beaming footage back and forth, trying to get what we want from the field.

"Don't go far," Alexandra instructs me before crossing the newsroom to Will.

"Here," a production assistant says, taking a working script from the pile under his arm and shoving it into my hand.

I take a seat in the corner and flip through it. Out of the corner of my eye I see young Jim come in with a tall, thin, absolutely terrified-looking woman behind him. I get up and walk over. "Alexandra's tied up for the moment."

"This is Edith," Jim says. "From research."

"Edith, hi," I say, holding out my hand. "Sally Harrington."

The hand that takes mine is shaking and I feel awful. Poor Edith is like so many researchers I've known over the years: brilliant, cripplingly shy and not quite working on the same level as the rest of us. She is somewhere around fifty; her brown hair is heavily streaked with gray, and is tied back with the same kind of yarn I imagine she has been using since the late 1960s when it was popular.

"Alexandra wanted to ask you about the photographs you captioned for us," I say. "The ones connected with the Presario-Arlenetta story."

Edith gives an involuntary shiver and gathers her cardigan in one fist over her breast. "I told them," she whispers in a slight rasp. "I told them not to push me out of my specialty."

I try to appear encouraging. "What is your specialty?"

"Health, science, mathematics. And cooking. Those are my designated areas."

"So why do you have to work on this mob stuff?"

"Because they've downsized our department from six people to three," she hisses with sudden vehemence, knuckles turning white against her sweater.

Ah, passive-aggressive. Why am I not surprised.

"When was this?"

"Last month."

"I see," I say, thinking this over.

"And we don't have the stacks to support this kind of research, and I, for one, do not trust that computer," she suddenly rushes on. "I told my supervisor the computer can only recognize what it has been programmed to recognize but I don't think anyone has—" She abruptly stops, clamping her mouth shut.

Research is part of the electronics division, and is offered as a service to DBS News. We do not carry a line in our budget for it. I have no idea how the overall Darenbrook Communications empire works financially, but I have worked for privately held companies before, and so I know chances run high that the accounting practices were purposely designed on a broken abacus, meant only to be fully understood by those who deliberately broke the abacus in the first place. In other words, I have no idea if our division actually pays for research or not, and thus, whether we have any say about how the department is run.

"Now that I have an explanation," I tell Edith, "I'm sure Alexandra will—"

"Oh, God, don't tell anyone I said anything!" she pleads, releasing her sweater to grab my arm with alarming strength. "I don't want to lose my job," she agonizes. "Oh, my God, it's her. I can't!" She turns to flee, but this time I grab her arm to make her stay put.

I look over my shoulder and see that it's Alexandra approaching. "It's okay," I say to Edith, giving Alexandra a warning look. The anchorwoman kicks her head to the side, indicating she'll wait near by. I take a step forward, bending to look under Edith's hanging head in an attempt to see her face. "What's the matter?"

"I couldn't possibly meet her," she whispers in a rush, her back stiffening.

I blink. "You've never met Alexandra?"

After a moment, she shakes her head. "No," she whispers.

"And you've worked here how long?"

"Six years."

Edith must have gone to amazing lengths to avoid such a meeting, since Alexandra makes it her business to meet every employee. I don't have time to figure out all of poor Edith's neuroses, but I do know what needs to be done. "Trust me," I say quietly.

"But I don't even know who you are!" she whispers harshly. A studio technician walks by, raising his eyebrows, as if he finds it unusual to see me holding on to a neurotic researcher who's trying to bolt.

"Pull yourself to*gether!*" I command under my breath, and I give her arm a gentle yank, prompting her to turn around. She wrests her arm back and grabs her cardigan over her breast again.

"Alexandra?" I call, and she looks up from the script in her hand, smiles slightly and walks over. "I'd like you to meet Edith, who has been working in the research division for six years."

I know Alexandra well enough to know she will read the situation correctly. "Edith," she says, offering her hand, "what a pleasure. You've done so much wonderful work. It must be very interesting."

Slowly, in a jerky movement, the hand comes down from the sweater and takes the anchorwoman's. Alexandra shakes it, releases it, and to cover the silence, continues, "There is a part of me that has always longed to be a researcher. It's so rewarding. Although with the computers these days, I'm not sure it's as much fun as it used to be. When you used the stacks."

"No," Edith says quietly. "It's not."

"Well, it's very nice to meet you. Perhaps sometime you'll let me visit your work area and you can show me what resources we have for you to use." She offers one of her better smiles. "Perhaps you have some ideas for improvement."

"I—that would be fine," Edith says, starting to blink, as if waking up. "Thank you." The researcher smiles slightly, then, lowers her eyes, glances shyly back at Alexandra and walks purposefully out of the newsroom.

"What on earth was that about?" Alexandra murmurs out of the corner of her mouth.

"They fired three researchers and left three—she's terrified she'll lose her job. She's supposed to be science, math and cooking or something, and she says the computer's not complete and we don't have the stacks to cover something like identifying old mobsters." I look at her. "Do we pay for access to research?"

Alexandra shakes her head. "No. We did a deal to cut our overhead. Why?" She looks at me.

"I think we're getting what we pay for, don't you?"

She presses her mouth into a line, considering this, but not commenting on it. "By the way," she says instead, "I will need you in the field tonight. Is that okay? And you'll be out of the office tomorrow."

"Sure."

"Great," she says, moving away, eyes returning to the working script in her hand, "you'll be leaving right after the newscast."

I know better, but when she's a few steps away, I can't resist letting her know I know what she has in mind. "Atlanta, right?" I call.

She turns around. "No, New Jersey. My house."

CHAPTER THREE

At six forty-five I take a break for dinner and wander outside to the dog run to see how Scotty's doing. He's having dinner, too. All of the dogs are in separate cages for this, each with their own bowl of food as provided by their owners. Everybody else's bowl seems to be made of pretty swanky ceramic, I notice, as compared to Scotty's plain old blue plastic one from K-Mart.

When I go back upstairs to my office, I find that Alexandra has locked herself in her office to rewrite the introductions to various news segments. She is a perfectionist in this regard, although I've seen her wing it many times in the studio when need be, seemingly flawlessly revising her narrative as she speaks.

I check my watch. Seven-thirty. Hour and a half to air.

"There you are," Will says, swinging into my office. "Look at this, will you?" He tosses a video over my desk, which I catch. "Give me some notes on what you think." And then he is gone.

I come out from behind my desk, throw the tape in the VCR and sit on the small couch to watch.

This is interview footage with a self-described former

member of a satanic cult in Georgia. This must be what Jim the intern was talking about, the assignment Alexandra had been thinking about sending me on.

I watch for a while and see a host of problems. The producer has disguised the man's identity by having him sit in the shadows and scrambling his voice. The picture and sound is so distorted it could virtually be anyone, man or woman. Secondly, it is what he is saying. Beyond the sensationalism of the words *Satan, satanic* and *sacrifice,* the content is virtually useless "They have hundreds of members," he says, "organized in cartels of baby-sitters. The whole eastern seaboard is infested with cult members."

"And they are baby-sitters?" the producer asks.

"Yes. To begin recruiting the children into the cult."

The interview goes on and on and the producer presses for details, any detail at all, but the guy won't give any. He just keeps saying they—whoever *they* are—are daily brainwashing thousands of children in their care, initiating them to the rites and rituals of satanism, including sacrifices.

I sit down at my computer to dash out a memo to Will.

I have watched forty-five minutes of the mystery interviewee from Atlanta who claims he is a former member of a satanic cult, which is organized as a cartel of baby-sitters that are systematically brainwashing the children in their care.

Despite the attempts of the producer to gain any specifics from him, I still have not the slightest idea who he is talking about or whether they actually exist. He doesn't have to name names, but he does have to profile at least one or two actual members: religion, age, profession, etc. Also, how do they recruit members? (For example, how was he recruited? How did he find out about them?) When do they meet, where do they meet, how often, how are the leaders determined, who makes up the rules? ANYTHING.

Also, where are their satanic icons kept? Together or kept by individual members?

About the children. Surely at least one child must have surfaced by now who has been exposed to this abuse. Or parents who know of this. How about an expert in the field? ANYTHING.

In short, while I know for a fact this kind of abuse has and does occasionally take place, but this guy is utterly useless. It all sounds like b.s. The lighting is just too bizarre and his voice sounds like Donald Duck. I can't imagine anyone believing anything he says. I certainly would not use any of this. If the producer insists he's legit, that the story has legs, my vote is to approach the Atlanta paper to partner the story. There is tons of research to do and, frankly, if our producer submitted this to us, then I have less than zero faith she has the capability of producing a legitimate story.

I leave the video and memo on Will's office chair and saunter back into the hall in time to see the back of Alexandra sailing toward the elevator. Time for her to change clothes and hit makeup.

I walk back into my office and startle young Jim, who had been looking at some of my things framed on the wall. "I have stuff for you," he says quickly, pointing to three large plastic storage boxes stacked next to my desk. "Alexandra says you are now in charge of all the Presario-Arlenetta archives."

"I am, am I? What do you suppose that means?"

"I think she expects you to check all the labels and captions, and then catalog everything for her."

I let out a small laugh. "Yeah, right." I open the top box to look inside. Papers, pictures, videotapes, piles of stuff. I drop the lid again, wondering when I'm going to have time to do this. "Listen, Jim, it looks like I am going out of town tonight."

"That's what I heard," he says, excitement creeping into his voice.

I glance over. "So you're still game? Taking Scotty tonight and house-sitting? Bringing him in tomorrow?"

"I am, like, so psyched," he says, grinning. "I already went down to meet him, Scotty, I mean. He's a great dog. He gave me his paw."

"All part of his plot to convince you to let him out, no doubt," I say, smiling, walking back around my desk to sit. "This is great." I start writing out directions and lists for him. "You don't happen to know, do you, what's going on at Alexandra's farm?"

"Something to do with Rocky Presario, I think."

"That's odd," I murmur, writing. "No one's said anything. He does have a place in Jersey, but I thought his interview was in a couple weeks."

"I know that actress lady called Alexandra yesterday," my new ally and stool pigeon Jim tells me.

"Lilliana Martin?"

"Yeah."

Lilliana Martin is the granddaughter of Rocky Presario and the sister of Jonathan Small, the man on trial for the murder of his cousin, Nick Arlenetta. It's possible the interview with Rocky has been moved up, but it doesn't make sense that I don't know about it. It must mean there is something about tonight or tomorrow I won't like, and that's why Alexandra hasn't filled me in.

"I'm writing some lists out for you, Jim. First off—" I look up at him "—promise me you won't look at whatever I've left out."

He frowns slightly, unsure what I mean.

"Mess," I explain. "I think there's a damp towel over the back of a chair, sneakers in the middle of the floor, probably socks, too, maybe a bra on the bed—"

He lowers his eyes at the last, smiling, swallowing, a tinge of pink in his ears.

"I *think* I made the bed," I continue, writing out Scotty's feeding instructions and where the food is. "But before you think I'm some sort of nut, I am subletting this apartment— I am not a woman who buys big round beds."

"I'm not going to sleep in your bed," he says quickly, sounding faintly horrified. "I'll just sleep on the floor."

"You'll sleep in the bed," I tell him. "First of all, because Scotty will expect you to, and second of all, there is so much bed and very little floor. It's this enormous, round, weird bed, but it's comfortable." I finish writing and hold out the lists to him. "The door to the backyard is in the bathroom, you can't miss it, but if you're not too tired, I wish you'd take him for a run in the park either tonight or in the morning. If you can't, just let him out back to do his business. There are some plastic bags to clean up after him." We go over the address and the instructions and I thank him profusely. I look up the number of the veterinary hospital in the neighborhood and give him some money for cabs and to get something to eat, since I think there's celery and orange juice in the house, that's about it.

Then I hurry downstairs to sub-level 2, just off the studio, to makeup. Alexandra is not here yet. The three chairs in front of the room-length mirrors are empty, and Cleo, the stylist, is checking over her inventory of cosmetics, brushes, combs, clips and curlers. She glances up and smiles at me in the mirror. She is a hip little lady of unknown age, and today is featuring a leopard-skin leotard, skintight black jeans and black spiked high heels. She also wears those Lina Wertmuller kind of glasses.

"Going on the air tonight, sweetie?"

"Afraid not," I answer. "I'm here strictly in a handmaiden capacity."

"Oh, that's definitely you, Sally," Alexandra says, breezing past me to climb into Cleo's chair. "A handmaiden."

Cleo deftly takes off the anchorwoman's strand of pearls and hands them to her, then sweeps an apron over Alexandra's pale gray dress. She leans forward to take a closer look at Alexandra's face. "When was the last time you slept?"

Alexandra does not answer right away. She's irritated and I don't blame her. You do not want to be told you look like hell thirty minutes before you do a national newscast. On the other hand, I suppose Cleo has to say something as a disclaimer for the end product she sends into the studio, because viewers notice everything, and if Alexandra is not her usual self, DBS will be deluged with calls and mail about it.

"Just see what you can do," Alexandra finally says.

"Sweetie," Cleo says, grabbing her hand, "it's me. I didn't mean to hurt your feelings."

"Cleo," she says, taking her hand back, "you're not hurting my feelings. You're right, I'm tired and I've got a lot on my mind. Could you please just try your best—" she takes a breath and forces a smile "—and do your magic." Then she looks over to me, holding out a script, finger marking the page. "Did you see this?"

I take the script from her and read. It's the weather segment. At DBS our meteorologist, Gary Plains, does a general report and forecast of the country, then the affiliates drop in their local forecast, and then we come back to Gary, who introduces a spectacular video of some kind of extraordinary weather that is occurring somewhere in America. In tonight's script he will be talking about a lightning storm in Nebraska. "It reads okay," I say, looking up. "What's the visual?" and then I see in the production column it says ROLL MISSOURI. "We're using tape of Missouri for a story about Nebraska?"

"Exactly," Alexandra says, closing her eyes so Cleo can dab on foundation.

"I'll check on it," I promise, sliding the script back into her lap and heading for the door as Dash Tomlinson, the sports editor, comes in.

I hurry to the newsroom to find Hailey, the assistant producer who helps on the weather. "We didn't get anything usable from Nebraska," she explains. "The transmission tower outside Lincoln got blown out in the storm. This is the same kind of lightning, though."

I look at her straight in the eye. "Are you absolutely sure of that?"

"Well," she wavers, "not absolutely, abso*lute*ly sure—but pretty sure. Sort of."

"Okay, come on," I direct, leading her in search of Gary Plains, who is paged and located in the company cafeteria.

Actually no, the meteorologist tells us, the lightning is not really the same, the kind in Nebraska would be closer to the ground and the footage they pulled from the archives is from the Ozarks.

Alexandra is ten minutes into the newscast before we finally fix it. Gary finds storm footage from South Dakota from five years ago he says is similar to the lightning storms in Nebraska, and so we rewrite the story to cut twelve seconds off the top to accommodate the ten seconds Gary needs to explain that the footage is the same kind of lightning, but is not of Nebraska and why.

It's done, finally, and the final segment of the script is slipped in and the proper video cued up. I slip into the control room to watch the rest of the newscast.

I love it in here. We have two rows of seats in the back. In front of us, across the center console, sits the assistant director, the director, the technical director and down in the corner, the audio director. There is a window to the studio surrounded, floor to ceiling, with monitors. What's so neat is to see how many separate sources go into the actual newscast, how many hundreds of people whose work is smoothly coordinated to present a single stream of information about what has gone on this day in the world.

Print journalism is so different. It is, for one, so incredibly slow. Nowhere else is it more evident to me than when I'm sitting in here, watching the virtually instant transmission of stories from thousands of miles away. I think of the presses, the printing, the folding and collating of newspapers, and then the lumbering forklifts that have to move the tons of paper onto the loading docks, where those same old diesel trucks—not so different from the ones used seventy years ago—are laboriously backed up to the dock, and where those same kind of big beefy union men are still heaving bales of papers by hand, pile after pile. And then trucks roll out, some driving for hundreds of miles at night, all to get that news story on the reader's doorstep when TV has already been covering the same story for at least eighteen hours.

Brevity is the name of the game in TV, though, and we will never cover any aspect of the news as thoroughly as the newspapers can. But newspapers demand literacy, and they demand time, two of the scarcest commodities in America today.

I am always slightly startled by Alexandra's presence on-screen. TV takes her striking features and makes her a raving beauty. Only, perhaps, is her brilliant smile accurately translated in electronics. It is a warm, vaguely stunning smile on camera or off.

But she is getting older. I was looking at some tapes from six years ago the other day, and sitting here now I notice the increasing lines around her eyes and mouth. I wonder if anyone has hinted yet about what is happening to the lids of her eyes, and what will happen to them in the coming years, faster and faster, unless she has something done.

Thirty-seven. She's practically like that boy in the bubble, she's spent most of her life hermetically sealed in a radio or TV studio. How does a girl from a Kansas farm end up with a life like this?

The weather segment is not great, but at least we're not a bunch of liars, trying to pass off pictures of the Ozarks as Nebraska. At the end of the newscast, when the studio lights come on, Alexandra, as she always does, thanks the studio crew, comes into the control room to thank everyone here, and then swings into the newsroom to do the same with the support staff. I follow, waiting for instructions.

"Got your things?" she asks, heading for her dressing room.

"All set."

She looks back over her shoulder. "What about your dog?"

"Jim, the intern, is going to house-sit for me."

"Good," she says, waiting half a second for me to come up alongside her. "I think he's very good."

"I do, too."

"Think he can help you on the Presario-Arlenetta material?" She opens her dressing-room door and gestures for me to go inside. It's not very big, but it's nice. It has wall-to-wall beige carpeting with some kind of little blue designs in it, pale beige wallpaper, some landscape paintings nicely framed in wood, a large vanity table, closets and a door leading to a full bathroom.

"What is it, exactly, you wish me to do with all the Presario-Arlenetta material?"

"Create a special," she says, slipping into the bathroom and closing the door halfway. I hear the zipper on her dress and the bang of a hanger on the back of the door. "I sent up everything we have to your office. Now I want you to work on your pal Lilliana and see what you can get from the family. Pictures, letters, anything."

"I think they destroyed most of everything when they went into the witness protection program."

"I'm sure you'll turn up something," she says, coming out in a robe and throwing panty hose and underwear into the hamper. "She trusts you like no tomorrow. I had quite a talk with her yesterday."

"So you understand my reluctance to do anything that could compromise my credibility as a witness in her brother's trial," I say.

"On the other hand," Alexandra counters, putting her pearls away in a jewelry box on her vanity and proceeding to hang the dress up in the closet, "since it is her brother who's on trial, maybe Lilliana is a better judge of what you should or should not do." She looks over at me. "We've had to move the interview with her grandfather up to tomorrow, and she's insisting you be present for it."

"But I thought—"

"Her brother's defense team is advising Lilliana," Alexandra continues, "so if they think you can be there—off the record, of course—then I don't see how we can object." She takes a step toward me. "Because those are the conditions she's set for this interview—that you be there. So I said okay."

What am I going to say to that? "But I'm still not clear what my role is supposed to be."

"Your role is to produce a special for *DBS News Magazine*," she says, sounding slightly impatient. "Which means

I'm pulling you off everything else to have you focus entirely on this."

"You think I can produce a special on the Presarios and still be a credible witness for the defense?" I say, amazed. "The prosecution's going to accuse me of trying to throw the trial by producing a nationally televised show sympathetic to the Presario family."

"Well, aren't you?"

"Well," I falter, "I don't know. *Are* we?"

"It's a newsmagazine special, Sally," she says, gesturing. "This is not breaking news, this is a news-making special. If one set of people wants to talk to us and no other news group, that's news. The Presarios want to talk to us, and Jonathan Small is the defendant on trial. You're going to produce a special that includes the history of the people we are going to talk to, that's it."

"But we need to bring up the opposing viewpoints, on behalf of those people who won't appear on camera for us," I maintain.

"It's your special, Sally, so make the decision."

I feel like I'm in some sort of face-off. "Of course I'm going to present opposing views," I say firmly.

Alexandra flashes a smile. "Then what's the problem?" She turns around and moves back to the closet, looking inside.

"I guess there's not a problem," I mumble, "but if I'm going to be hanging around with Lilliana again, God knows there'll be one."

The anchorwoman laughs, peeking around the closet door at me. "I have every confidence in you, Sally."

Behind my cynical exterior, of course, my mind is racing. When Alexandra says I'm producing a special for her, she has deliberately left open exactly how long this special might be, or the form it might take. Which means if we get all the interviews I am hopeful that we will—with Rocky Presario, with Frank Presario and the two kids, Jonathan Small and Lilliana herself—and can come up with previously unseen and unpublished materials regarding the history and path of one mafia family gone straight—photographs, anecdotes, letters, diaries, things like that—we could practically have a miniseries on our hands. And Alexandra said it twice: I am producing a special, which means I'll get the producer credit.

This is big time.

"Can you let me have Jim Reinemann full-time on this?"

"Sure," she agrees, pulling a hanger out of the closet with blue jeans on it, and two others with a T-shirt and an ironed blue-jean shirt.

"Cool," I say.

"But there's one thing I need you to do for me this week," she adds, moving over to the built-in dresser to take out panties and a bra. "I need you to cover for me."

My heart leaps, visualizing anchoring the news.

"Not in terms of the newsroom," she clarifies, "but in terms of covering my absence with everyone."

My heart sinks. Put on camera and yanked off, all in the same moment. "Sure," I say.

"I—" she begins, walking to the bathroom. She pauses a moment and then turns around in the doorway to look at me. "It seems that I've got cancer. And I don't want to freak everybody out."

CHAPTER FOUR

Alexandra has breast cancer, but if there is a good kind to have it is what she has been diagnosed with: a malignant tumor in her left breast, caught in the early stages by the second mammogram of her life. "I had a baseline done when I was thirty-five," she explains in the back seat of her limousine. She is now freshly scrubbed, her hair still wet from a quick shower at West End. "I had it done so there would be something to compare future mammograms against." She sighs, looking out the window. "I'm having a lumpectomy day after tomorrow."

"I can go with you if you like," I offer quietly.

She turns to look at me. "That's all right, thank you. What I need for you to do is cover for me at work. I told Will I'm going to be off the radar for a few days, working on something connected to the Presarios. I'd like you to back me up on it."

"Certainly," I say. I try to mind my own business but I can't. "Will you have radiation afterward?"

"Yes," she says, nodding. "Six weeks, they say."

"Then you'll be done with it," I say, trying to sound cheerful. "You know how effective this treatment is, don't you?"

"Yes. It should be all right. I just don't want people panicking." She looks out the window again and then abruptly turns back to me. "It's not that I want to hide it, Sally, that's not it. The second I know I'm going to be all right is the second I will go public with it. I swear. It's just that—" She reaches forward to open the refrigerator and take out a small bottle of Perrier. She offers one to me, which I accept. She always uses a glass, but not this time. She flips off the cap with an opener and sips directly out of the bottle as if it is something other than water. I follow her lead.

She swallows, lowering the bottle to her lap. "My father is very ill right now." Alexandra's father, Paul Waring, the retired congressman, is back on the family farm in Kansas. "My mom has all she can handle right now. So I don't want her to hear anything about it until I know everything is okay."

I'm tempted to ask what she will do if everything is not okay.

"I've also been putting off an arthroscopic procedure on my shoulder." She touches it and keeps her hand there. "Where I got shot years ago."

Alexandra was shot on national television while conducting an interview on the stairs of the Capitol building. If you ever wondered why the press can't stand on the stairs of the Capitol building anymore, now you know.

"So I'm going to get a bone chip and some scar tissue taken out the same day."

"Your doctor will let you do that?" I blurt out. "The procedure on your breast is not heavy-duty, but it is surgery and—"

"Thank you," Alexandra says sharply. But then she lessens her tone of voice. "I've heard it already, Sally. And thank you for your concern, but this is what I'm doing. I'm only telling you as a courtesy for doing me this favor."

"It's just that since my mother went through so much with her cancer," I persist, "a tremendously more aggressive form of cancer, I guess I feel like I know something about it."

"I can appreciate that," she says with finality, but then adds a slight smile to soften it.

We are suddenly a little shy with each other. Medical stuff is always like this.

"Not to change the subject," I begin.

"Oh, please, change the subject," she begs me. She looks so tired and now I know why. She's terrified. It doesn't matter what the doctors tell you, the word *cancer* scares you to death anyway. I remember so well, because my mother had that same look Alexandra has right now, and had that same strained pitch to her voice after she had been diagnosed. Only mother's cancer had been lymphatic, and her treatment had been drastic and long.

"If my presence at the Rocky Presario interview is supposed to be off the record, I don't think I should arrive in an official DBS News vehicle tomorrow, do you?"

"You're still hung up on the California prosecutor."

"Well, it's one thing for me to be working on a special, and it's another to appear to be influencing the course of an interview. Do you know what I mean? I can always present all the original footage and material I was given to create a special out of, but how can I prove I didn't tell Rocky to say something at the time of the filming?"

Alexandra chuckles. "The way that mind of yours works. Well, what is it you suggest?"

I check my watch. It's close to midnight. "We could swing by Newark and I could pick up a rental. Then I'll follow you out and drive it over to Rocky's tomorrow. It may seem like a petty distinction to you, but I would feel a lot more comfortable doing it that way, if I'm not officially supposed to be there."

Alexandra picks up the in-car phone and tells the driver to head for Newark Airport.

An hour and a half later, I am following the taillights of her limo down the road of Alexandra's farm. We parallel two open fields and then sink into a wooded area, the new spring green of the trees lofting high overhead as a cover, and emerge into a clearing ablaze with light. The farmhouse is a quietly magnificent place. Set on top of a rise, it is a white Victorian with a porch extending all the way across the front and around the side. A lawn rolls down in front, gently leveling out to a small pond and flower gardens.

The limo pulls off to the right, around the circular drive in front of the house, and Alexandra rolls down her window to tell me to park in the back, by the barn. I drive down there and find the spot she mentioned. I don't know how to describe it other than to say it's a kind of a Victorian gazebo for cars. Or maybe it is an old carriage port, but if it is, then shouldn't it be attached to the side of the house? Whatever, there is already a big blue Chevy Tahoe parked there and I slip my white Ford Taurus into the other space.

I hear the whinny of a horse. Beyond the barn is a stable, a paddock and another outer building. Directly behind the house is a swimming pool. Alexandra has quite a bit of acreage and leases the land to local farmers. The agricultural use gains her some kind of tax concessions. Regardless, this whole exercise is a very expensive proposition, and developers salivate at the thought of Alexandra ever selling.

I walk back to the front of the house, where the driver is bringing our bags up the stairs. I follow him inside and say all the appropriate things one should say when a farmhouse is both beautifully and comfortably furnished. It's not a fortune in antiques or anything; her taste is a lot like mine. She likes real wood, she likes natural fabrics, she likes brass. It is very nice, and yet retains the atmosphere of a farm.

I follow Alexandra upstairs, where on the landing she turns left and points me to go to the right. At the end of the hall a door is open and I walk in to find what amounts to a suite: a bedroom with a queen-size bed, a full bathroom and a separate sitting room.

Alexandra calls down the hall that there is a snack to be had in twenty minutes if I'm interested. I'm interested.

So after I freshen up I go downstairs to the kitchen. "I have some homemade vegetable stew," she says. "And I can offer a slice of garlic bread."

"Sold," I say, wandering over to the bay window to look out. There's not much to see in the dark, so I sit down and watch her. That's when I notice a photograph of Georgiana Hamilton-Ayres by the telephone, the actress who has been romantically linked to Alexandra for a while. She is looking at the camera while a horse is nuzzling the side of her face. No one speaks of this relationship at DBS, but then, no one dares to speak about Alexandra's personal life, period.

But now I'm in her private home, for Pete's sake, and her girlfriend's picture is plainly sitting there in front of my face.

"Did you know," I say conversationally, "that when Frank Presario went into the witness protection program, he changed Lise's—" I pronounce this *Leeza's*—"name to Lilliana because he saw Georgiana Hamilton-Ayres's mother on the front of the *New York Post*?"

"I think I heard something about that," Alexandra says, peeking in the oven to check on the bread.

"He said he saw a picture of Lillian Bartlett on the stairs of some courthouse, dragging her daughter behind her." The former Lillian Rosenblatt of Brooklyn, New York, who had became a reigning movie queen of the late 1950s and early 1960s, had married the financially compromised and rather eccentric Lord Hamilton-Ayres of Scotland. After the free-spirited (read, pill-popping, heavy-drinking) Hollywood beauty managed to pull her husband's ancestral estate out of hock, he kept her there as a virtual prisoner for the duration of her pregnancy. A healthy little Georgiana had been the result. Lillian later bolted with the child to Hollywood, where she resumed her wild ways, and thus began a very long, very public custody battle.

While Lillian Bartlett would for years run from one scandalous romantic mess to another, and Lord Hamilton-Ayres grew even dottier—roaming the castle, talking to ghosts, taking up causes like the reinstitution of iron horseshoes— Georgiana grew up virtually in the public eye, smiling sweetly and acting pretty normal, which of course she wasn't. She became a major motion picture actress in her own right and although she was never as voluptuous as her crazy mother, she too became somewhat of a sex symbol.

This is who Alexandra Waring has allegedly been involved with for a few years now. There had been a marriage somewhere in Georgiana Hamilton-Ayres's past, and certainly Alexandra had been very publicly engaged at one point, but now people pretty much assume they are gay, or are sort of gay, or something, but since they're both so talented and attractive, the rumors don't seem to have diminished their appeal to the public. On the other hand, I can't imagine what kind of life it is they share.

"I should get a copy of that front page for the special," I say out loud.

"It would make a good visual," Alexandra agrees, "although I'm not sure how much Georgiana's going to like it. Her parents are still in court, if you can believe it. Thirty-some-odd years and they're still at it."

"Frank liked the name Lillian," I continue, "but he loved the name Lise, so he stuck the 'a' on the end and thus Lilliana was born. And it's all because of a picture she was in as a child," I summarize, nodding to the photo of Georgiana Hamilton-Ayres.

Alexandra shakes her head, laughing softly to herself. She is standing at the stove in her socks, stirring a saucepan. "That is the most roundabout way of trying to make polite chitchat without sticking your nose in my business I've ever heard."

"Well," I say, "I'm tempted to ask how she's doing, like I would inquire after anyone's—" Now I am stuck. Anyone's what? Friend? Lover? Girlfriend? Other half?

"She's shooting a movie in British Columbia," the anchorwoman replies, and by the tone of her voice I know this is supposed to conclude this part of the conversation. After a moment, she turns to look at me. "I'm sorry, I didn't mean to be rude."

"Don't worry about it," I assure her, getting up. "I was just going to go into your den and look for something to read, if you don't mind." I move toward the doorway.

"Sally—"

I turn around.

"Sit." She proceeds to get me a beer out of the refrigerator without asking me if I want one. She plunks a glass down in front of me, twists off the top of an Amstel Lite and starts pouring. "We have to have this conversation at some point anyway. You're working too close to me not to."

I don't say anything.

"Truth is," she says, putting the bottle down and sitting across from me, "Georgiana and I are in a funny place right now."

"Hmm," I say in acknowledgement, sipping the beer. It is icy cold and tastes wonderful. "Heaven knows, I know what that's like. Although I'm not sure any of my relationships have ever been anywhere *other* than in a funny place."

She smiles a little. "So, I don't want to confuse the issues right now. By dragging my health into the picture."

I nod. "So you don't want to tell her."

She shakes her head. "No."

"I can understand that," I say quietly.

The anchorwoman gets up, picks up the empty beer bottle and walks over to the sink to rinse it out and place it on the counter. Then she opens some cupboards to take out plates and put soup bowls on them.

"Relationships are hard enough," I say. "I can't imagine what it's like with the demands of your careers."

"I'll say," she says, bending to open the oven again. The garlic bread smells divine. She leaves the door open a crack and tosses the pot holder on the counter. "Somehow you don't think about things like career demands, not in the beginning, when you first meet each other."

"I think it's wonderful and amazing that you've been able to have anything at all," I say. She looks at me, frowning slightly, confused, I think, by what I mean. "I think it's wonderful you went ahead and pursued the relationship you wanted, that you got to explore it, and got to keep your job while doing it. Under the circumstances, I mean. Let's face it, a whole lot of jobs at DBS News depend entirely on you."

"DBS News has given me tremendous support. And protection. In a lot of ways, DBS made it possible." She turns to the saucepan, sighing heavily suddenly, bringing her hand up to her forehead.

I wait a moment and then say, "It's a lot, I know. But this, too, shall pass. You just need time. At least, that's what my mother always tells me."

She drops her hand. "Your mother is a very wonderful person."

"Yeah, I know. Maybe we should both take her advice."

Alexandra picks up the pot holder and opens the oven again, this time taking the garlic bread out. I don't say anything more about anything we've talked about thus far and nor does she. Instead, we sit down and eat supper—it is out of this world—and talk about horses. She owns two.

CHAPTER FIVE

Blame it on my white Anglo-Saxon Protestant heritage if you like, but I strongly resist the notion of a magnificent drive purposely lined with trees other than oak, maple or elm. Maybe even beech. Or birch, if they can survive. So when I see two large redbrick columns, topped by delicate gold metal lanterns, that mark the beginning of a long stretch of Japanese maple trees, I know I am traveling into unfamiliar cultural territory.

I follow Alexandra's limousine in my rented Taurus and am mildly astonished to realize that the gravel we're driving over is crushed marble. The Presario house soon comes into view, a tremendous, heavy, redbrick mansion, sort of pseudo-Mediterranean, with white wood windows and a lot of white wrought iron. I follow the limo around the circle in front to the huge double white front doors.

A tall, dark, stocky man in a blue suit hurries to my window. "If you don't mind, Ms. Harrington, we'd like you to park in the back. If you go around the side there, you'll see the other DBS News vehicles." I guess retired mafia dons don't like Ford Tauruses or something in front of their mansions, but since the man has gone to the trouble of somehow recognizing me, I dutifully follow his instructions and drive around to the back. I see one of our mobile trucks and two of the company cars, and park in the space nearest the house.

As I climb out, a small window opens on the second floor and an older lady says, "You! You late with the breakfast!"

I look up at her. "Excuse me?"

"Oh!" she says, covering her mouth. "I sorry. You the wrong lady." And she slams the window shut.

One of the grips comes dashing out to get something from the truck and I follow him back inside the mansion, flashing my DBS badge to another large man standing just inside the kitchen door. I am led into the living room, where the producer of credit, Mitch Randall, has been setting up with the crew for hours. Like all the DBS News people, Mitch gives me a long look when I arrive because he hasn't figured out yet what it is, exactly, I've been hired to do. Am I an extension of Alexandra's power, am I an extension of Alexandra's capabilities, or am I simply a snitch? Healey O'Baird, the best crew manager DBS has, is here, and so are the best two cameramen, Hector Vega and Peter Zu. Actually, Peter is a former Hollywood cinematographer, so it's no wonder why Alexandra likes him. And even Cleo's been brought out here to make sure visual justice is done to the don.

I've never met Rocky Presario, although I certainly have heard a lot about him. Rocky was one of the great East Coast labor organizers and later building contractors, and it was his son, Frank, who tried to clean up the unions under his father's control, which, in the 1970s, had expanded into Atlantic City. That's when all the family's problems started, when the Arlenetta branch of the Genovese crime family in New York tried to take over the Presario unions and failed because of Frank. Nick Arlenetta then put the hit on Frank Presario, and Frank's wife, Celia, was killed instead. This would pit cousin against cousin for the next twenty years, culminating in Frank's son, Jonathan, shooting—some say executing—Nick Arlenetta earlier this year, prompting "The Mafia Boss Murder" trial in L.A.

The notes I have provided Alexandra with for today include a family tree that looks like this:

Joseph Arlenetta—m—Gina Presario
<u>(died in prison)</u>   (sister of)

                Rocky Presario—m—Isabella Gallini
                              <u>(died nat. causes)</u>

Nicky Arlenetta   Frank Presario—m—Celia Bruno
(murdered)   <u>(I. Frederick Small)</u>   (murdered)

Rose   Taylor Presario (later) Jonathan Small

Theresa   Lise Presario (later) Lilliana Martin

Clifford
(murdered)

Michael

Rocky's granddaughter, the actress Lilliana Martin, makes her entrance in sweatpants and a bare-waisted T-shirt that serves to get people's attention fast. She is not tall—a little over five foot four, maybe—but is so sleekly fit, and has this bleached-blond thing going on with her long hair, that she appears larger than life. She has brown eyes and dark eyebrows, olive skin, a brilliant smile and a large chest (which, at the moment, the crew seems particularly taken with). It's interesting, though, that despite the dyed-blond showbiz sensationalism of her hair, Lilliana's face is one of marked intelligence. She's a complicated young woman with an extremely complicated past and I have learned to be slightly wary of her.

Don't get me wrong, I like Lilliana. And I admire her. But she's kind of dangerous, a daughter of secrets who has spent her life using her looks and acting ability to fool the world. And to hide the loneliness that has tormented her since she was a child.

Lilliana greets the crew and gives Alexandra a warm welcome. The two women talk for a bit, turning toward me, and Lilliana smiles and gives me a little wave. Then she comes over. "Stick with me," she murmurs, elbowing me, "and you'll be president of DBS in no time."

"More likely I'll be six feet under," I say. We've been through a lot, Lilliana and I. "How's your brother?"

"Miserable, but hopeful, as we all are." She purses her lips slightly, eyes working down me. "My but you're looking very official."

I smile. "Yeah, and you, too."

"I was just working out," she says, which cannot be further from the truth. I've seen Lilliana work out and she gets drenched from head to toe. More likely she just rolled out of bed and dabbed on that scent of musk I smell. Now she is giving a catlike stretch, distracting the boys from their jobs. "She's going to be good to Poppy, isn't she?" she asks me, eyes on Alexandra.

"I think you'll be pleased."

"She looks different than on TV," she muses, checking her out. "So she and Georgiana Hamilton-Ayres...?" She looks at me quizzically.

"Why, are you interested?"

"Not my type," she says. She rubs the back of her neck, making her shirt rise tight against her breasts. The boys are beside themselves. She nods toward Hector. "Though I find him rather attractive."

I resist wanting to say that in the right mood Lilliana seems to find almost anyone attractive. (I think of my friend Michael Anderson, who has a lifelong specialty in complicated women, and wonder if I might recruit him to occupy Lilliana's time and keep her out of trouble. No, I think a second later, I couldn't do it to Michael.)

She smiles, slinging her arm through mine. "Come on, I want to talk to you," she says, pulling me out of the living room. We walk into the foyer, which, like the outside of the house, is a bit over the top. The white marble floor is rather pretty, but there is gilding all over everything, and the black wrought-iron staircase that sweeps down from the second floor doesn't seem to fit. Then there are all these marble statues around, sitting on fancy pedestals.

Lilliana plunks herself down on the second-last stair and looks up at me. "Thank God you guys came. We're all so bored. Jonathan's lawyers won't let us do anything, say anything, go anywhere, nothing. My agent's sent me a hundred scripts and I have to put everything on hold until they say so."

"Really?"

"Yes, really, and I'm bored out of my skull."

"Well, so listen," I tell her. "I've got something you can do. Something *really* interesting. Alexandra's just put me full-time on a special. Or specials."

"Of what?"

"Of your family."

"What, you mean like the interviews with us?"

I nod. "She wants me to do all the research and dig up whatever new background stuff I can. The more visuals I can come up with—pictures, newspaper clippings, yearbooks, wedding albums, home movies, videos..."

"Yeeessss," Lilliana prompts in a low, expectant tone of voice.

"The more airtime we'll get to present the facts behind your brother's case."

"That's what the lawyers want," she says. "But in a controlled way. They pretty much told Poppy what he should say today. I'm not sure when they'll let Dad or me do our interviews with Alexandra."

"Probably when they can trust what will come out of your mouth," I say honestly.

"Alexandra did say she could wait on us for a while."

"So the thing is," I resume, "we have the interviews, but the more pictures and things I can find no one else has seen, or published in a long time, the more time we'll get to make the public sympathetic to Jonathan."

She meets my eyes. "And what exactly do you want of me?"

"I was hoping you'd work with me on it."

"Work on it, like how?"

"Well, I was thinking, if anyone knew where such things existed, the kinds of things I'm looking for, it would probably be you."

"No, it would be Dad," she corrects me.

"Well, right. But he's in California."

Lilliana's eyes have focused on something behind me. "I think I know where there might be a few things of Mom's." She has a thought, her eyes sweeping back to me. "We could do my mother's story, couldn't we?" She starts to get excited, her eyes taking on a new light as she says, "Obviously you can't talk to her, but if I could find some letters of hers— You know, I have a letter she wrote me once! From Italy. When I was little. It's this wonderful letter about her and Dad visiting relatives and how she had found a doll for me."

"That's exactly the kind of thing I'm hoping for," I tell her.

"I think there must be things somewhere." She squints, thinking. "When Dad put us in the witness protection program, he was supposed to get rid of everything. But I can't believe he destroyed it all. It must be somewhere..."

"So," I say, bending nearer to lower my voice, "my thinking is this. If we have the interviews with your grandfather, your father, your brother and you, and we can find enough visuals and letters and things, then I'm going to push we produce something like a miniseries. Tell the whole story, from beginning to end, starting with your great-grandfather getting off the boat from Italy."

She frowns a little. "Not like *The Godfather.*"

I hesitate. Much of the recent Presario family story is about their struggle to break free of organized crime roots and take their interests legit, but the fact still remains, Lilliana's grandfather is a retired mafia don, her cousin murdered her mother, and her brother murdered her cousin. In other words, the family story is blood and money from the word go.

"It is the story of an American family," I say carefully, "whose ancestors began on the wrong foot, but whose descendants were determined to live the American dream. Your great-grandfather was an immigrant stonemason, your grandfather built construction unions, your father cleaned up the unions and was forced to give up his identity. But in his new identity he reeducated himself and became a major computer chip maker. Your brother went to Harvard and is—was—head of production at a major Hollywood studio.

And you, little Lise Presario, had foster parents and a made-up life for years, but nonetheless have become a major acting talent in your own right. That's the story. And what a story it is."

I swallow, standing up straight, waiting for her reaction.

She is thinking, eyes moving around the foyer. They come up to me. "Where would we work on this?"

"Wherever you want," I say. "I'd prefer West End because I can set up a dedicated working space for us. I'm sure we could work something out about a hotel in Manhattan."

I can tell she's still trying to think this through.

"Look, why don't you talk to your brother's lawyers and run it by them?" I suggest. "Take your time. I have a lot of work to do as it is. Anything I might be able to find through you will be gravy. So I'll get started and you just get back to me when you can."

She's looking at me with the strangest expression. "Lilliana," I say, dropping down in front of her, "you don't have to do this. In fact, it may be something that's too much right now, too emotional, too stressful. With everything that's going on with the trial."

"It's not that," she murmurs, dropping her head for a moment. When she raises it again I see that her eyes are red, that she is trying not to cry. "I need to do something," she whispers. "I am so angry and so screwed up over all this. I can't believe Jonathan's in prison. I can't believe that scumbag Nick murders like a hundred people and they put Jonathan in prison. They should be holding a parade in his honor for doing what the feds couldn't do. Which was to stop him."

"I know," I say softly.

"Excuse me, Sally?" the grip calls. "I'm sorry, but Alexandra wants to see you."

I tell him okay, I'll be right there. "Well," I say to Lilliana, "just let me know what you want to do. You've got all my numbers." I pause. "And remember, you don't have to do this. And if you just need someone to talk to, you know you can always call me. I'm going to do this program as a part of my job, but I also want to do whatever I can to help you. And your family." I pause again. "I better go."

"Yes," she says, watching me stand up. She smiles a little, rubbing her eye a minute, and then gets up too.

Back in the living room, which is now practically a full-fledged TV studio, the grip hurries over. "Sally, can we get your keys? They need to move your car."

"Where are you parked?" Lilliana asks me.

"Just outside the kitchen."

Lilliana frowns and looks over at the tall dark man standing by the other door. "Jocko, why do you have to move her car?"

"It would be better if it were on the other side," he says.

"Other side of what?" she says, annoyed. "Leave her car where it is and go get Poppy. And where's Marvin?"

"He's coming," someone says.

In a moment a very distinguished-looking gentleman walks in and Lilliana waves him over. "Did you go over everything with Alexandra Waring?"

"Yes," he tells her.

"Then go over it again with Sally, here, please." She looks at me. "It's the terms of the interview, okay?" She touches my arm briefly, before moving away. "You'll be hearing from me. Soon."

Marvin is evidently a cross between a lawyer and a bouncer. "I've told Mitch Randall and I've told Alexandra Waring and now I am telling you, Miss Harrington, that if Miss Waring strays from the questions she submitted and we approved, Mr. Presario will be taken from this room and the film in those cameras will become history. Do you understand?"

"I understand," I say.

He recaps the specific no-no areas Alexandra cannot talk about: Jimmy Hoffa, an accountant named Clayo Partella, a dancer named Bambi, the Wildwood Galleria Shops, toxic waste in Bayonne, hotel labor contracts in Atlantic City and anything connected with the construction of the Brendan Byrne Arena.

Rocky Presario finally arrives in the room, on his own steam, but barely. Leaning heavily on a walking stick, he shuffles in. He is perhaps five foot seven and heavyset, and still possesses a good head of hair, white with a little dark gray here and there. His face is deeply lined, his small eyes deeply set, but they are glittering, alive.

Alexandra shakes his hand with both of hers, holding it for a long while as she leans close to whisper something only he can hear. He smiles, then barks the deep, raspy laugh of an ex-smoker and knocks the side of her leg with his stick. "You're a pistol. Eh, what did you do to my living room? Looks like Hollywood in here. What am I, a big star like you, Leeza?"

"That's right, Poppy," Lilliana tells him. "We even have a makeup lady for you."

He turns to Alexandra. "Make me pretty, huh? My nose has been busted six times, I don't think you can do much about it."

Everybody laughs. He is cute. Hard to believe he was, in his day, probably a killer.

"Eh," he says again, looking around, "where's the crazy one? Little Leeza's friend. Sally. Who is she?"

Alexandra points me out. I walk over to say hi.

"You!" He chuckles, swinging his stick out to bump my leg. "You are a spicy nut, cookie."

I smile. I don't think anybody's ever called me cookie before, and I am quite sure I've never been called a spicy nut.

"You help my grandson," he tells me, his head leaning close and his voice taking on a serious tone. "He's a good boy. He did what he had to do."

"I understand that, Mr. Presario. That's why we're here. To get to the truth."

I back off to the corner, out of the way, as Alexandra takes over. She is so smooth it makes you wonder a little about her sincerity in life. She coddles and cajoles Rocky just the right way and we can all see him falling for her.

"Oh, boy, she's trouble," Lilliana whispers, moving over to stand next to me .

"She wouldn't do anything that would hurt him," I whisper back.

Lilliana gives me a look. "How do you think she's gotten where she is? By letting people only talk about what they intended to talk about? Get real."

"She won't do anything to compromise the interview," I insist, making the audio engineer hiss at me to be quiet.

And so begins the first interview Rocky Presario has had with the press in his fifty-year career as a crime boss.

Alexandra talks to him for almost an hour and a half straight. The cameramen have worked with her before, knowing that she likes to keep going as long as the subject lasts, and they time their video cartridge changes so at least one of the two cameras is always rolling. With the exception of pausing to sip water several times, Rocky seems very happy to be on camera, very happy to bask in the attention of the pretty anchorwoman. And he talks. Boy, does he talk, and it is, in fact, Alexandra who has to carefully steer him away from the no-no areas. For the first hour she has him talking about his childhood in Fort Lee and his nine younger brothers and sisters, and how he dropped out of school to help support the family by working a cement truck for a Gambino construction company and ended up rising through union ranks to president.

While Rocky whitewashes his story to sound like an all-American rags-to-riches tale, he is not shy about the origins of his brother-in-law, Nick Arlenetta's father, Joe. "My sister Gina got tripped up by this guy," he explains, "and there was not much I could do about it, if you know what I mean. Those were the olden days and the right thing to do was to get married, so they got married—and it was a very beautiful wedding we threw, in Fort Lee, but let me tell you about this Joe Arlenetta. He worked for the Genovese family, you know who they are? Well, this Joe was a tough, not educated, not worldly, but a muscle, and he muscled his way into the hotel and restaurant unions. Maids, waiters, catering, you know. Took the money off the top.

"Now, of course, with me being in construction, Joe was naturally interested in how our unions worked and he had this kid, Nick, his oldest, who was nothing but trouble."

Rocky describes how Nick was arrested for running numbers as a kid, and how Rocky took pity on his older sister, Gina, and gave her money to send Nick away to military school, how Nick ran away and lived with a gang in the Bronx and how Nick was arrested for murder.

"But by now you had your own children," Alexandra says.

"Oh, yes. Frankie. My Frank. Good boy. While Nicky was killing people in the Bronx, my Frankie was at the seminary."

Alexandra's eyebrows shoot up. "Seminary?"

"Yeah, my wife thought we should have a priest in the family, that's the way it was back then, and that's what you did, sent the eldest. But Frankie was no priest. I mean, he's a good boy, through and through, but—but, you know—" He shrugs. "The life of a priest was not the life for him."

"So he left the seminary?"

He barks that raspy laugh and covers his mouth, struggling to stop. I wonder if Rocky has emphysema. He takes some water, wipes his eyes and blows his nose with his handkerchief and resumes. "He left the seminary and married this wonderful, beautiful girl, Celia, beautiful Celia from Rosemont College."

Alexandra asks if Celia Bruno was, in fact, related to Angelo Bruno, the don of Philadelphia. "Angelo was a man of business, I know that" is all he acknowledges. "Anyway, Nicky went to work for Joe, his father the tough—nearly broke Gina's heart—but what was she gonna do? At least Joe would look out for him, or at least that's what she hoped. While my Frankie's graduating from Georgetown University, her Nicky's arrested again for slitting the throat of some fag waiter in midtown. So you can see what kind of trouble's coming."

He explains how Frankie became a union executive. "There was an old style of doing business before, you see?" he says. "My Frank wanted to bring us to modern times. Good work, good money for all."

"It has been said that Frankie tried to get organized crime out of the unions," Alexandra says.

"Oh, well, everyone wanted organized crime out of the unions," Rocky says with a hint of a smile. "None more than me. It was terrible, that organized crime."

Beside me, Lilliana has clamped a hand over her mouth to keep from laughing.

"But Nicky, that Nicky, he wanted to bring the New York crime families into our New Jersey unions and it was my Frank who stood up to him. And then Nick tried to push his way into Atlantic City, and Frankie blocked him and—" He sighs heavily, shaking his head, suddenly looking very old. "My Frank suffered the worst pain a man can have."

He explains how Nicky Arlenetta put the hit on Frank and the bomb that was placed in Frank's car ended up killing his wife, Celia. He explains how, shortly thereafter, Angelo Bruno was found slain in his car. And how Frankie Presario went to the feds and turned state's evidence against the Arlenettas, and how the old tough Joe Arlenetta was convicted on racketeering charges and was sent to prison, where he died. He also tells how Nick Arlenetta not only ducked the hangman's noose again, but any kind of prison sentence. "He let his father take the fall. I ask you, what kind of son is that?"

As Rocky recalls the day he had to say goodbye to his widowed son, Frank, and his grandchildren, Taylor and Lise Presario, his eyes fill with tears. He describes how little Lise became Lilliana and had to go into a foster home somewhere in the Midwest, and how Frank and Taylor, now Frederick and Jonathan Small, disappeared.

Now, almost two hours into the interview, Rocky speaks of Joe Presario's fourth child, Cliff, who became so ashamed of his father and brother that he changed his name. Rocky's eyes mist over as he describes how Cliff grew close to him, how Cliff became practically a son. He describes Cliff's collegiate achievements at NYU and how Cliff joined one of his unions in New Jersey as financial executive.

"That must have angered his brother Nick," Alexandra remarks.

Rocky grins, showing the last gasp of a full-set of tobacco-stained teeth. "Nicky at least had the sense to be scared of me," he says. "So he had the sense to leave his brother alone. For a while. Until Cliff went to Los Angeles to bring in the AFTW into Hollywood."

"The American Federation of Technical Workers," Alexandra says. "This was a comparatively new union, of computer workers."

He nods. "Good organization. They needed a union. This new technology—it wasn't right to have them in the truckers' union."

"What happened then?"

"Nicky wanted in." He smiles a little, eyes glittering. "Which is what we were all waiting for." He leans forward. "My nephew, Cliff, you see, was doing business with a family all right, just not the one Nicky hoped. He was doing business with my grandson, Jonathan Small, who was just made head of production at Monarch Studios. And Cliffie was hanging out with a glamorous actress—" He laughs, coughing, grabbing his water to clear his throat. "Lilliana, my little Leeza. All grown up and that stupid Nicky doesn't even know who she is. And my Frankie, the president of one of the largest computer chip companies in the United States. My family was doing business with Cliffie all right." He leans forward toward Alexandra to point his finger. "The family was going to give Nicky the business and how." He's thrown into another fit of coughing.

Rocky proceeds to describe how, when Cliff wouldn't play ball and let Nick move the Mob into the AFTW, Nick ordered the murder of his brother. Then he describes how Nick almost succeeded in killing Lilliana. "He murdered his own brother, was determined to kill my granddaughter, and he was determined to find and kill my son. The police could do nothing to stop him and so I ask you," he says, leaning forward again, narrowing his eyes at Alexandra, "I ask you what you would do."

"I would hide my family," Alexandra says.

"We did. And he came after them still. So what would do you then, eh? Let them live in fear until they are murdered, one by one?"

"I would defend them," Alexandra says.

"How?" the old man demands.

"In whatever way I could."

"And if it meant killing Nick before he killed your family?"

"If there was no other way, I would probably kill him," Alexandra admits.

There is a long silence while Rocky Presario takes measure of the anchorwoman. Then slowly he nods, satisfied. Finally he turns to the cameras, blinking against the light. "I am finished," he announces.

CHAPTER SIX

Driving back to Manhattan, I wonder if Alexandra will use her admission in the interview, that if someone was threatening to kill her family and she felt she had no other choice, she would probably kill him. To show this part would violate a basic tenet of journalism, that the purpose of the interview is to reveal the interviewee, not the interviewer. On the other hand, Rocky was pointing out the essential point in the upcoming "Mafia Boss Murder" trial, that Nick Arlenetta had murdered Jonathan's mother, vowed to murder his father, murdered his own brother and very nearly murdered Jonathan's sister without the authorities being able to lay a finger on him, so Jonathan Small was forced to kill him first.

This all sounds pretty good until you understand that Nicky Arlenetta had not realized that Jonathan Small was his cousin. And so, when Jonathan had cordially invited him to Monarch Studios to discuss union negotiations, Nick had been expecting to be recognized as the unofficial new union boss. Instead, he found a 32 mm gun pointed right between his eyes. And that was that; in the next moment he was dead. Regardless of the circumstances, premeditated murder is virtually indefensible. To carry it out, it means someone had to very carefully and quite deliberately choose wrong over right.

It's rush hour as I approach the Lincoln Tunnel, and since the inbound traffic lanes are reduced to accommodate exiting commuters, the delay is as long to get in to the city as out. But I make it through, finally, and surface in Manhattan, and head uptown to the car rental place at Fifty-sixth Street and Tenth Avenue. I hand the car over to an attendant, who prints out a receipt on a handheld device, and then I grab my bags and dash to the street to catch a cab.

I check my watch: six-twenty. Okay, I've got to get my story straight at DBS. Alexandra has gone off the radar to do some work on the Presario-Arlenetta story. She'll be back on Monday or Tuesday. When I asked her why she wasn't coming back to West End to do the newscast tonight (her surgery's scheduled for tomorrow at 7:00 a.m.), she looked a little annoyed, but said she needed to do some things with her lawyer before going into the hospital.

That's when I realized how shaken she was by the diagnosis. One time I had to go back to my gynecologist to have a second Pap smear taken because the results of the first had been slightly off. "I'm sure it's not serious," the doctor told me. "It could be a problem at the lab, but I need to do another to make sure." By the time I was back in his office, I had myself dead and buried, and my will had finally been executed. The point is, when all of a sudden you are forced to think of your own mortality, a lot of us panic, because all of those things we meant to do about our estates are still undone—so we drop everything and do it, fast. Evidently Alexandra was no exception.

"Hi, Benjamin," I say to the anchorwoman's secretary, taking the last turn into my office.

"Alexandra's not coming back, right?" he calls.

"No, not until Monday or Tuesday," I confirm, turning around.

"Will wants to see you," he tells me, resuming his typing on the computer. "I think he's in the newsroom."

I drop my overnight bag and briefcase in my office and circle my desk to check my voice mail. There is a note on my chair, under which I find the keys to my apartment. "As per Alexandra," the note reads, "I've put all the P-A materials in a secure work space. I've got a final tonight, but will be in first thing tomorrow if you need me. Jim Reinemann." I glance over; indeed, the boxes are gone.

There's nothing important on my voice mail; I check my e-mail. I'm in luck, not much there either. Maybe word has spread in advance that for the time being I've been pulled from the day-to-day news operation.

I hustle downstairs to the newsroom. The assistant producer tries to give me a script but I wave him off, explaining I've been assigned to something else for a while. He frowns a little and then blurts out, "What the hell do you do, anyway?"

"The right thing, clearly," I let him know, moving on. I find Will in the satellite room, trying to help the techs sort out an international transmission problem. When they decide to reroute a transmission through the company's other satellite, Will tells them to let him know the outcome and then focuses his attention on me. "How did it go today?" he asks, lightly putting his arm around me to steer me down the corridor to the newsroom. It's a gesture of camaraderie and I find it nice. Will is a gentleman and one never needs to worry on that score.

"Very, very well. She got him talking for two straight hours. We thought she had him around her little finger, until he got her to admit that put in Jonathan's position, she'd probably have killed Nicky Arlenetta too."

He stops short to look at me. "No way."

"Oh, yeah," I tell him. "And then Rocky said that was it, he had nothing more to say. And the interview was over."

Will makes a face of mock horror, dropping his arm. "How did Alexandra react?"

"She was as surprised as the rest of us, I think. And actually very pleased. I think because it was an honest kind of interview." But then I start laughing. "That is, if you can call an interview with a retired mafia don—who claims he was always working to get organized crime out of the unions—*honest*."

He chuckles and we walk on. "Was Lilliana there?"

"She had all the guys drooling."

"Did you talk to her?"

"Yeah. And she wants to help. She's going to look for material."

"That's great," Will says, stopping again. "Look, Sally, I gotta tell you, I'm sorry to be losing you right now—"

"You're executive producer of the magazine show, too," I remind him. "You're still my boss."

"Yeah, right, I'm the boss of you just like I'm the boss of Alexandra," he says with a laugh. He looks at his watch. "I gotta move. We're trying Paul Levitz in the anchor slot tonight."

Paul is the editor and segment anchor for business and the economy. He's been around a long time—I think he is sixty-something—and as far as I know, this is the first time he has filled in for Alexandra. *Good for him*, I think, although I'd gladly mug the guy so I could anchor instead. Alexandra did try me out once, not long ago, introducing an experimental new category called "Crime and Punishment," but I have not been invited back into the studio in that capacity since. I am very grateful for my opportunity at DBS News, please don't get me wrong, but I can't help wondering if I'll ever get back on the air as a reporter. Or as something.

What is the point, after all, of being a journalist who has inherited some good looks from my mother unless I use them on TV? (Unfortunately, in this line of work, as you may have noticed, everybody tends to be good-looking.)

"Needless to say," Will says, "unless for some reason Alexandra needs you to work different hours, there's no reason for you to keep the vampire schedule."

"On this project? Frankly, I think I'll be working all hours to get everything that Alexandra is hoping for done."

"Well, you'll do great, I'm sure," he says. He walks down

the hall, but then turns around. "Do you know exactly where Alexandra is?"

I shake my head. "No. She really wants to be off the radar."

He nods, looking vaguely puzzled, and I wonder if she's ever done this before, gone off the radar without telling Will where she is. Somehow I doubt it.

I suppress a yawn, wondering if I might be able to slip out of West End and go home early. I could go for a run with Scotty in Riverside Park, get something good for dinner and curl up with a movie and today's newspapers. Kind of a mini-vacation. Sounds like an excellent idea to me, so I go back up to my office to gather my things, tell Benjamin good-night and head to the dog run.

"Hi, Scotty boy!" I call. Scotty starts dancing, running in circles and then leaps up on the wire wall of the run. I liberate him from the cage, explain to the attendant I will feed him later, and snap on his leash for the trek home.

We round the side of the complex to the carport, hoping there might be a cab. We are in luck and the driver agrees to take Scotty. Scotty jumps in the back seat and I climb in after him and close the door. The next thing I know, there are sirens screaming and a cop car pulls in front of us, and another pulls in behind us, blocking us in, and officers are jumping out. Scotty, of course, has gone crazy.

"What the—?" I say out loud.

"Sally Harrington?" a cop barks through the speaker on top of his police car.

I laugh nervously, thinking this must be a joke.

"Sally Harrington," he says again.

I get a tighter grip on Scotty's leash and roll down the window. "Yes?"

I see a police officer hustling everyone back into West End reception.

"Leave the dog in the car and get out slowly," the speaker barks.

I get out of the cab and manage to close the door on Scotty, who is now in a fury at the window. "Both hands on top of the car," the speaker barks, and so I turn around and I kind of laugh again because this is getting so weird, and I put my hands on the top of the taxi cab.

I hear Jackson Darenbrook's voice yelling in that drawl of his. Since he is the owner and CEO of the whole darn shooting match, I guess he's entitled. "Creepin' crickets, what are you doin'? That's one of my best news producers you're manhandling!"

A policewoman has come forward to pat me down while her partner holds a gun on me. "Back off, mister," the cop tells Jackson.

"I'll back you right off my property, Officer," he retorts.

"Sally Harrington?" the woman officer says. "You're wanted for questioning in connection with a murder. Will you come with us please to the precinct?"

"Get the goddamn lawyers down here!" Jackson yells, flapping his arms to nobody in particular. "Where the hell is security?"

I see the head of security, Wendy Mitchell, come jogging out of the building. She comes over and talks in low tones to the officers. Another one comes over and there is quite a conference. Wendy cautions Jackson to be quiet and, amazingly, he remains so. I hear Wendy say, "I know we can work this out," to the officer as they walk over. "Tell the detectives we'll set up the room right now, it's theirs."

The officer nods and goes to his patrol car to radio in.

Wendy comes over and murmurs, "Did you just return a rental car?"

"A couple of hours ago, why?"

"Evidently," she says under her breath, eyes scouting the scene, "you returned it with a dead body in the trunk."

CHAPTER
SEVEN

"A dead body?" I nearly shriek. Wendy's look makes me lower my voice. "I never even opened the trunk. It's got to be someone else's."

She looks at me. "The car or the body?"

"I don't know anything about any of it," I sputter. Of course, I have just spent the day at a retired mafia don's house, so I suppose if something like this has to happen, it's going to happen on a day like this. "Who is it?"

"If they know, they're not saying," she says. "We're trying to talk them into talking to you here. At least until I can get a criminal lawyer to join us."

She nods to a cop. And then waves at another. "Right inside there, I'll bring her. We'll have coffee."

I walk inside with Wendy and the female officer just as a camera crew comes piling out of the newsroom corridor. "Oh, no," I groan as the camera lights go on.

"Guys, stop!" Wendy yells from behind me.

They don't, of course, they're newsmen. I push the elevator button and give the camera a little wave.

We ride upstairs and are directed to the windowless conference room across from Jackson Darenbrook's office in Darenbrook I. I take a seat and the police officer stands by the door and we just kind of look at each other. A half an hour goes by and still no one comes in. Now I am getting worried.

"Could you just ask someone about my dog? If he's okay?"

The officer nods and walks outside. In a minute she comes back. "Someone's looking after your dog at the—dog run?"

I say yes, the dog run.

"And they fed him, he's fine."

"Thank you."

I sit and she stands for another fifteen minutes.

Finally there is a knock and a man comes in who identifies himself as Detective Albert Lorenzo. Wendy comes in behind him and I hear Jackson Darenbrook yelling, "You don't say a word, Sally, not a word—" Detective Lorenzo looks at Wendy, who says something to Jackson, and in response Jackson kicks the conference room door open—prompting the police officer to take out her baton—and points his finger at the detective. "She does not say a word until you confirm the victim is NOT, NOT an employee of DBS!"

"Mr. Darenbrook—"

"Goddamn it, I mean it!" the billionaire yells, picking up a chair and hurling it into the wall with a crash.

He has gone crazy, clearly.

"Jackson," a strong voice says and I turn around to see Will in the doorway. "It's okay, Alexandra's just off the radar right now, working on something. She's not missing."

And then I get it. Jackson Darenbrook thought the body in my trunk might be Alexandra.

"Oh, no, Jackson," I pipe up. "I left Alexandra there. She's not missing, she's working on something."

He is panting, his color starting to return to normal. "You saw her? With your own eyes?"

"Yes, I swear. I saw everyone from DBS. Whoever this is, it's not one of us."

Jackson cranes his neck a bit, gripping it with his hand a moment, and then turns to Detective Lorenzo. "I don't think much of your technique."

"And I don't think much of yours," the detective replies, looking at the chair lying on its side in the corner. There is a huge gash in the drywall.

Jackson turns to me. "The lawyer will be right here. Not a word until then."

We all just sit, watching Jackson pace the room. Finally I turn to Detective Lorenzo and ask him if it would be possible for me to make a phone call. He says yes, but tells the female officer to accompany me.

We walk across the hall and I sit down in the reception area outside of Jackson's office. "Thank heavens you're home," I say to Doug when he picks up the phone. Doug Wrentham, the boy I fell in love with at seventeen, is now an assistant D.A. in New Haven. Doug, like me, is much better at his job than his love life. "It seems I may be in need of a good criminal lawyer."

"I can call Hugh Keefe," he says, referring to one of the best defense attorneys in Connecticut.

"No, I need one here, in Manhattan. DBS is getting somebody, but I'm thinking maybe I need my own counsel."

"What is the charge, Sally?" I love Doug in his lawyer mode. He is unflappable.

"It's not a charge, exactly," I say. "It's more like asking me why I returned a rental car this evening with a dead body in it." The police officer's eyes are on me, impassive, impossible to read.

A moment of silence. "Whose body?"

"I have no idea."

"Sit tight, listen to the lawyer they get you, and I'll be there within two hours," he tells me.

I return to the conference room to find the president of DBS, Cassy Cochran, in the conference room, as well as a well-dressed man who is introduced as my attorney. There is also an additional detective.

"Are you all right?" Cassy asks me, standing up when I come in.

"I'm fine."

"They're going to ask you some questions now," she explains.

"Fine," I say, shaking hands with the attorney and sitting down next to him.

It was Cassy Cochran, no doubt, who must have talked her husband, Jackson Darenbrook, into leaving the proceedings.

There is another knock on the door and a wagon of coffee, water, Danish and fruit is rolled in, just the kind we always get for meetings. "Please help yourselves, Detectives, Officer," Cassy says. And to get things going, she gets up and moves over to the wagon and asks them what they would like. All three take a cup of coffee. I do, too. And so we begin. They ask the questions and I answer them, and slowly but surely we cover the ground of last night and today. I was accompanying Alexandra Waring to New Jersey in preparation for an interview the following day. Today. We left West End last night about eleven-thirty. We drove to Newark Airport, to the rental car agency, where I rented the white Ford Taurus at close to 1:00 a.m.

"I wanted a compact," I explain quickly, "but they said they didn't have one. I asked them what kind of cars they had, and the guy said he had a Probe, but then when I said I wanted that, he turned around and said, no, he didn't have it after all, he only had one white Ford Taurus, take it or leave it."

Everyone is looking at me and I know I must be getting tired. "What I mean is," I try to clarify, "you should check out the car rental agency, because they forced that particular car on me. It's not one that I chose."

I tell them we drove to Alexandra's farm, where we spent

the night. No, I never opened the trunk. I had thrown my overnight bag in the back seat and my briefcase in the front seat. I tell them about driving to Rocky Presario's in the morning and quite naturally, their interest picks up. I explain that my part in the interview was done by four o'clock and I left shortly after that. I got tied up for a while at the Lincoln Tunnel, but reached the car rental place about six-thirty.

"The attendant says you didn't even take your receipt, that you jumped out of the car and ran down the street."

"I did take my receipt," I say, and ask if someone can get my briefcase so I can show it to them. The policewoman leaves the room. "And the reason I ran off was because I saw an available cab. It was rush hour. Trying to find one on Tenth Avenue can be a nightmare."

We spend some time on names and addresses. Alexandra's farm, Rocky Presario's home, the names of the DBS News crew who were there. "And where can we reach Ms. Waring now?" Lorenzo asks.

I hesitate. "Well, actually, she can't be reached. She's on an assignment until Monday."

"Are you telling me she can't be contacted?"

"Um, yeah. As we say, she's off the radar until Monday."

Lorenzo looks to Cassy. "Is this normal? For your anchorwoman to be completely out of touch with the newsroom?"

"Uh," Cassy says, thinking this over, "if it's necessary. If whatever she is working on requires complete confidentiality."

He turns to me. "Aren't you her personal assistant?"

"I'm her assistant producer," I say.

"Then you must know how to reach her."

Uh-oh, I knew this was coming. I can't lie to the police, but I also gave my word to Alexandra. "I have an idea where she might be," I admit, "but it would be of no help to you." *Because I'm not going to tell you.* Fine line all this is, but what can I do? She's having a lumpectomy in the morning and I'll be damned to put her through this tonight.

"As soon as Alexandra becomes available," Cassy says, "you have my word she will contact you. First thing."

The police officer returns with my briefcase and I dig out my receipt from the car rental agency and hand it to Detective Lorenzo. He glances at it, nods once and looks back up at me, passing the receipt on to his partner.

"You drove to Alexandra Waring's last night and spent the night," he rehashes. "You followed her to Rocky Presario's home, a known organized crime figure, and you drove back to Manhattan carrying a dead body in the trunk of your car, and Miss Waring is suddenly unavailable."

"It wasn't sudden," I say. "She had planned it carefully. Her trip." I'm tired and I'm starting to lose patience. "How was she supposed to know someone was going to leave a body in the car I rented?"

"So you think the body was in the trunk of the car at the time you rented it," Detective Lorenzo says. He leans over to confer with his partner. Suddenly he stands up. "Thank you, Ms. Harrington. I trust you will continue to be available to us?"

"Uh, sure," I say.

Cassy stands up and touches my arm to follow her out. We walk down the hall and into her office, where she closes the door. "Good Lord," she sighs, rubbing her eyes.

"Tell me about it," I say.

She drops her hand. "Where *is* Alexandra?"

I can't even begin to go into the complexity of Cassy Cochran and Alexandra Waring's relationship, but I was told directly that Alexandra does not want her to know about her breast cancer, so I'm not about to tell her.

I am beginning to resent enormously the position the anchorwoman has put me in.

"She's doing something on the Presario story."

Cassy frowns. "What?"

"I'm not sure. She may be with one of them."

She squints slightly. "Like who?"

"I'm not sure," I say.

She studies my face carefully and looks as though she might say something, but changes her mind. "Okay, then," she says, turning to walk toward her desk, "when she surfaces, she surfaces, and we'll take it from there." She turns the corner of her desk and glances back. "Doug Wrentham's in your office. I think your dog's up there, too."

"Thanks," I say, turning to the door.

"Sally—"

I turn around.

"Is there something you want to tell me?"

"About the body?"

"About anything," she says evenly.

"No," I say quietly, cursing Alexandra.

She pauses and smiles suddenly. "Tough day. Go home and get some sleep. Stick close to the office though, will you? Next couple of days?"

Upstairs I find Doug and Scotty dozing in my office with the TV on. Scotty perks up and trots over to say hello while Doug shifts his position slightly, nestling the side of his face in his arm along the back of the couch. He has come dressed in lawyer attire, a well-fitting Brooks Brothers suit, suspenders, pale blue shirt, a red and blue striped tie (which I gave him) and black-tie oxfords. His jacket is slung over the arm of the couch.

Whatever Doug's faults may be, the cut of his jib is not one of them. He is the kind of man one instinctively likes. A good-looking ex-athlete in a suit. Well-spoken, deliberate, he is essentially a kind and fair man. His first wife left him for their stockbroker because, she said, Doug was boring. I know what she meant, but I also knew the statement to be unfair. At the time he had been practicing corporate tax law which, regardless of how well it paid, bored him to death. On top of that, his wife wanted him to be a socialite with her and he hated that. She loved tennis and hated football and he tried to accommodate her and, well, why wouldn't she find him dull if she had no respect for his interests and dragged him around in a world that held no interest for him whatsoever?

See? I'm defensive of him. And yet, I left Doug, too, just in the last year, to be with someone I found more exciting. On the other hand, a year ago, it was Doug who had started playing around with someone other than me....

Can you tell what's going on here? That Doug and I were madly in love in high school and part of college, and then he went his way and I went mine and two years ago we found each other in Castleford again, and so at the time it seemed as though it was meant to be, that *we* were meant to be, and so we started all over again. But we have much unfinished business. I love him, but can I spend my life with him? He loves me, but is it more as a friend than a wife? Or what is a wife? He doesn't know, he had one already and it was a disaster. Mother thinks both of us are in some kind of delayed adolescence; I think we're a couple of worka-holics who can't devote enough time to sorting out our per-sonal lives.

I suspect Doug is still seeing someone, but we have not discussed it. Actually, we have done an amazing job in the past month of talking without saying anything.

I am so relieved he's here. As if he hears my thoughts, his eyes open. He smiles a little, "Hey, jailbird."

"Creep," I mutter, bending to kiss him on the cheek. "But thank you for coming, although I guess you didn't need to."

"I was too curious not to come," he admits, stretching. "What's going on?"

I give a brief overview of what happened, who was in the conference room and what I told them.

"And they wouldn't tell you who it is?"

"They won't even say if it's a man or a woman."

"That's creepy."

"Tell me about it."

"But you saw Alexandra Waring before you left, right?" he says, getting up.

"Why does everyone keep thinking it might be Alexandra? Yes, I saw her. She practically walked me out to the car. So I know it's not her."

"But you don't know where she is."

"I'm telling you, Doug, it's not Alexandra."

"Don't get annoyed, I know you're tired," he says, slipping on his jacket. "The reason why people panic is because she's been a target in the past."

I sigh, rubbing my eyes. Doug walks over and puts his arms around me. I let him and rest my head against his shoulder. "Come on," he murmurs, "let me take you guys home."

Down in the garage I see that a police car is still here, but no one stops us as we reclaim Doug's Saab. Scotty hops in the back seat with my stuff and we cruise up West End Avenue to 100th Street, where Doug drops us off as he zooms around to a parking garage around the corner. (It's not the Saab being stolen he fears but the habit New Yorkers have of bouncing off cars as they parallel park.)

I let myself in the brownstone and check the mail. A few bills. I unlock the foyer door, hold it open for Scotty, close it securely behind us, and then walk past the staircase to the door to the apartment. There are three locks on the door, including something called a police lock.

"Oh my," Mother said when she first saw the apartment's big round bed. "Is the owner a—a man about town?"

This was Mother's way of asking me if I was renting from a *sex fiend.*

The owner of the apartment is a young actor who found work in L.A. and I am subletting it furnished. He gave me a hard time about having a dog here, but once I agreed to outright buy his sheets and bedspread for the eight-foot circular bed, he relented. (A wise move on his part, I guess. The bed is so low and round, you see, there's no way I can explain to Scotty that this is NOT the largest L.L. Bean dog bed in the world.)

Scotty jumps on the bed and waits for his leash to come off.

The apartment is a perfect place for me and Scotty. It is a very large studio, facing south, so during the day, sunshine streams in through the bars that cover the big bay window. There is a Pullman kitchen that extends back, and beyond that, a bathroom, where there is a door that leads outside to a small, enclosed backyard. Mother rather liked the apartment and admitted that she had never actually been north of Lincoln Center on Manhattan's West Side in her life, except once when Daddy dragged her to a party at Columbia University. But that had been ages ago, before I was born, and she remembered very little about it except a girl named Alice from Barnard who wore plaid pants and kept trying to flirt with Daddy.

There are a few tasteful prints of classic paintings from the Metropolitan Museum hanging on the walls; there's a wonderful old fireplace (which doesn't work); bookshelves on either side of the bay window; and the ceiling is still in pretty good shape from the 1920s, boasting a large, carved plaster ring of ivy in the center. The wood floors have been redone, the throw rugs aren't bad, and there is a nice wooden table and three chairs in front of the fireplace where I can eat, and a built-in desk in the corner where I can work.

I let Scotty out the door to the backyard and use the bathroom, checking myself in the mirror after I wash my hands. I give my hair a few brush strokes although I don't see what the point is, I'm a mess. Scotty starts barking outside and I call him in. The intercom rings and I hurry back to buzz Doug into the building.

"I know," I say to him as he sees the bed. "As Mother says, 'It's just that bed, dear. You walk in and it's all you can see.'"

"I think this bed is just great," Doug announces, flinging himself down on his back and pulling me down with him.

Scotty jumps up, too, thinking it's the old days of the three of us.

"I hope you don't have to wear that suit to work tomorrow," I say, trying to figure out if this is something we should be doing, lying on this round bed together, clothes or no clothes, "because it's going to be covered in dog hair."

Doug props himself up on one elbow to look at me, loosening his tie. Then he softly bonks Scotty on the nose, playful. "I was thinking about taking tomorrow off. A personal day." He looks at me, eyes crinkling in a smile. "I told Hank—" his boss "'—I gotta get Sally out of jail,' and he never even questioned it. Why is that, do you suppose? It was just like, 'Oh, sure, tell Sally I said hi.'"

I smile, thinking how much I miss Doug sometimes. "He just doesn't want to get involved."

"So I can stay," Doug finishes.

I guess he thinks he is staying over. If this is good or bad, I can't make up my mind.

"Relax," he murmurs, brushing the side of my face with the back of his hand once. "No expectations."

The trouble is, I can think of nothing better than making love with Doug right now, but it is so complicated, this relationship, and I don't know if I can follow up with the rest that he will assume: that we are officially together again.

He gently touches my lips with his forefinger. I kiss it softly, once. His hand lowers, landing softly on the base of my neck. His eyes on mine. His hand trails down over my blouse.

I don't resist.

He undoes a button, and slides his hand over my left breast, closing around it, his eyes narrowing slightly, as if he is in pain. "I've so missed your body," he murmurs, kissing me lightly. "I've so missed everything about you." His eyes lower to concentrate on opening my blouse. I have not moved, still undecided.

He reaches behind me to unhook my bra and in one

movement has pushed it up over my breasts so that he may hold them, and he pulls his lower body in close against me, so that I can feel him starting to well up against my thigh. His mouth is briefly at my neck and then drops urgently to my breast.

The sensation travels straight down between my legs. And as I start to give over to it, I think how he's changed, he was never this aggressive before. And then I think, he's barely even kissed me, but he's got my blouse off, and my skirt riding high—

And I know in an instant what the last girlfriend must have been like. And I think how ironic it is that she was probably with Doug the way I had been with Spencer, feeling absolutely sexually free. One thing's for certain, Doug learned from her how to start making love with all of their clothes on, because, before this, Doug never got any of the disrobing moves right. He could never seem to get a blouse undone, certainly not a bra. And now he does. Effortlessly.

Takes a lot of practice.

And then I wonder where they made love, Doug and this woman, and I wonder if they made love at work somewhere in the courthouse, and I wonder if maybe this woman was actually more than one woman, but had been two—

"What's wrong?" Doug whispers, hanging over my face.

"I can't concentrate," I say.

He looks at me, clearly debating whether or not to try and talk me out of this mood. And then I wonder if he realizes how different he is with me now, that after all the times we've made love over the years, he's never acted this way, never, and I can't help but wonder about who he's been with that he's so different.

I wonder if he can guess how it feels as though a part of me has died with my failed relationship with Spencer Hawes. That I had completely trusted him and wholly gave myself over to him, sexually, and how unnerving it is to have Doug returned to me from another woman in this liberated way.

Oh, hell, I don't think Doug is thinking much of anything except what a pain in the ass I am.

He pulls away and I draw my blouse together. I murmur apologies, rolling off the bed, deliberately avoiding the sight or touch of anything in the vicinity of his pants, because I know me, and I know that same visual confirmation of his desire that got me as a teenager could get me now.

I drag myself into the bathroom to wash my face, button everything up and brush my hair. I come back out into the kitchen and give Scotty a Milk-Bone. "You're different," I say without looking at Doug, taking two glasses down from the cupboard.

He is sitting on the edge of the bed, folding his tie neatly and tucking it into his jacket pocket. "I imagine you must be different now, too."

I open the refrigerator. There is a carton of milk that wasn't here before. Oh, right. The intern, Jim, he was here last night. "Would you like a beer?"

"No thanks," he says. "I think I'll be driving back tonight."

I look at him over the door. "You don't have to go back. It's just that I'm not quite ready for—"

"It's better if I go," he says abruptly, standing up. "I just wanted to make sure you were all right."

I close the refrigerator door, open a bottle of beer and pour some into a glass. "Do you want some water or soda or something?"

"No thanks," he says, coming in to stand behind me. He puts his hands on my shoulders.

"Who is she?" I hear myself ask.

"Forget it, Sally, it's not important."

"It is important, Doug," I say quietly, "because whoever she is, she's changed you." I take a sip of beer.

"I've been in therapy, Sally. Maybe it's that."

"No," I murmur, shaking my head. I step away from him, walking back to the main room, and notice there are some flowers in the middle of the table. The intern? "It takes a lot of practice to be that smooth," I say, hating myself for doing so. "When was the last time you were with her? A day ago?"

"Sally, come on, don't do this," he urges, coming over to stand behind me again. This time he holds me around the waist.

I take another sip. "In the two years we were together, I couldn't change a thing about our sex life." I put the glass down on the table and turn around to look at him. "Somebody waltzed in and changed everything."

He simply looks at me, faint color in his cheeks. This is the way he looks when he's trying not to lie, when he opts to say nothing at all. Finally he says, "I haven't asked you about your sex life in the past few months, although I certainly got a good idea from the gossip columns."

Spencer Hawes may appear as sort of a bad boy in my life now, but when I met him it was as though my sexual life had only just been born. With Spencer, it was the first time I felt like a partner, not like an outlet or a feel-good tonic. I felt as if I was exploring, happily, joyously, actually, rather than playing a quick game of hit-or-miss, which toward the end with Doug, had been more miss.

Don't get me wrong, I enjoyed my time with Doug, but I didn't have any idea how much better my sex life could be. (There's something to be said for keeping the girl down on the farm, as it were.) And when I got a glimmer of that, that there was a sexual life of proportions I had never dreamed of, I'm afraid there was no calling me back, or holding me back, I wanted so much to see what it was all about. What I was about.

It wasn't the sex, of course, as we all come to realize sooner or later. It was Doug and our whole way of communicating with each other, a way that worked when we were teenagers and had not altered much, and thus began to fail us as adults. It had to fail. I blamed Doug mostly at the time because it was so easy to. He was the first to admit that he was shut down in ways that used to drive me crazy. Not only was he shut down at times, he would so firmly shut me out. That's the way it was, I figured, and so we staggered on.

And then I met Spencer Hawes.

When I left Doug, he finally did what I always wanted him to—he went into psychotherapy. He tried one more time to see if I would come back to him and then gave up. I was the one who called him when things with Spencer first went awry. And he was the one who warily kept his distance, but nonetheless stood by my side when I brought public humiliation on my family.

Doug.

I've been loath to admit it for years, but I know I have to get some kind of help. Maybe if I call it counseling instead of psychotherapy I'll go.

"Call me," Doug finally murmurs, drawing me close to kiss me on the forehead. "Sally." I look up. "We'll take it slow and figure it out. Okay? Don't make any judgments, decisions. Give it time."

I nod, stretching to kiss him briefly.

After he leaves, I lock all the locks, and Scotty and I go into the backyard for a final good-night trip. I sit on the stair and watch my dog circle, sniffing, whizzing here and there as if any other animal might ever venture here. A light goes on in the apartment building opposite and I see an old man peering down at me. He suddenly yanks the shade down.

Scotty and I go inside and I change into a nightie, pour the rest of my beer down the sink and brush my teeth. I climb into the big round bed and turn off the light.

I am so glad I didn't sleep with Doug, I cannot tell you. I am not ready. We're not ready. We don't know what the heck we're doing.

Curled up at my feet, Scotty starts softly snoring and I smile, thinking, well, all is not lost.

I get out of bed and get down on my knees. Sometimes you just need to do what your parents taught you as a child, and prayers, I don't think, ever wear thin. Certainly not when you have a life like mine.

PART TWO

Suspect

CHAPTER EIGHT

As Scotty and I leave my apartment building to go to work, two gentlemen climb out of an illegally parked Ford Crown Victoria and block the sidewalk. Scotty gives a warning bark and I don't stop him. The men stop. One reaches into his jacket pocket to withdraw his ID, making everyone else on the street stop dead in their tracks to watch the new neighbor get busted. "NYPD," he says. "I'm Detective Sergeant Gleason and this is Detective Czychek. You met him last night."

I may have met him, but he didn't say a word last night and he doesn't now.

I shorten the leash and tell Scotty to sit and he does, although he gives three sharp barks of warning until the detectives stop closing in on us. Now he simply growls, showing his junkyard-dog fangs. (That's my Scotty boy!)

"We were following up, to see how you are," Detective Gleason says.

"Better, thank you," I tell him.

"And we were wondering if you'd like to accompany us to the morgue to view the deceased," he adds.

"No thank you," I say.

"Aren't you the least bit curious who he is?"

"So it is a he," I comment. I look at Czychek. "You weren't saying last night."

"It is a he," Detective Sergeant Gleason confirms. He raises a hand to add something but Scotty barks at the movement, and it startles the detective. He looks around at the people lingering on the sidewalk, watching. "Maybe we should go inside to talk."

There's no point in being rude. I just hate how they've conspired to corner me without a lawyer. Reluctantly I lead them into the apartment. I put Scotty in the bathroom with a couple of Milk-Bones, tell him to stay and shut the door. When I come back into the studio, Gleason points to the front door and says, "That's an illegal fixture, Miss Harrington, did you know that?"

"What is?"

"That lock."

He is referring to the police lock, the solid steel bar that fits into the floor and then angles against the inside of the door when you lock it.

"If you were unconscious and there was a fire, nobody could get in," he says, knocking the door with his knuckles. "Plated steel. Even we couldn't break it down."

"Drug dealers use them," Detective Czychek says, speaking for the first time.

"So do people who don't like burglars breaking down their doors with sledgehammers," I say. "Look, I'm subletting this apartment, what do you suggest I do?"

"Dismantle it," Gleason says. Then he looks at the round bed, and then at Cyzchek. They exchange smiles and I am ticked off.

"I told you, I'm subletting," I snap.

Scotty starts barking and clawing at the bathroom door. I think we both need to calm down, so I offer the police coffee, which they say sounds good. I direct them to sit at the table while I make it, and open the door to the bathroom to tell Scotty to cool it. He does, collapsing with a groan in the doorway.

The detectives settle around the table and I call Benjamin to tell him that I've been detained and will be in the office as soon as I can.

"Nobody cares where you are," he points out. "You're on special assignment."

"Just pretend," I tell him. "Is Jim around?" While he goes off to find Jim Reinemann, I fix a tray for the coffee. Jim finally comes on and I ask what he's doing. He says he's in the conference room where he moved the Presario-Arlenetta materials and is having some equipment set up in there. I tell him good, I'll be there soon. Then I check my voice mail. Nothing burning. I call Cassy Cochran's office and tell her assistant, Chi Chi Santiago, that I am at home with two detectives from the NYPD. "No, I don't need the lawyers here," I say, making sure the detectives overhear.

Chi Chi says, "I think you should have a lawyer," and I call out to the police officers, "DBS insists I need a lawyer. Do I need one?"

"Not unless you killed this guy," Gleason says good-naturedly.

"Not unless I killed this guy," I dutifully report to Chi Chi.

"Cassy's going to have a stroke," Chi Chi says.

"I'll see you very soon," I promise, hanging up.

We sit down around the table with the tray of coffee and some crackers. Scotty has combat-crawled his way across the floor to lie under my seat, which I don't realize until I feel his cold wet nose on my ankle. "You must know by now," I say, pouring a cup of coffee for each of us, "that I had nothing to do with the death of this person."

"No, you just drove him around a while," Detective Sergeant Gleason says.

I resist the urge to laugh. This is so ghastly it's funny. I mean, where is the reality quotient here? I rented a car, I returned it, and there's a body in it.

"So you were at Rocky Presario's yesterday," Gleason says, looking at his notes.

I nod. "Yes."

"So that's where you got the body, we're thinking."

"Could be," I acknowledge. "Although I was parked right by the kitchen door, where the crew was going in and out most of the time. My money's still on the car rental place at the airport."

Detective Czychek gives a slow smile. "You have a thing for dead bodies at airports. You, uh, failed to mention last night you were implicated in the murder of Cliff Yarlen at JFK not long ago."

"Nobody asked me," I say, sipping my coffee.

"Cliff Yarlen was Rocky Presario's nephew. Is that correct?"

"Yes," I confirm, setting my cup down. If there is only one thing I've learned of late, it's best not to volunteer information to the police.

"Who else had the keys to the car besides you, Ms. Harrington?"

"No one."

His eyebrows rise. "No one? At any time?"

"No one, at any time."

He looks down at his notes for a long while, pausing once only to sip his coffee. Finally he looks up. "You never gave the keys to Alexandra Waring?"

I shake my head. "No."

"And no one drove the car but you?"

"No one drove it but me."

Suddenly Detective Czychek takes out a photograph from his breast pocket and drops it on the table. It is a morgue photograph. I know because I've seen quite a few, most reporters have.

The dead man is on the young side, maybe in his early thirties. White. Military-style haircut. He is shown in profile only, which makes me believe there must be a lot of damage on the other side.

"Do you recognize him?" Gleason asks.

"No," I say, staring, shaking my head. "No. I don't think I've ever seen this man before." I look up. "Who is he?"

"We're working on it," Gleason confesses. He pushes the picture toward me with his finger. "Are you sure?"

I pick it up and earnestly study the photograph. I shake my head. "I see what you see. A white man, maybe thirty-three, looks ex-military, or a ball player, maybe. Gunshot to the head."

"Who told you that?" he demands, jumping down my throat.

"What?" I put the photo down.

"Gunshot to the head? How do you know that?"

I point to the picture. "That's the only reason they do a profile, at least that's been my experience. It's almost always a gunshot to the head, unless someone's smashed in the head with a sledgehammer or something."

He relaxes slightly and takes a big swig of his coffee. While I'm watching him, Czychek speaks. "You have a gun permit, Miss Harrington."

"Yes," I acknowledge, looking at him, "although I haven't shot in at least six months."

"Do you own a gun?"

"No. I usually borrow a friend's when I go to the range."

"What caliber?"

"Twenty-two. Um, that's the only caliber we can use at the Castleford Gun Club. It's a smaller, older place. You have to go to Wallingford to shoot anything bigger."

"Have you ever shot anything bigger?" This is from Gleason.

"Yes."

"Like what?"

"Uh, a shotgun, you know, for trap. I haven't done that in a couple of years. Um, I've shot an old Colt 45. It was part of a museum fund-raiser for the Colt museum in Hartford. And I've shot a Parker shotgun a couple times—they were made near me, a lot of families have one. Handed down, you know." I've got to watch it; I'm doing my habitual babbling again.

"Your mother owns a Parker shotgun?" Gleason says.

I look at him. "Yes. It's in a gun safe."

Gleason returns to his notebook again and Czychek just sits there. I finish my coffee and pour myself a little more.

"You never opened the trunk of the rental car," Gleason says without looking up.

"No."

"You didn't put your overnight bag in there?"

"No. I tossed it on the back seat. I put my briefcase in the front."

I focus my attention on Czychek. "What about the car rental place? *Have* you talked to them?"

"It's being covered," he assures me.

And that's the last they say for quite some time. So I just sit there, looking at Czychek, who is just sitting there, looking at me, Gleason reads his notes and Scotty licks my ankle.

"I think you need to be very careful, Ms. Harrington," Gleason finally says, closing his notebook and putting his pen away. "You hang out with a very, very tough crowd."

I frown.

"You used to go out with that book editor," he tells me. "The one that got the hell beaten out of him. You were the last person seen with Cliff Yarlen before he got his head shot off. You run around with Jonathan Small," Gleason continues, "who's on trial for murder. And now you're carting around dead bodies." He narrows his eyes. "Last night you were entertaining a Connecticut prosecutor." He smiles slightly, glancing over at the round bed.

I take a slow, deep, breath and stand up. "Unless you urgently need me for something else, I've got to get to work," I say, putting the dishes on the tray. Neither police officer is moving. I bring the stuff into the kitchen and leave it by the sink. Then I come back to leash Scotty and pick up my briefcase. "You're welcome to stay," I say, "but you've got to remember to set the spring lock before you leave. And remember, you mustn't use that police lock."

The detectives look at each other and get up. "No, that's all right," Gleason says. "We need to be getting along."

They file out into the hall wordlessly and continue outside. I lock the door, and Scotty and I walk out to where they are standing on the stoop. Detective Gleason has just lit a cigarette. "We can reach you at work?"

"Yes," I say, edging Scotty and myself past them down the stairs. On the sidewalk, I turn around, waiting to be dismissed.

"Be very careful," Gleason says to me.

"I shall. Thank you."

"We don't want the next body," Detective Sergeant Gleason says, exhaling a cloud of blue-gray smoke, "to be yours, Miss Harrington."

CHAPTER NINE

After I reach West End and drop Scotty off at the run, Benjamin grabs me on my way into my office to say Jessica Wright has been waiting to see me. I throw my briefcase down and walk back up the hall to the office belonging to the hit talk show host. Her secretary waves me through and I knock on the frame of the door.

"Come in!"

Jessica's office is something between a collage in progress and a DBS time capsule. Every square inch of the office, identical in size to Alexandra's, seems to be covered with framed photographs and memorabilia. The connection between the photographs is the green-eyed extrovert extremis, with long auburn hair, who appears in every one of them.

"I was told you were looking for me," I say.

"Give me one second," she pleads, studying something on her desk. I sit down in one of the two chairs that face her and wait. Finally she murmurs something to herself, makes a mark with a pen and looks up. "We're doing a show on astronauts," she explains. "It's the strangest thing, but the more I find out about these guys, the more I feel like I'm interviewing Evel Knievel."

I like Jessica enormously. She's kind of a wiseass and requires being the center of attention in almost any room she's in, but there is something inherently inspiring and uplifting and fun about her. She's also very smart. Guys are nuts about her. (Her chest is a television legend.) Women like her, too. Heck, everyone seems to like Jessica and that's why her ratings stay up even when she herself says it feels as though she's doing the same old thing these days, over and over. I'm afraid I tend to agree with her. I think she is repeating herself on the air, and yet those ratings stay up.

I wonder how Will, her husband, feels about having so many guys drooling over his wife all the time. Surely he sees it even here, at West End. And there are the baby rumors, that Jessica and Will are trying to conceive. What happens to the talk show then?

"Like Evel Knieval how?" I ask.

"They lived for danger, these guys. They're thrill seekers. The danger in space turned them on, made them feel acutely alive, high almost. And then once it was over, when they were grounded, all they talk about is getting depressed and losing their zest for living. But ask them about the old days, about something blowing up and them nearly dying, and their eyes light up and their hearts swell with happiness. And then you ask them about what they're doing now, it's like sitting through a bad eulogy at a very sad funeral."

"They sound like retired journalists." I laugh.

"And TV talk show hosts." Jessica gives a toss of her hair, focusing her large green eyes on me. "The feds arrived here this morning looking for Alexandra. Will tells me you've been chauffeuring somebody in the trunk of your car?"

"Some dead guy," I say. "All I did was rent a car and return it and there he was. Two detectives just grabbed me at my apartment." I blink. "The feds were here?"

"Yep," she says, nodding. "And Cassy's made Will put a lid on the whole thing, Feds' request."

"Huh," I say. "I wonder if the NYPD knows. Usually when the feds get involved, the locals get pushed off. And the guys who came to my apartment today are not acting like that, that's for sure."

"Pity the gag's on," Jessica says. "Last time we put you on the air with dead bodies, the ratings went through the roof. First time I ever got a decent lead-in rating from you guys," she jokes. Her expression grows more serious. "Are you all right?"

"Yeah, fine, thanks."

"So where is Alexandra Eyes, anyway?"

"She's working on something," I say, feeling horribly uncomfortable. Jessica Wright is Alexandra's best friend. "And she wanted to be off the radar."

Jessica holds her chin in her hand, considering me. "Something's up."

I don't say anything.

"You guys were at the farm, she did an interview with the godfather or something, you come back with a body and Alexandra takes a pass on being here?"

"I'm sure she doesn't know," I say, relieved I can take an honest tack.

"Frankly, Sally, I think you're full of it," the talk show hostess tells me, standing up. She's in jeans and a T-shirt and within the hour will no doubt change into one of her signature TV outfits, consisting of a low-cut silk blouse, miniskirt and cowgirl boots. I stand up, too.

She takes a step toward me, pointing a finger. "Tell Alexandra Eyes she's a jerk next time you talk to her, will you? And tell her I know something's up and I'm going to give her one—and only one—chance to tell me what it is." She retracts her finger and shakes her head, smiling slightly. "Hiring you is either the smartest or dumbest thing she's ever done."

"Definitely the smartest," I tell her.

The talk show hostess sashays on out of her office. (That's the only way one can describe Jessica Wright's walk, kind of a graceful, country-cowgirl sway—although she's originally from Essex Fells, New Jersey.) "I hope so," she calls back.

I return to my office and start wading through e-mail and

phone calls and quickly feel incapacitated. I'm not supposed to be doing this, I think, I'm supposed to be working on the Presario-Arlenetta special. In that light, however, I guess that means I should return Lilliana Martin's screaming voice mail about what the hell is going on, why have I sicced the state police on her grandfather?

I call Lilliana's number but the answering service picks up. I leave a message that I'm at West End, will be here for a while, and am very sorry for the confusion, but there wasn't anything I could do about it. "Call me and we'll talk." I hang up and try to face some other stuff that needs answering, but my heart feels heavy, suddenly, and for a second I'm almost ill.

I try to shake the image of the dead man's face. It's awful when death becomes real to me. I think of my father.

I wonder how Alexandra is doing, whether she had the surgery this morning as scheduled. I don't even know where she is to check on her.

I wonder if I should call Doug, thank him for coming in last night. Thank him for letting me throw him out; tell him we were being watched by the NYPD?

I want to start looking through the Presario-Arlenetta material, but I'm unable to face some of those pictures in the files just yet—other bodies from other times—and decide instead to swing over to the company cafeteria to pick up something to eat. Halfway there, I find myself detouring to the dog run to see Scotty.

I feel homesick, suddenly, longing for where Scotty can just run around outside and where I have all my things together in my own little house. And my car. When you grow up driving a car, you never get it out of your system. You want to just get in and go. The novelty of subway, buses and cabs lasted, for me, I think, about five minutes.

Maybe it was the police coming to the apartment. I feel violated, like my new life has already turned stale.

The dog run Darenbrook Communications built is very cool. There are actually three, used according to each dog's temperament and compatibility. The three runs meet in a hut, where the dogs can go inside to bark at each other through the chain-link fences. Today there are only three dogs and they're all together in one run. I walk into the hut and find Scotty taking a nap. The barking of Jessica and Will's dog, a wire-haired Jack Russell terrier, wakes him up. As soon as I let myself in the run, Scotty's all over me and so is the Jack Russell, and Scotty growls a little bit at the competition but then gets used to it and concedes half of me to his new pal.

I pet them both and then my heart turns a little when I see the third little dog come in, that unidentifiable scruffy little black something whose eyes are shining hopefully in my direction. "Hello, little muppet," I murmur, rising and moving toward it. Scotty tries to block me. I tell him to sit and he does (the Jack Russell doesn't do so well, jumping up on me), but the little one is fearful and won't come any closer, so I simply scoop it up in my arm to pet it.

"That's Mr. Peterson's new dog," a voice says from behind me. I turn. It's young Jim Reinemann.

"What kind is it?" I ask, peering at its little face, rubbing it behind the ears. "It's a boy," Jim says. "His name is Blackie."

I smile. Langley Peterson is just the sort of man to name his dog Blackie. Functional, kindly, to the point. Langley is the CEO of the electronics side of the Darenbrook Communications empire and is married to Jackson Darenbrook's sister, Belinda. His wife is a pistol; in a way she reminds me of a more refined Jessica Wright, with that kind of buoyant spirit. Langley is a very nice man. Jessica calls him "Mr. Mitchell," in honor of the actor that played Dennis the Menace's father on TV, and he does resemble him. Tall, a bit gangly, with glasses, he is a number cruncher at heart and looks vaguely paralyzed whenever decisions are demanded that don't have numbers attached to them. Given the personalities at DBS, this happens quite a lot. Cassy Cochran's his baby, though, and they work together as a team. The fact that they are in-laws means what, I have no idea.

"They have another dog, a big wolfhound," Jim continues,

"but Mrs. Peterson keeps him with her most of the time. This is Mr. Peterson's dog."

I kiss the little fellow softly on the head. "But what kind of dog is he?"

"Nobody knows. He thinks pit bull-Chihuahua-Scottie or something."

"Something black, I should think," I offer, rubbing his little head. "Hello, Blackie."

"Mr. Peterson's kids were having soccer practice in Central Park a couple of weeks ago and they found him tied up to a tree. They waited hours and nobody came." Jim lets himself into the cage and Scotty runs to him, making me want to say, "Hey, watch the loyalty, bub."

"Good for Langley," I say, putting Blackie back down. Immediately he skitters off, wary.

"He's so much better than he was already," Jim comments. "God only knows what he's been through."

"Scotty was like that when I got him. It just takes time, good food, reassurance and lotsa, lotsa love." I smile, watching the little guy. "I can see from his coat he didn't have a great diet." Scotty has come back to me to look up and whine. "Whatsamatter, boy?" I tease. Then I squat and give him a big hug. "So," I say, standing up and moving toward the door, "you've got us all set up in a conference room?"

As we leave the dog run and walk back to Darenbrook I, to the cafeteria, Jim eagerly tells me what he's done. I pick up some soup and salad and seltzer and we continue to Darenbrook III.

He has done a good job and I say so. He is like one of the better study partners you find in college, the one that is highly organized and not a procrastinator. He's set up two extra tables along the wall of the conference room and has unpacked the boxes of materials and placed them in stacks, with neat little signs as to what they are. He's brought in a TV and VCR, a magnifying glass, a laptop computer and printer, and various supplies.

"The only other thing we need," I say, "is a steel filing cabinet. Make it two. It can either be the horizontal kind, with two drawers, or vertical with four. Because I'm going to want to put segments in chronological order. So if you can imagine making a file—for example, Rocky Presario at cement factory 1955, and Rocky Presario at cement factory, 1965—there should be a lot of files hanging in between."

He doesn't quite get it.

"So when we've cataloged everything, all our materials," I explain, "we can start with the first file in drawer one and then see how the whole story unfolds from there, chronologically. And visually. We can use the material anywhere we want in the series, but we have to lay out the whole story first, as it happened, for two reasons."

He appears acutely interested.

"One, to see where the holes in the story are. If we have a big gap of time between files, we know that's the time period we need to focus on researching. And then two, after we have the story laid out chronologically, we can instantly see by the files where the *visual* holes are."

"Wow," he says softly. "You're good."

"No," I say matter-of-factly, taking the lid off my soup. "Just a little more experienced. The thing is—" I look up "—we're talking about seventy years of two major storylines, which, twenty years ago, split into four, and then ten years ago, into six storylines." I sigh. "That is a ton of research."

"I'm psyched," he tells me.

I smile. "I know you are, which is great, Jim, because it's going to be a project like this that will land you a paying job. Here, or just about anywhere in town." I sip the soup. It's very good. Minestrone. They have excellent food at West End, and having witnessed the tantrums of the Darenbrook Communications CEO when he is displeased about such things (he wants West End to feel like a second home for his employees), I am not surprised. "By the way," I add, "there is one rule in here. No food or liquid on any table where we have materials out. So we need another table, over there in the corner, to put coffee or soda or food on as we work."

"Consider it done."

He watches me eat and I try not to notice it, becoming increasingly self-conscious. Fortunately my parents were the sort who told me and my brother as children that if we didn't have good table manners, we could never eat with the queen, and so, intrigued by the possibility of being entertained in a palace should we ever run into a queen, we paid attention to learning them.

"Can I ask you something?" he finally says.

"Sure."

"I heard some guys in the newsroom whispering something about you and a dead body. When I asked Will about it, he said the story doesn't exist."

I roll my eyes, swallowing. "Officially, the story doesn't. Unofficially, between us, it seems I brought a passenger back to Manhattan yesterday in the trunk of my rental car."

His eyes grow wide and he takes a seat across from me. "Who?"

"Nobody seems to know at the moment." I'm losing my appetite, fast. I pat my mouth with my napkin. "I can't say anything more. Except that it hasn't been particularly pleasant."

He's still watching me.

"Why don't you see if you can get those filing cabinets?" I suggest.

"Yeah, sure." He scrambles to his feet. And then hesitates. "I think you're really great, Sally," he says. "I'm really honored and happy you chose me to work with you." I see the admiration of a certain kind in the young intern's eyes and I make a mental note to be very careful not to hurt his feelings.

And, somehow, get him over those feelings. Fast.

CHAPTER
TEN

The telephone rings at eight-thirty Thursday morning and I wish Scotty would answer it. I still don't know where I am half the time in this apartment and it takes me a minute to remember I have to get up and cross the room. (Round beds, you see, at least this one, do not have headboards or room for end tables.) Scotty stretches his legs forward on the bedclothes, yawning.

"Hello?"

"Hi, Sally, it's Alexandra calling."

"Oh," I blurt out, waking up in a hurry. "How are you?"

"I'm all right, thanks. It went okay."

She certainly doesn't sound okay. She sounds terrible, and I suspect she is in pain. I wonder if it's the shoulder or the breast. Or both.

"So is everything okay?" she says after a moment.

"Um," I say, thinking maybe Alexandra should have a little bed rest before I tell her that I've been driving a dead body around the tristate area and the police and the feds and everybody else on the face of the earth want to know where she is. "Um, well," I say this time, "in terms of the newsroom, yes. In terms of the Presario-Arlenetta case, there may be a bit of a—well, twist."

"What kind of twist?" She sounds tired and not really up to this. Heaven only knows what she'll want to do if I tell her.

"The New Jersey state police descended on Rocky's the day after we were there," I say.

"Why?"

"They're looking for something, but I'm not sure what. Lilliana is incommunicado at the moment, and the authorities have been to West End."

Pause. "They're looking for me, aren't they?"

"Well, yes," I say. "But I've put them off until Monday. I've put everyone off until at least Monday, saying that you're away. So you can relax."

There is a sigh. "I must confess," she says, "I'm not feeling much like seeing anyone, much less dealing with anything."

"Well, look," I suggest, "why don't I come and see you— if you're in New York—"

"Oh, I'm here," she tells me.

"Good. Then I can see you for a bit, fill you in on what's going on and get you anything you might need. Do you need anything?"

"No. Thank you. But maybe it would be good if you came. Maybe at eleven?"

I look at the clock. "Great. What hospital are you in?"

"Actually, I'm not in a hospital."

I frown. "So where are you?"

I have just enough time to sail into the office and clear the decks before going to see Alexandra. From now on, I only want Presario-Arlenetta information pouring into this office and the rest of the news operation can bug Will or Alexandra directly. On the e-mail front, I forward each message to the appropriate person in the newsroom and then e-mail each sender back, saying that until further notice, I have been put on special assignment. Then I return the calls left on my voice mail, explaining the same. Then I try to reach Lilliana Martin again, to no avail, and leave her another message. Then I say to heck with it all and dash over to the conference room.

The table for food and drink is in place in the corner. Two new filing cabinets are sitting here, still in packing cases. Pleased, I leave a note for Jim about stuff I'd like him to do, plus a list of books I want him to get, and then dash down to reception to get a cab. On the way across town, I stop at a Lincoln Center florist.

I check the address Alexandra dictated to me again. Yep. It matches the brass plate embedded in the East Side brownstone the cab has stopped in front of. The building is not dissimilar to the one I live in, but it has been sandblasted clean and boasts an enormous awning, supported on two highly polished brass poles. A uniformed doorman opens my cab door for me.

"I'm here to see A. Bonner," I tell him, giving him the name Alexandra told me to use. He walks into the foyer and picks up a telephone. In a few moments a young woman comes downstairs and asks me to follow her into a tiny elevator. We ride up to the top floor, four, where she leads me over an antique Oriental runner and ushers me through a double set of walnut doors.

My boss is lying in a hospital bed. With the exception of the bed, the room looks like something out of an Edith Wharton novel, with vaulted ceilings, wood moldings, mahogany furniture, a fireplace and a large chinz-covered chair in front of a large bay window. Alexandra is lying on her right side and does not look very well. She looks thin and terribly pale and her eyes are uncharacteristically dull. She tries to smile. "Hi."

"Hi. These are for A. Bonner," I say, walking over to put the basket of flowers on a small bookcase next to the fireplace. I smile brightly, walking back.

"A. Bonner is feeling blah," she confesses quietly.

"Not for long," I promise, pulling up a chair.

She tries to smile. "Thanks for coming."

"You're welcome." I see a flicker of something cross her face. "You're in pain."

"A little," she admits.

"It's not the lumpectomy, is it?"

"No. It's here." She points in the general direction of the left side of her collarbone, and for the first time I notice the bandages just below the neck of her dressing gown. "They scraped it all out. There was a lot more stuff in there than the doctor had anticipated."

"What, like calcium deposits?"

"It was a combination of scar tissue and bone chips. They thought there was one chip, but there were three." She closes her eyes a minute and then opens them again. "I've been having all these flashbacks. About before DBS even existed." She smiles and this time flinches for real.

"So they did do both procedures?"

"Yes. My new doctor did the—you know."

"Lumpectomy," I say, hoping she will get used to the word.

"And my old doctor, the orthopedic surgeon, did the other."

"I've never heard of two surgical procedures at the same time."

"They had to. Because I said I wasn't coming back."

I look around. "But what *is* this place? Don't they know Johnny Walker's not the mayor of New York anymore?"

"The new doctor owns it, I think," she says.

"And they operated on you here?"

"The operating room's on the second floor. It's licensed for certain surgical procedures. There's two of us in here right now, I think."

Duh, finally I get it. I know out in L.A., Cedars-Sinai hospital has private suites to hide wealthy patients who pay way up and over to make sure their medical procedures remain secret. Most often this means plastic surgery. The lumpectomy performed on Alexandra's left breast was most likely performed by a plastic surgeon, and this is most likely that doctor's private facility. I never knew what famous rich people in New York did to insure their privacy about such matters, but I guess now I do. "So who's the other patient?"

"I have no idea," Alexandra says. "Which I believe is the point."

A nurse comes in and asks Alexandra how she is feeling. "Okay," she says, looking not okay at all.

The nurse looks at me as if for help. I know the look from my mother's medical trials.

I look at Alexandra. "So what are you taking for pain?"

"Some Tylenol," she mumbles.

"Tylenol? You've got to be kidding." I say. "After surgery? After two surgical procedures? What the heck is the matter with you?"

"I want a clear head," she says, closing her eyes.

I look to the nurse. "And what do you think about this?"

"She hasn't gotten much sleep," the nurse says carefully, not wanting to alienate her patient.

"You don't have to talk about me in the third person," Alexandra says, eyes still closed.

"This is crazy," I tell her, prompting her to open her eyes. "You're staying here a day or two, so why don't you just take what the doctor prescribed and get some rest? If you want to be back in action next week, there's no way you're going to be in any shape to do it unless you get some sleep."

I'm not sure if the look Alexandra gives me means, *Please talk me into it, I'm dying,* or *As soon as I get back on my feet, I'm gonna slug you,* but I'm determined to stand my ground. "Here's the deal. You take your medication and I'll tell you what's been going on. You don't—and I won't."

"Why don't I just fire you and be done with it?" she says, starting to laugh, but it hurts and she winces. She sighs and looks at the nurse. "Beth, thank you, I think I will take those painkillers."

The nurse quickly leaves before Alexandra changes her mind. In a few moments she is back, needle in hand. After she injects Alexandra and leaves the room, I tell the anchorwoman about driving back to Manhattan, the body being discovered at the car rental place, the police raid on West End, the feds putting a gag on the story, the police at my apartment yesterday. I figure I might as well highlight the fact that in order to cover for her, I've had to lie to the police, to say nothing of Cassy, Will and Jessica, all of whom, I suspect, know I'm not being truthful.

This only seems to amuse her.

"So where did you get this body?"

"I have not the slightest idea."

"And you don't know who it is."

I shake my head. She asks me to describe him again, which I do. It doesn't ring any bells with her, either. "So either it was in the car when I picked it up," I conclude, "or someone put it in the trunk at Rocky Presario's."

"Didn't somebody move your car there?" she asks.

"The big guy, Jocko, wanted to, but didn't. The car was sitting right by the kitchen door the whole time."

She is looking at the fireplace, thinking. After a moment, "They've probably served a warrant to search the farm."

I look at her.

"It's either there or the airport, isn't it? Where you got the body?"

I feel a bit stunned. That thought hadn't occurred to me, that the body had been put in my trunk at Alexandra's. It would have been easy. The keys were sitting there in the car all night.

"I wonder..." Alexandra lets her voice trail off as the nurse pops her head around the door.

"How are you feeling?"

"It's just starting to work, thank you," Alexandra says. She waits until the nurse leaves. "My poor farmers are probably scared to death, and no one knows where I am."

"Maybe the body belongs to one of your farmers?" I say.

"No. Ten to one it's something connected to the Presarios." Her eyes meet mine. "You know what this means, don't you?"

I shake my head.

"It means this story is going to grow even bigger and we should run the Presario special two hours a night, Sunday through Thursday, 7:00 to 9:00 p.m. Better yet, let's run it during November sweeps."

One of the great aspects of being the "other" broadcast network is that DBS can do crazy stuff the others can't. The seven-to-eight time slot usually belongs to the local stations, where they normally run game shows and other syndicated shows like *Inside Edition.* What Alexandra's talking about is running a two-hour special each night for five nights running, ones filled with love, sex, marriage, murder, the mob and Hollywood. Sweeps is the week the ratings are determined for the network. The higher the ratings, the higher the ad rates.

"But the trial is supposed to start in September," I point out.

"I wouldn't be so sure about that," she says mysteriously. "Look, Sally, I know it's a lot of work—"

Ten hours of programming on one subject. Tell me about it. That must be some drug she's on.

"But if you just gather everything you can find and catalog it, and the material's there, Sally, you know it will write itself. And that's what I want you to do. Write it."

Great, so now I'm the producer and the writer and a star witness in the case I'm covering. No conflict of interest here!

"The other part I want to see happen," she adds, "is a tie-in book published. So call Kate Weston at Bennett, Fitzallen & Coe today and sound her out. Tell her we'd design camera-ready mechanicals, but they'd have to do an instant book. And drop ship it."

I dated a book editor long enough to know this means we'll design the whole book and all the publisher has to do is print it and ship it, skipping all the other normal production work on their end.

My stomach has begun to hurt. "And who is writing this book?"

Alexandra yawns. "You know you can do it, Sally."

"Oh, God," I say.

"It will be almost all photographs," Alexandra says. "We'll just get a designer on board, adapt it from each hour's script." Her eyelids are beginning to grow heavy. She yawns again, eyes closing. "I'll write some of it. We'll all write some of it. It will be great."

I sit there, watching as the anchorwoman falls asleep. I'm hoping the operations and drugs have altered her mind and she will come back to sanity sometime over the next few days. Research, produce, write and edit a ten-hour mini-series. You and an intern. Oh, and write a book while you're at it.

Quietly I gather myself together and go.

CHAPTER ELEVEN

During the cab ride across town to West End, I call Kate Weston's office at Bennett, Fitzallen & Coe. Kate is the editor-in-chief and I know her rather well because my ex-boyfriend, Spencer Hawes, is an executive editor reporting to her. As a matter of fact, it was largely Spencer's role at Bennett, Fitzallen & Coe that swayed my decision to get involved with him in the first place. No, wait, that's not quite accurate. I had already gotten involved with Spencer, but it was after talking to his colleagues and his subordinates that I decided to try and forge a relationship out of what had already transpired. Spencer is beloved there, as a hard worker, as one who delivers on his promises, and as an accessible mentor to the younger staff.

Our relationship failed, ultimately, as I guess almost all relationships do that are born out of rash impulse and initial soaring highs. (Of course, what do I know? I am thirty years old, unmarried, and have three failed relationships behind me: Doug—twice; an Adonis in California whom I'm not even going to honor by using his name; and Spencer.)

Before I talk to Kate I have a good idea what she's going to tell me, but for the sake of my sanity I've got to go through the motions. I explain to her the project we're working on and she agrees with Alexandra; she thinks it could work as a book. Good true-crime books tend to do well, and she knows for a fact that several writers are covering "The Mafia Boss Murder" trial, but no one for Bennett, Fitzallen & Coe. And if DBS can get exclusive materials and interviews from the principals of the case, she sees how our book could be THE one. "The key," Kate says, "is to get it out just as the trial starts, before any of the exclusive information comes out at the trial. Now, you said November, and the trial's scheduled to begin..."

"September," I say. "That was a concern for me, too, but Alexandra seems to think that's not a real date."

"If it were my son or brother on trial," Kate says, "and I knew DBS News was planning a documentary series that could help him, I'd get that trial postponed so fast it would make your head spin."

"I think that's what Alexandra's thinking is." Now comes the part I dread.

"Look, Sally," Kate says, "I'm not sure if you're going to want to hear this, but the one who has done this kind of tie-in book successfully—"

"Is Spencer," I finish for her.

"Is that going to be a problem?"

"No, of course not. We were just calling you first as a courtesy, to see if you're interested."

"We're interested and Spencer's the editor to do it. I'll stick my head into his office and tell him to expect your call."

I hang up and look out the window a few minutes. I don't feel like talking to Spencer. There are lots of other publishing houses, but DBS already has a working relationship with Bennett, Fitzallen & Coe from when they published Jessica Wright's autobiography. And I'd be a fool to go to anyone else, particularly when I know, for a fact, that if this tie-in project is to work, Spencer is the one who can make it happen.

I make the call and mercifully he's not there. So I arrive back at West End, check into my office, stop to say hi to Scotty, pick up some lunch and head for the conference room in Darenbrook III.

I am thrilled at what I find. Jim has followed my instructions to a T. The filing cabinets are unpacked, the files are ready to be used, and the boxes of materials unpacked. As I requested, there are also a couple of video racks, a nice pile of blank index cards with filing cards—white, yellow, orange, blue, red, green—four large bulletin boards and all the other supplies I requested—pens, erasers, grease pencils, photo loops, masking tape, and on and on.

"This is absolutely fantastic," I tell him, returning to the eating and drinking table in the corner. "Now sit down a minute and let me explain the method to my madness." He sips on a bottle of water as I explain my preferred method of cataloging. "We've got five major characters in this series. Nick Arlenetta, Rocky Presario, Frankie Presario, Lilliana Martin and, of course, Jonathan Small. I want to assign a color to each character. For example, we'll make Lilliana pink, Jonathan blue, Rocky green, Frankie yellow and Nick orange. Let's say we open a box and on top is a newspaper clipping about the arrest of Nick's father, Joe Arlenetta. Since that reflects directly on Nick, I'd simply record the date and the event on an orange card and stick it in the card file. Then you put the clipping in the filing cabinet under the appropriate date. Both the file and the cards are going chronologically. So then the next thing we have is a photograph of Lilliana and Cliff Yarlen. I take a pink card, date it, and write down the event. You put the photograph in the last part of the file for most recent."

He is hanging on every word. "So what happens is, as we go through, cataloging video, clippings, photos, our research accumulates in chronological order in the file. And by color coding each event by character—using the different colored cards—we can see in a glance, just by looking at the top of the card file, who we have the most on, at what periods, and who we do not have enough on. So every day we can see how balanced the series is. For example, I suspect we will have tons of stuff for Jonathan and Lilliana for the 1990s, but probably nothing from the 1970s, not unless Lilliana surprises us."

"And how does this work with the interviews?"

"We'll have the transcripts of the rough cut Alexandra wants to use and then we'll literally cut up the script by each event that is discussed, date them and file them. Hopefully, by then, when you file that part of the script, you'll find some kind of visual already cataloged there. And that's something we can use as a visual during the interview. To break it up, make it more interesting."

"This is so friggin' cool," he says. "I thought you'd just be like computerizing everything."

"Eventually, when I start writing, I will. I'll be writing and scanning stuff in, but this is an old-fashioned but extremely efficient way of organizing large bodies of material coming from all over the place. As you do it, you can see the whole cloth of it."

He smiles in admiration at me.

There is a knock at the door and Benjamin sticks his head in. "A Spencer Hawes from Bennett, Fitzallen & Coe? Says he's returning your call?"

"I'll be right there," I say.

"Who's he?"

"He could be our book editor," I tell him, getting up. I look in my briefcase for the hastily scribbled notes I took while talking to Alexandra.

"We're going to do a book?"

"We'll see," I say.

As I get out of the cab on Fifty-seventh Street, I drop my notebook in the gutter, I'm so nervous. A nicely outfitted businessman stops to help me gather the papers, while the cabdriver yells, "You close the door! I go!" and starts honking the horn.

"And I deport you if you don't shut up!" I yell back, amassing my papers back between the notebook covers and standing up.

The driver's dark eyes flash white, and while he turns around in his seat to consider this threat, I remove myself from between the cab and the curb. "You be nice," I add as I close the door, "because this is America!" He roars off.

"Never thought of posing as immigration," the businessman says, smiling.

"I'm lucky he didn't run me down," I say, smiling back. "Thank you."

"No problem," he assures me. He looks at his watch and shrugs, "My train," and hurries off.

At the entrance of the restaurant, I take a deep breath. I haven't seen Spencer in months, not since he was lying in a hospital bed in Long Beach, California. (Our initial encounter with Lilliana's "family" landed him there.) I talked to him once or twice, but that's it and it was a while ago.

The maître d' comes over. "I'm here to meet Spencer Hawes."

"Ah, yes, right this way," he says smoothly, leading the way. It is a nice restaurant, well lit. When I spoke to Spencer he kept insisting we meet for dinner although I explained dinner hours were normally working hours for me.

I clench down hard on my back teeth when I see Spencer because he is so familiar and yet, by this time, so weirdly— How can I explain it? Spencer's so *over there*, in another world, while I'm *over here* in this one. Used to be we felt like we were in one small, safe, cozy world, and nothing could have been farther from the truth.

"Hi," he says brightly, pushing his glasses higher on his nose and standing. He holds out his hands to take mine and kisses me on the cheek. He is wearing one of my favorite jackets, a navy Ralph Lauren blazer, which we bought together one lazy Sunday afternoon at the Clinton Crossing outlet stores.

We settle into our chairs, Spencer leaning forward, eager to talk, me feeling glued to my seat, my hands clutching the notebook in my lap. The waiter comes over and Spencer says he took the liberty of ordering me a glass of Chardonnay; if I don't want it, he adds, he can send it back, not to worry. I tell him that's fine and sip it immediately and feel grateful for its warmth. I sip again and try to hear what Spencer's saying. I'm looking at his cheek, his ear; I look down, glance at his eyes, his mouth, down to his hand, and I'm scared I might start to cry. It's not that I miss him; it's that I was so totally his for a while, so totally committed, so in love. I thought he was the man I was going to spend my life with. I wanted to know every inch of Spencer, inside and out. Now I am looking at him from across the table, remembering so well how each of his features feels under my hand. How his hands felt on me.

"Let me do a brief overview of the book we have in mind," I suggest, as if this book idea is more than seven hours old. "And then you can react, okay?"

He looks vaguely surprised, as if he thought this dinner was merely a ruse, that there wasn't really any business to conduct.

"Okay, this is it," I begin, taking a breath and removing the sheet of notes from my notebook. I start reeling off the project, a ten-hour docu-series on "The Mafia Boss Murder" trial, the marriage of Rocky Presario's sister to Joe Arlenetta, Joe's son Nicky killing Rocky's son's wife, Frank turning state's evidence and Joe dying in prison, Frankie going into the witness protection program with his kids, only for the three to resurface years later on the West Coast as a microchip maker, a movie studio head and a movie star. It would include the murder of Cliff Yarlen, the mob infiltration of unions, the kidnapping of book editor Spencer Hawes—

"And no doubt you'll run pictures of me all beat up," he says, laughing.

That's when I notice the faint scar to the right of his eye, the faint line to the right of his mouth, and the slashing mark on the back of his hand. He had been very badly hurt.

"Well, yes," I concede.

"Lot of cool pictures," he acknowledges. "We've got Hollywood, a firebombed mansion, dead bodies—"

And so we talk on, working through our lists, what would be in the book, when could we deliver, about a packager Spencer knows who might pull it together for me, about marketing, advertising, promotion— "You know," he says, "you and I might be the best ones to promote it. Hell, we were there!" and we laugh, because it's true, it would be quite an angle, the fact that the author and editor were themselves dragged into the middle of "The Mafia Boss Murder" case. He reaches to pat my hand and ends up holding it. "We would be fantastic on tour together."

The waiter comes to take our order and I take the opportunity to pull my hand back. After the waiter leaves, I ask,

"How come there are never waitresses in good midtown restaurants?"

"Because the money is too good," he says easily.

"Well, that stinks."

"Then do something about it, Sally. You're a media maven now."

"Okay, I will," I say, and as I make a note I think that this idea may not be wholly unrelated to the project at hand—since midtown Manhattan restaurants were part of the Arlenetta Family's territory.

While Spencer explains some of the production and sales demands of our proposed project, he eats veal chops and I eat seared tuna. I adore beef and am only eating fish tonight because I've had cancer on my mind ever since I saw Alexandra this morning.

"What pleases me," Spencer is saying, "is how much you know about the process."

"Well, you should be, you taught me everything I know."

"But I didn't know you were really listening!" He laughs. "I come out of work some nights and I'd talk to the towel rack if I thought it was listening, about everything that went wrong during the day."

I lean over to extract a piece of paper from my notebook and hand it to him. "Sorry, it was clean when I started," I explain, "but it's been lying in the gutter."

"I'm not even going there." He smiles, reading the sheet quickly. "Don't use this for comparison," he says, reaching for my pen to cross something out. "That book bombed beyond belief. It's what's called an instant remainder." He reads on. "This one's good," he says, circling it. "And this one—you know, I can probably get this author to help you. You'll have to pay him, but he's a walking encyclopedia on organized crime. As you can see, that's what he does, compiles one mafia yearbook thing after another."

"And they do pretty well?"

"Yeah. People like to read about organized crime." He hands the list back to me. "This is fine. Just write up a couple pages of narrative, give me an outline, some sample photographs—"

"I was going to do a mock-up of some pages, I can do that through the textbook division."

"Cool," he says. "But don't let them talk you into using a textbook designer, okay? You want this dramatic, hip and alive. It's got to look like something. Maybe you can get a designer from one of the Darenbrook magazines."

"That's a thought," I say, writing this down. "And what about color? Do you think we need color?"

"No," he says. "I mean, with the exception of Lilliana, what's there to look at?"

"Blood," I say honestly. "Pictures of murder victims and crime scenes."

He squints, scratching the back of his head. "No, I don't think so. Color will just jack the price up and we're going to have a hard enough time coming up with a package that people will want to buy as a book when they can see it on TV."

I sit back, allowing the busboy to take my plate away.

"So I think we're done," Spencer announces, folding his hands on the table in front of him. He offers a gentle smile. "So can we talk about something other than work?"

I smile back and feel a small ache. Do I miss Spencer, or do I miss feeling so close to someone? Of feeling confident of someone loving me, even though I know it's often easier to love just about any woman other than me. "So how is Verity?" I ask.

Spencer and Verity Rhodes have a long and complicated history. She is the editor of *Expectations* magazine and gave me my first big-time assignment, a profile on Cassy Cochran at DBS. It was through Verity I first met Spencer; and it is for Spencer that Verity is currently battling her tycoon husband for a favorable divorce. I could frankly care less about Verity or her ex, Corbett Schroeder, but they do have a young son I very much wish the best for, as I would for any child with or without messed-up parents.

"It's a very difficult situation," Spencer says, sounding tired.

I bet he is tired. And I bet he must be having second thoughts. It's one thing to be lured into a flier with a very attractive married person, but it is a whole other thing to deal with the horribly debilitating aftermath of actually acting out on it.

"Corbett wants custody of Corbie."

"Who has him now?"

"Verity, on weekdays, Corbett, on weekends. He's threatening to move to London, though, and take Corbie with him."

"Surely there is a way to discredit someone like him as a father," I say. "This is what, like his third marriage?"

"Fourth."

"So he's got one kid who's like seven and another kid who's like forty-seven?"

Spencer smiles. "Thirty-nine."

We look at each other a moment and then I have to look down at the table. "Are you living with her?"

He shakes his head. "No, not right now. We can't." As if he hears my next thought, *What are your plans with Verity?*, he adds, "I think Corbett will draw this out as long as he can. For years. I think he wants to make sure Verity can't have another child with someone else."

Someone else. As if there's anyone else but Spencer in her life.

"I wouldn't worry about that," I say. "Nowadays it's possible to have children almost forever. She can always put some eggs in storage."

He looks at me and swallows, looking back down to the table. "I don't know how it's gotten so complicated."

The waiter brings us coffee. When he leaves again, Spencer stirs his for a long time. Finally he puts the spoon down and looks at me. "Don't you think it's ironic that as soon as we stopped seeing each other—" he swallows "—you moved to New York?"

"No," I say. "I just got the job."

"But don't you wonder...?" His voice trails off and he is frowning, waiting for my answer.

"No," I tell him.

He drops his eyes and reaches for the cream. "I don't believe you," he murmurs.

"You can believe whatever you want." I'm angry, suddenly, because I am thinking about how Spencer's rotten stinking affair with Verity Rhodes ended up with my mother nearly being driven from Castleford. It's a long story and one which, if I wish to remain even civil to Spencer this evening, I am best not to think about right now. "I've got to get back to the office," I say, taking my napkin out of my lap and putting it on the table.

"Sally—" He's got his hand on mine.

I look at him.

"You were the one who called it off," he murmurs.

"I know."

"So it's got to be you," he whispers, leaning forward, "if things are to be different."

I sigh, closing my eyes and taking my hand back. I reopen them and stand up. So does he, holding his napkin over his lap.

Oh, God.

"I've got a lot of work to do," I tell him. "That's all I can focus on right now. So do whatever you want to do, Spencer, but don't figure me into the equation."

He starts to say something, but I mumble, "I've got to go," and hurry out. I don't want to know what he is going to say.

"Hey, guess what?" Jim calls when I come into the conference room. "Lilliana Martin's been calling you and I don't think she's mad at you anymore. Maybe she'll help us."

"That's good," I say, grateful to focus on something else.

"She wants you to call her at this number at exactly eleven o'clock tonight," he says, excited, handing me a piece of paper. I look at my watch. Eight-thirty. I want to work for a while in here. I wish I could bring Scotty up, but sometimes he likes to chew on things, so I can't risk it. I do, however, send Jim home, claiming there is work I have to do alone.

"But it's only eight-thirty," he says, disappointed.

"Look, Jim, you're going to have so much work to do, I can't tell you. And if Lilliana is going to help us, there's a good chance I might have to go to her for a while, maybe in New Jersey or California, which means you'll be alone with all this mess."

His face falls. "I thought you were going to work on it here."

"If she cooperates, I doubt it. It might even be better if I work with her somewhere else." *Like a thousand miles from Spencer.* "Hey, cheer up," I say, giving him a playful punch in the arm. "This is a project of a lifetime."

"Yeah," he says, not sounding the least bit happy. "I was just kind of hoping to work with you. I learn a lot from you."

Finally the door closes behind him and I am alone. I get up and do a few stretches and then sit down to work. I adore research like this and it doesn't take long to lose myself in it. At ten forty-five the alarm on my watch goes off and I head for my office. I search for my notes for Lilliana, find them, read them over and make some new ones. At exactly fifteen seconds before eleven I dial the number. Sure enough, the actress answers.

"My assistant said you didn't sound quite as furious with me as you were before," I say for openers.

"Oh, I'm not. You didn't tell me somebody put a dead body in your trunk. It wasn't from here, by the way."

"We're not supposed to be talking about this," I say. "The feds have put a lid on it."

"I wondered why I hadn't heard anything on the news," Lilliana says. "The state troopers descended on us at dawn, for Pete's sake, with a fistful of warrants. And all they said to us was there was a signed statement from Sally Harrington indicating a murder may have taken place on the premises. I thought you'd gone out of your mind."

"I wouldn't do that to you."

"Well, anyway, I've skipped out of Poppy's, Sally."

"Where are you?"

"At a friend's," is all she will say. "And I'm looking around for those materials you mentioned."

I brighten instantly. "Really? And is there material, you think?"

"I've already found some."

"You're kidding! That's great! That's really wonderful, Lilliana, because we're going all out here, and we really want to do the best job possible. You haven't happened to talk to your brother's defense counsel, have you?"

"When I've had the New Jersey state troopers on Poppy's property? You bet I have."

"I mean about the idea for a series."

"They think it's great. They just want to be able to see it, though—"

"I can't promise that. It would taint the whole credibility of the project."

"I don't know how it can have any credibility with you involved anyway," the actress says.

"Thank you, Lilliana."

"You know what I mean. How unbiased are you supposed to be about Nicky? He was going to kill you, too, it was only a matter of time."

"That's Alexandra and Will Rafferty's role," I say. "They're the final judges, the final arbiters."

There is a weird, dull cracking sound behind me. I swivel my chair and see a dent at the edge of my window, with something that looks like a pond ripple around it.

I swivel back around and focus on psyching Lilliana up to find as much background material about her family as she can. She promises to stay in touch.

"Oh no, vat is dat?" Gertie, the cleaning lady, says minutes later, climbing up on a chair, trying to wipe the dent and ripple off the window with her rag.

"I think a bird or something flew into it," I say.

She frowns a little and mutters something in Polish and wanders back out to her cart.

A few minutes later, the night maintenance engineer, Edwardo, appears in my office to look at the window. "I think a bird flew into it," I tell him.

"This window's going to cost a fortune," he tells me seriously. "You didn't do anything to it, did you?"

"No, I was just talking on the phone and I heard this sound and when I turned toward it that's what I saw."

"You didn't throw anything? Or back your chair into it?"

Now I'm getting annoyed. "No. I told you. I was just sitting here talking on the telephone and a bird flew into it."

"You saw this bird?"

"No, I didn't see this bird, but what else could be flying around outside?"

"A bat," he says. "It's nighttime."

"Fine," I tell him, "a bat. It must have been a bat." I stand up, gathering my stuff to leave. I'm not going to get anything more done tonight.

Maybe five minutes later, as I am leaving my office, a security guard comes running in, shuts off the lights and flies across the room to pull me to the floor. "Stay down," he commands me.

"Yeah, okay," I say, knowing this is probably yet another of the incessant and insane security drills they have at West End. So I lie there on the floor as the guard crawls around my desk and turns on his penlight. Then he crawls back my way and tells me to follow him on my hands and knees.

We crawl out of my office and he slams the door behind us. I get up just as two other security guards come running down the hall. As I am ushered down the elevator to reception, I see that people from the newsroom have been herded out, too.

A police car arrives with its lights flashing and someone says a helicopter's overhead outside, sweeping the complex with a searchlight. "You don't suppose someone's been kidnapped again?" someone whispers.

"No, it's probably a bomb scare."

"Then why are we still in the complex?" someone else says. "Sally, do you know what's going on?"

"I don't have the slightest idea," I whisper back. The police officers are conferring outside. A cab comes flying in and Wendy Mitchell, head of security, jumps out. She is a tall woman, with short brown hair, streaked with highlights. There is more discussion. Then Wendy comes in, looking around. She sees me and comes over. "They want you to make a statement," she says. "It's okay, I want you to do it."

"A statement about what?" I ask, confused, walking out with her. She tightens her grip on my arm and turns to look at me. "I don't know what the hell's going on," I tell her.

She yanks me close. "Sally," she says under her breath, "someone just tried to shoot you."

I blink. "No. A bat flew into my window. Ask Edwardo."

"The windows on your floor in Darenbrook III," she continues, "are made of bulletproof glass. I'm telling you, Sally, it was a bullet, not a bat, that hit your window. Someone tried to shoot you."

CHAPTER TWELVE

Scotty got a chauffeured car all to himself. No kidding. That's the solution Cassy Cochran came up with when Wendy Mitchell demanded I be kept on a secure floor of a hotel that did not take animals. So I kissed my Scotty boy on the nose and put him in the back of a car and gave the driver directions to Doug's apartment in New Haven. I don't dare send him to Mother's at this hour, because regardless of what I tell her she'll never sleep. Doug, on the other hand, is more—well, accustomed to my life.

"Are they sure you were the target?" he asked when I called.

"I'm certainly not," I said in a low voice, because I did not wish to be overheard. "You can't see through the windows from the outside. They're mirrored, day or night. They could have been shooting at anybody or anything, or just at the complex. I talked to one of the security guys and he says it couldn't have been a very high-powered gun, because there's barely a dent, and if it was, say, a high-powered rifle, there would have been cracks, lines in the glass, not this little ripple thing."

"I don't know, Sal," he sighed, "this has been quite a week."

"So can I send Scotty to you? He'll be in a gray Lincoln

Town Car. He won't have sunglasses on, though, so you'll recognize him."

"Of course I'll take care of him," he said. "Just keep me posted."

"As best I can," I whispered. "The lid's come down on this big time."

"After the Jessica Wright incident, I'm not surprised," he said.

He is referring to how, a few years ago, despite all sorts of extreme security measures, the talk show hostess had been kidnapped.

I wondered, as I hung up, if Doug still had the couple of cans of food he used to keep for Scotty in the old days.

Now I am sitting in Cassy's office with Will, waiting for someone to come in and talk to us. It's nearly 3:00 a.m. and we can see that the huge outdoor tents we occasionally use for events down in the park are set up on the roof of Darenbrook I. Tonight, however, they are being used to shield the scene from overhead news helicopters, for beneath the tents, studio lights have been set up to illuminate every nook and cranny of the roof for investigation.

It is an eerie scene, made stranger by the lack of uniforms on the investigators. I don't know where the police are anymore. I don't know who these investigators are. I do know from Will that there were no radio calls on the shooting, but that a secured alert had been sent that an act of terrorism was, or had been, taking place at the West End Broadcasting Center.

I look over to see that Will's head has fallen back against his chair and he is dozing. There is a legend that circulates around West End about his ability to catnap anywhere, a skill developed by his years in the field. Alexandra told me that before she came to DBS, when she was a reporter at another network, she and Will went on a stakeout outside the Georgetown apartment of a congressman who was under indictment for fraud. Will went to make a phone call in a nearby coffee shop, and a half hour later Alexandra wondered where he was, so she went into the coffee shop and found him asleep in the phone booth.

I get up and walk over to the window, looking out at the scene. Beyond West End, in the night, a large boat is sailing up the Hudson River.

The office door opens and a bleary-eyed network president comes in. Cassy's blond hair, streaked with gray, is usually swept up neatly on the back of her head, but now is hanging down all over the place, the clip barely still in. It is a little funny to see her dressed in a warm-up suit, but I guess those were the first clothes at hand when she was called in the middle of the night. "Unbelievable," she mutters, striding across the office to the small entertaining area she has in here. "Who wants orange juice?"

Will wakens with a start and raises his hand. "Orange juice," he says sleepily, rubbing his eyes.

Cassy's rummaging around over there. "Sally?"

"No, thanks. So what's going on?"

"So we're in lockdown," Cassy says. "The FBI's here, they're going through everyone in the complex. How I'm supposed to keep this quiet, I have no idea."

"There weren't that many people here," I say.

"Enough to start rumors," she says. She walks over to hand Will a glass of juice and takes a large sip of her own, her eyes moving to me over the rim of the glass. She swallows. "I'll give you this, Sally, it's not often I find someone who has just been shot at standing right back up at the window again."

I realize what she means and flinch slightly. "Oh. Right."

"Oh, right, she says," Cassy says to Will, collapsing on the couch next to him. "Who does that remind you of?"

"It's just I don't think the shot was meant for me in particular," I say, moving away from the window. "To be honest—" I sit down in a chair and lean forward slightly, resting my elbows on my knees and holding my chin in my hands "—I should think if it was meant for anyone specifically, it would have been Alexandra. Her office is right next to mine."

"What do you mean, *if* it was meant for anyone?" Will picks up.

"The shot was way up here," I say, jumping up to illustrate. "If someone was trying to shoot me or Alexandra or whomever, wouldn't they be a little better shot? A low-caliber gun? Across the park? What kind of assassination attempt is that?" When they don't say anything, I add, "Believe me, if it was supposed to be a hit, no one would try it with a Mickey Mouse gun from two hundred yards away."

Cassy puts her glass down and starts undoing the clip in her hair. "One of the FBI agents said essentially the same thing."

Will screws up his face. "Who cares if it was a hit or some freak taking potshots? The point is, somebody was running around the complex wielding a gun! What the hell is that about, how the hell did that happen?"

Cassy shakes her hair out and quickly gathers it together, twists it up and secures it in place with the clip. This is the first time I've ever seen her hair down and I know it sounds funny, but I find it a bit unsettling. I wrote an entire profile of this woman for *Expectations* magazine not long ago, and yet this is the first time I've glimpsed the sexuality—or is it sensuality?—she so determinedly conceals. Cassy is one of those gifted women in their early fifties who have spent their entire lives playing down their looks in the corporate frontier. As a result she emits a controlled vibe of extreme attractiveness, but which is vacant of sexual overtone. It's hard to describe; Mother, I'm sure, would say I'm simply describing a well-bred lady who believes there is a proper time and place for everything.

Cassy looks at Will, depressed. "I'm afraid this is not good for Wendy."

"I thought she was supposed to be in charge of security for *us*," Will says, "DBS News. I don't get how she got stuck with the whole place."

"A moment of irrational exuberance, I'm afraid," Cassy sighs. "I think when Jessica was brought back, we were all so grateful to Wendy for everything she had done."

"So now they'll fire her," Will surmises.

"I don't know." Cassy drags herself to her feet. "I don't know anything anymore," she continues, walking toward the door. "I don't know who was shooting tonight, I don't know who the shooter was shooting at—" Her eyes dart to me. "I don't know where Alexandra is."

I try to look innocent.

"Sometimes I think—" she says loudly, opening her office door.

"Hello," a male voice says.

"Hi," Cassy says, sounding none too delighted. "Come in. Sally, I think you've met Agent Alfonso before, of the FBI?"

I do know him. He gave me a ride once, in a helicopter. But that had been in L.A. "Hi, Agent Alfonso."

"Hello, Sally," he says.

Cassy introduces Will and comes back to sit on the couch. Agent Alfonso sits in a chair next to me, focusing on me, explaining they were called in. The natural question, he explains, is who do I think might wish to shoot me? I tell him basically what I told Cassy, I didn't think it was directed at me personally.

"The weapon appears to have been a handgun. A twenty-two." He looks at me expectantly, waiting for me to respond.

"You haven't asked me yet about the dead body in my rental car day before yesterday," I remind him.

"I don't think this is necessarily related, do you?"

This is the exact opposite of what I expected him to say. Usually the authorities immediately assume everything is related and then start discounting elements, one by one.

"Do you *know* about that case?" I persist.

"Yes."

"So you know a lot more than we do," I say. "Because I'm not sure I could dismiss, out of hand, a dead body, a mafia don's house and a shooting—" I snap my fingers "—just like that."

"Well, you can think whatever you like, Sally," he says easily. "Fact remains, it's our responsibility to ferret out the truth."

"So why are you looking at me?" I ask. "If you know so much, you know I don't know what the heck is going on."

He turns to Cassy. "She is much like I remember."

"Look, I'm beat," I plead. "I've got a huge project on my plate and I just want to get some sleep and get back to work, okay? I can sack out in the conference room, I don't care."

"You'll go over to Hotel Bernier," Cassy says, referring to a small luxury hotel DBS often does business with.

"Fine," I say, getting up. "May I go?"

"You can go," Agent Alfonso says amicably.

Suspicious, I edge toward the door. "So what are you guys going to do after I leave?"

"Nothing, I hope, I'm half-asleep," Will says.

Cassy looks at me. "We will discuss keeping the lid on this, Sally." She waves her hand. "Go. Get some rest."

In reception there is a security guy waiting to take me over to the hotel. I don't see Wendy around and wonder if they've already fired her. I feel kind of bad.

"I don't have any clothes," I remember on the way over. "Whatever I had was up in my office."

"A fancy hotel should be able to help you out," he says.

That concludes our conversation.

I check in at the hotel and am given a key to an elevator that takes me to the top floor. The room is small, but very nice. In a moment, a porter appears with a packet of Woolite. I call room service and order a fruit-and-cheese plate, strip my clothes off, wrap myself in a hotel robe, wash my underwear and blouse in the sink and hang them up to dry. I give them a head start with the hair dryer. The food arrives and I set it out on the foot of the bed. Then I jump in the shower and try to wash everything away. I put the robe back on and come back, to sit on the bed, watch *Headline News*, and enjoy the food.

But I am lonely.

Maybe, I think, New York is not for me.

Maybe...

CHAPTER THIRTEEN

I awaken at ten on Friday morning with a plan. I can either succumb to these crazy circumstances, or I can detach with an ax, mind my own business and do the work I want to get done.

Guess which plan I choose.

I leave the hotel, stop at a branch of my bank to do a little business, and hail a cab to West End. The complex, I find, is amazingly quiet. I am waved through the guardhouse, scarcely acknowledged in the drive when I'm dropped off, and I breeze past security in reception. Upstairs at my office, however, I find myself thwarted, since my office is locked with a key I evidently do not possess. I walk next door and stand next to Benjamin until he gets off the phone. "When do I get my office back?"

"I didn't know anyone took it," he says, writing something down in Alexandra's message log.

Benjamin might not, I realize, even know what happened here last night.

He twists around to look at me. "Where've you been? I've called your apartment ten thousand four hundred and seventeen times. Alexandra's been trying to reach you. She said you were supposed to call her this morning."

Oops. I completely forgot.

"I told her," Benjamin adds, "I didn't know how you could call her since you supposedly have no idea where she is."

I smile slightly. "What did she say?"

"She just laughed." He lofts one eyebrow, curious. "So where is she?"

"I'd like to get into my office," I say, ignoring the question. "Can you please call somebody?"

"Suddenly, she has a broken hand," he comments to a nonexistent audience.

"Then tell me who to call, and give me a phone. I don't have one. There's no phone in the conference room."

"Use Alexandra's office," he says, kicking his head toward it. "And *call* her, will you? And I'll call maintenance." The last is said with all the energy of having achieved the final four stairs atop the Empire State Building. "Oh," he calls out, "and those are for you."

I follow the direction of his hand to see a huge vase of flowers, wrapped in clear wrap and a big yellow bow, sitting on the floor by the filing cabinets. They are gorgeous, a mix of tulips and irises and roses and lilies and other flowers I don't even recognize. I snap up the small envelope that's attached on my way into Alexandra's office.

If Jessica Wright's office is a collage in progress, Alexandra's is the agricultural belt of the indoor complex. She's got an amazing number of trees and plants in this office, all of them evidently thriving. Of course, she keeps a humidifier going at least half the day, which is good for her, too, I imagine, since all the electronics in the building dehydrate us all.

I sit down in the anchorwoman's leather chair and dial her number, opening the florist envelope afterward.

You're already my favorite author,
here and in all the world.

Love,
Spencer

"Hello?" Alexandra's voice says.

"Hi, it's Sally."

"Not another romance," she says. "Not already."

At this, I jerk to attention. I am getting accustomed to Alexandra's intuitive gifts, but this is too weird. "What are you talking about?"

"You forgot to call me this morning," she reminds me. "And you weren't at your apartment this morning. What am I supposed to think?" She is teasing, which is unusual. She must still be on painkillers.

"Actually, you could say I was away on company business." And then I quickly explain what took place last night, and reiterate that the lid is clearly on, that I'm not sure even Benjamin knows what happened.

"No, he knows," she says. "He told me about it earlier. He's just doing what he's supposed to do, pretend it never happened."

My admiration for Benjamin increases. He's American, but there's definitely a streak of the inscrutable East still running through his blood.

"How are you feeling?"

"I was better before I talked to Benjamin," Alexandra admits. "According to him, I have ten thousand messages, nine thousand of which are from various branches of law enforcement."

"They're waiting for you to reappear," I confirm.

"I know. And actually, I've been given the option of staying here through the weekend. The next patient doesn't come in until Monday night."

"I think that would be an excellent idea," I tell her.

"My orthopedist thinks it's a good idea too. He doesn't want me to try and use this arm for a few more days." She sighs. "But I've got so much to do."

"And when don't you?" I say, reading Spencer's card again. "Look, the work will get done whether you're here or not. You are sorely missed on the air, I'll grant you—the mail's already starting to come in." Distracted, I'm not sure if she's just said something or not. "So your shoulder's killing you, huh?"

"Yes," she admits.

"How's the other—incision?"

"Fine. Really, just fine."

I stick Spencer's card in my pocket to keep from looking at it.

"Sally, do you really think the shot was arbitrary?"

"It sure seems like it," I say. "Just some nut out there."

"On top of Darenbrook I?"

"You can get up there from the outside," I say. "They've got that iron ladder on the back that goes up to the satellite dishes."

Silence. And then, "I can't very well pretend we don't have bulletproof glass and reinforced concrete for a reason."

I swivel in her chair to look outside. "How many things like this have happened, anyway?"

"I'm not even sure. We don't talk about it. Sometimes I'll walk through reception and I'll see something strange going on outside, like security hustling somebody off somewhere, but I've learned not to ask about it." Pause. "I know when the crazies come, security always takes their pictures and run them through the police department, but frankly, I prefer not to know how often it happens. It's too scary to try and live your life. You know?" A sigh. "But that's TV, isn't it?"

"I think it's fame on any level," I say, thinking of the nuts who used to come see me back at my hometown paper. "I don't see anything unusual outside, as we speak," I tell her. "The tents are gone, the lights, there's no one out there. It looks like it does any other day."

"Cassy must be going out of her mind."

"Pretty close," I say, swiveling back, "but I think she's relieved that neither you nor Jessica were here. Or any of the on-air talent. By the way, Cassy's made it very clear she thinks I'm lying to her, that I know where you are."

We talk a little while longer, about the Presario-Arlenetta material in the conference room, and arrangements for next week upon her return. Then the door of her office swings open and Cassy's very tall, very angry administrative assistant, Chi Chi Rodriguez, is standing there glaring at me. I quickly tell Alexandra I have to go and hang up.

"Where have you been?" Chi Chi demands. "Everyone's looking for you!"

"I'm right here," I say, standing up. "I work here, remember?"

Will appears from behind her. "Damn it, Sally," he says. "You can't just disappear."

"I'm right here," I say, annoyed. "I don't know what you're talking about!"

"You were supposed to have someone from security come and get you this morning," Will says, clearly exhausted.

"Nobody told me," I say lamely, but it's the truth.

Will and Chi Chi look at each other and Will runs his hand through his hair and says, "Just forget it, Chi Chi. Tell Cassy this is not going to work. Since nobody seems to know what anybody's doing, I'm just telling Sally to do whatever she thinks best."

"She's not going to like it," Chi Chi says, walking out.

"Like any of us do!" he snaps. Will turns to me. "Wendy resigned this morning and everything is absolutely crazy here. And you know what? I've got a news operation to run, so Sally, you're on your own. If you want security or whatever, go downstairs and get it. I can't put up with this bullshit anymore, I've got a job to do."

I don't take what Will said personally in the least. Alexandra's not here and I've been pulled out of the newsroom; he's got his hands full. He's also been up all night, I have no doubt, and he's worried.

I walk outside, where Benjamin reports that as soon as maintenance has replaced the glass in my office, it will be turned back over to me. I pick up the flowers and head for the conference room. When I open the door, Jim leaps up from in front of the filing cabinet. "My God," he says, walking over to me, looking as if I might drop dead at any moment. "Are you all right?"

"I'm fine," I say cheerfully, moving past him to put the flowers down on the food table. "So how did you hear?"

"Everybody's talking about it," he says.

"Just make sure you don't." I rip off the wrapping and throw it away. I start arranging the flowers a bit.

"Did someone send those to you?"

I glance over my shoulder. "Yes. The publisher who's hoping to do a tie-in book with us." I turn around and smile.

"Oh, Sally, wait until you see," he says suddenly, beaming, hurrying over to the video deck. "Look at what Mr. Graham found for us!"

Mr. Graham, I think, must be around ninety years old, because he was headquartered with Edward R. Murrow in the BBC building in London during WWII. Alexandra hired him years ago to work on developing a historical documentary-video line, which in large part meant handing him a checkbook to buy every usable foot of old newsreel film he could find. Some of these archives had lain dormant in company and individual vaults for years, and Mr. Graham succeeded in garnering quite a collection and not for a whole lot of money. After all, as he would tell you, he shot a lot of that footage himself way back when!

And how his efforts have paid off. First came a videotape series on World War II; then World War I; then the Korean War; modern histories of Russia, China, Africa and the South Pacific followed; and then a variety of shorts that were largely used in schools. The newsroom was thrilled because each year more and more of the collection was being put on digital record, making the archives increasingly and almost instantly available to use in newscasts. Then came the huge boom of extended cable, and the producers for the History Channel, the Learning Channel and Discovery Channel and the like all came knocking, begging, actually, desperate for the historic visual materials DBS News now owned.

I watch over Jim's shoulder as he backs to a particular frame, freezes it, and then excitedly looks to me for my reaction.

"That's Vito Genovese," I say, recognizing the figure that is mugging for the camera in all his finery.

"And that's Joe Arlenetta," he says, pointing to a badly dressed laborer in the corner of the frame, standing outside the restaurant with a pile of linens in his arms.

"Cool," I say, sitting down.

I end up mesmerized. It's just too cool, this material. Minutes turn to hours—I send Jim out for food—and we view and catalog all afternoon and then into the evening. You have to understand that while I worked for a magazine in Los Angeles, I was never allowed to work on any of the really big feature stories. And while I was able to write four major, multipart feature stories for the *Herald-American* in Castleford (I even won a couple of prizes, which was nice), this is the first time I've been able to really sink my teeth into a very big, very long, very complicated story that is absolutely dying to be told.

History was my minor in college. And there were times I was so in love with it, I flirted with the idea of going into academics, with an eye to teaching and writing books. It's the puzzle nature of history that I love, I think. It's never finite, it's never complete (despite what many titles claim); as we progress intellectually and technologically, new tools, new sources reveal themselves, and the next thing we know, generally accepted facts about the past are suddenly shown to be less than factual, and the truth, in pieces, finally begins to emerge. (Only to change again in another generation!)

Photography is so new. Audio is so new. Video is so new. Imagine if we could have had any of it two hundred years ago. We do have computers now, so we can try and re-create the atmospheres and textures and the mechanics of a period, but the spirit of the times is so much harder to get our technology around. So far (Still! After centuries!), we can only somewhat succeed in re-creating the past by writing about it. I always think of this process, of writing about history, as the fourth dimension, where the world can be reconstructed in anyone's mind.

And now I get a chance to reconstruct some recent history and I have everything at my disposal. This is not like writing a book; this is like re-creating a whole world, and I think it is the most amazing thing I've ever been asked to work on. (Of course, I think this about almost every project at the beginning, or else I could never do all the work to finish it.) Maybe, I think, this whole time I was more broadcast-oriented than print-oriented. But who cares, because I have never been happier than right now, sorting through ten thousand bits of the puzzle.

I love this job.

At around eight I send Jim uptown to get my Jeep from the garage. He's back by nine but it is eleven o'clock before I am serious about getting on the road. I'm going home this weekend, I've decided, and I'm taking a pile of stuff to read. "I also need to find my dog," I tell Jim as I start packing a box, "who is in downtown New Haven." I glance over. "I hope you take some time this weekend for yourself. You've been working very long hours all week and they don't even pay you."

"I don't mind," he says. "So if you don't, I'd like to come in over the weekend."

"Well, sure, if you'd like."

I finish packing the box and pile a few books on the table. "Let me take those to the car for you," Jim offers, coming over.

"Thanks. It's a little heavy."

"Can someone help you on the other end with it?"

I laugh a little. "I'm not helpless, Jim, although I probably don't look very fit at this point."

"You look so wonderful I think you could probably do anything." He says this with such sincerity, and in such a hushed voice, it stops me dead in my tracks, my eyes frozen on the books in front of me.

Silence.

Finally, I look up. His face is pink, his ears burning red, but his eyes are on me.

"Thank you," I say. "If you could just take that box," I continue matter-of-factly, picking up the books, "I'll take these."

He hefts the box up against his chest and I open the door for him, hold it, and we walk together through Darenbrook III toward the elevator. It's pretty quiet. When the newscast ends at ten, the network runs the evening taping of *The Jessica Wright Show* and then West End quickly empties out. I babble about something on the way down to reception. I sign out with security—nobody seems to give a damn about me tonight, that's for sure—and we cross the garage to my Jeep. I unlock the car and put my books on the floor of the front seat. Then I open the back hatch, Jim slides the box in and I close it.

"Thank you," I say.

"You're welcome," he says, just standing there. Waiting. If he were a porter, I would assume he is waiting for a tip, but since he is a young college intern, I'm not sure what is going on. Or maybe I do and feel awkward handling it. I've got to do something, we can't just stand here looking at each other all night, which, evidently, Jim is quite happy to do.

I can't believe the thought I have next. I'm thinking that I could just ask him to hop in and I could take him anywhere, and spend some or all of the weekend making love. He is not married. He does not have a girlfriend. He is twenty-one. He is crazy about me. Of course, he is interning at DBS and this is unthinkable.

In comparison to Doug and Spencer, though, he seems like an uncomplicated gift from the heavens. Straightforward lust. After he has me, and has me, and has me (one would hope), his infatuation would turn to dust and vanish with the next female breeze of something new.

I'm going into psychotherapy, I decide. I have to before I completely destroy my entire life.

I hold my hand out to Jim and he takes it, and I give him a warm, firm handshake before pulling my hand away. "You are terrific. Thanks for all your help this week. Hopefully, next week will be nothing but fun. Okay?"

He smiles, showing all his teeth. "Okay."

I turn to walk around to the driver-side door. Jim tears around me, beating me to the door so he can open it for me.

"Thank you," I say, getting in and pulling the door closed behind me. I roll down the window.

That face. So young, so earnest. I am back in high school, stuck forever. My body grows older, my spirit more cynical, but the desire edging what feels like everything I do remains adolescent.

"Please be careful, Sally," he says quietly. "And take your time driving. It's late." I imagine he's using the same tone of voice his father does with him.

"I shall," I promise, starting the car.

"Say hi to Scotty for me," he adds.

"I will." I put the car in Reverse and wait for him to move away before I start moving. I back out of the space and turn the wheel, put the car in drive and pull out.

I look in the rearview mirror and see him standing there, watching. I know that look and my heart goes out to him. It's no fun falling in love with the wrong person. Even if you don't know yet that that's what's happening.

PART THREE

Sensation

CHAPTER FOURTEEN

I call ahead on my cell phone to find that Doug is at home. I don't know if he's alone, but I carry on with the assumption that he is. I explain that I'm just leaving New York and can't possibly reach New Haven until at least twelve-thirty. Does he want me to pick Scotty up tonight or wait until morning?

"What do you say, boy?" he asks my dog. "You want to see your mama and go home?" He laughs. "He says he's a mama's boy and wants to go home. We'll be waiting!"

I smile, hanging up.

I crank up the volume on my tape deck and make excellent time on 95, swinging over to the beginning of 91, and taking the first exit downtown. New Haven has vastly changed since I was a child, a time when rich parents sent their kids to Yale wearing bulletproof vests. Downtown was a nightmare, but it's come back mightily in recent years, starting with the renovation of the Shubert and Palace theaters, and the new courthouse on Chapel, all of which spawned a series of new restaurants and cafés. Understand, it's still not the greatest neighborhood, but at least it's an urban destination where you can hang out at night.

Doug lives in one of the few high-rise apartment buildings. It's actually owned and operated by a Manhattan realty group. His apartment is thoroughly modern, with a large living room and two spacious bedrooms that have spectacular views of Yale and the New Haven Green. Since we first hooked up again two years ago, Doug and I have spent many, many nights walking the streets around here, eating out, catching a movie, sitting in a bookstore sipping cappuccino. In New York, this is a matter of course, but in New Haven, I will never again take for granted the great strides the city has made.

I pull into the underground parking garage and leave my car with the attendant. I am buzzed into the building lobby and sign in with the night concierge, who calls up to Doug's apartment. I've always liked this building. It has a lot of young families living here, usually waiting to find a house. And while kids are encouraged, dogs are allowed, too.

I take the elevator up to seventeen and my Scotty comes bounding down the hall to greet me. I lean over and give him a big hug and smile at Doug. He's standing in the door-way of his apartment, featuring his idea of pajamas: gray sweatpants and a Jack Daniel's T-shirt. From here, he looks about as old as Jim the intern, but as I draw closer, the wear life has given him comes into focus. Golly, he's only thirty-one. Why do we feel so old?

I end up staying for a beer, and we sit at his breakfast bar, talking. I tell him more about the shooting, and how things were today.

"So Wendy's gone?"

"Apparently," I say, sipping. "Poor Will was one step away from a fit. He basically told me I'm on my own, the system's failed."

Doug frowns slightly. "That's not good, Sally."

"I know, but what's the alternative? I'm certainly better off out here this weekend, while things get sorted out there."

His attention, I notice, is drifting. Either he's tired, bored or has something on his mind. "What exactly are you doing this weekend, anyway?" he asks me.

I look at my watch. "The weekend's practically half over." I look up. "I have a ton of reading to do." I yawn. "I'll probably run, and enjoy the peace and quiet."

"Well," he says, leaning forward, "I have a suggestion."

I blink in surprise. It seems like forever since Doug has suggested anything other than my going to bed, to therapy or to hell.

"Have you played golf yet this year?"

"I barely even played last year."

"Then I think we should play tomorrow," he says, putting a hand on my knee.

"Careful," I say, "these pants are so dirty they can walk by themselves at this point."

"It's going to be beautiful out," he continues, his dark brown eyes sincere. "So you do your work, then we can go to the club around four-thirty, play maybe nine holes, and then have a bite to eat after. At the clubhouse."

I can't help but smile. It's a great idea and I love him for thinking of it. Both of us have always worked too much and we always say we need to do things, get more activities in our lives, and right now, the way things are between us, this is exactly the way we should spend time. Fresh air, exercise, an infuriating game to play. Hmm, time together, just hanging out. Heaven knows, we need it.

Sometimes I am so sure I love him. Love him more than all. Ever. And then the doubts begin. And the arguments.

"I think that is the most excellent idea I've heard in some time," I tell him. I smile, meeting his eyes. Then I lean forward and we kiss once, lightly. "Let me go so I'll be ready to play tomorrow," I say, sliding off the stool.

As Doug accompanies us down to the garage, everybody is happy, especially Scotty, who is dancing around us. I pay the garage fee and tip the attendant, kiss Doug good-night again, and then Scotty and I take off for home. It is a twenty-five-minute ride.

The cottage I rent is on one of two remaining farms in Castleford. The icy winters of central Connecticut and the twisting dirt road that serves as my driveway are the main reasons I drive a Jeep. The headlights bounce crazily over the trees and bushes as we near home, making the last turn. I pull up in front of the cottage and Scotty jumps out, shooting around to the backyard, tripping a motion detector that turns on the front-porch light. I have to make three trips to get all the materials into the house, while Scotty dashes around, this way and that, marking trees and rocks to tell all that this is his world and he is in charge.

Within minutes of locking the front door, I am nestled down under the covers of my very own sheets, in my very own bed, with no noise whatsoever outside. Scotty holds his head up a minute, waiting for sounds of cars and trucks and city, but they do not come. He lowers his head and sleep comes easily to both of us.

In the morning, Scotty and I take a ride into town to the post office to pick up my mail. I say hi to four different people, two I recognize and two I don't. Although Castleford has nearly sixty thousand people, it is my hometown. My father was born and raised here. If you ask people about Wilbur Harrington, they'll simply look at you a while with a baffled expression, but then if you modify it to, "Dodge Harrington," their faces will light up and they'll say, "Oh, Dodge Harrington! He was a legend on the football field. Smart boy, too, went on to Yale and played for them. Parents were as rich as Croesus but didn't have a dime for him. Father blew the fortune and then blew out his brains, a pity. The mother's dead now, and poor Dodge was killed, murdered they say now, but then, we don't talk about that much around here."

They don't talk about my father's death because the man responsible for it, Phillip O'Hearn, is the largest employer in town. And I don't know about where you live, but in Castleford and every other former industrial city I know of, the economy has not been great and good jobs are hard to get.

Let me explain. For almost a hundred years, the name Castleford was synonymous with good jobs, good housing, good schools and good people. In our large inner city, tremendous factories were built on the railroad. Around the inner city, then, were rooming houses, beyond them, elegant avenues of town houses, which in turn gave way to a few massive estates and an outermost ring of farms. The standard of living was excellent. Food and natural resources were abundant, the factories grew, an influx of foreign labor came in to man the machines while the previous laborers rose to the middle class. The schools improved, the roads were paved, the library was built, fortunes were made.

Probably the best indication of how things were back then are the number of churches that remain in Castleford. We have not one, but two enormous Congregational churches, two large Episcopal churches, two large Baptist churches, two Methodist churches, a tremendous Universalist church, one very large synagogue and then a series of Catholic churches whose establishment largely followed the immigration pattern into the city: two Catholic churches were built for the Irish, one went up for the Germans, one for the Northern Italians, one later for Southern Italians, followed by another church for French Canadians, another for the Poles, another for Puerto Ricans, and most recently, one for Dominicans.

Only, there are no factories anymore. What lures people to the inner city now is subsidized housing projects built in the 1960s. Instead of the country clubs and theaters and grand hotels and roller rinks and amusement parks we used to be known for, Castleford has increasingly taken on the burden of caring for the poor, maintaining the only welfare offices, soup kitchens, homeless shelter and out-patient drug and alcohol program in the area.

What we have to do, my mother, Isabel "Belle" Ann Goodwin Harrington, says, help people rise in society the way people before us helped our ancestors. That is the role of the city.

Yeah, well, Mother's sort of an idealist, and while there are many wonderful people who feel the same way she does, a lot of inherited wealth has skedaddled at the first opportunity. Don't get me wrong, Castleford has wonderful places to live. Heaven knows, our mountains and our parks are unbeatable. Our spirit, too, I like to think, is invincible. But where even twenty years ago we had thousands of good-paying jobs—in insurance, aerospace, defense systems, tool and die, automobile parts—most of those jobs have disappeared or relocated out of state. So it's not just blue-collar jobs that have evaporated, but white-collar ones, too, and the divide between those who have and have not has never been more pronounced.

Phillip O'Hearn is one of the few employers left who pays good wages.

After picking up the mail, Scotty and I continue to the grocery store to pick up a few things. We know a lot of people in here, too. Then it's off to Mother's to say hi. Her house, the house I grew up in, which my father designed and built, is set back off the road. Before I even turn into the driveway I can see that Mack's new maroon Outback wagon is parked out front. Mack is my mother's beau.

As we pull in, Abigail, Mother's golden retriever, nearly cuts me off. She knows my car and goes into this routine every time she spots it. The point is to make me stop so she can trot in front of the Jeep, plume tail held high, and properly lead me in. During this little parade Scotty is barking through the glass at Abigail, the pitch of which makes me wince.

I park and let Scotty out and the two dogs go tearing around the house. I yawn and stretch—my back is bothering me, lack of exercise, no doubt—and follow the dogs. It is gorgeous out. To the right of Mother's is the old Harrington estate, now a convent. To the left is a farm. Behind the house runs Mother's five acres, which has a backdrop of the Connecticut Mountains upon which sits our city's castle, now one hundred years old. (About a sixth of our mountains are missing, by the way, having been excavated for brownstone in yesteryear and carted off to build New York City.)

"What a nice surprise, sweetheart," Mother says, taking off her gardening gloves.

She is a looker, that mother of mine, a kind of aging beauty in her late fifties who seems to be taking on a special glow of late. Her honey-blond hair, streaked with gray, softly hangs around her face; her blue eyes, much larger and bluer than my own, are bright. Her smile is loving, gentle, which is Mother's essential nature.

The apple's not supposed to fall far from the tree, but hell if I know what orchard I came from in comparison to Mother. And my younger brother's no picnic either, although while I'm usually right there, in your face, Rob is withdrawn and rather secretive, currently focusing on his career as an avalanche blower-upper in Colorado.

I walk to the backyard with Mother and she points down to the pond, about six hundred yards past the fields, where Mack Cleary can be seen standing, talking to someone. "He's talking to Mr. Rogers—" the farmer whose family has been here about three hundred years "—about putting in a fountain, to get some oxygen into the water."

The pond, dredged by my father's father in the late 1920s, has long been half strangled by an increase in weeds. It desperately needs to be dredged, but no one has that kind of money these days, not for a pond as big as this. Mack is, however, a retired scientist, and I have every faith he'll figure something out. He loves to fish and everybody knows the pond has bass and a few trout left over from being stocked in the 1930s.

Over on the left of Mother's property stands a small greenhouse Mack built for her from scratch. She has had astonishing success with it, her entire summer garden already started in there, just waiting for consistently temperate nights to make the move outside.

I watch her resume working the soil. The crocus and daffodils have come and gone, the tulips are just starting to go. Very soon the whole yard will explode into changing colors until October. A lot of Mother's flowers are perennials, but she plants a great many annuals too, and lots of vegetables, hence the greenhouse. For a girl who grew up in old-school Newport, she sure has a thing for dirt.

This is the first spring Mack has been on the scene. As

much as I hate admitting that my mother, after all these years, has a lover, I have to say that Mack is a gentleman and an excellent choice. He is a widower with grown children, and is not interested in a housekeeper, or nurse, or younger woman. He wants a partner. He met my mother at a Wesleyan reception, where he teaches physics, and asked her out, the first woman he had asked in the three years since his wife died. I strongly suspect that he has asked Mother to marry him, and I strongly suspect that it was Mother who advanced the idea of spending occasional nights together until she makes up her mind.

My mother, you see, became a widow at thirty-six and until Mack, has never really even gone out on a date. It was not for the lack of being asked. She is a beauty, there's no doubt about it, and I well remember after Daddy died that many married men acted funny around Mother. To her credit, Mother kept them at bay when, perhaps, it would have made things financially easier if she had maintained a "special" friendship somewhere along the line. But she didn't, and she went back to work as a schoolteacher, and with her parents' help, managed to hang on to the house Daddy had built. She pooh-poohs her achievements as a widow, but I certainly don't. Mother is my hero.

I tell her about the Presario-Arlenetta series Alexandra has assigned me to produce, and she gets as excited as I do. She knows how much a project like this would appeal to me, and she wants to know all about the materials I have. So I tell her about everything, about the conference room and Jim and the video and the clippings and the photos and Lilliana looking for stuff, about going to Alexandra's farm and Rocky Presario's mansion, but refrain, wisely, I think, from mentioning the dead body I transported in the trunk of my car, getting grilled by the cops, and then being shot at the night before last at work.

"It just sounds wonderful, dear!" she exclaims. She sees Mack hiking up across the field. "You must tell Mack. He'll be so interested."

I explain I've got to get home and get to work, that I promised to play golf with Doug this evening and have dinner. She smiles. "Where are you playing?"

"The country club."

"Good for you," she says, returning to her digging. "You know, dear, I may have been wrong about Doug. He seems to be evolving." She looks up. "Don't you think?"

"What, you mean like from a Neanderthal?"

"I'm serious. He's different. He treats you differently."

"I guess," I say noncommittally. "He's been in therapy."

"You mentioned that. Well, it's none of my business, I realize, but I wanted to say something. I may have been too hard on him in the past. But then, I didn't think he would ever—" she glances up at me again "—grow up."

"Hint taken," I tell her, moving on to say hello to Mack. We chat for a minute and the three of us agree to have dinner tomorrow night, since I won't drive back to the city until Monday morning. Then I can relax and we can discuss my project, and they can tell me what's been going on out here, which usually means my mother trying to remember everything she heard at the hairdresser's.

I whistle for Scotty and both dogs come bounding up the field. Mother walks me to the car. "Give my best to Doug, will you?"

"Sure." I look over to find her smiling at me. "What?"

"My little girl," she says, taking my hand and giving it a squeeze. "I'm so very proud of you."

I squint slightly, out of the corner of my eye, suspicious.

"You are," she says, smiling, "a young lady of the world. And you are my daughter."

I laugh, shaking my head. Who am I to disillusion my mother?

CHAPTER FIFTEEN

"Wow," Doug says appreciatively, holding his hand over his eyes to follow my ball. "Too bad we're playing the second hole instead of the seventh."

I jam my three iron down into my bag and sling the bag over my shoulder, dreading the trek out to the adjacent fairway. Our golf game is not going terribly well, but at least I'm outside and hitting the ball hard. That feels good.

"Are you going to tell me what's wrong?" Doug asks, walking by my side.

"What makes you think something's wrong?" I ask, feeling sick inside because he's right, something is very, very wrong.

He points to my ball as a response.

We stop on the edge of the fairway, waiting for the foursome on the seventh hole to tee off so I can play my ball.

I'll tell you what's wrong, I feel like crying. *Mother's selling our house!* But the news is still too new and hurts too much, and I am desperately trying to keep down my feelings of panic and dread.

My brother, Rob, called me just before I left my house this afternoon. He called to warn me that Mother's planning to tell me the news tomorrow night, that she and Mack are getting married and want to build a house in Essex.

"Essex?" I said, the wind literally knocked out of me.

"Sally, I know." Rob said, "I feel the same way. But you can't ruin it for Mother, you just can't. You can't fly off the handle and freak her out, because you know you're the one who can make her change her mind. Make her feel guilty."

Never in my wildest dreams did I ever think Mother would sell the house Daddy built for us. Never in my wildest dreams did I ever think Mother would leave Castleford.

"They found some land on the water," Rob says.

Castleford was Daddy's hometown, not Mother's, although she's lived here for thirty-two years, gave birth to two children here, was widowed here and valiantly raised us here by herself. She had grown up on the water. She swam, she sailed, and loved to walk the beaches. Like Mack.

"And she's scared to tell you," Rob finished. "You know how scared she must be if she told me first. To practice, I guess."

I wonder if Mother is leaving because of Phillip O'Hearn. Because Phillip O'Hearn humiliated her, all of us, by distributing a certain video of me all over town. (Yes. It was a video of me and Spencer having sex. No. We did not know someone was filming us. It was awful. Truly awful.) Or maybe she can simply no longer abide living in the same town as the man who killed Daddy.

No, I know that if Mother wants a new life, she has to leave Castleford. It would be the only way for her and Mack to begin again without ghosts at every turn.

Good God, Castleford without Mother? Rob's not coming back, I know that. What on earth would be left here for me?

I look at Doug and know that I will feel better telling him about it. "I'll tell you all about it later," I say. "And I'm going to cheer up, promise. I'm not going to ruin our evening."

I've always enjoyed playing sports with Doug. Part of it could be because it was while watching him play sports in high school that I fell in love with him. He's not a great athlete—his best friend, Chris, was, and got a full ride to college—but Doug is a well-rounded athlete, pretty good at just about anything he centers his mind and practice on. And more than that, he's a confident, generous player. He never throws a game to anyone; and he never offers instruction unless asked, and if asked, offers it in a way that never offends.

He's at his best-looking, too, I think, when he's in play clothes. I've always had a thing about his thighs and, I don't know, I'm always so proud of him that he is so smart and lawyerly in his suits and yet so appealing in his shorts.

The men have teed off and are walking down the hill and so I quickly scoot out in their fairway to play my ball. There is no way I can get to the green from here, not unless I chop the big oak tree down, so the safe shot is to use one of my low irons and go under the tree, back into the fairway.

I'm not a bad golfer; I just have a bad temperament. When I hit it well, I'm the greatest golfer who ever lived, mishit it and I vow I'll never play again. As a result I am always emotionally exhausted and rarely make it to eighteen holes anymore.

"Sally!" an older man hails from the foursome playing through on seven. "That's not little Sally Harrington, is it?"

I grin. It's Mr. McCann, one of my father's best friends from childhood. I walk over to shake hands and kiss him on the cheek. "How are you, Mr. McCann? I haven't seen you in a million years." (When did I start sounding like Mother?)

"Well, we moved some time ago," he explains. "Down to Florida."

"You and the rest of the aerospace industry," growls one of his companions. It should be explained that those of us who remain in Castleford have not taken it particularly well that so many of our industries have moved south.

"So you're visiting?" I can't stop smiling. I remember Mr. McCann so well from when I was little. He had a boat moored in Guilford and used to take me and Rob and Mother and Daddy out sometimes on Long Island Sound. We have movies of it.

"Yep, yep," he says, nodding his tan round face. "Had some business, decided to stay over and see some of the guys. See the old hometown." He looks around the course. "Isn't quite what it once was, is it?"

"Officers of the club aren't the caliber they were once, either," another man says.

He catches my interest, because Phillip O'Hearn is the current president. "Sally, I don't expect you to remember me," the man says, stepping forward, "but I was a friend of your father's. Hal—"

"Bernstein," I supply. "How wonderful to see you, Mr. Bernstein. You're still here in Castleford, aren't you?"

He smiles, pleased I remember him. "Oh, yeah. Hanging on. Fine printing isn't dead yet, we've still got that here in Castleford."

"Guys," cues another player. "People are waiting to tee off."

"Going to the clubhouse after?" Mr. McCann asks me, moving away.

"Yeah. That is, if I ever get back on the fairway." I select a club from my bag and see Mr. McCann squinting in Doug's direction. "That's Doug Wrentham, Mr. McCann."

"Oh, yeah, Jack Wrentham—I knew his dad—the insurance guru from Seattle. Used to play with him here. Where is he?"

"Back in Seattle."

Mr. McCann laughs, shaking his head, and the foursome move on.

I quickly square off with the ball to get out of here before I am alone and am exposed as the one holding everyone up on the tee. I swing and I don't know how it happens, not with a four iron, but I loft the ball into the big oak and the ball bounces off the tree, back to pretty much where I started from a stroke ago. Well, at least I'm on the fairway of the right hole.

Doug is laughing as I walk back, and I softly kick him in the seat of the shorts and ask for some help. I get a quick set of instructions: he pulls out my five wood, makes me line the club with the ball, move my feet to form a triangle (my father did this with me when I was seven, thank you) and when I protest I'm too close to the ball, he disagrees, saying that's the problem, I'm standing too far back. I swing and, damn it, it flies straight and true, landing maybe four yards off the green.

He doesn't dare say I told you so, but the swing felt so good I thank him and ask him to keep an eye on me for the rest of the game. "Not a problem," he tells me over his shoulder.

My game improves and so does my mood. (Although, every time I remember about Mother, I must admit, I feel sick with dread, and then try to shake it off and think about something else.) It's a wonderful evening out; the sky is blue, the sun is sinking to the west, casting a rosy glow over the mountains. And the grass and the trees—is there anything more lush and green and beautiful than Connecticut in the onset of summer?

I feel increasingly close to Doug as we play, walking with him, talking and laughing and agonizing, watching those thighs, those familiar hands, the shoulders... I smile, noticing how his neck has gotten sunburned, even in this pale warmth. Between panic attacks at the thought of Mother selling the house, I feel comforted. I feel, well, married. Rather, I feel as if I might want to be married.

He is a wonderful man. Complicated, intensely private, often uncommunicative. But then, I don't know, that could be changing. Something's definitely happening with Doug.

The clubhouse is in a beautiful spot. In its heyday, the dining room had the best food in town and the men's golf locker room swarmed with recent immigrants who would practically lick the members' shoes clean, carefully maintain their clubs and even launder their clothes. There was a sauna for men, a hot tub for men, a resident masseuse for men.

Across the way from the clubhouse had been the gorgeously landscaped Olympic-size pool and a series of cabanas with restaurant and bar service. There had been a wading pool and playground for little ones, surrounded by a charming picket fence. There had been trapshooting, paddle tennis, clay tennis courts, and under the clubhouse, even a bowling alley and casual grill.

Well, so goes the economic well-being of a region and so

goes its country clubs. Membership is way down and dues have skyrocketed. The men reluctantly had to give up part of their domain to build a women's locker room to lure dues-paying members. The sauna and hot tub and laundry services are long gone, and so is the bowling alley. The INS has cleaned out the cheap labor who have been replaced by surly types who lease better cars than the members drive.

The kiddie pool has been filled in, the rusting playground equipment dismantled, the fence taken down, and the whole area is now covered over with those evergreen bushes and wood chips I've come to associate with the demolition of Castleford. There is no more trapshooting. The clay courts are now covered with all-weather surface. There is paddle tennis in the winter, but the warming hut is gone. The casual grill has been moved upstairs, trying to cover the fact that the once-thriving dining room has been down-sized to half.

I know, this all sounds very depressing, but the club is nonetheless still located on one of the most gorgeous spots on earth. The grill and the dining room still look out over the eighteenth green with the backdrop of a lake and the Connecticut Mountains. The membership is still made up of relatively rich people, but the caliber of the membership's character, I'm afraid, is going the way of other luxuries.

Mother and I share the yearly dues; the biggest financial obstacle new members face is the large initial bond one must post, which, in our case, was posted thirty-two years ago by my maternal grandparents as a wedding present to my parents. After Daddy died, Mother maintained only a house membership, wanting to preserve the option for me and Rob to join the country club as adults at very little cost. When Doug and I got back together two years ago, we ended up splitting the reactivation of the family's golf membership. The very first day I took Doug as a guest on the course, he learned of the club's tax woes with the IRS. To make a long story short, Doug ended up supervising the club's case in exchange for a membership bond. So now we all belong.

Only Mother's leaving now.

I want a drink.

As we approach the entrance to the grill, my former boss at the *Herald-American*, Alfred Royce Jr., comes out to greet me. Al is fourth-generation Castleford rich. This means regardless of what he did or did not do in life, he grew up knowing he would have a lot of money and a guaranteed job in one of the family's businesses. Al went to boarding school and Dartmouth College and came home to run the paper, although his sister is forever suing him for control. For whatever charm Al lacked as a boss, he is respected in Castleford as old school, and if indeed his family began their fortune by slaughtering Native Americans to take their land, it is not, the community feels, Al's fault.

So Al, in many ways, represents the respectable rich in town. At sixty, he is one of the youngest ones left, for his contemporaries, and even his own children are long gone, pulling their money out of Castleford to move to snootier circles in which they believe they truly belong. Al has also been in love with my mother for years, and it is for that reason, I have no doubt, he gave me a job in the first place. We did not, shall we say, get on swimmingly.

"Sally, Sally, Sally," Al bellows, holding out his arms, a motion that makes me want to run for the hills. "It seems like forever."

"It's been ten weeks, Al," I say, getting pulled into his embrace. He's drunk, I realize, so I will forgive him a little. I push myself off his chest. "You remember Doug Wrentham?"

"'Course, of course," he says, abandoning me and vigorously shaking Doug's hand. "Sally, my girl," he says to me, still shaking Doug's hand, "how are you?"

"Just fine, Al," I say, trying to edge around him. "We were just going into dinner."

"Ah, come on," he cries, grabbing my arm and trying to pull me the other way, "have a drink with me out on the terrace. It's nice out."

I know an attempt to get rid of me when I see one. "What's the problem, Al? Who's in there? As if I don't know."

Immediately the joviality vanishes from his face and he takes on a dire look. "We're entertaining a banker," he whispers, breathing scotch into my face. "The club's gotta refinance, we can't blow this."

"And you won't," I promise him, prompting him to look at me with watery, drunken, but hopeful eyes. "My problems with O'Hearn are private, not public," I say, although we all know this isn't quite true. I had, in the past year, gone on national television to accuse him of murder, and then, most recently, had arranged for the FBI to pick him up for questioning in the middle of the country club ball.

"We're just going to have dinner," Doug tells him. "Sally won't do anything. And for Pete's sake, the grill can use our business, I should think."

Al seems easier after Doug says this, and moves out of our way. We walk into the grill and I see Phillip O'Hearn sitting at the head of a table of six. Doug asks for a table on the other side of the room, and when we are led over there, he holds out the chair that has its back to O'Hearn's table.

"Does he see me?" I ask casually.

"He sees you, all right."

"Good." I smile, opening the menu.

We order a large bottle of Pellegrino to quench our thirst and glasses of house wine. Doug is going red, I am going white. It is beautiful outside, my body's had a little exercise, and the wine is seeping warmth inside.

I'm also sitting in full view of Phillip O'Hearn who is scared of what I might do.

Life is good.

In about thirty minutes the O'Hearn table clears, and the waiter comes over to tell me that before Mr. Royce left, he had instructed him to bring us a bottle of cabernet.

The waiter holds the bottle in Doug's direction, who shrugs, smiling, saying sure, and the waiter pours a little in a fresh glass for him to taste. When he gives the nod, the waiter pours wine for both of us. Fortunately, we have both ordered beef.

"This is about nineteen times better than the house wine," Doug says, savoring it.

The food is actually pretty good tonight, or maybe it's the wine, who knows. And over the wine I tell Doug about Mother. He murmurs all the right things and I feel better. It turns to night outside, and we talk, watching the meager number of members.

Out of the blue, Doug says, "I've done pretty well with my investments."

I look at him, frowning slightly. He graduated from law school seven years ago and went into tax law for almost five to meet his student loans (and the social aspirations of his wife), leaving to be a prosecutor at about forty-three thousand a year. "How could you have investments?"

He shrugs. "The one good thing shithead did for me."

Shithead is the stockbroker his wife had left him for. They are married, live in Hingham, Massachusetts, and have a baby.

"Cisco. Microsoft. Intel. I had it in my Keough, sold it all a year and a half ago, and I converted all the money into Roth IRAs." He lowers his eyes, sipping the last of the wine. "I can use that for a down payment on a house."

I'm not sure I've heard him correctly. I'm not great on red wine, particularly when preceded by a glass of white.

"Doesn't affect my government pension at all," he adds. He glances up. "I had to have something, somewhere, I knew, if I wanted to go into public service." He gives a sarcastic laugh with a shake of his head. "So shithead gave me good advice. And then he took my wife, but—"

Our eyes meet.

"But that was a very good thing," he finishes.

There is a sudden bark of laughter and I turn around to see Mr. McCann coming out of the dining room. Unlike Doug and me, who are still in our golf clothes, his foursome had showered and changed into slacks and blazers and ties to eat in the dining room. He looks as though he's been having a great time. He crosses the room to us and slaps me on the shoulder. "So how's that beautiful mother of yours?"

"Excellent," I say. "You should give her a call, she'd love to hear from you, particularly when you look so well." Lest he get the wrong idea, I hastily add, "After all these years, she's seeing someone and it's turned rather serious."

"Good for her," he declares, making a cheering sign with his arm. "She was a very beautiful woman."

"She still is," I tell him.

He looks across the table at Doug and suddenly sticks out his hand. "Kevin McCann, Doug, I know your dad."

Doug says hello, stands up to shake hands and invites him to join us.

"No can do, the wife is waiting for me and I'm in trouble as it is." He closes one eye and holds a hand up to whisper, "Good old martini madness, you can't beat it." He leans down to whisper in my ear, "So are you two—?" His breath is hot.

"Oh, gosh, I don't know," I say honestly, turning to smile at him.

"Don't wait too long to find out," he advises, pointing to me to accentuate the point. "You're young, yes, but not as young as you think. The things you think matter now—" he snaps his fingers and then spreads all of the fingers of the same hand, like a magician does when something has disappeared "—will soon not matter a whit. Not one whit. And that's when you'll want your best friend at your side, someone you know, someone you love, someone you can count on. Because kids, that's what it's all about."

He bids us farewell and shoves off, prompting Doug to lean across the table. "What was that last bit about? I couldn't hear."

"He wanted to know if we're an item." (There I go again, sounding like Mother.)

"What did you tell him?"

"I said I didn't know." I excuse myself to use the ladies' room. On the way there, just inside the hall leading to the rest rooms, I run into Phillip O'Hearn. Although I hate him, I have to admit he doesn't look particularly evil. He is maybe six feet tall and used to be balding, but now has nearly a full head of gray hair (Plugs? Hairpiece? Who cares, except maybe his woman on the side?), has a little paunch around the waist and wears contact lenses. He is never seen with anything other than expensive clothes, cars and cigars. His wife, too, I understand, has become rather expensive to maintain.

Phillip O'Hearn went to school with my father, eighth grade through high school. When Daddy graduated from Yale and returned to Castleford with his architectural degree, Mr. O'Hearn was already married with two children and was digging sewer trenches in Hartford. Daddy bought his old friend a complete set of tools from an estate sale and got him into a good construction crew in Castleford. Two years later, Daddy threw him his first job as an independent contractor and O'Hearn never looked back.

The problem was, Mr. O'Hearn was winning new construction jobs by underbidding everyone, and the reason why he was able to do this was because he was using, whenever he could, black market building materials that had failed safety standards. The long and the short of it is that years later, when Daddy realized what O'Hearn was doing, that O'Hearn had even used sub-standards materials in the construction of the Castleford High School gymnasium, causing part of the roof to fall in, Daddy was going to do something about it.

But my father was murdered, the evidence destroyed, and twenty-one years later Phillip O'Hearn is a multimillionaire and applauded as the largest employer in town.

O'Hearn hesitates only a fraction of a second when he sees me. Then he boldly looks down at my breasts, and then back up to me, the side of his mouth curling in a sneer.

So I slap him. I just haul off and slap him so hard he falls sideways, crashing into the wall. And then I continue to the ladies' room.

While I'm in here, I think of a hundred things to say to him, to do to him, but when I walk out of the ladies' room and back to the grill, O'Hearn is nowhere to be found.

So I return to our table, acting as if nothing has happened.

"Let's move out to the terrace," Doug suggests. On the way out, he orders a couple of brandies and I ask him who it is he thinks is going to drive. "Oh, we'll figure it out," he says, putting his arm around me. We settle on the love seat in the far corner of the stone terrace. The waiter brings our brandies and I ask for two espressos.

I leave my brandy untouched as Doug sips his, watching the night.

He takes my hand, gently. "I never apologized for the other night. In New York."

"No need to," I murmur back.

"I have something I want to say."

I wait, listen to the crickets, wondering if they hop around the greens at night.

"I want us to go to counseling together, Sally."

I don't know what I expected, but this isn't it. After a long moment, I pull my hand away from his and lean forward to take a sip of the brandy. It is powerful stuff. I put the snifter down and stay sitting up. "I don't even live here anymore, Doug."

"Yes, you do." He puts his hand on my back and starts to rub it. "This is your home, Sally. Maybe not seven days a week, but it will always be your home."

I sigh, looking down at the candle on the table. "I have no faith," I say quietly, "that some third person is going to have a magic formula that can change us back to the way we were, Doug."

"I don't want to be the way we were," he says, sitting up next to me. He kisses my cheek. "I want to move on to a better life." He kisses my ear. "With you." He kisses my neck. "I love you," he whispers.

The waiter clears his throat, coming over with the espressos. Doug falls back against the cushions. After the waiter leaves, he says, "It's normal to be nervous about seeing a therapist."

"It's normal to be nervous we've grown too much apart," I tell him. "And I'm not convinced I need a third person to tell me that."

"Sally," he says, sitting forward again, "the road we've been on—"

"I'm sick of roads," I say irritably. "That's the problem. You want to stick to a road and all I want to do is run to the horizon and see what freedom feels like for a change." I look at him. "All my life, Doug, I have known exactly what to do, what was expected of me, whether it's schoolwork or money or Mother's illness or being with you. I was told exactly what I had to do, how to do it, and by God, I did it. And now I'm in a place in life, for the very first time, when I am free to do whatever I want."

"Oh, hell, then just go," he says, surprising me. He pulls away to the other end of the love seat and takes his brandy with him. "It's not like there aren't choices for me now, too. It's not as if I might not like to clear out of here and move on. Be with somebody who's normal, not to have to fight and argue all the time—"

"Then why *don't* you go off with someone normal if it's so great?" I turn to look at him. "You left me and got married to someone else, and when that didn't work out, you came back here to me. And then you walked out again. And now you're back. Maybe that's exactly what you need to do, Doug, is get the hell out altogether. Go to Seattle, Chicago, San Diego, I don't know. Go to friggin' France, just *do* something if you're so unhappy. I don't know why you stay here."

He doesn't say anything but finishes off his brandy.

"Look," I say, "you're a man. You can go anywhere you want and I guarantee you, there will always be at least five eligible women to settle down with. And you'll be a lot happier with almost any of them than you would be with me. Because no matter what you say, Doug, I know you want a life that is comfortable and predictable, and that is exactly what I can't give you."

"I want you," he says, reaching for my cognac.

He's drunk. I sip my espresso.

"And you, Sally," he continues, "are drive and ambition and passion. You are also crazy. But try and tell me you don't want children, and you don't want a stable home for your children. Because I know you, Sally, much better than you know yourself—"

"Ha."

"And sooner or later, our priorities are going to become crystal clear and then it won't be complicated at all. You'll know your place is with me. And my place is with you."

He's drunk all right.

"Right now, Doug, I just want to settle into my new job, do some good work, and get some sense of where I'm going. At this rate, I might end up on the other side of the world."

He starts laughing and it doesn't sound very kindly.

"What?"

"You'll never leave Castleford," he says.

"Yeah, well, maybe that's just exactly what I want to do." I stand up. "I've got to go."

"Oh, come on, Sally," he says, grabbing my wrist.

I shake his hand off. "I'm going to go sign for the check." I walk into the grill and go over the bill with the waiter and sign for it. Doug hasn't come inside yet, so I continue outside, deciding to wait two more minutes. Then I remember he has the keys to his car.

Doug comes lumbering out of the grill, thumbing the waist of his shorts. "That was good."

I shake my head, ready to kill him.

"I don't know why you're in such a hurry," he says, coming down the stairs with exaggerated care.

"I've got a lot to do," I say, starting down the path to the golf shop, where we are parked.

"Sally," he whispers, coming up behind me in the shadows, to grab me from behind. He chuckles and buries his mouth into the base of my neck, making sounds of satisfaction.

I have to admit, it is not an unpleasant sensation.

He brings his head up, breathing in through his nose. "Do you remember the first time we were here? Do you remember that smell?"

I smile. I have to. We parked over in the parking lot, by

the golf shop, on our first date in high school. We sipped beers and Doug was too shy to speak and a security guard caught us. Doug had lied our way out of the situation with amazing fortitude, I thought at the time.

"It's the lilacs," I say.

"I just love you, Sally," he whispers. "I'm sorry, I can't help it. I don't want other women, I want you." He's kissing my neck again and his hands have come up around my breasts. "I just want you. And want you," he murmurs, and he keeps his left hand on my breast and drops his right arm around my waist to pull me tight against him. I feel his erection against me.

I can't tell you how strange this is. Doug is a man who has always acted as though he was ashamed of his desire, trying to hide it until it was time to put it in and then he would practically freeze, as if scared of moving, scared of climaxing right then. It made me crazy after a while, and unless I was so excited, so ready and dying for him to slip inside me, there was rarely time or movement enough for me to fully join him.

And here he is, crushing my derriere against him, grinding into me, his left hand deftly sliding under my blouse and over my bra.

And me? I am standing here, amazed, incredulous, thinking this is not a Doug I recognize. Suddenly he sucks a breath in through his teeth and roughly turns me around, holding me around the waist, looking at me, pressing himself against me. He takes my hand and brings it down, then, pressing it over the swelling in his shorts.

I have touched Doug before, obviously, but it has been virtually without his permission. He would always take my hand quickly away and flip me on my back to enter me. But now, now he keeps his hand over mine, guiding me to press down on him, rubbing, rubbing, and he moans suddenly, hoarse, letting his head loll back.

Does he want to climax? Like this? I don't know. I don't know what's going on, this is so strange, so wonderful. He brings his head down, and then suddenly half carries me like a linebacker through the bushes, which scratch us both, and we run into something, a golf cart. He fumbles a moment, pushes me past it, and we both stumble and fall to the ground. Gravel is scraping my back. He undoes my shorts and yanks them down. He pulls at my underwear. He yanks them off impatiently and looks down at me, his eyes glittering, catching light from the parking lot. He undoes his belt and lets it flap open. He unhooks his shorts and jerks his zipper, fighting with it, and then yanks his shorts down, his Jockey shorts, and is lording over me on his knees, holding his gleaming self in his hand. He reaches for my hand and brings it to him, guiding me to gently stroke it. "All I want is you, Sally," he whispers and he eases himself down as I angle myself up, knees wide and I guide him toward me. He pauses, looks at me, says, "I only want you" and pushes himself in, divinely pushing his way in up to the hilt. "You're mine, you're mine," he says, closing his eyes and staying up on the palms of his hands as he begins to thrust, twisting, jamming, going after me. He has me gasping, crying, and, finally, convulsing around him, whimpering, and shaking with each spasm. He freezes, coming, and then collapses on me. The gravel digs into my spine and I wince, but I don't dare move.

Not now, not now. My hand falls to his back; it is slick. We are wet, soaking. His face is in my neck, his hair tastes salty.

He says something I can't make out and rolls over, pulling me on top. His hands detect the gravel embedded in my flesh and he laughs, pulling my hips tighter against him. "I love you," he whispers, and we lie there, murmuring to each other, until we hear laughter in the parking lot. Hastily we try to dress, Doug falling over and scraping his knee. "Shit!" he yells, and I tell him to shh, but it's too late. The security guard is coming this way, the flashlight swinging. I dive back through the bushes and Doug staggers after me and we burst out laughing, holding hands, hurrying down the path to a place where we can pull ourselves together.

On the way home I realize I left my underpants somewhere out there. We laugh, but I feel giddy and scared and happy. As though we have achieved something, been somewhere few have. At my house, Scotty is overjoyed to see Doug, and when he comes in, I think about making love again, but now Doug surprises me for a second time tonight. He wants me to make coffee and to sit with him at the kitchen table for a while. I want to say, why are we sitting here, why aren't you screwing my brains out in the bedroom, in the living room, all over the house, my God, who knew, Doug, who knew? But something tells me not to, to follow his lead, which is one of shyness, a shyness I remember, and then, I think, don't push it, this is still new for him, let it go.

After a half hour, he kisses me lightly on the lips, no passion anywhere, and leaves to go home.

I am utterly confused. I also have a number of painful wounds on my back from the gravel. But after a stinging shower, in bed, I feel the after throb down there between my legs, the slight soreness and burning that tells me how much Doug really does want me.

CHAPTER SIXTEEN

I awaken in the morning with a twinge. My back has stiffened and I have to laugh as I try to get out of bed, wondering what on earth got into us last night. What on earth has gotten into Doug. Amazingly, I am not worried about him, and I am not worried about me. Certainly, from a more generous point of view, I can see that last night was good for Doug; he was able to reclaim something, take back some ground to stand on. It was also a kind of victory over Spencer for him, too, I think, because the fact is, no matter what happens down the road, Doug knows I can and will sexually respond to him big-time. That will no longer be a problem in his head. That's not it, he will know. Sex is not why we're apart.

As I slip on my running clothes, my casualness about last night quickly starts to fade.

I love this man. I always have and I always will. Whether we can be together is an issue that will take time to figure out. That much I know. But one thing did happen last night for me. It alleviated an enormous amount of guilt I have been carrying. Doug is not a proud man, but for him to think that I left him because I preferred someone else sexually—merely sexually—was, in my mind, unforgivable. Because that wasn't why! That wasn't it! But until last night happened, there was no way I could convince Doug of that. So good for him.

But now the question is, how do I feel?

I rub my eyes, ignoring Scotty's dancing around me, beginning to feel overwhelmed. I live and work in New York now, and Doug lives out here. Do I encourage him to look for a job in New York, as he has offered in the past? But what if he does and it all blows up again, what right do I have to mess up his career?

And what was last night really about for me? Was it reenacting our teenage years? Or was it about me and Doug now? Or, more to the point, how much did it have to do with my sadness about my mother getting married again and leaving Castleford? Did I reach for Doug because...

Oh, to hell with it, I decide. I should just write down on my calendar for tomorrow at 9:00 a.m.: "Resume freaking out about Doug."

It's cool and drizzling out this morning, but Scotty and I go for a run anyway. I have very little breath—why does this surprise me as I haven't run consistently for weeks—but nonetheless I push myself because I need to clear my head.

Simply, I need to work.

We cross the fields of Brackleton Farm. I wonder what was planted this year and if the third-generation heir, my landlord, will be able to continue his strip-mining operation on the hill. He's gotten by Castleford zoning laws by claiming he's building a lake, and first we watched the topsoil leave to start lawns in other towns, and then we watched him make a cool couple of million blasting rock for gravel. At this rate, the lake will become the sixth Great one, with a depth of over a hundred twenty feet. Thank heavens the trucks exit the farm from the other side, out onto Claremont Road, where the neighbors—upset at their ceilings and walls cracking from the rumbling tonnage of the rock trucks—continue to unsuccessfully petition City Hall.

It has crossed my mind to try to buy some of Brackleton Farm and save it. I even went so far as to check the records at City Hall to determine what parts are considered wet-lands and would be, in terms of real estate, comparatively valueless (read, lowest taxable rate). There is not as much as one would think. No, Castleford is in a funny place. Land is at a premium, but housing can go for nothing. The trick is, how do we clear the thousands of acres in the inner city of abandoned factories and industrial works without disturbing God-only-knows what lies under it?

It's not going to be easy to stay on in Castleford without Mother. If I do, it will mean a level of commitment I'm not sure even Daddy would possess if he were still alive.

I try to hop over a stone wall, but slip, and Scotty circles back, thinking this must be some new kind of game. I tell him to get moving, Buster, and he scampers over the wall and finally I get over it, and we take a shortcut home through the woods. My legs are killing me and my breath is shot, but Scotty keeps dancing around me, teasing, as if to say, *What's the problem, lady?*, and as we emerge from the woods, near the house, I lunge and catch him, scooping up all eighty pounds of him in my arms. I kiss his fluffy neck and put him back on the ground. (He loves this. It reminds him of his puppyhood.)

Glancing ahead at my driveway, I stop short, because parked next to my mud-splattered Jeep is a limo. It's not just any limo; it's the kind you'd never dream of riding in voluntarily, not unless it was a joke or something, because it's a garishly white, city-block-long freakmobile. The driver-side door opens and a huge, dark-haired fellow in a blue blazer heaves himself out. Scotty starts barking, fangs gnashing, and he charges ahead, spreading his four legs in a stance, ready to protect me.

"As long as you don't come near me," I call, "he'll be okay."

The linebacker guy ignores me, opens an umbrella and moves to the rear of the limousine to open the passenger door.

"I come bearing gifts!" Lilliana Martin calls, stepping out. The actress is in tight blue jeans, probably size four or something, and a cotton sweater. Her hair and makeup are perfect. I look down at my wet, mud-splattered self and my big wet mutt, whose muzzle is shedding drops of water with each ear-piercing bark, and wonder what is wrong with this picture.

Lilliana has taken the umbrella from the driver and is

making her way through the wet toward us. "You must be Scotty," she says to him, bending slightly and holding out her hand to him.

He is such a wuss. He licks her hand and offers his paw. Lilliana laughs, delighted, straightening up to look at me. As for her muddy hand, she looks around and I offer the end of my T-shirt. "Thanks," she says, using it. "So, Will didn't reach you," she surmises, smiling. "I didn't mean to come unannounced."

"Don't worry about it," I say. "Go up to the porch and get out of the rain. I just need to towel off in the back and I'll meet you at the front door."

I drag Scotty with me to the back door, where there is a small mudroom off the kitchen, where I towel off and take off my soaked sneakers. Then I towel off Scotty, which normally he loves, but since there are strangers about he is still determined to bark, and each sharp, ear-splitting bark goes right through my head.

With another clean towel slung around my shoulders, I hustle to the front door to let Lilliana in. Following on her heels is the huge guy carrying a large, blue, sealed plastic crate. Scotty starts barking again and I send him into the kitchen, closing the swinging door behind him.

"I got so excited by what I found," Lilliana says, "I went to West End. Some kid called Will up, and he said you were out here and he'd call you."

I can see the blinking light of the answering machine from here. My cell phone, I know, is turned off. The big guy mumbles something and goes back outside. "You found something?"

"Lots of stuff," she says happily. "You know, I always wondered what Castleford was like," Lilliana says, looking around my living room. "This is charming."

"You never even heard of Castleford until you met me," I point out.

"Yes, I had," she says, whirling around to disagree. "One of Poppy's brothers worked in a silver factory here. He was an artist. He etched patterns in silver plate." She smiles, looking around. "I do so like this."

I try to see the cottage through her eyes. Being from Southern California she'd call it a bungalow, I think, built in the 1920s like so many were in Los Angeles. The living room is oblong, with a fireplace at the far end that has built-in bookcases and two small windows on either side. At the near end, toward the kitchen, perpendicular archways serve to frame a little corner dining area, which I have always used as an office. For a change, this area is fairly neat at the moment. There are two freestanding bookcases along the two walls, a computer, printer, fax machine, ancient desktop copying machine and four wood filing cabinets.

The living-room furniture is a bit of this and that from the Goodwin and the Harrington families, which means each piece is old and will last forever. I also have two pretty nice wingback chairs I rescued from a great-uncle's estate, along with a small brass fender set. I have a mahogany coffee table that desperately needs to be refinished, so it is covered with old magazines and books. Only the couch is fairly new, a pullout which serves as my guest room. On the floor I have a twelve-by-fourteen red, blue and gray Oriental rug, which is now in its very last gasp of threadbare glory. Once upon a time, my mother crawled around on this rug on the bedroom landing of the Goodwin house in Newport.

"Do you mind if I look around?" she asks.

I shrug, toweling my hair dry. "Sure."

"This is the house where Cliff visited you," she says, walking toward the kitchen, "when he thought I had run off with you." She turns, a twinkle in her eyes.

I pick up the handset of my answering machine to listen to my messages. There is only one. "I already left a message on your cell phone, Sally. It's Will. Listen, Lilliana Martin stopped by the studio this afternoon, looking for you, and I think she might be heading out your way. It seems she's found some of what you asked her to look for and she's very excited. Whether this is good or bad, I leave that determination to you." A laugh.

Ah, the good old days when the answering machine was the only thing I had to check for messages. I dig my cell phone out and check for messages. Two. From yesterday. One is from Will and the second is from young Jim, sounding on the verge of a nervous breakdown. "Hi, Jim Reinemann and it's about five-fifteen. I don't know if it means anything, but Lilliana Martin just stole a card out of Benjamin's Rolodex. Now the cards go from 'Harrington Hams' to a 'Reverend Hart,' so I think she must have taken your card with your home addresses and phone numbers. Just wanted to let you know. Hope everything is okay." Pause. "You can call me if you need anything," and he leaves his home phone number.

I wander into the kitchen to find the actress.

"Oh, this is wonderful in here," Lilliana says.

I have to agree. Mother chose the pale yellow paint and made the white lacy curtains. The real touch was the wallpaper she selected to put up on only one wall, where the table is. It's from France, I know that; how else to describe it? French country, with pale yellows and browns and oranges in a gentle swirling pattern. All I know is, it always feels like a perfect summer day in this kitchen, offering a warm, bountiful, secure feeling, not unlike Mother's kitchen. The table is rather nice too. It's a circular oak table, which Mother claims is from Daddy's frat house at Yale. They were going to throw it out but Daddy rebuilt it and refinished it and it was up in our attic forever, until I moved here and she said I could have it. If you look on the bottom, there are about a hundred initials carved there.

"I love the feeling out here," Lilliana says. She peers out the back window. "Nice yard, private, beautiful woods." She turns around. "I'd have a hard time leaving here for city living."

We walk back through the living room to the bedroom, which is also a pleasantly large room. Lilliana even checks out the bathroom. "Nice big tub," she comments.

"Actually, I put that in there," I said. "There was a halftub, and I'm a big bath person."

"Me too."

I am still wet, my hair plastered against my skull, and my wet T-shirt and shorts are making me shiver. "So what's in the blue box?"

"Oh!' she cries happily. "Come, let me show you."

I'm dying for a hot shower, but she looks so excited, I follow her back into the living room, where she struggles with a securing strap around the box and then finally manages to raise the lid. Inside I see piles of old photographs. Some are color, but a lot are those old black-and-white kind that were processed and returned in plastic comb bindings.

She beams at me. "Dad checked with my great-aunt Sophia and guess what? She had these squirreled away." When I don't seem to get it, she nearly cries, "These are our family pictures!"

My eyes fly open wide and I squat next to the box and pick up a photograph. Excited, Lilliana drops down next to me. "That's my mother, Celia Bruno, with her cousins at the beach. I think it's Wildwood."

Her mother is a thin little girl, wearing a bathing suit that has a skirt. She is laughing, showing off for the camera with a bunch of other kids.

Lilliana takes the photograph from me and checks the back. "Yep. And that," she adds, turning the photograph over to point to the man in the background, "is Angelo."

"Angelo Bruno, the don of Philadelphia?"

She makes a sound of assent and drops that picture to reach for another, murmuring, "I haven't seen these in years. A lot of them, never. Look at this. That's Jonathan."

Lilliana's brother is but a few months old in this picture, a sweet little baby, dressed in a white christening gown trimmed in lace. What's so remarkable to me is that as part of their new identities in the witness protection program, Jonathan and his father had assumed the roles of lapsed Jews.

"And this is my first communion," she says, pulling out a picture of a dark-haired little girl all in white. Even at six or seven Lilliana was attractive, but without the blond hair and Hollywood glamorization of her adult life, she was all innocent dark eyes, dark hair and olive skin, a lovely testament to her heritage. Clearly she takes after her mother when it comes to physique, because her father is short and stocky.

"Oh my God," she murmurs then, pushing back some

photos to seize a black manila sleeve. She undoes the flap and opens it, sliding out a 5 x 7 that instantly brings tears to her eyes.

I move closer to see. It is a family portrait. A very young, almost handsome Frank Presario is standing proudly behind his wife, who is sitting in a chair in front of him. Frank's hands are resting on her shoulders. Celia was a pretty woman with well-defined features and lovely, soft-looking black hair swept up on the back of her head. Standing next to her, holding her hand, is young Taylor (later Jonathan), about five or six, wearing a little gray suit with shorts and a cap. Sitting in her lap is young Lise (Lilliana), maybe three years old, wearing a pink dress with smocking and Mary Jane shoes.

It is an all-American portrait of two young, hopeful parents and their children. Of course, this was not a typical family. Young Frank was already heavily committed to dragging his father's union interests out of organized crime and into legitimacy.

And Celia, in a few short years, would be dead.

I am a bit overwhelmed by the box Lilliana has brought to me. These pictures alone could make our series, because they are unpublished—no, more than that—no one even knows these pictures exist! "Do you suppose there are any photographs of the Arlenettas in here?" I ask.

"There's got to be," Lilliana says, eyes still on her family. She blinks a couple of times and then carefully returns the portrait to the sleeve. "Aunt Gina was a lot older than Dad, but he used to see her and the kids on Sundays. By the time I was born, Nicky was already in the rackets."

My body gives another involuntary shiver. I'm freezing.

"Go, take a hot shower," Lilliana says. She points to my room. "Go now, before you get pneumonia."

I stand up, rubbing my arms. "This is really wonderful. I can't tell you what this will do for the series, to say nothing of the book."

"Book," she says. "What book?"

"I thought I told you—we might be able to have a book tie into the series."

Slowly Lilliana stands up. "You're kidding."

I shake my head.

"But won't that kill any deal for my autobiography down the road?" she asks.

"No," I say. "Not unless you're going to put everyone you've slept with in this one."

She throws her head back and laughs. "Oh, you're catty, Harrington." Then she snaps her finger and points to my bedroom. "Go!"

I take a very hot shower and begin worrying about legal clearance for the photographs. Also, shouldn't we be paying someone to use them? Shouldn't we be crediting the Presarios in some way? Well, we have to do that. Don't we? I'm starting to get nervous about the possibility of this series turning into the Presarios' autobiography, as opposed to a program produced by a news department.

Well, I'll just have to check it out with legal, and with Alexandra. *Just assemble the facts and the visuals and the audio, Sally, and it will be a team effort from there.*

When I'm finally warm, I climb out of the shower and get dressed. As I stand in the living-room doorway, I watch Lilliana as she scours my bookcases, bending occasionally to scratch Scotty behind the ears. When she moves, so does Scotty, and he gets another scratch. Suddenly Lilliana looks back over her shoulder at me. And smiles. "You read a little bit of everything, don't you?"

"As does every good reporter, I should hope," I say. "Listen, Lilliana, I think I should sign some kind of property release on behalf of DBS News for these pictures. I'm scared if I don't, someone somewhere down the line is going to lose something."

"Well, they can't do that," she agrees, turning around.

"What I will do is take them back to West End and get them duplicated right away."

"But couldn't we," the actress begins, perching on the arm of the couch, "just hang out here a little while? And make a list?"

"It would be better to do it at West End," I say. "The less we handle and transport the photographs, the better."

"The less I'm handled and transported," she declares, sliding off the arm onto the sofa with a bounce, "the better."

I look at her a moment, trying to figure out where she's coming from. With Lilliana, it is strongly advisable to determine this as soon as possible.

"I'm sick of New York," she complains. "I'm sick of people looking at me." She stretches across the couch, looking up at me, not quite giving me a come-hither look, but not quite offering up normal guest behavior, either.

"Perhaps you could try driving around in something less conspicuous than a fifteen-mile-long limousine," I suggest.

"It's like Alcatraz at Poppy's house," she huffs, sitting up. "I'm sick of hotels, I'm sick of room service, I just want to be somewhere quiet. Like here. I like it here, Sally. Please, can't I just stay here? Tonight, at least? On the couch?"

Yeah, right, like I'm going to put a movie star on my pull-out couch. "Well, at least tonight, sure," I say. "Why not? But I'll take the couch."

The next thing I know, the driver is bringing in no less than three large suitcases. So much for a spur-of-the-moment visit.

"You've got to get rid of that car," I tell her. "All of Castleford's probably on the phone now trying to figure out who it is that came to town in that thing and where did she go."

As if to confirm this scenario, the telephone rings and I run to the kitchen to pick up the cordless. It's Mother, wondering when I'm coming over for dinner.

"Well, actually," I say, edging back into the living room, "I'm not sure if I can."

"I thought you weren't going back until tomorrow morning."

"I'm not. But some work just arrived here. With someone I need to work on it with."

"Then bring whoever it is with you," Mother says. "I'm roasting an eight-pound chicken. You don't have to stay long, dear."

Oh. Maybe that last part means she's not going to tell me about Mack and Essex tonight after all. If not, I might actually enjoy going over. I know Mother'd love to meet Lilliana Martin.

"Um," I say, "hold on." I walk to my bedroom, where I find Lilliana unpacking with alarming enthusiasm. Either she has a bag-lady mentality or expects to be here a while. "Lilliana? Would you like to go over to my mother's house for dinner tonight?"

"I'd *love* to meet your mother," she declares, opening my closet. "What's for dinner?"

"Roast chicken, stuffing and broccoli with a light cheese sauce," Mother says. "Good heavens, Sally, that's not Lilliana Martin, is it?"

"The one and the same."

"In Castleford," my mother marvels. "Pity I couldn't set something up at the cultural center."

"No, this is entirely off the record," I tell her. Lilliana is standing in front of me now, hands on her hips. I look at her. "Yes?"

"What's for dinner?" she repeats.

"Roast chicken, stuffing, broccoli with Mother's low-fat-but-tastes-wonderful cheese sauce."

The actress smiles. "Maybe I should be staying over there."

We set a time with Mother, Lilliana gets rid of the driver and the limousine, and then we sit down at the kitchen table to look through the photographs. I am blown away, the material is so wonderful, so personal. Hours slip by, half of which Lilliana spends on the verge of tears, explaining each photograph and describing the people in them.

Then the doorbell rings and Scotty starts barking, banging the table with his head as he scrambles to get up and to the front door. I frown, looking at the oven clock. It's a quarter to five, and I cannot imagine who's here. I know it's not a friend—all my friends call first before coming over because they know it drives me crazy to be dropped in on. (That's what I love about New York—you don't have to be home if you don't want to be, while out here, you're always stuck.)

Annoyed with our progress being interrupted, I reluctantly trudge to the front door to open it.

"Hi," Spencer Hawes says, leaning in to kiss me on the cheek. "I was hoping you'd be here."

CHAPTER SEVENTEEN

"I was driving back to New York," Spencer continues, "and I thought I'd stop and see if you wanted to get a quick bite to eat."

"Oh, my God, I don't believe it," Lilliana says, appearing over my shoulder. "It's the randy book editor."

Spencer does more than a double take. He actually takes a step back, touching his glasses as if he doesn't trust his eyes. "Oh my God," he finally counters, "it's the randy movie actress. Lilliana, how are you?"

And so Spencer comes into the living room and gives Lilliana a kiss, and the two are chatting merrily away, as if I'm not here. Within minutes Spencer's showing off his scars from his ordeal with the mob—which directly resulted from our first meeting with the actress—and when he pulls his shirt up and Lilliana starts tracing a scar down his side with her fingertips, I wonder what, exactly, I've gotten myself into.

I can't believe he just showed up. Evidently I missed whatever he thinks happened between us at dinner the other night that he feels free to barge back into my life like this.

"We have a lot of work to do," I say after Spencer tells Lilliana he won't show her the scar across his lower abdomen and the two laugh conspiratorially. (This is how my whole involvement with the mob began, with these two making goo-goo eyes at each other.)

"I'm going to be your publisher, did she tell you?" Spencer says.

"Really?"

"Really?" I echo. He looks at me. "Maybe I missed something, Spencer. I thought we had to develop the book a little more."

"Oh, well, if Lilliana's working on it," he says with a slight air of pomposity, "I can tell you right now, we'll do it. And it will sell."

"Then sit down there," I say, pointing to the chair at my computer, "and give me a memo to that effect." When he simply stands there, I gesture that he is to get on with it. "Give me the memo," I explain, "and I'll give you a glass of wine and a snack. And I'll show you some of what we've got for the book."

"We don't do deal memos in publishing," Spencer grumbles, heading nonetheless, I'm glad to see, to my computer.

"Well, you're doing one now," I tell him. "You also have to sign a confidentiality agreement for me," I continue, opening a drawer of my desk. I keep copies of the aforementioned agreement on hand and quickly fill in the blanks: the date, his name, his company's name, the material: "documentation and photographs relating to the Presario-Arlenetta television programming," and the damages: "$500,000."

"You breathe one word to anyone outside of Bennett, Fitzallen & Coe of what I am about to show you," I tell him, handing him the agreement, "without written permission from us, not only is the deal off, but B, F & C is going to owe DBS News half a million dollars."

"Oh, come on," he says, plunking down in the chair and pressing the button to turn on the computer screen. He's worked on this computer many times, in days gone by. "It'll never stand up in court."

"Try us," I suggest, leaving out the agreement for him to sign.

"This is very exciting," Lilliana says. "This series is really going to be big, isn't it?"

"Huge," I confirm. I motion for her to follow me into the kitchen, and after she does, I close the swinging door behind us. "I don't want him to see all of the material," I whisper. "The deal isn't done, not by a long shot. We need a contract first. And a check to use toward our expenses. Also, I don't want him trying to edit the thing before we even have an outline of the story." I smile. "Trust me, I know how he is, and he's a control freak."

"Oh, and you're not," she whispers back.

"Right. So listen," I whisper, "we'll sit in the living room and I'll bring out a few pictures, but we need to put him off until I get back to West End, all right? So don't let on there's anything else here."

"Crafty," she whispers back. She hesitates a moment and then kisses me lightly on the mouth and moves off toward the living room.

I blink a few times, recovering my composure from *that* surprise.

I don't know what's going on lately. I'm not that attractive, trust me. I must have a sign that says VACANCY or something.

I dig out a bottle of Chardonnay from the back of my refrigerator and open it. I also bring out an unopened bottle of Pellegrino water. (No way I'm drinking anything around these two.) I make up a tray with the drinks and wineglasses, then search around in one of the refrigerator bins and come up with some cheeses from Bishop's Farm someone gave me for Christmas. I search my cabinet and find a box of water crackers. I know Lilliana won't eat any of this (that's why she looks the way she does and the rest of us look the way we do) and so I put out some baby carrots and celery as well.

I bring the tray out to find Spencer and Lilliana sitting on the couch, talking in hushed voices. I put things out on the coffee table and realize the actress is bringing him up to speed on her brother, Jonathan, that he is in prison, although he seems to have special privileges.

"Such as?" Spencer asks, hand shooting out to take a piece of cheese.

"His girlfriend," she answers.

"Really, in the cell?"

"Yeah. Wild, isn't it?" She reaches for a celery stick. "We're praying, of course, we can get him out soon."

Spencer and I exchange looks. No matter how good his lawyers are, we both know no one is going to let Jonathan Small post bond when the charge is murder one, not in California.

Spencer drinks half a glass of wine while Lilliana and I drink Pellegrino. Unlike the actress, I dive into the cheeses.

We talk series, we talk book, and I am surprised at how much the project has already come into focus for me. Feed your subconscious and it's amazing how a storyline begins to form. I bring out a handful of photographs and Spencer is suitably impressed: Nicky Arlenetta flipping hamburgers with John Gotti in Queens; Rocky and Frankie Presario, the latter as a young boy, standing with Jimmy Hoffa; a magnificent wedding portrait of Frank and Celia; the family portrait with young Jonathan and baby Lilliana; Frank and Celia with Frank Sinatra at the New Jersey Arts Center; Lilliana and Jonathan in bathing suits, as children, standing with their cousin, Cliff Arlenetta (later Yarlen), whose brother, Nick, would one day murder him.

In no time it is six o'clock. I explain to Spencer we are going over to Mother's for dinner, and he does not try to get himself invited, because he is, I know, scared of seeing Mother. He thinks the world of my mother and spent a lot of time with her, telling her the truth about his life, about his past, and about how meeting me had changed everything. He told her I was the love of his life, that he would do anything to marry me and settle down. So he doesn't particularly want to face her right now, not when he would have to explain to Mother how, within days of our breakup, he effortlessly switched his undying devotion to a married woman.

Lilliana excuses herself, wanting to change for dinner, leaving me and Spencer alone.

"So were you and Verity out for the weekend?"

He cinches up the side of his mouth. "I really don't feel like talking about Verity, if you don't mind."

I could be nice and let it pass, or I can be mean and press him about it. "Why not?"

He looks at me. "You know why."

I give him a skeptical look. "No, Spencer, I can honestly say, I have no idea why."

"Because I'm still in love with you," he says.

There is a banging sound in the bedroom.

"No," I say, my attention returning to him, "you're still in love with Verity. That's why you went straight back to her."

He shakes his head. "You left me. She came to me. I was sick, I was in the hospital."

I fight the urge to burst out laughing. He looks so serious, so earnest, and I wonder how he can honestly sit there and tell himself he is unhappy because he is still in love with me. Heaven forbid he should link his unhappiness with the fact he has chosen a married woman over forty who not only has a young son, but a billionaire husband determined to destroy their lives. Sometimes men are so fundamentally dumb I can't believe it.

"You know you have to see this through with Verity," I say softly. "Frankly, you owe it to her. You can't interfere with a family's life and then quit when you get what you said you always wanted."

"But Sally," he begins, moving across the couch toward me.

"*Don't*," I say.

He looks at me pleadingly a moment, sighs, lowers his head and falls back against the couch. "My life is a complete and total nightmare."

"I have to get ready for Mother's," I say, fleeing to the bedroom. Scotty sticks around the living room, hoping for an opportunity with an unsupervised cheese plate.

All of Lilliana's suitcases are open on the floor, and I nearly wipe out, trying to walk into my bedroom without trampling her clothes.

"Oh, God," the actress says, "you're not sleeping with

him again, are you?" Lilliana is standing in front of my mirror, looking at me in the reflection while brushing her hair.
She has changed into some pretty beige slacks and a silk
blouse, gold earrings, a gold bracelet. It is a conservative out-
fit and very pretty. Mother will love it.

"No," I tell her, picking my way over to the closet.

She waits until I look over again and meet her eyes in the
mirror. "So who were you douching for today?"

"Lilliana!" I nearly yell, knowing she must have seen the
box in the bathroom trash basket.

"Just wondered." She shrugs.

"Just stop it and behave, okay?" I snap, trying to look
through the clothes in my closet, but she's already jammed
her own clothes in it already. "What the hell do you need a
beaded cocktail dress for?" I demand, yanking out such a
dress, in the color of red.

"Maybe she wants to take you out on the town," Spencer
suggests, leaning on the door frame.

The telephone rings. "It's probably Mother, wondering
where we are," I say, sticking the dress back in the closet
and walking defiantly over Lilliana's clothes to get to the
phone. "Hello?"

"Hi," Doug says.

"Hi," I say back, amazingly relieved to hear his voice. It
was so strange not to hear from him today. But then, after
last night (oh golly, was that really me, was that really us?),
he might well have been waiting to hear from me.

"You're not going to get her to sleep with you, you know,"
Spencer says across the room.

"I certainly won't be telling you about it if she does," Lilliana fires back.

Given that Doug has just heard this exchange, I don't
know quite what to say.

"You've got company," he observes.

"Lilliana came out to work," I explain.

"She won't do it," Spencer taunts her.

"*Hello!*" I call out. "I'm on the telephone, here, thank you!"

"That can't be who I think it might be," Doug says.

"Yes, it is, entirely and totally uninvited, I assure you."

"Well, she's certainly not going to screw you!" Lilliana yells.

"This is going to be some book collaboration," Doug speculates.

"Go to hell, Lilliana," Spencer mutters, leaving.

I clear my throat. "Lilliana and I are going over to Mother's for dinner."

"Oh, good luck with your mom." He remembers about Mother's plans. "It's probably just as well someone's with you."

"You are such a fuckhead, Spencer Hawes!" Lilliana yells, running after him.

Doug bursts out laughing and it is so good to hear him laugh. It means he does not feel threatened. I chose him last night, he knows that. It proved to him something he needed to know and he is not going to worry about that part of our relationship.

When I get off the phone and walk into the living room, I'm just in time to hear the front door slam and see Lilliana standing triumphantly at the window, arms folded over her chest. "That son of a bitch! Imagine talking to me that way!"

I walk over to stand next to her, watching Spencer climb into his car. "I feel sorry for him," I confess. I don't say that I also started to feel a lot of other things the other night when I saw Spencer, but last night with Doug has given me some kind of armor.

"You shouldn't." She looks at me, eyes narrowing slightly. "A guy like Spencer Hawes will never stop breaking your heart."

"I want him to publish our book, though."

"If it's any good, we can go anywhere in town," she assures me, moving away. "Get rid of him, that's what I say. Now, your mother," she adds, turning around. "I'd like to bring her flowers. Is there somewhere we can stop?"

CHAPTER EIGHTEEN

"We're late because that idiot Spencer Hawes stopped in," Lilliana explains to Mother as if they've known each other for years.

"Spencer? Really?" Mother is looking at me from across the kitchen counter, where she is arranging the flowers Lilliana brought.

Lilliana nearly brought the Super Stop 'n Shop management to its knees when she started pulling packages of flowers out of the cold case and began cutting them open, choosing only the freshest-looking flowers. When employees came running over to stop the madwoman and she turned around, they nearly died. "Oh my God, it's you!" exclaimed one worker. Lilliana held one long, elegant finger to her lips, saying, "Shh," but within moments half the employees in the store had run over to help her. Once she had assembled the bouquet she wanted, Lilliana paid the clerk for all the bouquets, handed her selection to me, scooped up all the unused bouquets and then waltzed over to give them out to people waiting in the checkout lines. By the time we drove out of the parking lot, it seemed as though half of

Castleford was trailing after us. "Well, this was a very discreet outing," I commented.

From my seat at Mother's kitchen table, I say, "Bennett, Fitzallen & Coe is interested in doing a tie-in book with our series."

"Spencer's trying to get Sally back," Lilliana tells Mother, snipping the bottom of another flower stem over the sink and handing it to her. "But she's not going for it. I think she finally knows the score with that one."

Mother's eyebrows rise and fall slightly, but she doesn't say anything.

"So what is this series you're working on?" Mack Cleary asks from the other side of the table

"I can't believe I cleaned the living room and we're all sitting in here," Mother says, sticking a fern into the back of the flowers.

"We're doing a series of programs," I explain to Mack, "that tell the whole history of the Presario family in America, and how, ultimately, that history led to the—incident— that Lilliana's brother is being tried for."

"Jonathan murdered a murderer," Lilliana translates matter-of-factly, snipping the bottom of a rose and handing it to Mother.

"Yes, I know that, dear," Mother says just as matter-of-factly. "It must be quite dreadful for you."

"It's Jonathan I worry about," Lilliana begins, and soon the two women are talking amongst themselves about family trials and tribulations, and the ways one can be supportive without interfering.

"Seems they've hit it off," Mack says quietly.

"Everybody hits it off with Mother."

He looks at me. "Are you all right? With Spencer and this book project?"

I smile. "Thanks. Yes. It's fine."

"I must confess, I always rather liked him."

"Me too," I say honestly. "I still do. And he's confused and troubled and I think he's just lonely." I kick my head in Lilliana's direction. "This is another one. I don't know how she survives. Make that, I don't know how she survived in the first place. It's quite a story, Mack, and not a very happy one, not for a little girl." I start telling him a bit about the story-line, the scheduled interviews, and then about the records and clippings and now, thanks to Lilliana, the personal photographs we have to use.

"I feel like I've been teased all week," I say. "I've got all this material ready, and it's been one thing after another keeping me away from it."

"Like what? What's going on?"

Well, if I leave out the dead body in the truck of my rental car, Alexandra having cancer, and being shot at in the office, it doesn't leave much for me to complain about to Mack.

"Oh, just stuff," I say.

"Just stuff," he echoes, grinning. He is a good-looking man, with twinkling blue eyes, neatly cut gray hair and a matching, closely cropped beard. He's a good teacher. (I sat in on one of his lectures at Weslyan). His three children are quite nice, too. The son is a financial analyst for one of the big houses on Wall Street, married with one son; one daughter is a medical doctor and is married, no children; and his youngest daughter is a lawyer, married with a new baby. They are pretty normal. What I mean is, they don't dynamite avalanches for a living like my brother does, or hang out with the mob like I do these days.

"Before your mother knew that Lilliana was coming," he says quietly, "she was hoping to speak with you about something."

Even though I know what that something is, out of habit my stomach turns over in fear. "The cancer hasn't come back—"

Quickly he reaches across the table to touch my hand. "No, no—no, Sally, I'm sorry, it's nothing like that. Your mother's health is excellent. She just had a complete physical."

"Thank God," I murmur. "I have a friend who had some surgery this week. Breast cancer. She's going to be all right, but it's got it back in my mind, you know?"

"If this isn't the single most beautiful bouquet in all the world," Mother announces, picking up the vase in her hands. "Now wait a minute," she says, hesitating. "I was going to put it on the dining-room table, but then we won't be able to see each other."

"Oh, let's just put it right here," Lilliana says, taking the vase from Mother and coming over to place it on the kitchen table.

There are two loud thunks against the sliding glass doors as Scotty and Abigail announce their arrival home.

"The children were the same way," Mother explains, sliding open the glass door to let the dogs in. "They always knew the minute dinner was going to be served."

We enjoy a very low-key and delicious dinner. For dessert, Mother has whipped up individual parfaits, with a layer of blueberries and a layer of strawberries between layers of fat-free vanilla yogurt. "A little early for Fourth of July," Mother says as we dig in, "but I thought Lilliana might be careful about desserts."

"Unlike us, right, Sally?" Mack says, patting his tummy. Mack is always doing sit-ups to counter what he says is his problem, sitting too much, while Mother tells him it's the wrong foods he eats, plain and simple. Since I am a great fan of the wrong foods, too (as well as the right ones, because, you know, I adore food, period), Mack and I have not been above meeting for lunch at, say, the drive-thru window at McDonald's in town.

At the conclusion of dinner, Mack announces he is doing the dishes, and Lilliana insists she is doing them with him. Mother says this just isn't possible, she couldn't possibly allow her guest to wash the dishes, and I interrupt to say that of course it's possible, particularly since Mother and I need a few minutes alone to discuss some things.

Mother looks at me, baffled, and then quickly looks to Mack, who shrugs. "I merely mentioned you wanted to talk to her."

"Then it's settled," Lilliana announces, jumping up and taking Mother's dessert dish and her own.

Mother is looking a tad annoyed with Mack. I know she

thinks this is not an appropriate time, but then, she doesn't know I already know what she is going to tell me.

"Let's just go outside," I suggest, moving my chair back to stand up. "And let's take these miserable beggars with us." The last is directed under the table to the dogs.

"Abigail never used to beg," Mother says nervously, following me, and I realize how much she does not want to have this conversation right now.

We walk, out of habit, I think, toward the pond. It was a favorite destination for me and Rob as kids—fishing, launching rafts we had built, deliberately falling in—and Mother always tried to be near by. At the end of Mother's lawn, however, tonight she stops. "I'm not in the right shoes." She walks toward the greenhouse. "Darling," she says in that you-best-listen-carefully voice, "Mack and I are talking about getting married." She stops walking to look at me. "What would you think about that?"

"I think it would be wonderful."

She smiles. "Thank you." She resumes walking and takes my hand. "I don't think your brother feels quite the same way."

"Oh, he may surprise you, Mother. I know he would feel better if he knew someone was watching out for you."

"But you watch out for me," she says, giving my hand a squeeze.

"No, it's time, Mother. It's time you had a life of your own." We walk a bit.

"I'm also thinking about taking early retirement from teaching."

Mack has probably done pretty well. His children are grown. I suppose they would have some sort of agreement about their estates.

I stop to look at her. "Mother, Rob called me yesterday and told me."

Her eyes search mine.

"He also told me about Essex." I struggle to smile. "You should do it. Absolutely. Start a new life with a wonderful man who loves you."

"Sally," she says, looking me straight in the eye, "it's important you understand. Your father built this house for me—" Her eyes fill with tears. "And I loved him—and besides you and your brother, I still love him more than anyone on earth. I do love Mack, I wouldn't marry him otherwise, but I cannot expect to give him what I should if I stayed on in this house. Because here I am still your father's wife. I will always be your father's wife."

I start to cry. I can't help it. I feel Mother's hand on my shoulder and I turn to sob on it as I did as a child.

"I know, darling," she murmurs. "I miss him, too. I will always miss him."

I cling to her, thinking about that night the police chief came to tell us that my father had been killed in an "accident." The night of the great flood. Finally I stop, and try to pull myself together. I step back, wiping my eyes. "I'm glad you're getting out of Castleford. The town doesn't deserve you."

Mother sighs, looking out at the horizon as if the answer is there. "It doesn't mean to me what it once did," she admits.

"How could it?" I say angrily. "When your husband's murderer fucking runs it!"

"Sally!" my mother gasps. "The *language*, please!"

We look at each other and start to laugh. "It's okay to call him a murderer, isn't it?" I say, half laughing, half crying, "I just can't use *that* word."

"That's right," Mother says, wiping a tear from her eye.

I try to smile again. "It will be fine, Mother." I reach out for her hand. "It will be more than fine. For the first time in your life, you'll have someone to yourself. The two of you can sail and travel and do whatever happily married people do."

"It's more than marriage," she says shyly, leading me by the hand back toward the house. "It's a second chance at life." Suddenly Mother hugs me like there's no tomorrow. "I love you, baby. I love you and your brother more than anything in the world."

"We know," I tell her. "And we love you too."

We separate, wipe our eyes and walk back up to the house.

Only now do I realize that we have easily been watched from the kitchen.

When we go inside, Mack pretends nothing is unusual, but Lilliana is not so tactful. "Why are you both crying?"

"Tears of happiness," I say. "Mother and Mack are getting married." I make my way around the counter toward Mack, whose hands are full of soapy pots and pans. "Congratulations," I say, giving him a hug, and I know he has sent a questioning look at my mother over my shoulder, because Mother says, "She knows all about Essex."

"So that's going to be a big change for you," Lilliana says during the ride home. "I was under the impression the only reason that you came back to Castleford was because of your mother."

I don't bother answering. I've got a lot to think about.

"So will you keep your cottage, or maybe get something somewhere else?"

"I don't know," I say, turning down my road.

"You're not going to the Hamptons, are you? Oh, God," she groans. "It's like so *over* out there, you know?"

"I think it's beautiful."

Rather than argue, Lilliana decides to be quiet.

"You're very lucky," she says to me later as we sit in my office area having a mug of herbal tea, "to have such a wonderful mother."

"Extremely," I agree. "She's my saving grace."

"Sometimes I can barely remember my mother," the actress says. "At other times, I can hear her talking to me. Not talking exactly, but letting me know, somehow, when she thinks I'm doing the right thing."

The comment raises my spirits a little. "I know what you mean. It's that way with my father. If you asked me what his voice was like, I could describe it, but I couldn't remember it. I just know when he's talking to me."

"Do you suppose we'll ever get over it?" Lilliana asks. "Wanting that connection? Missing it so much?"

"I don't know," I say honestly.

We decide to pack it in for the night and start work in the morning. I go into the bedroom first to change and use the bathroom. Then I come back into the living room and she goes in. I pull out the couch and make up the bed with linens from the hall closet. Scotty goes out to do his final business of the day and I knock softly on the bedroom door and Lilliana says to come in. All of her makeup has been removed, so she looks less actress-like and more like simply an attractive young woman. She has changed into an L.A. Lakers T-shirt and is tucked into my bed, the bedside lamp on and a book open in her lap. She has stacked her clothes neatly on an open suitcase and has moved the others under the bed so there is actually floor space now.

"May I get you anything?"

"Not a thing. I'm extremely comfortable and very glad to be here." She smiles. "I like your life. And I'm so glad you're through with Spencer," she adds. "He is no good for you."

"Do you mind if I take a pillow?" I ask, changing the subject. "I've got one, but I prefer two."

"Sure." She reaches next to her to grab one and offers it to me.

"Thanks." I hesitate and she looks up with a questioning expression. "I'm very grateful for your help today," I say quietly. "It's not the pictures—although I am overwhelmed by what you found—but for, um, being a friend, being so nice to my mother and Mack, and making a big deal over them."

"They are a big deal." She smiles.

"They don't often have Hollywood actresses to Sunday dinner. You were terrific." I sigh. "I guess you can tell I'm a little depressed about Mother moving."

"There would be something wrong with you if you weren't," she says softly. She reaches out to touch my arm. "Get some sleep. You're very tired."

"I shall," I promise, carrying my pillow to the door. "Good night, sweet dreams."

"You too."

I close the door and go to the front door to call Scotty. He comes bounding up and I lock the door behind him. I close the drapes over the windows, and then walk into the kitchen to check that door. Locked. I turn off the kitchen lights, close the swinging door and climb into bed. I start reading one of my mafia histories.

I think I'm going to have trouble sleeping, but Scotty drops off first, quietly snoring on his back, his four legs bent in the air. I put my book on the end table and turn off the lamp. I settle down under the covers, thinking I should make Scotty roll over onto his side to make him stop snoring, but I drift off before doing anything about it.

Suddenly I am sitting up, wide awake. Something has happened, although I'm not sure what. Scotty's jumped off the bed, barking his head off, and I hear a crash in the bedroom. "Lilliana?" I call, fumbling to turn on the lamp. Now I smell smoke, rubber burning, and some horrible chemical smell.

Scotty is barking furiously at the front door.

The bedroom door opens and Lilliana comes running out. "What was that?"

I race to the front door, flick the switch that turns on the outdoor floodlights and sweep the drapes open to look outside.

My Jeep is in flames. What's left of it, anyway. It's a burning, twisted metal mess, and a tree branch, high above it, I can see, is burning. "Call 911," I tell Lilliana. "Cottage at Brackleton Farm. Whatever you do, keep Scotty in."

I run outside and around the back of the house to the shed. I grab the garden hose and drag it around to the front, hook it up to the tap and turn it on. It is far too late to do anything about the car, but at least I can hose down the yard and the trees and the front of the cottage.

I hear sirens in the distance.

CHAPTER NINETEEN

"Who else was here, Sally?" Detective Buddy D'Amico of the Castleford Police Department asks as he surveys the living room.

I decide to take his question in the context of the last twenty minutes. "Nobody."

"You always sleep out here in the living room when you're here by yourself?" he continues, nodding to the pullout bed.

"Sometimes. If my room is a mess."

"And so your room is a mess now, I take it."

"Kind of." I'm not really sure I know how to play this, except to try and keep Lilliana out of this as long as possible. The explosion may or may not have to do with her.

Buddy and I went to high school together and have remained friends, particularly when I was working at the paper. He is a great guy, but anything I tell him tonight, when the police chief is here, I know, will end up in the headlines tomorrow. "I'm shuttling back and forth from New York," I explain, "and so I have a ton of clothes and stuff I'm moving. Let me just go and check on the coffee, Buddy, okay?" I say, edging toward the kitchen. "I mean, Detective D'Amico. "

Police Chief Morgan has his eyes on me and I don't know

if it's in suspicion or because he can't hear what's being said. He consistently fails the hearing test in his physical, but no threats can move his vanity to the point of wearing his hearing aide.

I hurry into the kitchen and nervously peek out the back window. Just before Buddy arrived, I had sent Lilliana—hastily clad in jeans and that Lakers T-shirt—fleeing into the night with a flashlight and directions. I hope she didn't get lost, and I dearly hope my friend can find her and whisk her away from this until I have a better idea of what's going on. Once I pushed her out the door, I packed all the photographs back in the blue plastic crate and sealed it up with packaging tape. It is sitting on the floor in the kitchen by the table. Then I called Doug and told him what had happened.

I pour the fresh pot of coffee into a thermos dispenser and place it on a tray with the cups, milk, sugar, spoons and napkins already there. I carry it out to the living room and put it down in my office area, asking if I can close up the couch so there are more places for people to sit.

"Fine," Buddy says. He holds his cell phone between his shoulder and ear, and helps me put the bed away and replace the cushions. "Tell the guys there's coffee," he instructs the officer near the door.

"Odd, very odd, Sally," Chief Morgan says to me as he helps himself to coffee. "Cars don't just blow themselves up in the middle of the night."

"I agree, Chief Morgan, and I'm racking my brain trying to think of anybody in Castleford who might want to do it." I say this because everybody knows I only have one enemy in Castleford and that's Phillip O'Hearn, so why not, I figure, push the investigation in his direction?

My friend Maggie, a lieutenant with the fire department, comes in. She looks tired but is her usual upbeat self. "Nobody in the explosion, thank God," she confirms to Buddy.

I must have looked startled, because Buddy says, "If the person doesn't know what he's doing, very often he'll detonate the bomb while installing it."

"Bomb," I repeat.

"Cars don't just blow themselves up in the middle of the night," Chief Morgan says again. "Maggie, want some coffee?"

"Thank you, I'm okay!" she calls, going back out the front door, where she stops to confer with someone coming in. It turns out to be another friend, John, the assistant fire chief.

"There's nothing left to tow," he tells Buddy. "We'll let it cool off and then we've got a flatbed coming to take it over to the lab." His eyes swing over to me. "Sally, what was that car?"

"A Jeep. Just paid for, too."

"Yeah, well," John says, "you've got a lot to be grateful for."

"A car can't just blow itself up," the chief says yet again, and I'm beginning to see why Buddy thinks maybe it's time for the good captain to retire.

I return to the kitchen to start another pot of coffee. A few moments later, Buddy comes in. "Do you want to call your mother?"

"I'd like to let her sleep until morning."

He's studying me as I study the coffeemaker. "So what's going on? Why would someone blow up your car?"

I look over at him. "There's only one person I know in Castleford that hires people to blow up things."

Buddy gets a pained expression on his face. He has to live and work in this town and Phillip O'Hearn can, and has in the past, made his life miserable. Things have only recently begun to smooth out for Buddy. "Why would he do this, Sally?"

"I saw him yesterday. At the country club."

Buddy sighs. "And what did you say to him?"

"Not a word. I went to the other side of the dining room and sat with my back to him. You can ask Al Royce, because he's the one who begged me not to cause a scene. The club's on the verge of collapse and O'Hearn was greasing some sucker for a loan, so who was I to interrupt the scam?"

He shakes his head. "Sally—"

"Look," I tell him, "someone blew up my car, and it just so happens that there is a man in town who has a long history of blowing things up. I didn't say a word to O'Hearn, but I did slap him across the face."

"I thought you said—"

"I saw him later, outside the rest rooms. He leered down my blouse and I slapped him. Knocked him over into the wall, in fact." I challenge Buddy with my eyes. "So you want a lead? That's the lead, I don't know what else to tell you."

He sighs again, but makes some notes in his flip book. Looking up, "No boyfriend problems?"

"None that would blow up my car."

"Anyone gunning for revenge? From something you wrote? For the paper?"

I shake my head.

"What about from working at DBS?"

I shake my head. I know I am playing with fire on this one. The feds have put a lid on this week's events at West End, but does this mean Castleford PD won't find out? When the feds find out my car has been blown up, they'll come out here. What the heck, let Buddy do his own investigation.

Buddy goes outside to review the remains of the Jeep, time passes, more coffee is consumed, and Doug arrives. He hugs me tight, kisses me on top of the head and looks meaningfully at me, knowing better than to say anything in front of Buddy.

"Counselor," Buddy says to Doug, "you wouldn't happen to know why anyone would want to blow Sally up the next time she drove her car, do you?"

Doug looks at me. "I would assume," he says quietly, "it would be someone who wishes very badly she would go away." He turns to Buddy. "The only one I can think of like that is Phillip O'Hearn."

"Not you too," Buddy sighs.

"Who else would do something like this out here?" Doug says.

"Who says it's someone from out here?" Buddy says. He turns to me. "And since when do you wear size six clothing?"

"I think you need a warrant to go snooping through my things, Buddy," I tell him.

"I saw the tag, it was right out there in the open," he tells me. "And who was that photographer that was outside? How did he get here?"

"From listening to the police scanner, I should think," I say, knowing full well that I called the photographer myself. A favor lent is a favor owed.

"I've impounded his camera."

"No way," I say, feeling a little combative spark firing up. "That film is mine."

"That film is mine until I give it back to you. Right now it is crucial confidential evidence in the investigation of attempted murder."

I give up and turn to Doug. "Will you get me out of here?"

He nods. "Of course. Let's get your stuff and go."

I pack up Lilliana's suitcases and Doug takes them out to the car. When he carries out the blue crate, Buddy wants to know what's in it. "Dog food," Doug tells him.

"Dog food?" I whisper outside in the car. Maggie and John are standing next to the soldered carcass of the Jeep and wave to me. I wave back.

"It's all I could think of," Doug says. He holds the seat forward and tells Scotty to hop in.

"Oh, hell," I mutter to Doug minutes later as we cruise the maze of the downtown municipal parking garage. "I specifically told him to bring her here."

We've been driving around and around in this place until we're carsick.

"Maybe he's hiding and doesn't know it's you in the car."

"Could be," I agree. I reach for the flask of brandy Doug brought and take a shot. Yow, that clears my head. "Well, I'll just get out and walk around."

"No, we both get out," Doug says, swinging into a parking place.

And so we leave Scotty in the car and start walking up and down the first floor of the garage with me softly calling, "It's me, Sally!" We traverse the second floor and finally, twenty minutes later, we're on the roof of the parking garage, getting blown all over every which way by the wind. The exercise is pointless, there are no cars up here anyway. But then I hear a car turning into the garage and Doug and I run over to take the elevator down. The elevator takes forever to arrive, so we bound down the stairs, reaching the first floor just in time to see the taillights of the car tearing up to the next level. We whirl around and run up the stairs, Doug pulling out in front. On the second floor we race over to the second row and wave at the car, which swerves, tires screeching, and then heads right at us, blinding us with the headlights. Doug pulls me back in between cars, and the approaching car, an old Impala, screams to a halt just before crashing and the driver-side door flies open. "Where the hell have you been?" Lilliana cries, jumping out.

"With the police, trying to keep you out of it," I say. "Where's Pete?"

"On the floor in the back seat."

I look at Doug and he walks over to the Impala, opens the back door and climbs in.

"That guy is an absolute fruitcake, you know," Lilliana tells me confidentially. "He wanted me to wear tinfoil on my head before he'd let me get in the friggin' car! I'm out there falling down in the woods and he's telling me to put Reynolds Wrap on my head!"

"He has a thing about radio waves—" I begin.

"And then he starts driving like I don't know what, raving about George Bush and the Masons, so I grabbed his hair and told him to pull over, I was driving."

I can hear the men talking in the back of the Impala, although I can only see Doug. My friend Pete Sabatino is a little crazy, having chosen a life of paranoid conspiracy theories over a more simple existence.

"But where have you been?"

"We came right here, but you guys didn't show up and he thought we better hide a while, in case something was wrong and they made you talk."

"Who made me talk?"

"I don't know!" the actress says, exasperated. "So we went behind some warehouse and now here we are."

I can't help it. I have to laugh. I am so tired and I'm so freaked out, there is nothing left but mild hysteria.

"I'm glad you find it funny," the actress says. "I want a cigarette."

The Impala door opens and Doug gets out, waits a second, and then my friend Crazy Pete comes out. "Thank you so much," I say, going over to him. "You really came through for me."

He grins. But then he sees Lilliana and his face turns to a scowl. "*She* took a lot of unnecessary chances."

I think Lilliana might lose it altogether and sock him, but she surprises me. "I owe you one, Pete. I'll make it up to you someday. Promise."

Pete suddenly looks around, his body turning in a twitchy motion. Out of the corner his mouth he says to Doug, "I think I should go."

"Please, go," I urge him. "Thank you."

Pete hurries to the Impala and gets in. I see him putting on a baseball hat, which I know is lined with aluminum foil, put the car into gear and drive away.

We walk to Doug's car and I squish into the back seat with Scotty and the blue crate. "You brought the pictures," Lilliana says, sounding relieved, turning around to look at me.

"And your luggage," I say. I sit forward. "So you've really quit smoking?"

"Trying."

I offer the flask of brandy Doug brought. Given the events of the night, he thought it might come in handy.

"Thanks," she says, and without bothering to ask what it is, takes a big jolt.

We hightail it to New York.

Story

CHAPTER TWENTY

"That's it!" Langley Peterson announces in an uncharacteristically loud voice. "Until all this is cleared up, Sally, you live at the Hotel Bernier and you work here. And that's *it*. You're either there, or here. You do not go anywhere else; you do not do anything without the security assigned to you at your side. Is that understood?"

"Yes, sir." I turn to Cassy. "I'll see if Jim Reinemann can stay at my apartment, and take my dog."

"Not until I get clearance," Cassy says. "We need to check out everywhere you normally would be. I don't want anything happening to him."

"I've got to get some things from my apartment," I say.

"Give security a list," she says, "and they'll get it."

Thankfully I don't have—at least I don't *think* I have—any fiercely private stuff in the apartment yet. I wouldn't be taking this nearly so well if I had love letters or weird underwear or something there.

"I'll say this one more time," Langley lectures me. "You are at the Hotel Bernier or you are here."

"Yes, sir," I repeat, as if taking an oath.

Langley turns to Cassy. "Now what about this mafia girl? What are we doing about her?"

I suppress a smile. *Mafia Girl.* Catchy title.

"Lilliana Martin is helping us on the series," Cassy says smoothly. "She's been taken to the Hotel Bernier already and has agreed to stay there, under our protection, for however long she works on the series."

"I hate to be tacky," Will Rafferty speaks up from the corner of Langley's office, "but this could blow our contingency budget for the year."

"It's not coming out of the news division so don't worry about it," Langley says. "Cordelia Paine holds half interest in the Bernier and they'll work something out for us."

Cordelia *Darenbrook* Paine is Jackson's older sister.

Langley focuses his attention back on me, pushing his black glasses higher up on his nose. "You seem to have a great deal of trouble attached to you, Sally. I certainly hope it's worth it." He turns away and I gape at Cassy, as much as to say, *I didn't do anything!*

She signals for me to cool it.

"In the meantime," Langley says, turning around again, "I want to know where the hell Alexandra is. You know, I *should* charge the news division for this—that'll make her appear."

"She'll be here tomorrow without fail," I say, prompting everyone to look at me.

"Nice of her," Langley mutters, striding across the office to his desk.

"If her absence could have been avoided," I add, "it would have been." No wonder Alexandra felt compelled to cram all her medical stuff into a few days; she's not allowed to be sick—heck, she's not even allowed to take a day off without everyone freaking out around here.

Langley dismisses us, and outside his office Cassy latches on to my arm. "I understand you're loyal to Alexandra," she says quietly. "But understand she is an employee of this network."

"I know."

She looks at me steadily. "Where has she been?"

"She was in the field," I say. "And then she had a problem with the scar tissue in her shoulder, from where she was shot."

Cassy nods, conceding this makes sense.

"So she had to get something done about it."

"Why didn't she tell me?"

"It just happened, there wasn't time," I lie. "So tomorrow is literally the first day she can physically get here."

She studies me a moment more. "Tomorrow. Without fail?"

"You know Alexandra."

"Yes, I do." She turns away, taking a breath. Then she turns back to me. "Get down to security and meet your bodyguard."

"Okay," I say, walking obediently to the elevator. I take the elevator down to reception and then run out to the driveway, jumping into the hired car that is waiting.

"So where am I supposed to say I had my shoulder done?" Alexandra wonders out loud while I hold the car door open for her. Gingerly she lowers herself in.

I had suspected these two procedures performed on the same side of her upper body would end up like this, seizing up her whole left side from her neck to her waist.

"Tell them it was here," I suggest when I climb in the other side of the car. "The closer you stick to the truth, the better."

"I know," she sighs, letting her head fall back against the seat.

Alexandra looks a lot better than she did on Thursday, but her carefully applied makeup may be responsible for most of it.

"Are you taking any painkillers?" I ask her.

"No, not since Saturday."

"So you haven't slept."

Her eyes look at me sidelong. "You're not my mother, Sally."

"No, but you are stuck with me," I remind her.

"It might be easier," she admits, "had I hired someone whose life is a little less violent." She tries to turn her head a bit. "Are you sure *you're* all right?"

"I'm great," I tell her. "Don't know what's going on, but I get to stay at the Bernier, work on this fabulous series, and you're coming back tomorrow. What could be better?"

Alexandra makes a sound of skepticism. After a moment she sighs. "I've got to get a handle on this. It's not making sense, what's going on." She squints. "And Will has no take on any of this? The body, the shooting, your Jeep?"

"Not really," I tell her, opting not to say I think Will wishes that, since I'm not helping him in the newsroom, I would simply go away and stop interrupting his schedule.

In the middle of Central Park West, between Seventy-ninth and Eightieth Streets, the driver makes a U-turn so the car can pull up directly in front of Alexandra's apartment building, The Roehampton. "See anybody?" Alexandra asks me, unable to freely turn her neck.

"Just the doorman."

"What about in the cars? Photographers or anything? That idiot from *The Inquiring Eye?*"

That idiot, I know, took photos of Alexandra and Georgiana Hamilton-Ayres walking through La Guardia airport a few months ago that ran in the supermarket tabloid under the heading of "Gal Pals in Paradise?"

"All clear," I report.

She takes a breath. "Okay, let's go." I take Alexandra's suitcase and open the door to get out. Alexandra slides across the seat to follow. By the time she reaches the doors of The Roehampton, her effort to move normally has made her break out in a cold sweat.

"Miss Waring, welcome home," the doorman says. "You've been traveling."

"Yes, for work," she says, not stopping.

"Where this time?"

"Not far," she says.

"Mrs. Roberts has been picking up your mail," he calls after her.

"Thank you," she says, pushing the button for the elevator.

The doorman is now staring at me. "Hey, didn't somebody blow you up or something this weekend?"

"Me? Naw," I tell him, turning to follow the anchorwoman.

Once we're safely behind the closed doors of the elevator, Alexandra closes her eyes. "Ow."

"We're almost there."

I unlock the apartment door for her. She is exhausted and I send her to her room to prepare for bed. I tell her I'm going to get her something to eat. She says she doesn't want anything, but I ignore her and go to the kitchen to see what I can find.

Her housekeeper, Mrs. Roberts, has prepared some dinners she can just zap in the microwave. They look a little much for the shape Alexandra's in at the moment, but then I find a can of hearty vegetable and garlic pasta soup. I heat it up. I also find some lite bread and toast two slices of that. I make up a tray, putting the soup, toast and a glass of Perrier on it. While opening drawers, looking for a soup spoon, I see a photograph of Alexandra and Georgiana Hamilton-Ayres sitting in the stands at a horse show.

For about the tenth time, I wonder if I should have tracked Hamilton-Ayres down last week and told her about Alexandra. And yet, how could I? It's none of my business. And if I were not together with my lover anymore, I wouldn't want that lover to come back because I was sick, either. Particularly if I had broken up with him. But that is not the feeling I get; increasingly I'm getting the feeling that Alexandra is the one who has been left.

I knock on her bedroom door and push it open with my foot to bring the tray in. The bed is turned down but she is not in it. "Sally," her voice comes from the bathroom. "I'm afraid I need your help."

Interesting choice of words. Only Alexandra would be afraid of needing help from anyone. I put the tray down on the foot of the bed and walk over to the bathroom door. "What can I do?"

"Can you get this blouse off?" The door opens and I feel badly, the shirt is hung up on her bandages and she can't get her arm out. She is thin. A lot of muscle, but thin. Carefully, I try to ease the blouse over the bandages and over her arm.

She sucks her breath in between her teeth. "I can't believe how much it hurts."

"Just be still, let me do it," I tell her.

She curses softly under her breath as the blouse finally comes off. She has no bra on, of course, for her left breast is still in bandages, too. I pull the door closed to give her privacy. "What about your other incision?" I call. "How does that feel?"

"Absolutely fine, wouldn't you know," comes the answer. "If I had just had that done, I would have been home the same day and at work the next."

Told you so, I think to myself.

I hear her gasp and then say, *"Ow."*

I leave her alone, not wanting to interfere. Finally the bathroom door opens and she comes out wearing a large button-down pajama top. "I can't believe you did that," she says, spotting the tray.

"If you don't eat something while I'm here," I tell her, "then I'm not leaving."

She eases herself into bed, glancing over at me. "So when was the last time you slept?"

"This morning. Scotty and I curled up in a conference room and slept for about four hours." I pick up the tray and bring it to her.

She falls back against the pillows. "It's so good to be home." I put the tray in her lap. "Eat."

She smiles, sniffing. "I love this kind of soup."

"Good." I tell her, "Eat." I walk back out to the living room to retrieve her suitcase. When I return, I'm pleased to see she is sipping the soup.

"Oh, don't worry about that," she says. "Mrs. Roberts will take care of it. She's coming in later."

I put the case down in the corner. "I'm afraid I've got to get going. I was supposed to meet my bodyguard and took the opportunity of slipping away before meeting him."

Alexandra's eyes widen over her spoon. "Uh-oh."

"Yeah," I agree. "I better get going."

She puts the spoon down. "Sally, I can never thank you enough."

"Just eat, and tomorrow tell everyone you had your shoulder done and I will be happy," I assure her. "And get to your radiation treatments on time, every day."

She makes a face. "Oh, that."

"When are you supposed to start?"

"Next week."

"Good. So you'll do it, and be done with it, and have a great life." She looks so helpless sitting there, I feel like giving her a hug. But I don't. You just don't give someone like Alexandra Waring hugs. I don't know why, you just don't.

I am not out of the car at West End three seconds before an iron fist has closed around my arm. "Right this way, Ms. Harrington," the security officer tells me, guiding me, whether I like it or not, toward another door into the building.

We enter the center where all the security monitors for the complex are located. Wendy Mitchell swivels around in a chair and stands up. "This is very, very serious, Sally."

"I'll say. I thought you resigned."

She takes a deep breath and walks toward me. Normally Wendy is not a very threatening-looking person. In my opinion she looks more like a lost member of the Daisy Chain. Her mother is, however, some kind of big-shot D.A. in Maryland and I guess what I see coming toward me now is a genetic transmission of intimidation.

"There was something I had to do before security was officially assigned to me," I tell her. "Now I'm yours. Whatever you want."

She walks straight up to me and I wait for the explosion. She's taller than I am and succeeds in looking down at me. "I do not want you dead."

I swallow. "Me neither."

"Then you do exactly as I say."

"Okay." When she doesn't say anything, I raise my right hand. "I will, I swear."

While still staring down at me, she says, "Slim," and a six-foot-four, absolutely tremendous wall of flesh appears at her side. "Meet Sally Harrington. Sally, Slim Karlzycki." We shake hands and I am dismissed.

"Hi, Jim," I greet my intern minutes later in the conference room. "I'd like you to meet my new associate, Slim." The bodyguard comes in, carrying the blue plastic crate belonging to Lilliana. "Slim, Jim," and I burst out laughing, shaking my head, because I'm losing it for sure. I direct Slim to put the crate on the large table in the middle, which is, at this moment, clear.

"So guess," I tell Jim, walking over to rip the tape off the crate, "what this is." As he approaches, I look over at Slim and point to the door. "Sorry, but this is confidential. You'll have to wait outside."

Slim appears to be accustomed to being asked to leave and good-naturedly lumbers away. When the door closes behind him, Jim leans forward to whisper, "Somebody blew up your house last night?"

"No, just my car," I say, lifting the lid off the crate. "How would you feel about staying at my apartment for a few days? With Scotty? Security says it's okay, if you feel okay about it. They don't think anyone's going to blow it up or anything."

"Sure. Anything I can do to help."

"Well, that would be an enormous help."

"But where are you going to be?"

"The Hotel Bernier." I nod in the direction of the door. "With, uh, Slim. Lilliana Martin's already there and she'll be coming back and forth to work with us."

"You're kidding. Lilliana Martin? The lady who stole your card out of the Rolodex?"

I laugh. Only a twenty-one-year-old kid would call a thirty-year-old actress *lady*. "The one and the same."

"But isn't she, like, dangerous? I mean, it seems like every time she's around you, somebody dies, or something blows up."

"She wasn't here when someone shot at me last week," I point out. I start pulling out things from the crate and notice that Jim is still standing there, watching me. "What's the matter?"

"I don't know," he says uneasily. "I guess I'm just a little more worried about you than you are."

"Don't worry about me," I tell him.

"I mean, I'm not looking for a free ride or anything," he continues, "but maybe I should hang out at the hotel, too. You know, just another set of eyes."

I smile. "Thank you, but that won't be necessary. What I do need is for you to stay at my apartment and take care of Scotty. For that you will have my gratitude forever."

"Okay," he agrees.

"But look at this!" I cry with excitement. I toss the lid of the box on the floor and start taking out pictures so he can see the spectrum of materials inside. I tell him about Lilliana digging up all the family's memorabilia at her Great-Aunt Sophia's house. "But I need everything in this crate to be duplicated right away. These are irreplaceable. We might use an original to shoot from here and there, later on, we'll see how it goes. But there's old super-8 movies, Beta tapes, cracked Polaroids, black-and-white photos from the forties and fifties, all kinds of stuff. Will's already set it up for you to work with the Nerd Brigade."

Jim looks as though I have kicked him in the teeth. "You mean work over there? With them?"

"Just until these are done. And then bring them to me as they're duplicated." I know that few people at DBS News like to work with the Nerd Brigade, the nickname of a very odd group of men over in the electronic's R & D division, but I'm afraid that's not what Jim is disappointed about. Frankly, I want some distance from Jim right now. I need to focus on work.

"I don't think you should be by yourself right now," he says.

"Slim's right outside." I mock a country twang. "Ain't nothin' or nobody's gonna get past him." I point to the crate. "Protect that with your life, please."

He puts his arms around the crate and I put the lid back on it, tapping it down into place. I accompany him to the door and hold it open for him. Slim is standing just to the side of the door, with his back against the wall, feet spread, trying to look massively discreet.

"Bring me each duplicate as they're made," I remind Jim as he moves down the hall. I sigh, leaning against the doorway, watching him, wondering if it's wise having him stay in my apartment. Well, who else am I going to get? I should have sent Scotty home with Doug.

Doug. I smile a little.

Something down at the end of the hall catches my attention. It's someone I think I recognize. As the figure draws closer, sure enough, I do know him.

Slim quickly moves to stand between me and the approaching man. Then he bursts out, "Hey, Sky, how're ya doing?" and my bodyguard, so help me, *hugs* the man I know is a federal special prosecutor, Sky Preston.

Why do I get the feeling people like Crazy Pete might be right to feel paranoid?

CHAPTER TWENTY-ONE

"Hello, Sally," Sky Preston says after his fraternal reunion with my bodyguard. "How are you?"

"Alive, thank you."

"You know," he says in a low voice, glancing over his shoulder before continuing, "either you've got it or you don't, and you definitely seem to have it. You're still walking and talking, Sally, while other mere mortals would be long gone by now."

"No thanks to you, I bet," I tell him. "Come on, let's go to my office. I only just got it back." I turn around, walking backward. "So how do you know my new pal?"

Both Sky and Slim smile. I find it very annoying.

"We've worked together before."

"Hmm," I say, turning back around. "And I don't suppose you have anything to do with Wendy being reinstated?"

"I don't suppose you know anything about what happened last night in Castleford?" he counters.

I glance back and then stand at the side of my doorway, gesturing for him to come in. "I could be just a happening kind of gal."

He smiles and looks as though he might like to elaborate

on this hypothesis, but doesn't as he walks into my office. I look at Slim. "You might as well join us."

"Not," Sky says, correcting me and reaching past me to close the door.

Wearily, I walk over to crash in a chair and watch as Sky sits on the couch. He is about five ten, hair light brown, close to the color of mine. His blue eyes are steady, always steady. "I was wondering when you would get to me," I tell him. "I heard you were here."

"You haven't been around much," he says. He looks over at the window. "We took that entire wall of glass with us," he remarks, casually gesturing. "Someone stood right across the way, over there, on top of Darenbrook I, and fired at this window with a twenty-two handgun."

"It wasn't at this window in particular," I insist.

"He fired three times until he hit it," he tells me. "I'd say he was rather persistent."

My stomach churns a bit. "And no one heard it?"

"He fired as the train was coming through."

True, occasionally Amtrak trains come rumbling down the Hudson line and they are loud.

"Look, Sally," he says, tugging slightly at the knees of his pants and leaning forward, "I know what's it like. To be a target. And that's why I'm here."

I feel a chill. Things are starting to sink in and it feels creepy. I think I liked it better when I was blissfully casual about everything going on. Particularly when I was convinced Alexandra was the target.

"I have a baby now," Sky says suddenly.

I blink, utterly surprised at the admission he has a personal life. "Congratulations," I say instinctively.

"But I just recently had to move my wife and child," he continues. "I had to move them to a whole other state because of retaliation threats."

"Perhaps you should consider a career change."

"My wife wouldn't stand for it," he says. "She's in my line of work too now."

"I think I knew that," I say. "Didn't she used to be on Wall Street or something?"

"Something like that."

"That's cool," I tell him. "What about the baby?"

"The baby's cool, too," he assures me, cracking a smile.

"Do you have a picture?"

He cocks his head to the side, wondering if I'm serious.

"Please, I'd love to see him."

"Her. She's a little girl." Slowly he reaches back to pull a wallet out of his back pocket. He does this slowly, I bet, because he still carries a gun in the small of his back the way he used to. He pulls a photograph out of the wallet and hands it to me.

I am a little surprised. I'm not sure what kind of woman I expected Sky Preston to be married to, but I did not think she would be the kind who would pose for a picture with her new baby and be making a face at the camera. I can't help but laugh.

"That's Mary Liz, my wife," he says quietly, smiling. "She's kind of a character."

"Your little girl is a knockout. What's her name?"

"Claire."

"Claire," I repeat admiringly, looking at the round-faced baby girl who has not a hair on her head. Suddenly another picture is pushed in over the one I'm holding.

"This is Mary Liz."

This photograph is a candid, showing a laughing, dark-haired woman on a sailboat, obviously having a glorious time. She is pretty, but heavier than I would have imagined. She has a most excellent smile—her teeth and cheekbones are terrific—and she radiates a healthy energy. I feel a twinge inside; perhaps it is envy. I wonder if one day I will have a husband who so loves me he will press my photograph into the hand of single women to show to whom he belongs.

"She's extremely attractive," I say, returning the photograph. I look up at Sky and find him a bit shy. I guess this means we're some sort of friends now, although I still don't trust him a bit, and I shouldn't think he would trust me particularly either. We've spent most of the time we've known each other lying by omission.

"Tell me about the sniper," I say as he carefully puts the photographs back in his wallet. "And thank you," I add, making him look up at me, "for showing me Claire and Mary Liz. They make me want to trust you, Sky, which I guess was the point."

"Maybe I just want to show off my family."

I smile. "And a beautiful family it is. Thank you."

He nods once, as if this is an acceptable apology for my cynicism.

"You said the sniper was a he," I prompt. "How do you know that?"

"We have a very good idea who he is. The field is narrowing rapidly."

"How so?"

He pauses. "We think the shooting, the bombing in Castleford and the body you had in the trunk of your car are all related."

I frown, putting my elbow on the chair arm and resting my chin on my hand. "Do you know who the body is?" I wince. "Was? In the rental car?"

He nods.

Nervous, I stand up. I don't quite know what to do with myself, but I can't sit still. There's something strange going on and it's giving me the willies. The New York police grilled me about the body in the trunk and then suddenly disappeared. Days later a special federal prosecutor is here to talk about it. It means the NYPD has been called off the case by the feds.

I walk over to the window, cross my arms and look out across the park at the roof of Darenbrook I. For a second I have the urge to hide, but I command myself to stay where I am. It is, after all, bulletproof glass and I am not a coward. "Who was he?"

"A part-time construction worker named Walter Learing," Sky says. "Thirty-one years old, lived outside of Pittsburgh, Pennsylvania. Ex-military, served in the army,

honorable discharge three years ago, private first class."
Pause. "Ring any bells?"

I shake my head, trying to see Scotty down in the run.
"None."

"He was arrested once on an illegal-weapons charge. A
machine gun."

My mind is racing. "We've been asking the affiliates for
leads on wacko groups," I say. I turn around. "Could this
guy have been one? Like a terrorist?"

"It's a possibility," Sky says.

My arms still crossed, I walk back to my chair. "So who
do you think the sniper here was?"

"The same person who put a bomb under your car. Walter
Learing's brother, Wilkie. He's been missing for over a week."

"L-e-a-r-i-n-g?" I spell.

"Yes."

"I see," I say, sitting down. "And what's his story?"

"Thirty-seven, owns a sporting and hunting goods store
outside Pittsburgh in a town called Harlen."

"Ah, guns."

"Lots."

I consider this and long for the safety of the windowless
conference room. "So what do you want from me, Sky?"

"For starters, I need to know where Alexandra Waring is."

"She's home. On Central Park West."

He looks surprised.

"I just left her there. She's had surgery on her shoulder,
so I wish you'd leave her alone until tomorrow."

Eyes on me, he pulls a cell phone out of his breast
pocket, and then looks down to frown at the screen.

"All electronic signals are scrambled here at West End," I
explain. "To avoid interfering with our operations. You'll
have to use my phone. Right there on the desk, help yourself."

He jumps up and hurries around my desk.

"Dial nine first."

He snaps up the phone and dials a number. "And she's
there, right now, at her apartment?" he asks me.

"Took her there myself."

"Alexandra Waring is in her apartment on Central Park West," he says into the phone. "No, I want you to get your ass over there."

I jump up. "I asked you to leave her alone until tomorrow!"

He frowns and turns his back to me.

"She had surgery, for Pete's sake!" I yell. "Leave her alone!"

He turns around, hanging up the phone. "Okay, okay, we'll talk to her tomorrow."

"Good," I tell him. "Now can I go back to work, please? And then you can just let me know when all of humanity is safe again?"

He holds up one finger while he finishes his call. He hangs up. "You're either here, or at the Bernier, right?" he drills me.

"Either here or at the Bernier," I confirm. "And I've got Skinny."

"Slim," he says. He picks up the phone to make another call. "Be careful, be smart, Sally. And for God's sake, don't go anywhere near Rocky Presario right now. And you'd be wise to make sure Lilliana doesn't either."

I scribble the names on a piece of paper and hand it to Dr. Kessler. He reads them, frowns, and says, "Who are dees people?"

Dr. Irwin Kessler is a genius. That's the good news. It is his brilliance in electrical engineering and physics that gave birth to the electronic operations of the Darenbrook Communications empire. The bad news is, he is eighty, his health has begun to fail, and no one knows what we will do without him. He is, incidentally, completely in love with Alexandra, which seems to be the only vulnerable spot in the man of science who survived prison camp in Nazi Germany.

"These are very dangerous men Alexandra's investigating," I explain. "She wants anything and everything you can dig up on them." I look at him steadily. "You know what I mean."

What I mean is tapping every electronic method, legal or illegal, to find what he can on them.

I point to the paper. "Those are their ages, and the town. Wilkie I think is i-e, but if nothing comes up, try e-y or just y."

"You know dis needs special clearances, mah dearrrr."

I look into the aging blue eyes behind the thick spectacles. "Alexandra said you would take care of it."

He takes the bait. "Veell see vat ve can find."

Feeling better about being kept prisoner, I hurry back to my office, type up notes on my conversation with Sky Preston and then dash off a confidential memo to Will, alerting him to the leads on the New Jersey body and the resulting story that could break. I find him in his office, screaming at someone on the phone that they *can't* be sick, *someone* has to anchor the news tonight. I hand him the memo and retreat to the conference room, outside of which Slim can finally sit because I have found him a comfortable chair.

I check the file drawers to see what Jim has been up to over the weekend. I start reading a batch of old newspaper clippings, and the next thing I know, five hours have gone by and I am starving. I take a break, going to the cafeteria for a sandwich, and bring Slim along and encourage him to eat.

Employees from the news division are walking in and out of the cafeteria, saying hi, but I feel like a stranger. Or that I'm being punished. Certainly I do not feel like a team member at the moment. After our dinner, we stop at the run to see Scotty. He is terrified of Slim's bulk, but eventually he comes around and lets him pet him. Then we go up to my office to make some calls. First, Mother, to let her know of course I am just fine, living the high life, and no, I don't know if Phillip O'Hearn had really arranged to blow up my car, but yes, that is what I indicated to the police.

"Oh, Sally," she frets.

"Oh, Mother," I say, "if someone wanted to hurt me, they would have hurt me. Please, don't worry."

My second call is to Doug, who tells me Castleford PD is screaming foul, because DBS is maintaining that I'm on "secured leave" and is referring all inquiries to an Agent Alfonso at the FBI. I give Doug the number of the hotel and explain that he is to ask for John Dailey if he wants to reach me.

Last but not least, I call the hotel and ask for John Dailey and am connected to a security person, who finally gets Lilliana on the phone for me. "So where are you?" she wants to know. "I thought we were supposed to be cell mates. I worked out in the gym, had a facial and a massage, a long bath and dinner and you're still not here!"

"They didn't put us in the same—" I begin.

"Oh, stop sputtering, Sally, it's a suite. You've got your room, I've got my room, and then there's a room off the kitchen where the biggest broad I've ever seen's sitting there packing. Her name's Racia."

"Packing?" I say. "Packing what?"

"A nine millimeter, I think."

If I hang around with Lilliana long enough, no doubt I'll get the hang of this.

I look at my watch. It's almost ten. "I'll be over shortly," I promise.

I return to the conference room and find Jim sitting at the table, his head resting on his arms. I touch his shoulder and instantly he wakes, jerking upright.

"It's late, you should go home," I tell him. "And you guys should sleep in." When he looks sleepily confused, I add, "You and Scotty, remember?"

"Oh, right," he says, yawning. "Sorry. I brought some stats of photographs back."

"Let's look at them tomorrow. I'm not coming in before noon and I expect the same of you. Do you have any classes tomorrow?"

He shakes his head, pushing back the chair to stand up.

"Here's some money for cabs and food," I tell him, pressing some bills into his hand. "Tomorrow you're going to have to get some more dry food for Scotty—"

He recoils from the money as if it's dangerous. "No," he says, sounding offended, "you don't have to pay me."

"This is house-sitting money, to run the house. To take my

dog back and forth to work, and to feed him. And to feed you, I might add. I'm not paying you. I mean, I should, and I will, if you let me, but this money is for expenses. So take it."

Reluctantly he opens his hand to take it. Suddenly I find that he has closed his hand around mine. It is not an aggressive move; it is more like a timid person's sudden impulse.

"So you guys go eat and get some sleep," I say, moving away toward the door. "And I'll see you tomorrow." At the door, I turn. "Thank you, Jim. And don't forget to lock up."

"I won't." He has streaks of scarlet down his neck. "Please be careful."

Slim and I take a Yellow Cab over to the hotel. At his direction we're dropped off at the side entrance, and Slim inserts a key in the elevator that takes us straight up to the top floor. The suite is marvelous. The floor is softly padded with deep, beige carpeting and the furniture is comfortably overstuffed. The view is of uptown Manhattan, not of the park or anything, but it is very pretty with all the lights.

Lilliana comes out to the living room in a silk robe that prompts Slim to avert his eyes and apologize. "I didn't know—" he tries to say.

"It's fine, don't worry about it," she tells him, swaying over—that's the only word there is to describe how she is moving—and shakes his hand. "Lilliana Martin."

"Slim Karlzycki," he mumbles.

"I think you go in there," she says, pointing.

"Where am I?" I say wearily.

"This way." The actress leads me down a short hall into a small but lovely bedroom. On the floor are two big black garbage bags stuffed with something. "They said they couldn't find your suitcases, " she explains.

"Nice," I say, dropping my briefcase and allowing myself the luxury of falling onto the bed in a heap. It's a great mattress.

"So I talked to Poppy today," Lilliana says, alighting on the edge of the bed.

I roll over to look at her. "You didn't tell him where you are, did you?"

"Why not?"

"I had a visitor today, Sky Preston."

"Uh-oh," she says. "That's not good."

"He told me very specifically that we both needed to stay away from your grandfather."

"I wonder why," she says, frowning. "Poppy's not going to do anything." Her robe has eased open somehow, showing the ample curve of her breast. I have no idea if this is on purpose and I have no desire to know. "I told him about the way your car blew up," she adds.

"And what did he say?" I ask, yawning.

"He said we need to find out if it was on a timer, or a fuse, or both. Also, what kind of explosives. If we can find out any of that, he says he might be able to help us."

I'm not sure exactly when I fall asleep. I know it must have been while Lilliana was there, talking. When I later awaken, I am still fully dressed, but have two extra blankets covering me. There's no pillow, though, and I can feel the imprint of the bedspread on the side of my face.

I peel off my clothes, slip under the sheets—they are heavenly—and sleep through the night.

CHAPTER TWENTY-TWO

I wake up early, around seven, and decide, what the heck, I'll go into work. I haven't had a single straight-shot day on this series and I have got to get cracking. Some guy is sitting in the living room of the suite when I come out, explaining that he will be with me until Slim returns at noon. "And what about Lilliana?"

He assures me she has her own bodyguard, in the other room.

There are no cabs downstairs and I ask the bodyguard if he minds walking. He minds. So we walk only maybe a block before he flags down one of those gypsy cabs you always wish you hadn't. My minimum requirement is for the car to at least have the same color paint on three sides, but my bodyguard does not share such snobbery. The smell of pot in the old Cadillac is overwhelming. Our driver, a cheerful Jamaican, has to restart the car every time he touches the brakes. Sometimes he restarts the car in neutral, while we're rolling, sometimes in neutral while we're at a stop. In either case, however, this requires that he drive with both feet, one on the brake and one on the accelerator.

We reach our destination in one piece, although we do raise several eyebrows as we spew fumes around the drive. I make my companion walk with me around the complex to see if by chance Jim has come in early with Scotty, but no such luck. There is just the little black mutt with the hopeful eyes, and I stop to say hello to him before continuing to the cafeteria for some coffee and yogurt.

No one is around on our floor in Darenbrook III and I'm thrilled. I walk straight to the conference room unmolested and unlock the door. I load a video into the player and watch copies of an old newsreel about Al Capone while I eat breakfast. When I'm finished, I am psyched and sit down with my coffee at the corner desk, with the laptop computer, and off the top of my head write what can only be described as a treatment. A script is the final direction; a treatment is a narrative that allows the writer to play writer, director, editor and producer, spinning out the framework of a series, the story it will cover and the visual and audio nuances that will highlight it.

I don't know where this energy is coming from this morning. It could be that the writer in me can no longer work in such a fragmented way and is demanding some sort of concentrated guidance. There is tons of information yet to be gathered from the files and photographs, but I have absorbed an enormous amount of material in the past months and do have a somewhat omniscient view already.

Frankly, if I do get knocked off, I'll be damned if this series won't get made and that I get a producer credit.

Besides, if we're going to get a contract out of a Bennett, Fitzallen & Coe, I need a proposal, and if I get a designer in here to do some sample pages, using a few of the unpublished photos Lilliana provided, I think Spencer will be able to push it through. And no matter what anybody says, any TV project that has a book attached to it has more validity in the eyes of the public.

At noon, there is a knock on the door. It is Slim, just wanting to let me know he is here. At twelve-thirty, I hear the door being unlocked and Benjamin pokes his head in to say

I am wanted in Alexandra's office. I smile, thinking, thank heavens! and hurry there. When I knock and walk through the doorway, a joyous Scotty comes bounding away from Alexandra over to me, nearly knocking me down. I laugh, squatting and giving him a big hug. I glance up to see Alexandra smiling and Jim standing shyly to the side.

"Hi, welcome back," I say to the anchorwoman.

"I would have been back before," she says, "but I had to have some surgery on my shoulder."

We play through this charade, and while Alexandra walks behind her desk in preparation to talk with me, I ask Jim if Scotty behaved. "He was great. We ran in the park this morning—"

"Did you, boy? Was it fun?"

"I see what you mean about keeping him on the leash," Jim says. "He wants to go into the Hudson in the worst way."

"And he's not a very good swimmer," I say, looking at my dog's eyes, which are shining with love. (It hurts my heart.) My mother's dog, Abigail, is a very good swimmer but Scotty isn't. As a matter of fact, I have had to jump into bodies of water three times in my life to pull him out before he went under for the last time.

I tell Jim to take Scotty to the run and I'll see him in the conference room.

"I've got Sky Preston on my case," Alexandra says after they leave. "He wants me to come out to New Jersey, to the farm."

"There's no way you can do anything," I tell her, "and still be upright for the newscast tonight. If I were you, I'd get briefed in the newsroom, take a nap, talk to Sky, take a nap, do the news and go home and go to bed."

"I want a report on the series," she tells me, ignoring my motherly advice. "I want a projected timetable, also the status of the book tie-in, and the schedule on that. I know you haven't had much time to work on it, but I want you to jot down your thoughts about the overall package. And I'd like this today. I've got to start running numbers on it and getting network clearances."

"Right away," I say, jumping up.

"One more thing," she adds, bringing me back. "Dr. Kessler is working on the Learing brothers for me?"

"Yes," I say, nodding. I lean closer. "The younger one was the body in my trunk. The older one's missing. The feds think he's after me. Wilkie Learing."

"Ah."

And then, pleased as punch with myself, I go next door to my office, call up the memo I already wrote for Will on the series timetable, revise it slightly and print it out. Then I write a brief where-we-are on the pending Bennett, Fitz-allen & Coe deal. Then I hurry to the conference room where I quickly reread my efforts of this morning, making some minor revisions and running it through spell check. I print it out and make a notation on page one that this is only a rough draft and is for Alexandra's eyes only.

I put the whole package together in an envelope marked CONFIDENTIAL, stamp it BY HAND, and happily deliver it to Alexandra within forty minutes of her having requested it. She is on the telephone when I come in and holds up a finger to signal me to stay a second. While still talking on the phone, obviously to someone out in the field, she opens the envelope and slides out the package. She tosses the envelope on her desk and thumbs through the papers, pausing at the first page of the treatment. Then she tells whoever it is to hold on, covers the phone and offers me one of her better smiles. "I knew I should hire you," she says, and I feel like a million bucks. "I can't believe you did this already."

The productivity lasts through the day. I don't know where Lilliana is—Jim's narrowed it down to the hairdresser's, the leg waxer's or a psychiatrist's office—and so I am free to concentrate (for a change) and work by myself. Jim comes in and out with copies of Lilliana's materials as they are made, and promises that tomorrow I'll start getting video copies of the super 8 and Beta movies. I barely acknowledge these visits because I do not wish him to linger. I want to run today, I want not to be distracted. I want to write!

"Have I done something?" he later asks.

"I'm sorry, what?" I say, looking up from the index card I've been writing notes on.

"You're so—I just—I mean, have I done something to upset you?"

I look at him another minute because my head's still not back in this world and I haven't processed what he's said yet. It's filtering through, though, and the image of Jonathan Small shooting Nicky Arlenetta through the temple is fading. "I'm just working," I say, sounding irritable. I catch myself, and rub my eyes. "I'm sorry, we haven't worked together before. When I'm really working, I'm on my own—I just shut out everything." I gesture to the file cabinet. "When we work on things together, that's different. It's a different mind-set. Than writing."

He nods. "Alexandra's like that too. But she locks herself in her office when she writes. I bet if I went in there, she'd be the same way."

"Maybe," I say, looking at my watch. "Good Lord, it's six o'clock!"

"I know," he says. "I only disturbed you because Lilliana's finally back at the hotel."

"Where has she been?"

"She went to the hairdresser, the leg waxer—" we both laugh at this "—and then had a two-hour phone session with her psychiatrist in Los Angeles."

"She told you this?"

"Yeah."

"It's a whole different world that woman lives in," I sigh.

"Anyway, she called to tell you she's not coming over today, but she wants you to come to the hotel and have dinner with her. If you do, she promises she'll come in tomorrow and work. If you don't, she's says she's going to be in a snit."

I frown. "I have to have dinner with her?"

"I'm just the messenger." He shrugs.

"Are you all right with staying at my place with Scotty again?"

"Sure! It's great. It's like a vacation."

It's been a very productive day, I think. Why not knock off early and get a good night's rest, and placate Lilliana a bit. I want her to watch those movies tomorrow.

I swing by my office to pick up my briefcase and find a hand-written note from Alexandra.

Sally,
This is wonderful. You'll see I made some changes. If you could give me a revised treatment next week, that would be great.

A.

I lift up the cover note and nearly drop my eyeteeth. *You'll see I made some changes.* I'll say! She's completely torn the pages apart, changing the order of not only individual paragraphs but entire pages! Then, to add insult to injury, she's changed the wording of half my sentences.

As I turn to the last page, angrily thinking that I DID mark it "first draft," I see that she has added yet another note:

S—
I know, I'd be ticked at me, too. Reread my changes, though, and you'll see they are stylistic not substantive. I am amazed how smoothly you've transferred your print talents to broadcasting as it is. You're terrific.

A.

Slim and I arrive at the hotel suite to find Lilliana suited up in sweats. "It's my evening," she informs me, and I try not to stare as I realize her hair color has changed from platinum blond to kind of strawberry blond. Reading my mind, she grasps her hair and curses, telling me, "Don't make me feel worse about this than I already do!"

First on Lilliana's agenda is working out in the gym. An Arab businessman is on the bike when we walk in and I think his eyes are going to bug out of his head while Lilliana does her stretches. Then she gets on the StairMaster, where she stays for one hour, while I stretch, run a while on the treadmill, lift a few weights and stretch again. By the time Lilliana gets off the StairMaster, she's climbed several miles and is soaked with perspiration. So is the Arab businessman, who at this point can barely pedal anymore, but nonetheless continues to try to engage Lilliana in conversation.

Back up in the suite, we retire to our respective rooms. I shower and wash my hair, change into a nightie and don one of the soft, fluffy terry-cloth robes the hotel provides. While I'm combing my hair out, somebody yells that the telephone is for me. I use the speakerphone in the bathroom.

"Sally, it's Doug," he says, sounding like the lawyer he is. "You're still under security watch. Yes?"

I laugh and say yes, it's a hardship, telling him about working out at the hotel, the bathrobes, the dinner we're ordering.

"You have to be very, very careful right now."

"We are," I say.

"Would you get off that space phone?" he demands.

I pick up the phone. "What's the matter?"

"The matter is, our office issued a warrant this afternoon for an unknown assailant for attempted murder."

"Unknown?"

"They found the remains of a timer and plastic explosives in the Jeep," he continues. "It's a classic hit, Sally, only the bomb was set incorrectly and went off by itself."

"Huh," I say absently.

"What do you mean, 'Huh'? This is how Lilliana Martin's mother was killed."

What I don't understand is, why would the warrant be for an unknown assailant and not Wilkie Learing if that is who the feds think set the bomb? But since the warrant does not have his name, one can only assume for some reason the feds have not told the local authorities. Which means... What?

Doug asks me about the sleeping arrangements, about how far, physically, is Lilliana's room from mine. "I'm going to demand DBS move her," he says. "There's no reason for both of you to get killed."

I assure Doug that the feds are all over everything here in the city and I am fine. Finally he gives in, muttering he's worried sick, and he supposes that maybe I am safest here, at the hotel.

With my hair still wet, I walk out into the living room where Lilliana is curled up on the couch with a room-service menu. She is back in her silk robe and I feel like a bag of laundry in comparison. "Who was that?" she asks.

"Doug."

"Oh, Mr. Cutie," she says, eyes on the menu. "I like him."

We order a light supper, soups and salads, and I go along with her on a bottle of white wine. We watch some television show, I don't know what, I've got too much to think about, and at nine turn to *DBS News America Tonight*.

"What's *happened* to her?" Lilliana says when Alexandra's face appears.

"What do you mean?"

"Look at her. Is she bulimic or something? She's got that self-inflicted sick look."

"She just had surgery on her shoulder," I say, sipping my wine to the point of emptying the glass.

"Maybe," Lilliana says, sounding doubtful. "Those are pain lines. But she's lost weight."

"I think she's been in some pain with the shoulder for a while," I say. "I think that can do something to your appetite."

"I suppose she can't be drugged during the news," the actress continues, picking at the fruit plate she ordered as dessert.

"You just saw her a week ago, Lilliana. You didn't say anything then."

"I didn't see her on TV. Everyone looks different off TV. So when I see her now, like this, I can see something's the matter with her, something's happened."

I reach over to put my glass down. "I think this is a very odd way to diagnose people's health."

Lilliana's eyes narrow slightly. "So there is something wrong with her."

"I told you, her shoulder," I say, getting up to go to my room. "Where she was shot years ago. Something about the scar tissue pressing a nerve."

Lilliana follows me, her silk robe swishing behind. "Her shoulder wasn't bothering her at Poppy's. What's wrong with her?"

I whirl around. "Nothing."

"Liar. What is it?' Her eyebrows rise slightly. "She isn't pregnant, is she? No, that's not it."

"Oh, for Pete's sake," I say, exasperated. "If you must know, she's undergoing some heartache. I don't think things have been going particularly well in her personal life." I walk back to my chair in the living room, which means Lilliana has just succeeded in chasing me around in a large circle around the room.

"*Ohhh*," Lilliana is saying, crossing her arms over her chest and cinching up the side of her mouth slightly. "I could see that one coming."

Sitting down again and reaching for the bottle of wine, I glance over. "How's that?"

"Well, her girlfriend, Georgiana, she always was a switch-hitter."

I resist making a crack, *Hey, isn't that funny? I know another actress like that.*

"And when she made *The Desert* this winter, I heard she had a fling with Alan Beardon—"

"You know this for a fact?" I snap. "Or is this just gossip?"

"Well," Lilliana says, gliding over, "everybody says she did."

"And have you done everything people say you've done, Lilliana?"

She smiles, eyes flashing. "I *wish*." She drops back down on the couch, drawing her legs under her and refocusing on the TV as Alexandra's image reappears. "She is intense, isn't she?"

"She's wonderful," I say. "Brilliant, loyal, terrific. She's much more, well, less like *that*—" I point to the screen "—and warmer. Shyer, too, in ways. I mean, she's not shy, but she has a—how can I explain?"

"Distance she maintains," Lilliana supplies. "Yes, I know, I met her last week, remember?" She looks back at the screen and tilts her head slightly. "It's my job to study people so I can portray them. And that is a woman in pain, who's masking it well, but not well enough to get by me."

I lower my voice to imitate the narrators of the newsreels I've been watching at West End and say, *"Lilliana Martin has spoken."*

CHAPTER TWENTY-THREE

The next day, Lilliana surprises me. Out comes a serious-looking pair of horn-rimmed glasses and presto, she turns into a worker. And I'm not sure why I am so surprised, but she writes rather well, too, so well, in fact, that as we go through the photographs, I find I can turn over the task of writing notations on the index cards to her. This does not make Jim very happy because it means I continue to send him over to bug the Nerd Brigade for the video transfers of those movies.

We have lunch delivered to my office, a request from Lilliana, who points out we're bound to lose momentum if we go anywhere in West End because of the sensation she is bound to stir. (Who says actresses are vain?) We eat and drink water and I point Scotty out to her down in the run. Jim joins us for a little while, and Lilliana makes an effort, asking him about himself, telling him that I said he was bright. He looks simultaneously pleased and tortured by the attention, and he never does, I notice, finish eating his tuna fish sandwich.

We go back to work in the conference room and look at some of the archival materials DBS had come up with before Lilliana came through with hers. "Good grief," she declares. "Where did you find this?"

I have to laugh. It is a color studio portrait of a raven-haired Lilliana sitting in a swing, dressed in a jungle costume. "What's the credit on the back?"

"Entertainment House," she reads, turning the photograph back over again to examine it.

"That's one of the stock houses. I don't think they actually own the rights to anything. They're usually shots from old press kits."

She's shaking her head, marveling. "I posed for this when I was in college. It was supposed to be publicity for *Tarzan*, but then the school canceled the production because their insurance wouldn't cover us swinging across the stage." She looks across the table at me. "You don't suppose I could get a copy of this?"

"Sure."

There is a quiet knock on the door and I get up to answer it. It's Alexandra. "I wanted to stop in and say hello," she says to Lilliana. "And to thank you for your help. And your expertise."

Something seems to happen to Lilliana under the anchorwoman's gaze. She seems to become, if you can believe it, uncertain of herself. The thing is, when Alexandra wants to be, she can be the most charming creature on earth, and this is one of those times.

"You're welcome," Lilliana says quietly, slipping off her glasses.

"We have every reason to believe that the series will help your brother," Alexandra continues, pulling a chair out to sit across from the actress.

"That's what his counsel has told me as well."

Alexandra suddenly smiles and reaches for the Tarzan photograph, but grimaces in pain.

"Sally told me about your shoulder," Lilliana says.

"A pain in the neck, literally," Alexandra says. I walk over to slide the *Tarzan* publicity photo in front of Alexandra, relating what Lilliana had just told me. Alexandra tells us there is a photograph sort of like this of her floating around, too, from a publicity stunt at a Kansas radio station. "They dressed me up as Wonder Woman, which was, may I add," she says, putting the photograph down, "the first and last time these thighs will go public."

This last statement provokes a flicker of interest in Lilliana's eyes and inwardly I groan.

"Sally has a real talent for this kind of work," Alexandra says, sifting through some of the index cards on the table. "I think you'll be very pleased."

"It's going to come down a bit hard on my grandfather, I think." Lilliana stretches her neck, trying to see what Alexandra is reading. "But given his past, I'm not sure there's any way around it."

"If you want the truth put out there about your brother," Alexandra agrees, "about how the event came to take place in your brother's office that day, I'm afraid you're going to have to present the past as truthfully as well."

Lilliana sighs slightly, flipping another photograph over. She laughs a little. "Look at this." She holds up an 8 x 11 black-and-white of Richard Nixon shaking hands with Rocky Presario. She reads off the back, "Saddlebrook, New Jersey, 1979."

"That reminds me," Alexandra says, turning to me, "do you think you could use that researcher, Edith? I think she's going to have to come over and work for us if she's going to have a job." She bites her lower lip. "She's not very good on people skills, is she?"

"No," I confirm.

"They want to get rid of her. They're trying to make her quit."

"What the hell is the matter with people?" I say. I well remember how odd Edith is, or, rather, how emotionally unstable—or SOMETHING—she is. But still, social skills have never been the prerequisite for a good researcher.

"I think she could learn a lot of things, don't you?"

"If she has the right resources, yeah." I can't believe Alexandra's going to hire this wacko. But then, poor Edith has worked here for six years, and I have worked with a lot worse. "Yeah, sure," I say, shrugging. "I've got lots of stuff she could work on."

"Whoever it is you're talking about," Lilliana pipes up, "she sounds perfectly dreadful. Sally's using that same tone of voice she did to talk me into trusting that kook out in Castleford the other night."

Alexandra looks at me with some interest. "Who was that?"

"Crazy Pete."

"Oh, yes," she says, nodding, "Mr. Sabatino."

"But you know," I say, "see all those books piled up over there?" I point to the three stacks of reference books about organized crime. "Edith could read those in preparation to fact check the series. It's not everything she's going to need, but it's a good start."

"Good. I'll see that she does," the anchorwoman says.

There is a knock at the door and Jim hurries in, waving the first video made from the Presario home movies. I tell him to cue it up, and Alexandra steps outside to tell Benjamin she'll be in here another fifteen minutes.

The video hasn't run thirty seconds before tears are streaming down Lilliana's face. The footage shows her grandmother trying to teach her mother, who is all of maybe six years old, how to ice-skate. It is very funny and very touching. They're in some kind of city park rink. Mrs. Bruno is very patient, practically walking on her figure skates, while young Celia staggers about on her double runners and spends most of the movie dangling from her mother's hand. "This has to be around '54, '55, Lilliana says. "Let's see, Mama was murdered in early '80."

Alexandra and I exchange glances.

"No," Lilliana says, sniffing and wiping her eyes with the back of her hand. "It has to be more like '52, '53. She was born in November of '48."

Suddenly little Celia is free of her mother's hand and she collides into the concrete side of the rink. A teenage boy, laughing, bends over to pick her up in his arms. The child beams and the boy evidently tells her to wave at the camera, which she does. Some large white dots pass over the screen and the movie is over.

I get up to bring some tissues to Lilliana. She wipes her eyes and blows her nose. "I think that might have been Chicken Man at the end," she says. "Uncle Angelo had most of the concessions in Philadelphia."

Alexandra looks to me in question and I shake my head, *I don't know.* "Who is Chicken Man?" I ask.

"Chicken Man Testa," Lilliana says, clearing her throat. She balls up the tissues and throws them, making the trash basket. "At least that's what they called him when he grew up." She looks to the ceiling, thinking. "Let's see, Mama was killed in '80—" She looks briefly at Alexandra and then to me. "Then Uncle Angelo was murdered—that was 1980 also—and Chicken Man took over Philadelphia. He tried to keep Atlantic City, but then Nicky got him in '81. He blew up the whole front of Chicken Man's house. That's when we went into the witness protection program, right after that."

I nod, not knowing quite what to say. I peek over at Alexandra and know she is thinking the same thing. That we treat Lilliana Martin as though she's the high-handed movie actress that she appears to be, when, deep down, she is still little Lise Presario, who, after her mother was murdered, was yanked out of her home and away from her family, thrust upon strangers in another state with another name, only to grow up and return to her family and endeavor to set right so many wrongs. It's a miracle this woman functions at all.

It also helps explain why she is such a good actress. Doesn't it.

CHAPTER TWENTY-FOUR

I'm not sure what transpired when we watched that home movie of Celia Bruno learning to skate, but something significantly—and instantly—changed for me about the series. I know it is completely commercial—the violence, the money, the power, the glamour—but I now find it impossible to separate the caliber of the series from Lilliana's future emotional well-being.

Why should I care? Well, first of all, I simply like Lilliana. She's definitely a high-maintenance kind of friend (my least favorite kind, thank you), but she doesn't use me up. In my presence she demands my full time and attention, but she isn't emotionally needy, or whatever that is that makes other demanding people feel so utterly draining. Do you know what I mean? The demanding friend who leaves you tired and smiling, as opposed to the demanding friend who leaves you feeling wasted and half-dead on the floor with emotional exhaustion?

We work very, very well together and fall into a routine that afternoon. I get up at seven-thirty and am at West End by nine; Jim comes in around eleven; Lilliana at noon. We work together until around two, when we have lunch in my

office, and resume until five, at which time Lilliana returns
to the hotel. Jim and I stay until seven and then I return to
the hotel, where Lilliana and I work out, eat a light supper,
watch the news and hit the hay. The bodyguards, mean-
while, shadow our every move.

Alexandra has instructed me that I am only to focus on
working with Lilliana while we've got her. I am not to worry
about anything else.

"What about Sky Preston?" I pressed her on Thursday.

"Don't worry about Sky," Alexandra insisted. "When I
want you to worry, I'll tell you. Right now there's nothing
for you to do."

"Well, what about those Learing guys, what's up with that?"

"I swear to you, Sally, the minute I have something for you
to do, for us to do—"

"Did you go to New Jersey? With Sky?"

"No," she said. "So I want you to do what I'm doing, and
that is, focus on work, get as much as you can get done, and
be grateful for the lack of interruptions."

Only from Alexandra would I take this.

I've got to admit though, working on this series is rock-
ing. It's fun. It is fascinating and challenging, like a big jig-
saw puzzle. The hotel is fabulous and so is the food. Lilliana
is really into this, too, and even Edith has tottered up to
prove that she can be, and is, worthy of her new position as
a DBS News researcher.

Lilliana and I occasionally allow ourselves the luxury of
discussing topics beyond the mafia. For example, Wednes-
day night she asked me about Doug, that cute lawyer that
drove us into New York in the wee hours of Monday morning. I told her he was an old friend.

"I love these friends of yours," she said, flicking through
the channels on TV.

"What's wrong with my friends?" I asked her.

"You're sleeping with him," she says, looking at me like
I'm an idiot. "What kind of friend is that?"

"I beg your pardon?"

She laughed. "Go ahead, try and deny it. The guy practically had a hard-on all the way to New York—"

"Lilliana!"

"And it wasn't for me, honey, because if it had been, I would have taken him up on it. How about we try this Nintendo stuff? Which game do you want to play?"

I have also been extremely pleased, over the last couple days, how young Jim Reinemann has successfully navigated through whatever feelings he thought he held for me. Or, more to the point, I think he's so wowed by Lilliana that I have become almost instantly old hat. Whatever, I am relieved we seem to be leaving all that behind, and he is taking very good care of my dog. Scotty's coat has never been so well tended.

On Friday morning, tired of Alexandra stonewalling me, I think I might try to find out what's going on by asking Cassy Cochran for permission to go to Connecticut for the weekend. This suggestion is met with stony silence. Finally she asks me if I'm out of my cotton-picking mind. (You can tell she lives with a Southerner.)

"Why not?" I ask. "I haven't heard anything, and no news is good news."

"What more do you need to hear? You were driving around with the dead body of some ex-military guy, his brother tried to shoot you, and when that didn't work, he tried putting a bomb under your car. I think you've heard quite enough. No, the answer is no, absolutely no, Sally, you don't go anywhere until we tell you otherwise."

"You're assuming all these events are related," I protest. "That bomb could have been meant for Lilliana."

"Oh, I see," she says with exaggerated care, taking off her reading glasses and tossing them on her desk. "You have all kinds of different people out there wishing you dead, so this was just a typical couple of days in your life and we shouldn't worry?"

"Maybe we should just ask Wendy."

"Maybe you should just get back to work," she suggests.

I sigh, getting up to leave. "I'm glad Wendy's back." No response as I walk to the door. I turn. "How did you get her back?"

Cassy looks at me without the slightest intention of answering.

I walk downstairs and outside into the square to see Scotty, who has begun to snub me. He doesn't understand why I won't come home with him at night, but keep sending him away with a college boy. I walk inside the hut and find Jim there, squatting down, having a visit with Scotty and the little dog with the hopeful eyes, Blackie. (Scotty has become friends with him and sometimes allows Blackie to curl up against him to sleep.)

I tell him about this weekend, that I'm still not allowed to go anywhere, but that I can get someone to take Scotty out to my mother's so he doesn't have to baby-sit. But Jim assures me he has no other plans.

"Are you sure?"

"Yes," he insists. "It's really terrific and I'm having a great time."

After visiting Scotty a while, we walk back up to the conference room together. Jim tells me that a Doug Wrentham called this morning. "Should I know his name?"

"He's a prosecutor in Connecticut," I say.

Doug and I have been talking every night, and I know he'd like to come in for the weekend. I wanted him to come in too, but after talking to Mother, I decided against it. "You need time," Mother advised me. "And you need quiet time. Battle fatigue and bunker mentality is not going to tell either one of you what you need to know." Mother, you see, believes that when something like my car getting bombed occurs, romance results whether it's warranted or not.

But our night at the country club last week is a memory hard to shake. In fact, it gets better and better every day.

Friday night passes and we come in to work on Saturday, even Lilliana, and I am beginning to anticipate starting to write the script sooner than I expected. It's coming together beautifully. I can feel the flow of the story and some of the older material, particularly about Rocky Presario and Joe Arlenetta in the early days, looks and feels like *The Godfather*, which is great, since we know that American audiences have insatiable appetites for this genre. We are not aspiring to attract merely an audience of true-crime buffs—whose numbers are legion these days, though, I must admit—but for a general audience. We need to capture the sweeping panorama of the Presario-Arlenetta families, and we've got to create a strong and irresistible pitch and campaign for DBS to execute.

The trick is, how do I prevent Lilliana from trying to rewrite her family's history without alienating her from the project?

"Yeah, sure," she says, "*The Godfather, The Sopranos, Good Fellas,* I know what you mean, Sally. But it's a— " She bites her lip, trying to think of how to express it. "It's a class thing I'm talking about. The people portrayed in those kinds of movies and shows are, well, déclassé, to say the least. I mean, take Poppy. He was a self-made man, granted. His father was a stonemason from the old country and he expected Poppy to be a stonemason too, and instead, he chose to fight his way up the union and go into construction himself and he became a very successful businessman."

I give her a look. "Lilliana, are you trying to convince me that your grandfather was not a mafia don?"

"He was the catalyst for legitimizing operations that were formerly controlled by organized crime."

"Which means?"

"That Poppy never sat around in his undershirt; he never used profanity; he didn't run around on my grandmother. He was always very well mannered and suitably dressed, as was his father before him."

I nod, conceding, "I understand."

"My father graduated from Georgetown University," she continues. "My mother went to Rosemont College. They were educated and refined people."

"So it's white collar versus blue collar, is that what you're telling me?"

"They've been white collar for at least fifty years," she says. "It's a much more refined world than people think. Even in Brooklyn. You met my cousin, Cliff—you think he was like Tony Soprano?"

Brooklyn born and bred, I remember Cliff Yarlen's attractive and extremely well mannered bearing. Yet his father and his older brother, Nick, were kingpins in the Genovese crime family. And I have to admit, the one time I met Nick Arlenetta, I couldn't distinguish him from any other wealthy businessman.

"If you take all the *Godfather* stuff to heart as you do this," Lilliana says, "you're going to serve up what people want to believe, as opposed to what is. The fact is, yesterday's organized crime families are more like the Rockefellers and the Vanderbilts today. No one cares anymore about how the original fortune was made; it's what the subsequent generations are doing with that money that matters."

"But Lilliana, look at your grandfather," I say. "Are you saying he doesn't fit the stereotype? The way he lives? The way he talks? What he looks like?"

"Okay, sure, Poppy's an easy target. He's old and of another era, and yes, his taste in architecture and furnishings is a little ethnic, but my father is much more typical. He's well educated, successful, and got out of the family business as soon as he could. And did a lot of good along the way, I might add."

She's right and she's wrong. True, many known organized crime families made their "do-it-or-I'll-break-your-face" fortunes in everything from protection rackets, construction, grocery store chains, retail, TV and movie production, magazine publishing, banking, real estate and on and on, but after they packed their kids off to Ivy League schools, those kids didn't resume shooting each other in the next generation like the Arlenetta and Presario kids did.

Lilliana leaves for the hotel around six. Jim and Scotty leave for uptown shortly thereafter, which leaves me happily alone with my piles of notes and files and videos. At seven forty-five there is a knock on the door and I walk over, expecting it to be Slim, asking what the plan for the evening is. Instead, I find Sky Preston and Agent Alfonso of the FBI. The agent and I shake hands hello.

"May we come in?" Sky asks.

"Actually," I begin, not particularly wanting these two to see what I'm working on, "I think we'd be more comfortable in my office." I pull the conference room door closed behind me and ask if they'd care for some coffee or water or something. They both decline.

For this interview, two against one, I opt to sit behind my desk. The two men take the chairs opposite it. I fold my hands in front of me and ask what can I do for them, apologizing in advance if I seem tired because I am.

"We need to clear something up," Sky says to me. "First, there's a Detective D'Amico at the Castleford Police Department—"

"Buddy."

"Who is convinced someone else was staying in your home in Castleford when your car exploded. Who was it?"

There's no point in lying to Sky. He probably knows who it was anyway. "Lilliana was there. There didn't seem to be much point in dragging her through the headlines. And if Castleford PD knew, everyone would know."

"Everyone knows Lilliana Martin was in Castleford," Agent Alfonso says. "You took her to some grocery store and nearly caused a riot."

I smile slightly. "Yes, I did. She wanted to get some flowers for my mother."

"So how did you get her out of your house without the authorities seeing her?" Sky asks.

"I sent her through the woods, and a friend of mine picked her up."

"Doug Wrentham?"

I shake my head. "No."

"Who?"

I sigh. "If I tell you, you'll try and question him, and you'll feed his paranoia for the next hundred years."

Sky turns to Agent Alfonso. "That's Peter Sabatino."

"Isn't that the guy—" Alfonso begins.

"No, that was his father," Sky says quickly. He doesn't have to say the rest, that *that* Sabatino was the man Phillip O'Hearn hired to kill my father twenty-one years ago.

"So Peter Sabatino picked her up?"

"Yes, and Doug came to the house to get me. We met them downtown and then Doug Wrentham drove us into New York, to here, to West End. And we've been under guard ever since." I lean forward slightly. "So tell me why you're asking."

"Just getting our ducks in a row."

I hate that expression. It implies that shooting is about to begin. "Okay," I say, "so now you know. Lilliana came from New Jersey to my house and that night my car was bombed. My question to you is, who was it meant for?"

He meets my eyes directly. "You."

I wait a moment. "Oh. And then it just went off?"

He nods.

"So why didn't whoever set it get blown up with it?"

"His name is Wilkie Learing," Sky tells me. "It could have been a faulty timer, we'll know that piece soon."

I scratch my head. "So why is Wilkie Learing blowing up my car? And by the way, are you guys going to help me with my insurance claim?"

"Wilkie Learing believes," Agent Alfonso says, "that you murdered his brother."

I frown. "And how was I supposed to do that?"

"You shot him out of a tree the night you were at Alexandra Waring's farm," he says. "And then you stuffed him into the trunk of your car to get rid of him later."

"Yeah, right," I say. "And he thinks I just dropped his brother off at the car rental place in Manhattan, that that was my clever way of disposing of his body?" I look at them. "I shot him out of a *tree*? What the hell was he doing up in a tree?"

"Preparing, we think, to shoot Alexandra Waring," Sky says.

I blink. "At least that part makes sense."

"He had an affiliation with an organized militia group," Sky says. "Outside Pittsburgh."

"Harlen," I say.

He nods again.

"And he was trying to kill Alexandra—why? To strike back at the establishment?"

"Something like that," Sky acknowledges.

"Okay. So, the question is, who shot Walter Learing out of the tree?"

Sky nods.

"Well, it wasn't me."

They sit there, waiting, and I don't know what they're waiting for. And then I do. They're waiting for me to say it was Alexandra.

I shake my head. "No, no, no. It was not Alexandra," I tell them.

CHAPTER TWENTY-FIVE

When Slim and I return to the hotel, we find the suite in chaos. It seems that Lilliana has ditched her bodyguard and has taken off for parts unknown. I call Rocky Presario's home in New Jersey.

"I'm sorry, Ms. Harrington," the housekeeper says, "but Miss Lilliana is not here." There is a pause and then a whisper, "I believe Mr. Presario thinks she's staying with *you.*"

"Oh, well, yes, she is," I say quickly. "She just took off tonight and I thought she might have taken a drive over there to say hello to her grandfather."

"No," she says, sounding worried. "Perhaps I should tell someone? Perhaps she needs some kind of assistance?"

"I don't think so," I say. "I really think maybe she got cabin fever—we've been working very hard, and things are coming along very well. I wouldn't even mention this to Mr. Presario, but if by chance Lilliana should swing by, just ask her to give me a call at the hotel, would you?"

"They're going to go bullshit!" Racia, Lilliana's six-foot-two bodyguard, cries to me and Slim.

"Just cool it for a minute, will you?" I say.

"You better call in," Slim tells Racia.

"You better not call in," I counter. "You better just sit down and relax and wait until she turns up. This is not your run-of-the-mill helpless damsel in distress, you know. This is a mafia princess who's been ducking and fleeing for most of her life."

"I think she should call in," Slim insists.

"And then what? Everybody freaks out and we still won't know where she is. And Racia will probably get fired. Just let me think a minute," I plead, holding my hand to my forehead. "Obviously Lilliana had something she needs to do, or wants to do, something she doesn't want us to know about."

And what could that be? I wonder, pacing in the privacy of my bedroom. Where would Lilliana go? It's Saturday night. Nine-thirty. I try to think of what we were talking about in the conference room this evening. The mob. White collar and blue collar, class. She left at six. Jim left five minutes later. Sky arrived at seven forty-five.

Jim never leaves before seven. But Jim left about five after six tonight. No doubt he had something to do. After all, it's Saturday night.

And Lilliana's gone somewhere she doesn't want us to know about.

Lilliana, who has been considering everything with two legs.

I burst into the living room and tell Slim I don't want any questions, but if he wants to come with me he can, but to just shut up and stay out of the way.

The light is on in my apartment and the blinds are drawn. I let Slim pay the cab and march up the stairs to the vestibule. I consider buzzing first and then say to hell with it. I unlock the vestibule door, hold it open for Slim, and then walk to my apartment door. I hear talking inside.

I hear Lilliana.

I hear Jim.

And I am livid.

I stick my key in the lock and turn it, and Scotty starts barking inside and I call, "It's me, Sally," and unlock the next lock. I hear movement inside, frantic whispers and Jim weakly calls out, "Just a minute!" There's more movement and whispering and I'll be damned if I'm going to wait, and throw open the door.

Lilliana is nowhere to be seen. Hiding in the bathroom, no doubt. Jim is standing in the middle of the room, looking absolutely stricken. He is fully dressed, so hopefully I'm in time. "Wait outside," I tell Slim, slamming the door in his face. I whirl around, nearly tripping over Scotty. "Where's Lilliana?"

He hesitates and then points toward the bathroom, from where Lilliana is just emerging. "Hello, Sally," she says coolly.

I can't even speak I am so angry with her.

"What brings you here?"

I turn to look at Jim, who now has turned his back to me. His hands are jammed into his pockets and he's looking down at the floor, as if he's being punished. "This is my apartment, Lilliana," I say menacingly. "If you want to pull this kind of crap, then you do it somewhere else. Not here, not in my home."

Her eyes widen a bit. And then her mouth opens and she simply stares at me.

"You've got it wrong, Sally," Jim says hoarsely, turning around. His face is scarlet, his expression is one of utter misery. He fumbles for the back of the chair and finally grasps it, pulling it out and collapsing into it. He doubles over, burying his face in his hands.

"What is going on here?" I demand. Scotty is dancing around me, wondering why I'm ignoring him.

"She was only trying to help me," Jim whispers. And then he begins to sob.

I turn to Lilliana, who sighs, closing her eyes. When she opens them, she walks over to pull out the chair next to Jim and she, too, falls heavily into it. "You have to tell her," she says to him quietly.

"Scotty, go over there and sit," I command. He flounces his tail at me, swinging around in the opposite direction and jumps up on the bed. I move closer to the table. "You have to tell me what?"

Jim stifles another sob, and shakes his head, face still buried in his hands. "I can't."

"You have to," Lilliana says gently, placing a hand on his shoulder.

I walk into the kitchen, grab a paper napkin and bring it back to push into Jim's hand. Then I walk back to the refrigerator and look inside, pulling out a bottle of Amstel, twisting the cap and taking a nice long swallow right out of the bottle. I walk back to the table and wait. Lilliana reaches up for the bottle of beer and I frown a little, but hand it to her. She does exactly what I did and sets it down on the table. The bottle is now two-thirds empty.

Jim finally pulls himself together. His hands are trembling, I notice, as he wipes his face. He stares down at the table and opens his mouth to speak. Then suddenly he jerks himself to his feet and lurches across the room to one of the bookcases. He reaches behind some books and pulls out a blue felt bag that looks like the kind Chivas Regal comes in. Eyes still down, he walks over, stops in front of me and says, "I knew it was bulletproof glass. I used a twenty-two, and you know I made sure not to aim anywhere near you."

I hear blood roaring in my ears.

"Tell her why you did it," Lilliana says.

"I didn't want you to go." He swallows. "I knew if I did it, they'd never let you leave West End. And I could work with you." He swallows. "I thought if we spent a lot of time together, maybe..." He raises his eyes briefly and lets them crash again.

"He told me because he knew he had to tell someone," Lilliana said. "He volunteered, Sally. I think it's an important distinction."

I'm just still standing here, looking at this kid who aimed a gun at my office window and fired. Not once, but three times. How the hell could he be sure the bulletproof glass was sound? He said he didn't aim anywhere near me, but what the hell, shooting across the park with a friggin' twenty-two? What kind of accuracy did a gun like that have, anyway?

I walk over to the telephone.

"Don't call the police, Sally," Lilliana says.

"I'm calling the car service," I tell her, picking up the telephone. "I'm sending Scotty out to my mother's." I look at Jim. "I want you to get your things together and get out. Now."

He looks to Lilliana and she nods. Shaking, he stands and moves to get his things. When he goes into the bathroom, Lilliana whispers, "What are you going to do?"

"I'm going back to the hotel and think about it," I tell her.

"You don't want him to kill himself," Lilliana whispers.

I look at her.

"If you leave him hanging, he's going to kill himself, I know he will."

I talk to the car service and Jim comes back out, stuffing things in a duffel bag. Scotty runs over to him, thinking they might be going on a trip.

I hang up the phone. "Where did you get the gun?"

"I own a couple," he murmurs. "Keep them at my parents' house upstate." He glances over. "I brought the twenty-two because it was the lowest caliber."

"How did you get it into the complex?"

"I didn't. I stashed it outside. Picked it up that night and climbed the satellite ladder. After I fired, I hopped the fence and took off."

Unbelievable. "Where's the ammunition?"

He hesitates and then walks over to the refrigerator. He opens the freezer, takes out a carton of frozen spinach and walks over to hand it to me. I pick at the packaging and find it is taped shut. Pretty heavy spinach. "Is there anything else?" I say to him.

"I would never hurt you," he says quietly. "I didn't mean to scare you."

"Of course you meant to scare me," I say. "That was the whole purpose, wasn't it?"

He looks down. "I have no excuse."

"You've got that part right at least," I tell him. I try to think, turning away. Lilliana's right, he might well kill himself before I decide how to handle this. "I want you to come to my office on Tuesday. At noon. If you're there, it's because you are willing to face up to what you've done— If you own up to what you did, and face it like a man, I will do what I can for you. Which may not be much."

He swallows, looking down at the floor.

"Or," I add, "if you want to bolt, and live the life of a fugitive, you've got about a thirty-six-hour head start." He raises his head to look at me. "I'll be disappointed if you run, but I'd also understand." I can't look at him anymore. I walk over to the table and put the bullets down.

"I deserve to die," he says miserably.

"Your parents' son deserves a chance to save himself," I say loudly, turning around. "*Don't* let your family down. Don't let me down."

He looks at me, flinching.

"Promise me you'll show up, or you'll run. Nothing else."

"I promise," he says, dropping his head again.

I walk over to open the door and hold it for Jim. He hands me the keys to the apartment and sadly moves along.

"Call Racia and tell her we're bringing Lilliana back," I tell Slim before slamming the door closed again. "This is unbelievable," I declare, spinning around to face the actress. "What the hell were you thinking? You're lucky he didn't get you up here to do God knows what to you."

"He's basically a good kid," she insists, grabbing the bottle of Amstel and draping one leg over the corner of the table. She tips the bottle and swallows it all down. "I'm not going to let you destroy his entire life."

"What are you going to do, have your grandfather give him a little career guidance?" I storm my way to the bathroom. Then I catch myself, sigh, and reluctantly walk back to her. "That was a stupid thing to say, I apologize. But I can't believe how friggin' stupid you are to put yourself at risk like this."

"He's a lovesick kid," Lilliana says, plunking the bottle down on the table.

There is a knock on the door. I yank it open. "We have a shift change coming up," Slim tells me, tapping his watch. I slam the door in response.

An hour later, the three of us are standing outside on 100th Street, watching as Scotty crawls up into the back window of the departing Lincoln Town Car, pressing his nose against the glass in a last desperate plea to stay.

It makes me want to cry.

Slim, Lilliana and I flag down a cab on West End Avenue and ride down to the Hotel Bernier. Lilliana and I are still arguing, which is quite a feat since I don't want Slim to know what we're talking about.

"It's psycho," I say.

"What is?" Slim asks.

"It's the kind of thing men do when they're in love," Lilliana says.

"What is?" Slim asks.

"No, it's the kind of thing that starts like this and ends up with him stalking and killing the woman—which in this case is me," I say.

"Who?" Slim asks.

"No, I disagree," Lilliana says. "He saw it as his only chance."

"Are you talking about that kid, Jim?" Slim asks.

"No!" Lilliana and I bark at the same time.

Back at the hotel, Lilliana does her best to placate Racia. Then Lilliana and I sort of make up over a late supper, and she asks me if I want to go to church with her in the morning. I suppose I'm staring because she snarls, "What?"

"I didn't imagine you as the churchgoing type."

"I think we can use a little of God's mercy on our side, don't you?"

"What are you?" I ask, fascinated. "I mean, what church?"

"Any Catholic church." She frowns, demanding, "Now what are you looking at?"

"Do you go to confession?" I ask, amazed.

"So what are you?" she demands. "What religion?"

"Congregationalist."

"What the hell is that?"

"Protestant."

"Oh, great, an infidel, I should have known," she declares, spearing her salad.

"So," I can't help but ask, "*do* you go to confession?"

"And what business is it of yours?"

"I was just curious." I sip my soup. "Maybe we should talk about something else," I suggest.

Lilliana drops her fork with a clatter. "I haven't been to confession in sixteen years, okay? Are you satisfied?"

"Yes," I tell her. "There's a very nice church around the corner. We can call the desk and see what time services are."

The telephone is ringing and I jump up to get it. "Hello?"

"Hi, it's Alexandra," my boss tells me. "What are your plans for tomorrow?" Only Alexandra can call at one in the morning and pretend it's office hours.

"Lilliana and I were going to go to church." Lilliana is frowning at me across the room, no doubt because I am an infidel.

"You better go early," Alexandra continues, "because I need you to take a ride out to New Jersey with me. Sky wants to talk to both of us at the farm."

I hang up the telephone and feel utterly wiped out suddenly. I tell Lilliana that Alexandra is picking me up tomorrow, plead exhaustion and excuse myself to my room.

I draw a bath and soak in it a while, eyes closed, trying to think. Or not to. I consider calling Doug and talking to him about Jim, but as an officer of the court, I know what he will feel obligated to do. Turn him in. And if I do that, Lilliana's right, his life will be destroyed. But the kid needs help. God only knows what he might do the next time he fancies himself in love with a woman he barely knows.

There is a quiet knock on the bathroom door. "Sally?" It's Lilliana. "Do you mind if I come in?"

I roll my eyes. Right, like I'm going to have Miss Body Perfect sitting here checking out my fatal figure flaws. "I'll be right out," I call, opening the drain. I quickly towel off and throw on the terry-cloth robe. I open the door. No Lilliana. I walk out and look in my bedroom and there she is, sitting on the corner of the foot of the bed, looking depressed.

"What's the matter?"

"I just called my father. You know, just to talk."

I think of the three-hour time difference in California.

"Somebody's put the hit on my brother," she says.

"Is he all right?" I ask, rushing over.

"He's okay. Right now. Dad says the word's out—two hundred thousand dollars for whoever knocks off Jonathan in prison."

I sit down on the bed beside her. Finally, I ask, "But who? Who's put out the hit?"

She looks at me, large brown eyes filled with worry. "That's just it. We don't know." She looks down. "It's pretty hard to protect yourself when you don't know who or what it is that's threatening you."

"Alexandra and I are going to see Sky tomorrow," I explain. "I think you should come with us, tell him about this."

She shakes her head. "No. I'm going to Poppy's. See what's going on."

"But you'll take Racia with you, right?"

"I suppose."

"You'll do more than suppose," I tell her. "You will not go anywhere without her."

We sit in silence a little while.

"They're going to kill him," she murmurs. "I can feel it."

"No," I tell her firmly, giving her hand a squeeze. "They'll protect Jonathan. And I know your dad will."

She turns to look at me, her expression sad. The next thing I know, she is kissing me.

I am so shocked I'm not sure what to do. It's not a major kiss. But then, it's not your simple "I like you" affectionate kiss, either. It's more like a meaningful warning of something very heavy duty that is about to come if I don't do something.

Too late. She's taken my hand and pressed it to her silk-covered breast. I gently pull back and bring my hand away, swallowing in apprehension as I do. "You're upset," I murmur. "This is not something you really want to do."

She looks at me for a long moment, her expression unreadable. Then she sighs. "You mean it's something you don't want to do." She stands up. "Good night," she says simply, sweeping out of the room, silk robe trailing after her.

Killer

CHAPTER TWENTY-SIX

"You look tired," Alexandra observes as the limo pulls away from the Hotel Bernier. Slim is sitting up front with the driver; the glass partition is up.

"I didn't get very much sleep last night," I admit, unsure where to begin my latest tale of woe. I shift in my seat to get a better look at the anchorwoman. "You, on the other hand, look wonderful. Better and better every day."

She smiles. "I'm moving a little bit better every day. But thank you, I'm feeling much better." A wave of something passes over her face and I know a change of subject is coming. "I hear through the grapevine you were pretty busy last night."

"Really? And what might you have heard through this grapevine of yours?" I ask, throwing a look of suspicion in the direction of Slim in the front seat.

"I heard that Sky and Agent Alfonso came to the office."

"Right."

"I heard Lilliana went AWOL and you went after her."

"Right."

"And then you went to your apartment, threw Jim Reinemann out and sent your dog to Connecticut in a company car."

"Hmm. Sounds pretty close to what happened." I glance out the window, still wondering where to begin.

"Was she sleeping with him?"

I turn, startled. "Who?"

"Lilliana. She didn't seduce Jim, did she?"

I almost say, *God, I wish!*, but shake my head instead. "No, nothing like that. They became friendly—" I hesitate. How do I say this? "He needed to talk to somebody, so he talked to Lilliana."

"About what?"

"He, um, sort of had a crush on me."

"What a shock," Alexandra deadpans. "A college kid in his first job, working around a pretty woman in authority. I am flabbergasted."

"Well, it gets complicated." She shoots me such a look, I can read her mind. "No, nothing like that!" I cry. "I would never do something like that!"

"Well then, what? Out with it, please, we've got a lot of things to go over before we see Sky."

"Okay, it's like this," I finally tell her. "He had a crush on me. He wanted to spend time with me. Last week I told him I might have to go away to work on the series for a while, to New Jersey or maybe California. He didn't want me to go, he wanted me to stay so he and I could get to know each other better."

Alexandra's waiting. "So?"

"So he went up on the roof of Darenbrook I and took a shot at my window to freak everybody out, so I wouldn't go anywhere, but would stay right there, at West End, with him."

She is stunned. "Jim?" she says incredulously.

I nod. "So he told Lilliana about it. And then I arrived—"

"How did you get there?"

"Well, I kind of thought what you did. I was nervous they were up to something. So Slim and I went up."

"Jim Reinemann," she repeats, looking straight ahead as if she is hoping she might not have heard the name correctly.

"Lilliana and I were scared he'd kill himself or something, so I made him promise he'd come to my office Tuesday at noon, to find out what I'm going to do." I think perhaps it's best for everyone concerned if I leave out the part about giving him the option of a thirty-six-hour head start if he decided to run.

"What do you mean, what you're going to do? You're going to call the police!"

"He told me what he did," I explain. "He gave me the gun. It's just a twenty-two—it's amazing he even hit the window from that far."

"Where's the gun now?"

"In the wall safe of my closet at the hotel."

She screws up her face at me in disbelief. "What are you thinking? He could have killed you!"

"He knew it was bulletproof glass," I say.

"Golly," she mutters in amazement, rubbing her forehead. "How can people be so stupid?"

"He seems to know a lot about guns," I continue. "In his eyes, I'm sure it was like a prank, you know? In comparison?"

"The man brought a gun to West End and shot at someone!" she nearly shouts. "We have put people in prison for a long time for a lot less!"

We ride along for a little while and she appears to calm down. Finally, I look over. "So what do you think I should do?"

She sighs, shaking her head. "I can't believe this. You're thinking about letting him go, aren't you?"

"I'm thinking he needs mandatory psychiatric help, and prison may not be the best place to get it."

"Just for the sake of argument," she says, "how would you determine how much psychiatric help is appropriate? And who would pay for this psychiatric care? He hasn't a cent to his name."

I sigh, nodding, looking out my window. "Thing is," I say quietly, "in a crazy way I understand what he did. You have no idea how many times I've thought about taking Mother's shotgun and shooting Phillip O'Hearn's windows out, just to scare the hell out of him."

"But you didn't do it," Alexandra points out. "Because someone could get hurt. And if you got caught, you know it would be the end of your career. And if you fancied yourself in love with him and did it? That would make it ten times worse—because what would it make you? A stalker and a terrorist, that's what. No way, Sally, the kid is sick and the authorities need to take over."

I sigh heavily and recross my legs, away from her, and lean on the door rest.

"This isn't about you, Sally," she continues. "This is about DBS and every employee who works at West End. You can't let some kid shoot at you across the park and let it slide."

"I'm not letting him off, okay?"

We ride along a while in silence. "I don't know who I can give you to assist on the series," she says. "Can Edith do any more for you?"

"Oh, come on," I say, irritated. "You've got me locked up with Lilliana and now you want to stick me in close quarters with that basket case, too?"

She looks at me. "What's wrong with Lilliana? I thought you liked Lilliana."

"Nothing's wrong, she's fine," I half snarl. I'm not doing a very good job of keeping my cool, but I am tired, and I am tired of living the life of a moving target. I want to go home, I want to pet my dog, I want to play golf with Doug. I am sick of this.

"Sally," Alexandra says quietly. I look at her. "You have been under an impossible amount of pressure the last couple of weeks. I appreciate that. And I appreciate you. But I can't help you unless you tell me what's wrong."

"I just told you what was wrong with Jim," I complain, "and you're yelling at me as though I haven't already told myself every single thing you just said." I gesture. "He's basically a good kid, okay? So I'm having a hard time wanting to destroy his entire life. Okay?"

"Okay," she says with finality.

Alexandra opens a bottle of water and pours it into two glasses. She hands me one and then opens her briefcase to take out some files to read. I look out the window, watching New York turn into New Jersey, wondering what is waiting for us at the farm. I peek at Alexandra out of the corner of my eye. Now she seems quite unaffected, content to sit back and read and sip Perrier.

"Lilliana says someone's put the hit on her brother," I finally say. I turn to find that I've gained Alexandra's interest. "Her father doesn't know who, but the word is out in the prison, anyone who does him in gets two hundred thousand dollars."

The anchorwoman considers this, absently sipping Perrier. "Interesting."

"And Lilliana made a major pass at me last night," I add. "I didn't even know what to say. Or what to do. So I'm certainly not convinced this living arrangement—or working arrangement—is a good idea."

"Was she upset? With you?"

"I don't know," I say. "It's not as if she hasn't made overtures before, but they were always kind of a joke, you know? And then out of the blue last night..." I let my voice trail off, wondering if Alexandra cares in the slightest about me, or just whether or not I successfully produce this series for her.

"It may be her way of coping."

I look at Alexandra.

"The stress. The kid, the gun, the hit on her brother—" She shakes her head, shrugging. "I've known a lot of people out in the field who are like that. It can be an instinct to alleviate pressure."

"*I'll* say."

The way I say this makes the anchorwoman laugh a little and then, finally, so do I.

"This way," Agent Alfonso says, leading us away from Alexandra's farmhouse. We cross the driveway and walk down the short side lawn to the beginning of what Alexandra says is a bridle path. We walk down into the woods, but then veer off, cutting through some bushes to reach an area that is sectioned off with yellow plastic tape. Sky Preston is standing there, by a large beech, waiting.

Sky points up. About thirty feet above us is a section of branches, also sectioned off with pieces of yellow plastic tape. "That's where Walter Learing was sitting. According to the marks left by the rifle resting on the tree," he continues, following with his finger the course of a long fluorescent-orange string that connects a tree branch to a window on the first floor of the farmhouse, "that is where he was aiming." He looks to Alexandra.

"That's the kitchen," she says. "The kitchen table is there, the stove and sink to the right."

His eyes move to me. "And were you ever in there, the night you stayed over?"

"We both were," I answer.

Alexandra absently touches her healing shoulder, walking around the tree, studying the tapes. "So where and how was he killed?"

"He was up there," Sky says. "He took a thirty-eight just here." He points under his right ear. "The rifle fell there." He points to the ground. "The body slumped over where the branches crossed." He moves around to the other side of the tree. "Someone climbed up." He illustrates this, swinging himself up and over the lowest branch, then pulling himself up to sit. "He climbed to here." He stands up on the branch and reaches up. "He grabbed the leg of the corpse and yanked it, so the body came down." He points to the branch he's standing on. "The right side of the face smashed down on that, shattering the cheek and jawbones after death."

We all look at the branch as if there is anything to see. There isn't. I have to turn away for a moment and catch my breath.

"He never knew what hit him," Sky adds. He jumps down.

"Could it have been two people?" Alexandra asks, crossing her arms over her chest.

"Two people...?"

"One who shot Learing and two of them to move the body?"

"Possibly," he says. "I will tell you this, somebody's been here before. We found evidence of camping back up in there—" He points into the woods. "Toward the north fence."

"Did he leave a car?" I ask.

"Not that we've found."

"So how did he get here?"

"Someone—maybe his brother—could have dropped him off at the highway," Alexandra says. "He could have hiked through the park and then come over the north fence."

"What about his brother, Wilkie Learing?" I look at Alexandra. "Sky tried to convince me last night he's the one who shot at me at West End," I say meaningfully. "And then blew up my car." I turn to Sky. "Have you found him yet?"

"As a matter of fact, we have," he says. "A group of kids found his body late last night in Fort Lee."

"Dead?" I ask.

"Very," Sky says. "What was interesting is that he had a thirty-eight slug in his head, too. And ballistics match it to the gun that killed his brother."

Alexandra and I look at each other, and then she turns to Sky. "Let me understand this. Why was Walter Learing here?"

Agent Alfonso steps forward and opens a small flip book. "Striking back at the media, the pawns of a tyrannical government. About you, Ms. Waring, in particular, he rants and raves about your father, a United States congressman for eighteen years who was, and I quote from his journal, 'determined to desecrate the Constitution by stripping Americans of their right to bear arms.'" Alfonso looks up, waiting for her reaction. We all are.

"So why have you brought us here? What do you want?" Alexandra asks him. "Surely you don't believe I killed him. And you must know Sally didn't."

Alfonso looks at Sky. "Somebody killed Walter Learing," Sky answers. "And his body ended up in Sally's car. And his brother, Wilkie Learing, did try to kill Sally not once, but twice. And now Wilkie Learing is dead, too, murdered last night. Who do you suggest I invite out here?"

Walking back to the limousine, Alexandra says under her breath, "I think we need to know a little more about the Learing brothers, don't you?"

"What did Dr. Kessler find out?"

"Not enough, clearly, because this still isn't making any sense."

Slim and the driver are standing outside the car, waiting. Alexandra stops and looks at her watch. "What do you say we go to Pittsburgh and look around for ourselves?"

My eyebrows go up. "To Harlen?"

"To Harlen," she confirms.

CHAPTER TWENTY-SEVEN

Alexandra hurries into the small structure that serves as the terminal for the Far Hills airport. "Hello, Miss Waring," says the young man behind the counter. "Not the greatest day for flying. We've got ten-knot gusts across the hills."

"Not the best, but not the worst," she says diplomatically, taking out her wallet. "We're going to need a Cessna one seventy-two." She pulls out a credit card and begins filling out forms.

"How long will you need it?" he asks.

"Eight hours should do it."

"Be sure to put the return time on the flight plan," he says, pointing to a line, "so we know when to turn the runway lights on for you."

I get this sinking feeling. "Who exactly is flying us?"

"I'm from Kansas," she says as if this explains everything. She smiles, glancing up. "It's practically our birthright." I turn around to find Slim standing there, not looking very happy either.

"Miss Waring flies nearly every weekend," the young man assures us. "When she's here."

Within forty minutes, we are sitting in a Cessna, taxiing

to the runway. Slim is in the front seat and Alexandra has instructed me to sit directly behind her in the back to compensate. It is horrendously noisy in here and I am grateful when Alexandra hands back some headphones for me to wear. I hear her gain permission to take off and seconds later we are buzzing down the runway. We're not even twenty feet off the ground when a gust of wind hits us and I shudder, curling into the side of the plane, unable to see anything but gray sky over the dashboard and below, a disappearing earth.

We ascend to an altitude of seven thousand feet. When the wind blows, we get tossed around like a kid's balsa-wood glider. Before taking off, Alexandra kindly showed me where the airsickness bags are kept. She also gave me a scratchy wool blanket. Once I get used to the idea that Alexandra really is comfortable flying and that her shoulder isn't going to suddenly come off or anything, I relax a little. In the headset I hear the control tower talking. Actually, I hear a LOT of control towers talking as we head west. Oh, God, we just bounced around again— and it's getting cold. I wrap myself in the blanket. Alexandra periodically hands a book of charts back to me so I can see what it is we're flying over. I have said the Lord's Prayer, I think, fifty times by the time we start to reach our destination.

"Do you see the airport?" she asks into the mike of her headset, craning her neck to see over the dashboard.

"No," Slim says.

"I do," I say. "Left, about ten o'clock."

"Thanks," she says.

Alexandra gets clearance to land and we circle once and then swoop in to land, the wind suddenly gusting, tipping the wings to the right, but Alexandra brings the plane back under control and quickly drops to the runway. We taxi in and park in the numbered space we've been assigned. My legs are a little shaky, and after he gets out, Slim wordlessly puts his hands around my waist to gently lower me to the tarmac.

Two younger-looking men come jogging out, greeting

Alexandra. They're introduced to me as colleagues from the DBS affiliate in Pittsburgh. Alexandra goes into the terminal to conduct some business and then joins us in the parking lot, where we climb into an unmarked Econoline van.

"So they're there for sure?" Alexandra asks the Pittsburgh guys.

"Sunday's the day they do their drills," the older of the two men, Jay, says, driving us to heaven only knows where. We've left the main highway and are on a two-lane road, wooded hills rising around us.

"How many in this group?"

"We think it's twenty-eight members. Walter Learing hung out with them, we know that for sure. His brother owns a sporting goods store in town."

"Owned," I say.

The younger one, Micky, turns around in his seat to look at me.

"He was murdered last night. And his body dumped in Fort Lee, New Jersey."

"No shit," Micky says appreciatively.

"Tell me about this sporting goods store," Alexandra says.

"It's almost all hunting stuff. Guns, bows, knives, army fatigues, you know."

We turn off the pavement and onto a dirt road. There are NO TRESPASSING signs everywhere. We bump and jostle our way through the woods and come upon a large clearing. We boldly drive up to where a group of cars is already parked. They are mostly four-wheel-drive vehicles and a couple of trucks. "Look at that—every vehicle is American made," Alexandra notes. "Slim, stay in the car." The four of us climb out.

"This is private property," a voice booms at us from the woods.

"Yes, sir, I know," Alexandra says, stepping forward. "I'm Alexandra Waring of DBS News."

"I know who you are and you have sixty seconds to get off this private property!"

"Or what?" she says, walking toward the sound of his voice.

"A citizen is allowed to protect his property," the voice says.

"I have no cameras, I have no recorders," she says, standing still. "I only wish to speak to the leader of the militia. I believe it's Captain Post?"

I hear men talking, but I still can't see them.

Alexandra turns around and waves for me to come up.

Oh, great. Now we'll both get shot by these right-wing crazies. But I do as I am told and walk up to stand next to her.

"I know you've been hounded by the feds," Alexandra calls. "I know the AFT has been hassling you, too." She is referring to the Department of Alcohol, Firearms and Tobacco. "But I need to talk to you about one of the men who has been associated with you. A man who was recently killed. His name was Walter Learing."

There is silence.

"I've been told he was a member of your militia. I don't believe it. Or if he was, then I think he was using you. He was sent to infiltrate your group. I know, for a fact, that the feds are lying to me. And I am trying to find out why."

There are a few whispers and then a man in complete camouflage togs, including a hat, black shiny boots and a field belt with a pistol in the holster, appears. He also has a semiautomatic slung over his shoulder. He counts his paces off, gives Alexandra what looks to be an authoritative salute, and I am amazed to see Alexandra return a salute equally accomplished. "Captain James R. Post?"

"Yes, ma'am, The Free Man's Militia of Western Pennsylvania."

"This is a colleague, Sally Harrington."

"Ma'am," he says, tipping his hat. Only now do I notice that seven other men, also in fatigues, are standing in the nearby woods, watching. They are evenly spaced, about five yards apart, and each is resting a semiautomatic on the ground between their legs.

"Thank you for speaking with me, Captain."

He nods again.

"Walter Learing was shot and killed on my farm in New Jersey last week," she says.

No reaction.

"The FBI has told me he was preparing to shoot me, but someone shot him before he got the chance."

Captain Post narrows his eyes and shakes his head in disgust. "That's what the FBI always says."

"That was my reaction," Alexandra agrees. "And it's the reason why I'm here this afternoon, to get some information from you firsthand."

One eyebrow travels up. "Such as?"

"Your code," Alexandra says. "You must have a code for members. The first part, I believe, would be that each member uphold the Constitution of the United States of America?"

"That's right."

"Would you agree, then, that if Walter Learing was, in fact, about to assassinate me, he was about to violate that essential first part of your code?"

"No member of the Free Man's Militia," he says tersely, "would harm anyone without provocation. As Thomas Jefferson clearly spelled it out, and I quote, 'The strongest reason for the people to retain the right to keep and bear arms is, as a last resort, to protect themselves against tyranny in Government.'"

Alexandra nods. "Is it possible that Walter Learing saw me—a symbol of the national media—as the pawn of a tyrannical government?"

"We know those boys over there," he says, kicking his head in the direction of Jay and Micky, "have been snooping where it's none of their business."

"Do *you* see me as a pawn of a tyrannical government?"

He grins. "Ma'am, I think you're just reportin' what they force-feed down the pipeline. I don't think you even have a choice anymore."

"I think you and your organization are being used, Captain Post, and no one from the police, or the Secret Service, or the FBI, or the AFT, has presented that possibility to me.

I arrive at this conclusion entirely on my own, based on my knowledge of the true intent and constitutional basis of your organization, and the facts of the case."

He cocks his head to the side slightly. "And the facts are...?"

"That Walter and Wilkie Learing infiltrated your group by offering deep discounts on weapons," she says. "And that Walter and Wilkie Learing have been dealing in the resale of unregistered and illegal firearms."

I turn to stare at Alexandra. "But I thought—"

"You thought militia groups are bad," Alexandra says, turning to me. "You thought militia groups are a bunch of wild revolutionaries determined to overthrow the federal government." She looks at Captain Post. "When, in fact, their purpose is to uphold and protect the power of the people as spelled out in the Constitution. The militia is the last resort against a tyrannical government—or tyrannical anything that threatens the Constitution, which includes organized crime groups, does it not, Captain?"

"You're pretty close, ma'am," he concedes.

"So do you understand why I'm here? Because the feds would like me to think the Learings are part of a crazed, right-wing militia group. Namely you. And I know that is bull. Whatever qualms you have with the national media, I don't believe for a second you would deliberately inflict violence on any member of it."

The captain is studying Alexandra carefully, like one might size up a deer in the sights of a rifle.

"I know there had to be someone behind the Learings," she says. "I know that if something happened, like this, or if they got caught, it was designed that all eyes would turn to your group." She bites her lip a moment. "I need your help to find out who it was. Who the Learings were working for."

"Wait here," he says, abruptly turning around and walking into the woods. One by one, each of the members turn and file in, squaring off to follow their captain.

"Everybody in Kansas in the militia, too?" I whisper.

She smiles slightly.

I look around. "They could just shoot us," I whisper. "And stick guns in our hands afterward and say we attacked them."

"They won't," she says.

"I don't think Sky Preston is a liar," I say then.

"I don't think Sky Preston always gets all the information he should," she replies.

That shuts me up. We've all heard conspiracy theories—heaven knows, Crazy Pete is forever offering them to me, chapter and verse—and I suppose there must be a grain of truth in them somewhere. And, I must admit, the debate over militia groups is tricky, because such groups *are* specifically spelled out in the Constitution, and it *was* the federal government that formed, in 1903, the National Guard that was supposed to take their place. The problem is, the National Guard is run and maintained by the federal government, which is exactly who the militia is supposed to defend the people from should the government go horribly awry.

The point is, we want to preserve the right for Americans to bear arms, but we also want criminals to stop slaughtering people in the streets. But if you take all the guns from the citizens, and allow only the police to carry them, that is, in the minds of many, as good as a police state—which is exactly what the Constitution warns against.

In a few minutes Captain Post comes striding back out of the woods. As before, his men fan out and position themselves in a half circle around us. He walks up to Alexandra and hands her a piece of paper. "This person offered to sell an illegal firearm to one of our men. He came to Learing's store. Nicely dressed, slick talker, from New Jersey. I know Wilkie does business with him."

"Was Wilkie a member of your group? Did he try to be?" He shakes his head. "No."

"So it was just Walter."

"Walter was never a member officially either," he says. "He never signed the pledge. In the beginning, we thought Walt was okay. But after this illegal gun incident—" He shakes his head. "We've got enough problems to deal with, what with the feds regulating us to death. Hell, ma'am, for all we knew, he could have been a fed."

Alexandra nods and holds out her card to him. "My direct number's on the back. I would be most happy to air the militia's views on our magazine show."

He looks cynically at her card and then at her. "But the question is, Ms. Waring, how long can you take the heat? When you'll be the only one telling the truth?"

"We'll see," Alexandra promises, and she extends her hand to shake his.

A few minutes later, we're on our way back to the airport. The name on the piece of paper Captain Post gave Alexandra, however, has jolted all of us with renewed energy.

I drag into the hotel suite at almost one in the morning. Lilliana is fully dressed still, sound asleep on the couch. Slim lumbers off to his room and I walk over to sit in a chair. Suddenly the actress starts, bolting upright with frightened eyes. "It's okay," I whisper. "It's Sally."

"God," the actress says, rubbing her eyes. She drops her hands to squint at me. "Where have you been? I was worried."

"Tell me about Michael Arlenetta," I say quietly, leaning forward.

"Mike?" She yawns, stretching. "I don't know," she says, dropping her arms. "He's the youngest of Joe's kids: Nick, Rose, Theresa, then it was Cliff and Michael."

"Is he, 'in the business,' as they say?"

"You mean the family business?" she asks. "I don't think so."

"Could you please call your father and ask him?"

"Now?"

"Please."

"I don't think Dad will know much if I don't," she says, pulling the telephone closer to her. "He's married, lives in Short Hills, I think, has kids, the whole nine yards." She looks at her watch and punches in the number.

Nervous, I get up and walk over to the bar to get a glass of water. Lilliana is talking to her father and motions for me to get her a glass of water, too, which I do. I bring it over and sit down, sipping, listening as Lilliana says uh-huh, uh-huh. Finally she says, "I didn't know that." Her eyes move to me. "I don't know, but I'll let you know. Promise. Yes. I love you, too, Dad. Bye." She hangs up.

"Well?"

"Michael's in the import-export business," she reports.

"It wouldn't be New World Import-Export by chance, would it?"

She raises an eyebrow. "As a matter of fact, yes." She sips her water and puts the glass down. "He deals in engines, sewing machines, blenders, all kinds of mechanical stuff. Dad says a portion of his business is also exporting stolen car parts from the operation Nick used to run."

"So Michael *is* in the family business," I say, leaning forward to push the phone back toward her. "Listen, Lilliana, you need to call your father back."

"Why? What's the matter?"

"Cousin Michael. I think he's just declared war with you."

CHAPTER TWENTY-EIGHT

"All right," Will says seriously, closing his office door. "Let's go over this." He sits down heavily on his couch, positioning a legal pad on the coffee table in front of him. "Okay. Walter Learing tried to become a member of this militia group."

"Right," Alexandra confirms. "The Free Man's Militia of Western Pennsylvania."

Will picks up his pencil. "Why?"

"He and his brother, Wilkie, were trying to find markets for illegal weapons in the Pittsburgh area. Walter approached the group, using his military credentials, and expressed interest in joining. He started attending meetings. Then he brought Wilkie to them, who offered militia members deep discounts on weapons."

"And those sales were legal, right?" Will says.

"Completely," Alexandra confirms. "It was all aboveboard, registered rifles and handguns, all the permits were in perfect order. So this went on for a couple of months, and Walter started practicing drills and maneuvers with the group. And then the Learings brought a stranger into the picture, a man who tried to interest one of the militia members in an unregistered assault rifle. The militia member reported it to Captain Post, and that's when they rejected Walter Learing's application for membership. At worst, they figured he was trying to set them up with the feds."

Will looks up. "They really have an application for membership? To a militia?"

"Oh, yeah, sure. It's all legal." Alexandra leans forward to toss a manila folder on the table. "Here's a copy of it. They're amazingly open about their membership and activities. They have to be, actually, because the feds are all over them, fearing, of course, something like Montana or Waco. I mean, think about it—large groups of men running around with assault weapons on military maneuvers every weekend?"

Will makes a note. "Okay, so Walter's application is rejected."

"Walter's application is rejected, but New World Import-Export in New Jersey," she continues, "offers him a special assignment. A rather lucrative one, in fact."

"And New World Import-Export is?"

"Owned by Michael Arlenetta," she says, "the youngest of Joe Arlenetta's children. It's based in Fort Lee, New Jersey, and is a cover to move stolen goods from Nicky Arlenetta's rackets—parts from stolen cars, guns, precious stones, laptop computers." She tosses another manila folder on the table. "This is what research has come up with for us."

Will looks surprised. "That Edith lady?"

Alexandra nods. "Working with Dr. Kessler."

"Huh," Will says, gathering all the papers together. "So who do you want on this?"

"I want to try Jay Sustito out of Pittsburgh," she says. "So we need to get him in today." She turns to me. "Sally, I feel badly about this. Normally you should be the reporter on this story. But under the circumstances, when both you and I are personally are up to our necks in this, someone else has to front it."

"I understand," I lie, ticked off that I have nearly been killed and Jay is being handed the story. Okay, okay, I'm not petty, I still get to produce the Presario series, but if this breaking story pans out, that Michael Arlenetta, cousin of 'The Mafia Boss Murder' defendant, Jonathan Small, has extended a twenty-year-old mob war against the Presarios, and hired a hit man along the way to kill a national news anchor, it's going to be pretty sensational. And there Jay will be, on television screens across the country, getting credit as the reporter on a breaking story.

"We owe you, okay?" Alexandra says. "I won't forget. Next time I'll stick you in front of the camera so fast it'll make your head spin."

I try to smile. Once again I've been made a star and yanked off the air in the same moment.

"Jay it is then," Will says. "He's a bit uneven, but we can whip him into shape pretty fast." He and Alexandra discuss producers and crews and decide on the roster. He sails outside to speak with his secretary and make a call.

Alexandra looks over at me. "Do you mind very much? About not going on the air?"

I consider lying again but think, why bother? "Yes."

She bursts out laughing. "Good girl," she tells me. "You're in the right business."

Will comes back, closing the door behind him. He sits down on the couch again and skims his notes. "Okay... Okay, so New World Import-Export hires Walter Learing to do—what?"

"Get rid of Sally," Alexandra replies.

My eyes fly wide open and I turn to her. "*Me?* I thought it was *you*."

"No," she insists, shaking her head. "The feds said it was me, but it was you,Sally, it was always you they were after, from the beginning."

"How do you know that?" Then I have a thought. "Oh my God, Alexandra, you didn't— You weren't the one who—"

"No, of course not." She turns to Will. "She's asking me if I went outside and shot Walter Learing."

"So who *did* shoot Walter Learing?" Will wants to know.

"Someone watching the farm," Alexandra says. "Someone who knew Sally might be in danger."

I frown. "Like who?"

"Well, let's start with the Presarios," Alexandra answers.

"And what might you be doing here, Alexandra?" Sky Preston asks, bending to speak to us through the open rear window of Alexandra's limousine. We are just outside the brick and iron gates of Rocky Presario's New Jersey estate.

"Just following up on a story," she says. "And what might you be doing here?"

"Waiting for a warrant," he tells her, "and watching to see who comes and who leaves until it arrives."

"We need to talk, Sky," Alexandra says, opening the door a crack and waiting for him to back away before opening it fully. Then she reaches forward toward the jump seat, utters a small gasp in what I recognize is pain, and so I quickly lunge forward to bring the jump seat down into position.

"Hello, Sally," Sky says as he climbs into the car. Alexandra closes the door behind him. He maneuvers himself around to sit across from us and I think how oddly familiar this seems, the three of us meeting in the back of a limousine, although we have never met like this before.

Sky sits forward, resting his arms on his knees. "I heard you flew out to Pittsburgh yesterday," he says to Alexandra. "Right after talking to us."

"That's right," Alexandra tells him.

Sky cocks his head slightly. "Are you going to tell me about your conversation with Captain Post?"

"Only that he has, to my knowledge, done nothing illegal, and that he did his best to protect the militia from infiltration by the Learing brothers."

Sky looks disgusted. "What did you *think* he was going to say, Alexandra? That he's happy to acknowledge a relationship with an illegal arms dealer and a would-be assassin?"

"Ah," the anchorwoman says, "so you did know the Learings were selling illegal weapons. Funny you didn't mention that, Sky. You told us Walter was a member of the militia, and that he initially was trying to kill me as—" She turns to me. "What did they say?"

"As a strike against the media," I supply, "the pawns of a tyrannical government. And Agent Alfonso read something that was supposedly from Walter Learing's journal about your father desecrating the Constitution."

We both look at Sky, who doesn't say anything.

"And then there's this little matter of you failing to mention the connection between the Learing brothers and Nicky Arlenetta's younger brother, Michael, and the fact that Michael has been supplying them with illegal weapons to sell."

Still he says nothing.

"So the question is, Sky," Alexandra continues, "why? Why wouldn't you tell us? Unless there's something else you don't want us to know."

"This is a federal investigation, Alexandra. And you know there is no way in hell we can share privileged information with the press, not even you, regardless of our working relationship in the past."

She meets his eyes for a full minute and then says, "Okay. You can get out now, we've got things to do."

"I wish you wouldn't go up to the house," he says.

"So what?" she tells him.

"Come on, Alexandra," he says, raising a hand. "You know I'll bring you in as soon as I can, but at this point in our investigation—"

"Fine, get out of the car," she says patiently. "Let us get on with our work."

"You can't have it both ways," he says, looking at me and then back to Alexandra. "You can't expect our protection and then run off and do crazy stuff. You can't expect our cooperation when you're obstructing the law."

"No one at DBS News is obstructing the law," Alexandra says sharply.

"Yeah, right," he says.

"This is not about your case, Sky," Alexandra says in a low voice, close to a growl. "This is about another case, the attempted murder of one of our employees and *your* failure to protect her."

His head kicks back. "What? Listen, someday you'll know just how much we have done to protect Sally—"

Alexandra leans forward menacingly. "You can't protect her, Sky, and I can go public with that fact anytime I choose."

"That's bull."

"Someone tried to shoot Sally in her office at West End and you still have absolutely *nothing* on it."

"That's not true."

"An act of urban terrorism directed at a major American

media institution and *you have nothing.* How do you think
the public is going to react to that, Sky? How do you think
the mayor's going to like it? The president? *I* know who tried
to shoot Sally Harrington and you still don't have a clue."

"The sniper is dead," Sky says.

"The sniper is not dead," she counters. "As a matter of fact,"
she says, turning to me, "maybe I'll interview the shooter next
week on the magazine show. What do you think?"

"I think it would be great," I say, playing along.

"Wilkie Learing will be linked to the shooting," Sky says.

"You mean you're *praying* Wilkie Learing can be linked to
the shooting," Alexandra tells him. "And if he is, we know
it won't be by any legitimate means."

Angry, he looks at me, but I'm not saying a word.

"It's not a pretty picture, Sky. The FBI is supposed to be
finding murderers and terrorists in New York City, not
shielding New Jersey mobsters and hassling weekend war-
riors on private property in western Pennsylvania."

He sits back in his seat as if to brace himself. "What do you
want?"

"I want a deal," she tells him.

He gives a sarcastic smile. "Of course you do. What is it?"

"For the next three months, DBS News gets a two-hour
lead on any and every aspect of the Presario-Arlenetta case
the feds choose to release to the public."

"And what do we get?"

"The West End shooter. Although there is a condition attached to that."

"Which is?"

"A sealed arrest warrant, no public disclosure, treatment at
a psychiatric facility and supervised probation. Also, victim no-
tification of the assailant's whereabouts for the next five years."

He turns to squint at me. "You're going along with this?"

"Completely," I answer. "In terms of the public, the incident never happened."

"I can't guarantee three months of advance leaks," he says
to Alexandra. "You know what it's like. Nobody knows who's
leaking what half the time. Besides, what if I get reassigned
to another case?"

"Your word that you'll honor our agreement—to the best of your ability—is good enough for me," the anchor-woman tells him.

He nods. And then sighs, looking to me. "You sure this is something you want to do?"

"Yes."

He turns back to Alexandra. "All right. Deal." He stretches forward and they shake hands on it.

"He's barely twenty-one, an intern, Jim Reinemann," she tells Sky. "Scholarship student at Columbia University. He thought he was in love with Sally and didn't want her to leave on assignment. He wanted to scare us into keeping Sally at West End. You saw the caliber gun he used. He knew there was bulletproof glass, he knew there was no way she could get hurt."

"Spell the last name," he says. As Alexandra complies, he writes it down in a small notebook. "And where's the gun?"

"I've got it," I say. "It's registered and he has a permit. He brought it to the city from his parents' house." I watch as he writes, and then add, "He told me of his own volition, Sky, what he had done."

"Stupidest smart kid I ever heard of," Sky mutters.

"That's why he needs help," Alexandra says. "And prison's not going to be the place."

"I told you, I'll do my best." He looks to me again. "Where is he?"

"Around," I say. "He'll be coming into my office tomorrow at noon. You can pick him up then."

He shakes his head, looking at me. "I don't even want to know how long you've known this, but the time and money we've—"

"She only just found out," Alexandra says. "We had no idea. And we'd still have no idea if he hadn't told her."

Sky nods, putting away his notebook. He glances outside at his waiting colleagues. "So what do you want with Presario?"

"So what do you need a warrant for?" Alexandra parries. "Who are you arresting?"

He meets her eye. "I don't think we're going to get anywhere on this."

"No," she agrees. She lifts the door handle and flings the door open. "See you."

"I wouldn't do anything to obstruct justice if I were you," he says, climbing out.

"I hope I don't have to sue you to make you stop saying that," she tells him.

He's out of the car and turns around, resting his hands on the roof of the limo and bending to look in at me. "You know, Sally, you're very attractive and everything, but you seem to create an inordinate amount of trouble wherever you go."

I open my mouth to protest.

"It's the natural fair-haired WASP thing," Alexandra says, waving Sky back to close the door.

"Be careful," he warns us.

After closing the door, Alexandra picks up the phone and tells the driver to head up to the house. Soon we are rolling over the crushed white marble, the Japanese maples moving past our windows. While I consider what is "the natural fair-haired WASP thing," Alexandra is holding a somewhat cryptic conversation with Will at West End on her cell phone.

"I want the A-team ready," she says, referring to the field crew of Mitch Randall, Healey O'Baird, Ned Dembrowski and Peter Zu. Will is evidently saying something, because Alexandra is listening. "No. I will." Pause. "No. I am." Pause. "No. Tonight. Absolutely." Pause. "Set it up." And then she hangs up.

"I wish I knew what was going on," I say as we round the circular drive in front of the Presario mansion.

"There's a method to my madness," Alexandra says. "Bear with me."

The car comes to a stop and we climb out. Alexandra leads the way to the front door, where she rings the doorbell. In a moment, Lilliana appears, dressed in a black pantsuit and very high heels. "Hi," she says warmly, as if she has been expecting us.

"Sky Preston's at the front gate waiting for an arrest warrant to arrive," Alexandra tells her.

The actress smiles. "So we've heard. Any idea who it's for?"

"Well, let's see," Alexandra says, "it could be for whoever shot Walter Learing out of a tree on my farm."

"Hmm," Lilliana says, mulling this possibility over.

"Or it could be for whoever shot Wilkie Learing through the head and dumped his body at the back door of New World Import-Export this weekend."

Lilliana glances over her shoulder and then steps outside, carefully closing the front door behind her. She leads us out onto the lawn, but her progress, with her high heels, is severely impeded. Finally she just slips her shoes off and carries them, leading us to the middle of the yard. "I didn't know Poppy had anything to do with it," she whispers to me, holding my arm. "I just found out. He had a couple guys watching me when I was at your house. They saw the guy set the bomb and they—" She grimaces slightly, glancing at Alexandra. "They took care of him. They couldn't remove the bomb without setting it off. So they set it off prematurely so no one would get hurt."

"So no one would get hurt," Alexandra repeats cynically. "This was right after they killed him?"

"So you didn't know," I say to Lilliana to make sure I've got this right, "that your grandfather was involved."

"Dad didn't know either, not until you told us last night about Michael and New World Import-Export."

Biting my lip, I look first at Alexandra and then back to the actress. "So all along your grandfather's known that Michael was a threat. That he might..."

She nods. "Yeah."

"And he didn't tell your father?"

She shakes her head. "No. Because of the trial. He wanted to keep him out of it, keep him from doing anything. Poppy's so torn up about Jonathan, it would kill him if Dad did something that could land him in prison, too." She hesitates. "And Dad might, if he knew I was in danger."

"Listen, Lilliana," Alexandra says, moving closer. "Michael Arlenetta wanted Sally killed. Do you know why?"

She shakes her head slowly. "I don't. I really don't."

"Walter Learing was sent to my farm to kill Sally," Alexandra continues. She hesitates a moment and then voices the question I've been both dreading and wondering about. "How did Walter Learing know Sally would be there?"

Lilliana swallows, looking at me and then to Alexandra.

"The only people who knew I was going to bring her out to the farm that night were you and me," the anchorwoman adds.

"Then it's got to be one of Poppy's people." Lilliana turns to me. "God, I had no idea, Sally. I'm so sorry." She looks at Alexandra. "Shit. Somebody tipped off Michael. Who? Poppy's got maybe eleven people working for him right now."

"And there's more, Lilliana," Alexandra says. "Not only is there a spy for Michael Arlenetta, but—" Her eyes move past us. "Oh, good, just the man I want to see."

Lilliana and I spin around to see Jocko walking down the front lawn toward us. The big man is in the Presario uniform of a massive blue blazer and khaki pants. "Jocko," the actress says, "you remember Alexandra Waring and Sally Harrington?"

She's being polite when all I can think of is how easily this guy could snap the three of us in two.

"Yes, nice to see you again." He nods. "I wouldn't interrupt, Ms. Martin, but there are some federal agents at the gate—"

"Who are about to serve a warrant for your arrest," Alexandra finishes for him.

"Mine?" he says, his eyebrows rising.

"For the murder of Walter Learing," she tells him. "But don't worry, they're only using it to get you out of here safely."

Lilliana looks at her.

"Your friend Jocko, here, is working for the FBI," Alexandra tells her. "The feds have been watching Walter Learing, and when he came this way, they notified Jocko. He went over to the farm, found the guy just as he was about to take out Sally, and was forced to shoot him first. He put the body in Sally's trunk, planning to get it out the next day while the car was here. It didn't work out that way, though."

I look up at Jocko. "Thanks. I think."

"How do you know he's a fed?" Lilliana says, her lip curling as she takes a step back from Jocko.

"When the body turned up, the NYPD was all over Sally, and the Jersey state troopers were all over your grandfather. Who else, Lilliana, could have called them all off? Poof! They all just disappeared the next day. Only the feds can do that."

"You son of a bitch," Lilliana tells him.

"So the feds are pulling Jocko out," Alexandra continues. "But what they don't know, and what Jocko doesn't know, is that Michael Arlenetta has someone here in Rocky's house." She addresses Jocko. "And I was about to advise Lilliana that instead of having Arlenetta's spy knocked off in yet another murder, maybe she should just turn the situation over to you. That maybe you could use it somehow, to the advantage of her family."

All this time the giant has been merely standing here, listening, occasionally glancing down the front lawn toward the gate.

"Shit," Lilliana says to Jocko, socking his massive upper arm. "You were practically family."

"I am family," he suddenly says. He turns to Alexandra. "I'm not a fed."

"Maybe not technically," Alexandra says.

"I'm not technically," he says quickly, offering this to Lilliana. "I had to do this or I—" He seems to be at a loss how to explain it.

"Or you were facing the music on other charges," Alexandra says. "It's okay, we know what Sky Preston is like, how he likes to work."

"Damn you, Jocko," Lilliana says, crossing her arms over her chest. To me, "Do you remember Joey? Who works for my father? On the West Coast? This is his brother. Supposedly. Son of a bitch."

"I'm Joey's brother, I'm *not* a fed, and I saved her *life*," he says, pointing to me.

"Maybe twice," I offer. "Somebody detonated that car bomb before it killed us," I remind Lilliana.

"And trussed Wilkie Learing up like a present and dumped him on Arlenetta's doorstep," Alexandra adds.

"You're not pinning that one on me," he tells her, pointing a finger at her. "I didn't do it."

"Here they come," Alexandra says, looking as a three-car procession comes up the drive. "Better make up your mind, Lilliana. Do you play along and keep Jocko's cover intact? Or do you want to tell your grandfather?"

"Jocko might want to redeem himself with the family," I speculate.

"I didn't do anything wrong!" Jocko nearly cries. "The guy was about to shoot you!"

"You've been spying on Poppy for the feds," Lilliana says, slugging his upper arm yet again.

"I've been watching out for all of you!" he insists. "I am here to protect you!"

"You have to choose, Lilliana," Alexandra says as the cars pull up around the drive. Sky jumps out, followed by others. "Play along with Jocko and find the spy, or blow the whole thing wide open."

Lilliana looks to me. "What do you think?"

"I'd back Jocko," I say. "So long as the feds don't know you know. I'd use it."

Her eyes travel to Jocko. "Why should I trust you?"

"Because I can tell the feds to take me out of here and I am out of it," he says. "But I want to stay and do my job, and that is to protect your family."

"John Xavier Costello?" Sky says as he walks down to us. "I have a warrant for your arrest."

"For what?" Lilliana cries. Oh, the actress, here she goes.

"For the murder of Walter Gideon Learing."

"That's the most ridiculous thing I've ever heard!" Lilliana claims. "Give me your walkie-talkie," she commands Jocko. As he starts to reach inside his jacket, two agents grab his arms and pull them behind him. As they handcuff him, Lilliana steps forward to snap the walkie-talkie off his belt and presses the talk button. "Get that lawyer out front, now. The feds are arresting Jocko."

As Jocko is read his rights, and Lilliana rants and raves that Sky Preston will live to regret this ridiculous and unwarranted arrest, Alexandra and I make our way back up to the limousine, where Slim has been standing, watching.

CHAPTER TWENTY-NINE

We're not done yet.

Alexandra's on a roll now. "What could be better for our series," she asks me as we drive through the city of Fort Lee, New Jersey, "than to have some up close and personal film of Michael Arlenetta?"

"Are you crazy?" I ask her.

"Nope," she answers as we pull into the parking lot of a Holiday Inn. Minutes later, we are let into a room where Cleo is waiting. While Alexandra showers and changes into the clothes Cleo has brought, I pace the room and try to give rational answers to the makeup and hair lady's questions. It goes like this:

"Why did I get yanked out here?"

"To pull Alexandra together before she gets in front of the camera."

"What's so special about this guy?"

"He hired someone to kill me."

"So now she wants to talk to him?"

"I guess."

"Is he like a gangster?"

"I guess."

"Are you going?"

"I guess."

Alexandra emerges from the bathroom and Cleo starts drying her hair. When they have graduated to the anchorwoman's makeup, Will arrives. "We're all set."

"What does he think he's doing?"

"An interview about a local charity fund-raiser."

"Good," she says, standing up.

We ride downtown and wind around some old factory buildings, pulling up to the back of a warehouse. It is not the greatest section of town. The crew has set up in an alley behind the building, next to the loading docks, which has been picked up and swept for the occasion. They have also draped some blue material over the brick wall for a backdrop and stuck an American flag in a stand. On camera, Michael Arlenetta might be mistaken for a White House staffer holding a press conference.

The van, I notice, is blocking all but a narrow passageway at the end of the alley. The logo on the van belongs to our New Jersey affiliate. Jay Sustito is waiting by the door from which, a moment later, Michael Arlenetta emerges. He looks like his brother Cliff, I think, but has narrow-set eyes and slicks his hair straight back. He is also shorter. And he is young. God is he young, or looks young, like he's wearing his father's suit to work or something.

I am taken aback for a second because I realize it is not Cliff he reminds me of so much, but his cousin, Lilliana's brother, Jonathan Small. They look amazingly alike.

"All right, Mr. Arlenetta," Jay Sustito tells him, guiding him before the backdrop, "before we start rolling the cameras—"

The cameras *are* rolling. The guys just haven't turned on the lights.

"I'd like to get a little background information on you."

"Yeah, sure," he says, nervously straightening his tie and then smoothing his hair back with his hand.

"Your brother, Nick—"

"Nick supported this charity," he says.

"Is that how you became involved?"

"Yes. The company likes to support local charities, and this was one Nick supported."

"And the company is—?"

"Well, it's three. NTA Enterprises, Imperial Consulting, and my own company that I built, New World Import-Export."

"So you're taking your brother's place chairing the fund-raiser?"

"Yes. He recently passed away."

"Are you also taking your brother's place in his businesses?"

"Not in all respects," he says, this time smoothing his hair with both hands.

"You're a very important businessman in the community," Jay tells him.

"Internationally," Arlenetta corrects him. "I do business in seventeen countries."

"So you were a businessman in your own right before your brother's death."

"Very definitely," he says.

"Importing and exporting machinery," Jay says.

"Mechanical parts, motors, machines," Arlenetta adds.

"Guns?"

"We import some guns. Collector caliber."

"And you sell those guns through dealers?"

"To authorized gun dealers," he says, frowning and starting to look concerned.

Jay doesn't miss a beat. "So when does the charity drive officially start?"

"Next week. With the dance."

"That's good. I think we might be able to send someone to cover the event. If you want."

"Oh yeah? That'd be great." He sniffs sharply, looking around. "Can we start? I gotta lot to do."

"Sure," Jay says.

Will walks up to him. "Mr. Arlenetta?"

"Yes."

The camera lights come on. "I'd like you to meet Alexandra Waring."

"You're kidding," Arlenetta says, squinting in the lights.

"Hello, Mr. Arlenetta," Alexandra says without offering her hand.

He smiles, showing nice teeth. "I didn't know you were coming. I thought it was just a local thing."

"I wouldn't miss this interview for anything," she tells him. "Okay, here we go." She turns to the camera. "We're in Fort Lee, New Jersey, standing outside the warehouse for New World Import-Export, the company owned by Michael Arlenetta. Thank you for making time to speak with us, Mr. Arlenetta."

"I always like to do my part for charity," he tells her.

"Mr. Arlenetta, this is the spot, is it not, where the dead body of Wilkie Learing was found day before yesterday?"

He stares at her.

"Wilkie Learing?" she says. "A gun dealer who did business with New World Import-Export?"

His face screws up into a sneer. *"What?"*

"How do you respond to allegations you have taken your brother's place in the Genovese crime family?"

"You've got to be kidding," he scowls. He turns to go inside, but finds the door won't open. He yanks at it.

"Mr. Arlenetta, sources allege you have renewed your brother's declaration of war against members of the Presario family."

He shoves Alexandra out of the way and walks through the cameras, only to find the trucks blocking most of the exit. "I'll sue your asses from here to hell!" he cries, moving to the small passageway and finding me in it, with Slim standing behind me. For a split second I see surprise in his eyes.

And I hear blood roaring in my ears.

Because I remember him now. His voice. I've heard that voice before.

I remember Michael Arlenetta.

Instead of trying to push past me, Arlenetta turns around and bulldozes his way through the crew back to the door. He tries it again, but it still won't budge.

"That's right," Alexandra tells him. "That's Sally Harrington standing over there."

"Open the goddamn door," he growls.

"You hired Walter Learing and his brother, Wilkie Learing, to kill her."

Arlenetta is now simply standing with his back to the camera.

"Shut the cameras off," Alexandra says, and the crew complies. She takes a step closer. "If anyone lays a finger on Sally, Mr. Arlenetta, what happened to the Learings will be kid's play compared to what's going to happen to you." She turns. "Will?"

Will trots over to remove a metal wedge from above the top hinge of the door. Arlenetta wrests the door open, but turns around to give me a parting look.

I am not likely to forget it.

Within seconds, Will, Alexandra and Slim have ushered me to the limousine. "I'll meet you in the office," Will tells us, closing Alexandra's door and speaking a moment to Slim.

Slim climbs in the front seat, making the whole limo rock, and the driver pulls out.

We ride in silence a little while, catching our breath. I watch as Alexandra pours two glasses of Perrier. "I know why Michael Arlenetta wants me out of the way," I tell her.

She looks startled. "You do?"

I nod and take a glass from her. "When Nicky Arlenetta firebombed the Presario mansion in Bel Air, he was there. Right after the explosion. He was calling Lilliana's name, looking for her." I take a sip, remembering how I thought Michael Arlenetta was help arriving, but how Lilliana had held me back, scared he could be follow-up to make sure she was dead. How right she was. "But Lilliana made me hide with her. Behind the hot-water heater. I heard him, though, and I saw him. But he ran away when the authorities arrived."

"And Lilliana didn't recognize him?"

"Lilliana hadn't laid eyes on Michael Arlenetta since they were seven years old," I explain. "That's when she was put into the witness protection program. He was as much a stranger to her as he was to me."

"Well, well, well," Alexandra quietly muses, sitting back in her seat, "what do you know? The witness for the defense in 'The Mafia Boss Murder' trial, Sally Harrington, can place Michael Arlenetta at the scene of the attempted murder of Lilliana Martin earlier in the year." She holds her glass out to me. "Here's to you."

We clink glasses.

"Good evening," Alexandra says into the camera at West End as if she has not a care in the world, "I'm Alexandra Waring and this is what's happening in America tonight."

The door to the control room opens and Lilliana slips in, looking around. She spots me and comes over to sit. "So aren't you ever going to get on the air?" she whispers.

"Hey," I whisper back, "what are you doing here?"

"Working."

I frown. "On what?"

"Great producer you are," she tells me. "I'm here to work on our series, what do you think?"

"But what about—" I lower my voice even more "—*everything* that's going on?"

She shrugs. "It can happen without me being there. They don't need my help." She looks at me. "But my brother does. We need this series, Sally. So I'm sticking with it until it's done."

I smile. "Really?"

"Really," she confirms. "And I'm going to behave." She laughs a little, moistening her lips and crossing her legs, eyes on the monitor. "For a little while, anyway."

"Shh," the assistant director finally says.

CHAPTER THIRTY

"You've got to have a dependable car," Doug says as we make our way through the front door of Mother's house.

"It's fine," I tell him, shifting my canvas bag over my other shoulder.

"What kind of car costs twenty-five hundred dollars?"

"The one I'm getting," I tell him.

"What are you young people arguing about?" Mother asks as we come into the kitchen.

"Maybe you can talk sense to her, Mrs. Harrington," Doug says, exasperated. "She's getting her check from the insurance company and wants to buy some bomb of a Bronco."

"It's not a bomb," I tell him, putting my bag down on the counter. I turn to Mother, who's standing at the table, wrapping a birthday present. "It's a four-wheel-drive Bronco, and I'm going to put eight hundred bucks into it. Art says it should be fine."

"He means around town," Doug protests, "not driving back and forth to New York."

"I don't know what's the matter with you," I say, opening the refrigerator. "Until the Jeep, I always drove a bomb car. As a matter of fact," I add, looking at him over my shoulder, "we used to drive *your* bomb everywhere, remember? " I laugh. "It had a hole in the floor. You could always see the ground moving."

He turns to Mother. "I don't want her breaking down on the Bruckner Expressway in the middle of the night."

"Scotty'll be with me, and I'll call triple A, what's the big deal," I say, pulling out a platter of fresh vegetables and dip. "Mother, can we steal some of this before you take it?"

"No."

I turn around to put it back in, but she tells me I might as well leave it out, Mack is picking her up in a few minutes anyway. It's the birthday of one of Mack's friends and they're going to the party in Middletown.

I look over the contents of the refrigerator again, frown, and try the cheese door. Success! An unopen container of Camembert.

"Sally," Mother says, measuring ribbon around her package, "why are you buying such an inexpensive car?"

"See?" I ask Doug, starting to prepare a plate of cheese and crackers. "It's not a bomb, it's *inexpensive.* You have no class."

Doug pulls out a chair and sits down. "She just got a check for nineteen thousand dollars from the insurance company," he snitches to Mother.

Mother looks at me, worried. "Darling, do you need money? I thought with the new job—"

"I have everything I need, Mother," I assure her. Humming, I take out a cold bottle of champagne from my canvas bag.

"Where did that come from?" Doug says.

"My house," I say, opening the cabinet. "Doug, can you reach the champagne glasses for me?"

"What's the occasion?" he says, standing up.

"All shall be revealed," I tell him. "Soon, very soon."

Before he can get the glasses, Mother makes him hold the ribbon so she can tie a bow. Once that is accomplished, she wanders over to the counter. "Something is going on."

"Yes, indeed," I confirm, cutting the Camembert. I offer her a small slice, which she accepts. Savoring the cheese,

Mother continues to study me. Doug hands me four glasses, two at a time.

The doorbell rings and a moment later Mack calls, "Hi, it's me!"

Mother walks out to the living room and I tell Doug to open the champagne. I bring the cheese and crackers to the table.

"I have no idea what's going on," Mother says as they come in. "But Sally's acting very strangely and she's buying a bomb car."

"Hey, Sally," Mack says, hand reaching for the cheese.

"Sit for a second," I urge them. "Just a half glass for them," I instruct Doug as he pours the champagne. I bring the glasses over to the table, return to the counter and pick one up for myself. Doug's just standing there, looking at me like I'm nuts. "Sit," I tell him. I walk around to the other side of the counter and dive into my canvas bag again. I withdraw an envelope and wave it. "This is it!"

Both men look to Mother, who shrugs.

I extract the letter inside and clear my throat. "'Dear Sally,'" I read. "'I am pleased to confirm you have been preapproved for a mortgage in the amount of two hundred twenty-five thousand dollars. As we discussed, this is a thirty-year, fixed-rate mortgage—blah, blah, blah.'" I lower the paper to see their reaction.

Silence. "Yeah, so?" Doug finally says.

I clear my throat while extracting a second piece of paper. "'Dear Sally—'"

"When do we get to drink the champagne?" Mack asks, eating another piece of cheese.

"'This is to confirm the appraisal of your mother's house and property located at 100 Douglas Avenue. At current market prices, she may reasonably expect it to sell in the neighborhood of two hundred thirty-five and two hundred sixty thousand dollars.'" I lower the paper and pick up my glass. "This is to me, the future owner of 100 Douglas Avenue."

"Oh, my Lord," Mother murmurs, tears springing into her eyes. She grabs Mack's hand.

"Holy crow," Doug says, blinking. "How much money do you make, anyway?"

"DBS helped me get the mortgage," I admit, walking over. "But I have to come up with twenty-five thousand for the down payment." I look at Mother. "So do you think that's fair? The property's appraised between two thirty-five and two-sixty, so two hundred fifty thousand? Would that be agreeable to you?"

In response, Mother bursts into tears and hides her face in her hands.

I look at Mack.

"I think that's a yes," he says.

Later, after Mother and Mack have left for their party, Doug and I walk the property. He picks up a ratty old tennis ball and throws it for the dogs. The ball soars, drops, and then bounces crazily off a tree stump, the dogs charging after it.

"It's an awful lot of house for one person," he says.

"Mother's lived here alone."

"Not just on weekends."

"I know," I sigh, bending as Abigail brings the ball back. "But I can't let it go, Doug. I have to hold on to it." I look at him. "It's my home."

"I know," he says softly.

I throw the ball and wipe my hand off on my jeans.

"I'm not saying you can't swing it on your own," he adds. "Because I know you can, because you can do anything, Sally, I'm convinced."

I smile.

"I just—" He shrugs. "I just think—" His eyes move to the mountains and then back to me. "I could swing half of the house."

I reach for his hand and bring it up to my cheek. "I need to do this, Doug. I don't know what will happen down the road, but I know for my head—and, I don't know—" I lower his hand and turn to look at the old Harrington mansion across the field. "The Harringtons need to stay on a while in Castleford. At least until things are set right."

He slides his arm around my shoulders and we walk toward the house. The dogs ignore us, tumbling around in a jumbled game of tag.

I look up and wonder if I'll ever be able to make love in this house. This house of my parents.

In a few minutes, I suspect, I'm going to find out.

I hope Slim isn't watching too closely.

PART SIX

Life

CHAPTER THIRTY-ONE

"Hey," I say quietly.

Coming off the elevator, Alexandra stops. "Hi. What are you doing here?"

"I thought you might like some company," I say, walking over to her.

Her eyes lower; she seems embarrassed. "I've got to go to, um..."

"I know," I tell her. "And I know you canceled your treatments last week." I take her arm. "So we'll go together, okay? For the first one?"

She raises her eyes and nods. "Okay." Her voice is barely audible.

"And that's exactly what you're going to be," I tell her. "Okay. Just ask my mother."

And so we walk outside, to where Alexandra's car is waiting.

About the Author

Laura Van Wormer was raised in Darien, Connecticut, and received a B.S. degree in Public Communications from the S. I. Newhouse School of Public Communications at Syracuse University. She joined Doubleday & Company as a secretary and worked her way up to the position of editor. As a freelance writer, she worked with the creators of the prime-time TV shows *Dynasty*, *Dallas* and *Knots Landing* to write coffee-table books about the shows.

Although *Trouble Becomes Her* is the third book featuring Sally Harrington (the first was *Exposé*, followed by *The Last Lover*), other characters in this book may be seen in the novels *Riverside Drive*, *West End*, *Benedict Canyon*, *Any Given Moment*, *Just for the Summer* and *Talk*.

Laura divides her time between Manhattan and her English-style, stone-and-stucco farmhouse in Meriden, Connecticut, where she sits on the board of directors of the Friends of the Meriden Public Library and the Augusta Curtis Cultural Center, Inc.